FALL ON ME

BROKEN #3

CHLOE WALSH

Fall on Me,
Published by Chloe Walsh.

Fall on Me,
Broken #3,
First published, August 2014.
Republished January 2018

Cover designed by Sarah Paige.
Edited by Aleesha Davis.
Proofread by: Brooke Bowen Hebert.

DISCLAIMER

This book is a work of fiction. All names, characters, places and incidents either are products of the author's imagination or are used fictitiously. Any resemblance to events, locales, or persons, living or dead, is coincidental.

The author acknowledges all songs titles, song lyrics, film titles, film characters, trademarked statuses, brands, mentioned in this book are the property of, and belong to, their respective owners. The publication/ use of these trademarks is not authorized/ associated with, or sponsored by the trademark owners.

Chloe Walsh is in no way affiliated with any of the brands, songs, musicians or artists mentioned in this book.

PROLOGUE

CAMRYN FREY

TURNING my key in the door, I smiled to myself as Lee's warbling voice filled my ears. She obviously thought she was alone. There was no other way to get that girl to sing – thank god for that because she held a note similar to the way an injured animal howled. I closed the door as quietly as I could and slipped down the hallway to his room. I wasn't going to bother Lee. She didn't need to know I was here or why for that matter. Or that I was leaving Colorado. I didn't want to burst her bubble. Not tonight. She'd been so excited when she visited last week to tell me her plan and all I could think of at the time was 'about damn time.' I knew what tonight meant for her and Kyle. It was the night she would finally come off her high horse and Kyle would become the luckiest son of a bitch in the world.

In the beginning, I hadn't thought Kyle would–or could–ever be worthy of my best friend. His asshole mood swings and her ignorant naivety blended together as well as oil and water. But after all they'd been through, and overcome, I was beginning to realize that there was never two people more suited. It tore my heart to think that I was leaving my old roommates behind... leaving him behind.

But I had to go.

I'd made too many mistakes.

If I had one wish, one do-over day in my life, I would go back to that morning in January. I would go back to that freezing cold morning and I would climb into the shower with my boyfriend, instead of answering his phone. If I had just let his phone ring, I'd never know and I could have lived in ignorance. But no, of course I'd taken the call and had my heart ripped to shreds and my world turned inside out. In an act of vengeance–because I was a get even kind of girl–and sheer fear over what happened to Lee, I took something away from Derek and in doing so, I lost myself.

After that day, after what I did, I didn't care. I'd been numb. I was still numb. I'd slept with Mike. I told him I loved him. All lies. All bullshit. I cared about him and for a while I'd thought I might love Mike. I tried to make myself love him, but all I'd wanted was...Derek. I knew I'd ruined everything. I was a big girl. I didn't want anyone's sympathy. Every time Derek called me or text, I'd been filled with such self-loathing and disgust with myself that I'd lashed out. I had used her words-her wrecking ball of a confession-to keep my guilt at bay. But it had always swamped me, because deep in my heart, I knew he hadn't betrayed me. Not like I had him. He knew about Mike, but if he knew everything...

Lifting his mattress, I slid the letter I'd written him underneath and I prayed with all my heart that he would find comfort in the truth. In knowing that there was never anyone for me but him. Not really. Not at all.

I knew I was being a coward and selfish and a million other horrible things, but he needed closure. And I needed forgiveness. When he read that letter he would know. Everything.

I couldn't stop myself from hugging his pillow to my chest, and inhaling his scent one last time. Oh god, even though I didn't deserve it, I secretly hoped he would follow me. I hoped he could find it in his heart to forgive me…

"This isn't going to make Kyle love you, Rachel. Killing me will only make him hate you more."

My heart rate spiked. The hairs on the back of my neck prickled.

Rachel.

Dropping Derek's pillow, I bolted out of his room towards the hallway with Lee's terrified voice screaming in my ears. *"Killing me will only make him hate you more."*

Over my dead body.

I'd ignored too many incidents. For years I sat back and remained silent while Jimmy Bennett beat her to a pulp. Over and fucking over. The marks...the burns...the tears of that five year old version of Lee huddled in our tree house–her face so bruised I could barely see her eyes through the blood and the swelling– penetrated my mind. A fire roared inside of me.

Vengeance.

I had to help her. I had to stop the fucking nut job aiming a gun at my best friend. On shaken legs, I pushed Rachel so hard that the gun fell from her hands, shooting off before sliding across the tiles of the kitchen floor. Grabbing her hair, I slammed her head against the door. "You bitch," I spat before slamming her head again. "How dare you? How fucking dare you point that thing at her?" How the hell Kyle and Mike had ever seen anything in this freak was beyond me.

"You're too late," Rachel cackled, not even trying to fight me off. "Poor little princess has a boo-boo."

My eyes followed where her finger pointed and my stomach lurched. I gaped in pure horror as Lee's frightened gray eyes fluttered closed. The hand she had pressed to her stomach dropped to her side. Her entire body slumped forward as she collapsed to her knees.

"Lee!" The roar that tore from my throat was that of a feral animal. Her stomach...Oh god, there was a freaking hole in her stomach. Fury–red hot burning rage–flooded my veins as I turned on Rachel. "You crazy bitch."

Digging my nails into her scalp, I dragged her forward. With every ounce of strength in my body, I crushed her head against the frame of the door. I couldn't think straight. I wanted to inflict so much pain on this girl that she'd never open her evil eyes again. She fell to the ground, eyes closed and unresponsive. I wished for her death. I prayed that I had taken her last breath. Spluttering noises drew my attention back to Lee. I had to force my eyes open as I went to her. "Lee, hang on. I'm going to get help."

"Cam..." she tried to speak but dark clots of blood spilled from her mouth.

She's dying...

Oh god, I knew she was. No one bled out of their mouth. No

one's blood was that black. She was going to die. That crazy fucking bitch had finally done it. Blood… All I could see was Lee's blood spilling from her mouth, her stomach. I could smell it. It was suffocating me.

"Cam…Get out of here…Run." Lee kept trying to speak to me and all I wanted to do was cover her mouth with my hand to stop the blood. I wanted to scream at her to keep quiet and close her mouth. There was so much of her blood on us–on the floor–that I couldn't imagine much more being left inside of her body…

Grabbing my cell phone I dialed 911. "I need an ambulance and the police." I glared at Rachel's slumped frame. "And a strait jacket. Thirteenth Street. University Hill. Hurry," I paused to stop my voice from rising to a scream. I didn't want Lee to hear my fear and right about now it was crawling up my throat. "My friend has been shot."

"Okay ma'am. We'll send someone out straight away," the voice on the other line said. I couldn't tell if I was speaking to a man or a woman. I couldn't think, period. "Is the wound visible through the clothing? Can you tell me where your friend has been shot?"

I looked down at Lee's stomach and flinched. "Yeah. In the stomach, I think."

Please don't die...

Please don't die…

"The paramedics are on the way, ma'am. I need you to put pressure on the wound," the operator told me. "Have you got a towel you can press to her stomach?" Oh my fucking god. I hung up before I could scream at the idiot. What the hell? I had just walked in on a shooting and now I was supposed to pull a towel out of my ass like I'd been doing the freaking dishes.

Asshole.

Shrugging off my jacket, I pressed it against her belly. Warm ooze seeped onto my hands. Blood. My mind was flooded with images of a blue eyed, eight week old baby looking for her momma. Her momma was dying in my arms. Oh god, how was I going to face Kyle? Should I call him? No…I needed to stay calm and stop her from bleeding out. "Lee, I have to put pressure on the wound. I need to slow the bleeding."

She looked up at me with her huge glassy eyes full of fear. I tried to smile to comfort her, but my jaw was strained so tight I could barely twitch my lips. "You need to get out of here," she coughed. "She could…wake up."

Shame filled me, mixing with the huge tsunami of fear in my gut, cracking my heart open. "Shut up," I hissed as I dragged her body into my arms and cradled her. I rocked her in my arms the same way I had all those years ago. She needed to live. This was so unfair. Everything she had endured. All her suffering. I couldn't stand this. I couldn't live with this…I battled down the sobs that were dangerously threatening to overpower me.

I was supposed to be leaving tonight for Ireland. I was leaving and I was going to let her down again. "God, I'm so glad I forgot to pack my swimsuit when I left," I lied. "That's why I came here. Me and Mike, we're taking a trip…" Bullshit. Truth was I hadn't seen Mike in days. Since the day I woke up and came clean with myself. The day I told him I was still in love with Derek– that I'd been consistently in love with Derek since I was nineteen years old.

I was going to Ireland alone. I needed to find myself again, but I didn't know if Lee was going to make it. I didn't want her last memory to be of me letting her down again. If she knew all the ways I'd let her down. The guilt I felt for her life turning out the way it did, churned in my stomach. Should I tell her what I knew? I couldn't. I *couldn't* do it. I just needed to hold her and keep her alive. My god, I needed to make this better. She needed to make it. I would do anything if she would just stay alive. I'd stay. I'd stay for her.

"Cam, I'm scared…" she gasped for air. Her body shook violently in my arms.

So am I…

The fear in her eyes was too much to take. At that moment, I would have done anything to trade places with her. "You better not be," I warned her. I was serious. She had too much to lose. Too many people to leave behind. "You have a beautiful baby who is depending on you. Focus on Hope. Put her picture in your head and keep it there. Do not lose focus."

"Get up." My head jerked up at the sound of Rachel's venomous tone. That bitch just wouldn't die… "Get out of the way, Camryn. She has to die."

Lee tried to push me away, but I held her tighter. This was not happening. Not on my watch. I needed to stay calm. I needed to talk this bitch down long enough for the cops to come and knock her out. Where the hell were they? "You don't have to do this, Rachel." I hated myself for even speaking to her, but I needed to slow her down.

"Cam, run...please move," Lee begged. "Do it. Do it...or she'll...kill us both."

I shook my head in disgust. How the hell was she asking me to do that, with a straight face? I looked at her face and I was transported back to a time when this girl had been a vulnerable child, begging me to run away with her. The life she'd endured from her father, from the bullies in school who had taunted her for being poor and for the clothes she wore, ate through me. It had broken my heart then. It broke my heart worse now that I knew. I wanted to tell her about her mother. I wanted her to know what I'd discovered when I'd stayed with my parents back in January, but she'd hate me for not telling her then. She would resent me and my parents. "And what kind of a person would that make me if I did that?" I demanded. She was trembling and terrified. So was I. But I couldn't...I just couldn't leave her.

Have you ever felt so much love for another person–such a pure, raw, overwhelming love and connection for another human being that you would put your heart, soul and body on the line to stop their pain? Have you ever owed another human everything you have? Have you ever known a secret about someone close to you that made you feel sick with guilt and unfairness? I have, and that's the way I felt for Lee. Our bond ran deeper than bloodlines. She was the other half of me. My sister...My best friend. I wasn't going to sit back and stay quiet this time.

I would NOT watch her die.

Setting Lee aside, I knelt slowly and tried some persuasion. "Rachel," I coaxed. "If you go now, if you run, you'll have time. Think of your family. You're twenty two years old and you're going to ruin your life. And for what, a man?" I cursed every inch of Kyle Carter's penis at that moment. "Don't be stupid. The cops will be here any minute. You're never going to get away with this."

Rachel's hand shot out so fast I didn't have time to defend myself before she grabbed my ponytail. "Do you think I care anymore," she screamed, eyes focused on Lee. I tried to free myself but the girl had trapped me. "I have nothing left to lose.

She took everything from me." Grabbing the back of my neck, Rachel shoved me forward. I hit the refrigerator so hard I was pretty sure my nose was printed on the door. Stupid bitch. *I have a photoshoot in Dublin next week...*

"It didn't have to come to this," Rachel roared. I shook my head to clear my vision. "If you had just left when I told you to...goodbye Delia."

"No," I screamed. A surge of desperation surged through my body causing me to hurl myself towards Lee's limp body huddled on the floor.

There was noise…pain…silence.

Heat encased my mind...burning though my body.

Everything stopped.

My heart.

My mind.

My body.

Light and warmth filled my soul. I closed my blue eyes and thought of his green ones.

ONE

PRESENT DAY

DEREK

I KNEW where I was going, and I also knew it was a really bad idea. It had been months. I needed to move on. I needed to get a life.

I needed a lobotomy.

Her headstone had been erected. It stood there in front of me, a constant reminder of who was underneath the ground.

Rest in Peace
Camryn Louise Frey
God's mercy shall never falter.
Nor shall the ferocity in which we love one another.
For it is cherished within the depths of our human hearts,
until we meet again.

It had been one hundred and seventy-seven days since she left me and one hundred and five since she left this world. Except she didn't leave. She was stolen–fucking robbed from me. First by Mike, and then by Rachel.

I leaned forward and stroked her headstone–something I did every day–as I placed the bouquet of lilies on her grave. "Happy birthday, babe."

Kyle didn't know I came here every day. I lived on my own now so it was easier to keep my shit to myself. As soon as Lee had been released from the hospital, he'd taken her and their daughter to stay at his hotel in Boulder, while he sorted out somewhere permanent for them to live.

He stopped by most days to check on me, probably because of how freaked out he'd been the morning when he came into my room as I was taking the meds I'd been prescribed after the shooting.

I'd been hung over to shit and holding a bottle of sleeping pills in my hands, so really, I couldn't blame him for jumping to conclusions. He'd thought I was going to end it, and to be perfectly honest, I still wasn't sure what I'd intended to do that morning.

My head had been all over the place. I'd been drinking at some crummy bar the night before and had brought home a girl–the first since she left me. And every second I'd been inside of her I thought of Camryn, which was wrong and messed up on more levels than I'd ever dare to think about.

All I remembered from that morning was that I'd felt like shit, I had been thoroughly disgusted with myself for using that girl. It hadn't stopped me from doing it though. I couldn't seem to stop myself from living like this.

"Hey, you."

The sound of her soft, familiar southern twang curled around my heart like a blanket of comfort. I turned and watched as my curly-haired, former-roommate made her way towards me pushing a stroller. I liked listening to Lee's voice. It was gentle and sweet. It reminded me of melted butter and Camryn.

I'd hoped I wouldn't run into her today. I knew she was worried about me and I didn't want to put her under any more strain. She had enough going on with her parents.

"Hey ice," I mumbled, jamming my hands into my jean pockets. Lee thought I called her 'ice queen' because of how screwed up and weird she was when she first moved here. But I actually meant Kyle was the ice–cold and hard as a rock. He'd been virtually impenetrable until Lee came along and softened him up. Hell, she'd turned him into a puddle of goo at her feet. Kyle called her his princess but she was his fucking queen and he protected her like their lives were a chess game. I'd seen the change in him the moment he set eyes on her in our kitchen. His stance changed, his whole body went on high alert and I reckoned if we were animals, he'd have marched straight over and marked his territory. Shit, thinking back, he did that anyway. Douchebag had almost taken her virginity in his damn kitchen…

Yeah, I'd been standing right beside Kyle Carter the night his world altered. He'd been ruined ever since. I knew the signs because it had happened to me with Cam…

She'd walked into my world when I was eighteen years old and had taken the air from my lungs and the earth from under my feet. She'd left a mark on me that could never be matched or would never fade. Well, she left two marks. One on my heart and the other on my ass.

Stupid poker game…

When Lee reached my side, she was slightly out of breath. A layer of sweat covered her forehead. My hackles shot up. "Tell me you didn't walk here."

"Please don't start as well, Derek." Her eyes dropped to the ground and I felt like a dick. "You're the only person in my life who doesn't treat me like glass. You're the only friend I have who treats me like I'm still *Lee*."

No, scratch that, I was a dick. I'd raised my voice knowing full well how shit like that affected her. But dammit, she was barely out of the hospital three fucking weeks and I remembered exactly how sick she had been–how close to death she was. It was amazing how quickly the human body could recover, but she shouldn't be walking down the stairs let alone the thirty minutes it took to get here. The girl had a death wish and Kyle was going to flip.

We stared each other down for a moment as a silent understanding passed between us.

'Back me up and I'll back you up. No questions,' her eyes begged me.

I nodded my silent response. ' I got your back, Ice.'

"Pretty flowers," Lee said in a soft dreamy tone. "Cam's favorites. She would have been twenty three today."

'I know' I wanted to scream. Her birthday wasn't something I was likely to forget. I'd celebrated the last four with her, three of them as her fucking boyfriend.

I'd spent my freshman year trying to woo Camryn Frey, finally winning her over the night of her twentieth birthday. Well, my ass wooed her more than my face. I lost a poker bet the night of her birthday and ended up getting a tattoo of a fucking penguin on my ass cheek. Cam had picked the design, a stipulation of the bet. I remembered being pissed as hell that I'd ended up with a goddamn penguin on my butt, however ending up with Camryn Frey naked in my bed that night had more than sweetened the deal. I'd been ruined the very first day she walked through Kyle's front door. Jesus, my stomach still flipped when I thought about it. I'd never seen legs like hers...so firm and slender and long. God, she had the most amazing legs.

I'd called dibs on her the minute she'd slipped down to her room with her pink suitcase to unpack. There was no way I was letting Kyle have her, though he hadn't really looked. I still found that crazy. Kyle was a huge player when we were younger, but he'd never looked at Cam like that. Well, he checked out her tits the morning she ran out of the bathroom butt naked, screaming about a spider trying to kill her, but I couldn't blame him for that. I ended up taking a very cold shower after that floor show.

"Did you have any trouble with reporters on your way here?" I asked, changing the subject before my brain exploded. "They've stopped camping outside the house." It was a relief to get up in the morning and not have vultures preying on the front door step looking for a scoop.

I'd been harassed in the weeks following Rachel's arrest, but Kyle and Lee had been tormented. Lee had been protected while in the hospital, but Kyle couldn't step foot outside the doors of the hospital or the hotel, without having a camera or a microphone shoved in his face. He had paid his legal team a small fortune to keep his daughter's face off the television and out of the papers, however there wasn't much he could do to protect his and Lee's privacy. The story was huge and I'd found out more about my best friend in the past four months than I had in the four and half years I'd known him.

Every detail of their private lives had been dragged through the press. Now the whole world knew about Kyle's relationship with Rachel Grayson and the twisted pact she had forced him into. Personally, I'd called bullshit on her lies years ago, but Kyle hadn't been able to see straight from guilt. Every sordid detail of his two year affair with Rachel–and Lee's miscarriage–was public knowledge. Kyle had been painted as a troubled orphan teenager who was thrust into power by his secret millionaire grandfather, targeted by an array of beautiful gold-diggers, only to lose his heart to a Louisianan bombshell with an empty bank account.

What fucking bullshit...

No one ever wrote about Kyle's decency towards his friends or the fact that he was the one who had pursued Lee. They never highlighted the fact that Lee had worked her butt off as a cleaner in his hotel for months without ever knowing the guy was loaded. I had been there. I'd suffered living in the house with that palpable chemistry buzzing between them. I'd watched their friendship progress to love. I'd witnessed their struggles, I knew the goddamn truth. Those two had been through enough heartache and it pissed me the hell off to read about their lives–our lives–being picked apart and scrutinized.

One particular newspaper seemed to have one hell of an informer. Just last month–when shit had finally started to die down–they had unearthed several details about incidents that happened during a house party last October. Kyle had been slated for his temper and accused of being abusive to Lee. More bullshit. Yeah, he had a temper that rivaled a lion, but the guy would never physically harm a female. As for hurting Lee? I think Kyle would tear the whole world apart if so much as a hair on her head was ruffled.

I banked my money on Dixon Jones being the rat. He'd never been a fan of Kyle. The fact that he'd shown an interest in Lee when she first moved here and how she'd turned him down for Kyle was probably his motivation. Well, that and the cash. There was a tidy sum of money being offered for information from the bigger newspapers.

Several foster families Kyle had lived with had come forward with stories about him and how he'd been a 'difficult' child growing up. Everyone had an opinion on their relationship and every newspaper covering the shooting had branded them 'the broken lovers.'

"No, but they still come to the hotel," Lee growled as she frowned deeply. "Not nearly as often as before, but some manage to sneak in. It's Kyle they want to speak to most. I guess he takes good pictures for the front page stories." She shook her head. "I don't know what they think they're going to find. The whole nightmare is a matter of public record." That was for sure. A living breathing nightmare.

"I really don't know why I'm here, Lee," I admitted, raising my shoulders in an awkward shrug. "Or why I keep coming here."

"I do," she said quietly as she stroked my arm. "You love her," she whispered. "And just because someone dies, it doesn't mean that your love for them becomes past tense. Emotions don't have an integrated app or warning signal to let people know when someone is gone. The heart has its own sat-nav. It always seems to lead us back to those we love, regardless of logic."

Shit.

"You should be a psychologist," I muttered, as I used my fingers to brush my hair out of my eyes. I used to keep my black hair shaved tight, but I hadn't bothered cutting it since Cam died. Truth was I didn't see much point in carrying out any grooming rituals besides the mandatory shit, shave and shower. There was no fucking point and I didn't care.

Fifteen weeks...some days it felt like it happened yesterday. Other days it felt like years had passed. The pain was the same. That was the one thing that never changed.

Lee smiled, but it was forced. "I don't think so, Derek. I'm just an experienced woman of heartbreak. The sat-nav of my heart is all kinds of crazy." Kyle's mini-me started crying and Lee bent down and picked her out of her stroller.

Hope was gorgeous. Even I had to admit that. She had a pair of lungs on her that rivaled any varsity football coach, but damn the kid was cute. I'd been unfortunate enough to witness her entrance into the world last May–well, her entrance into the back seat of Kyle's car.

Lee popping that kid out with Kyle perched between her legs waiting to catch her was something my eyes could never unsee. The demonic screams that had come out of her mouth were something my ears could never un-hear. I wished like hell he would change his fucking car and stop driving the maternity Merc. I would never look at a Mercedes the same way again–or a vagina.

"What's wrong, sweetie?" Lee crooned as she bobbed around with Hope in her arms.

"How'd you escape the guard?" I joked, trying to lighten the mood. If it were any other person I wouldn't bother, I wouldn't try to look normal and…stable. But this was Lee. She was as delicate as a flower. *Poor girl.*

Lee grinned. "I locked him in the bathroom." She turned to Hope and cooed. "That's right, isn't it? Momma locked your poor daddy in the bathroom."

"Nice," I chuckled. Lee had turned my hot-headed, temperamental best friend into a ball of mush. Kyle was whipped by the leading woman in his life. He bent over backwards for his two girls and damn straight he should.

After the way he had treated Lee in the beginning of their relationship– lying, cheating and generally being an asshole – I was surprised as hell that she'd forgiven him. She had a forgiving heart though, and it belonged to Kyle. The proof of which was hanging on her left hand in the form of a huge mother-fucker diamond. Yeah, he was also an over the top bastard.

Lee sighed heavily. "I swear, Derek, half of the time I feel like I'm drowning inside. Everything is upside down. I'm confused and scared. We have to be so careful around everyone, and Kyle freaks out if I move too far from his side. I shower: he's there. I freaking pee and he's outside the door shouting 'take a sample, princess,' or 'don't lock the door, baby.'" She bit down on her lip, clearly thinking of a plot I wanted no role in. "I understand why he's over-protective, I mean, of course I understand, but I'm worried about him. Do you think you could maybe have a word with him? Ask him to relax a little? I'm scared he's going to wear himself out."

I raised my brow and gave her an 'are you for real' look. "And you think he'd listen to me if I did?"

Lee chuckled softly. "No, probably not. He's as stubborn as a mule."

That was for sure. I'd known Kyle since we were teenagers. He'd been a hell-raiser then, doing whatever the hell he wanted, surviving on his wit and gut feeling. If he thought he was right, there wasn't a person on this planet that could talk the guy down. In the almost five years I'd known him, I'd only witnessed one person tame the beast. And that person was standing in front of me, holding his baby-spawn.

"He is who he is, Lee." I poked Hope in the belly and was rewarded with a huge gummy, one-toothed smile. "He needs control. It's just his way. Life knocked him on his ass as a kid and the guy just gets back up and keeps swinging. His intentions are good. It's his execution he needs to work on. He might have more cash than half of Boulder now, but the dude is street at heart. Rough rearing like that doesn't produce the most tactile people."

"It's not his past that bothers me," she said quietly. "I love him more *because* of what he's been through. What bothers me is the fact that I'm becoming too attached to him being with me all of the time, and then when he leaves, I'm a wreck. I'm too dependent on him, Derek. Most nights ,I can't even think about going to bed until he comes home, and even then he's only downstairs working. I'm craving him all of the time. I'm missing him as we speak. That's not normal. A woman isn't supposed to depend on a man that much, right?"

I smirked at her anxious looking expression. Poor girl was clueless. "That's not dependency you're feeling, sweetheart." I tapped my finger against my temple. "That's love. It's an evil, crazy bitch. Screws you right over."

She seemed to ponder that over for a moment before smiling. "Who's the psychologist now, huh?"

"Funny." I smirked. "Is he still pushing you on the whole Brady bunch, 'love your mommy' idea?"

I had to bite back a smile when Lee actually growled. "Yes," she hissed. "He is like a dog with a bone. And in this instance, he needs to keep that bone away from his bitch."

"Did you just call yourself Kyle's bitch?" I asked, not even trying to hide my grin.

"I meant it in a hypothetical way," she blushed. "As in...Oh never mind. I suppose you agree with him?"

"That you should make up with your mom?"

Lee nodded stiffly. "Yeah, do you agree?"

"No," I told her. "I actually think Kyle pushing you to talk to Tracy is about the dumbest thing he's done in months." I'd told

Kyle that very same thing but the idiot wouldn't back the hell off. I was team Lee on this one. Tracy had spent a year with Jimmy Bennett. Lee had eighteen of them. It didn't take a genius to figure out who had gotten the shorter end of the stick. "It's your choice, ice. No one can blame you for being wary."

"It's more than wariness, Derek." She paused to place a kiss on Hope's head. "I can't stand her," she confessed. "And I know that's a terrible way to feel because she saved my life when she gave me her kidney. But every time I look at Hope." Lee bit down on her lip as she shook her head in disgust. "Every time I look into my daughter's eyes, I remember what Tracy did to me and I am consumed with anger. I feel betrayed and abandoned."

"I don't blame you for feeling like that," I muttered. Lee was dealing with the biggest fucking shit bomb of all of us.

She'd been shot twice. Had been in a coma for weeks, only to wake up and find out that her best friend was dead. Worse again, the mother she'd believed to be dead actually wasn't and wanted to play happy families with her. And her dumb as fuck fiancé was all for it.

Lee was dealing and Kyle was pushing her. I'd warned him on enough occasions of what would happen if he pushed that girl too far. I was surprised as hell that she hadn't run screaming from Boulder. God knows I would if I was her. Shit was fucked up around this neck of the woods.

"That's because you know how it feels," she replied. "To have your whole world pulled out from under your feet. To be utterly betrayed, and then be expected to forgive and forget because of some redeeming, heroic act that wasn't in your power to prevent."

"Do you think it will ever go away?" I asked, knowing Lee would understand my question.

"I think in time it will become manageable," she replied. "I think it will become easier. But no, I don't think missing Cam will ever completely go away."

TWO

KYLE

"HOW FAST CAN we get this done?" I asked Kelsie Mayfield, my attorney, as we stood in front of the timber-framed, ranch style house on South Peak Road. The place was incredible, hidden well from the road and had more security than Fort Knox. Fucking perfect. I thanked my lucky stars the owner–some high-flying corporate monkey with a fondness for slot machines–needed a quick sale. I didn't consult my conscience when it came to the safety of my girls. His loss and stupidity was my gain. Their protection was paramount to me.

"I'll get right on it, Mr. Carter," Kelsie said as she pushed her glasses higher on her nose. "The owner says he'll be out before Christmas. You should have the keys by December at the latest. I'll have the paperwork drawn up and the fee transferred immediately."

"It has to be sooner," I muttered in irritation. Lee had been home three weeks and I wanted her out of that hotel room. Since she was still refusing to step foot inside our house on Thirteenth Street–and Christ, I didn't blame her–I'd decided on a belated birthday gift. A house. The one in front of me to be exact. I figured she'd like it. It kind of reminded me of her. Beautiful and untouched by the outside world with an air of loneliness…

Besides, this would be a positive move for both of us. After spending the last three weeks living in a hotel room with a five and half month old baby, I was starting to get antsy. Not to mention the fact that I needed her safe, somewhere away from the city and the drama. She needed to recover and I needed the peace of mind of knowing that she wasn't being harassed by reporters every damn minute she walked out the door. She'd been through enough and I sure as hell wasn't going to let anything else happen to her.

Lee Bennett ruined me the moment she walked through my door–all hips and curls–and continued to ruin me every day since. *Ruin me and drive me insane in the process.* Having spent a little under two years of her life with me, Lee had more scars and wounds on her body than when I'd met her. I'd let her down more times than I could count and she still remained by my side. That Friday afternoon three weeks ago, when the doctors had finally allowed me to take her home after twelve weeks in hospital, was one of the best days of my life. It was the day Lee Bennett had *finally* agreed to marry me. After months of asking–and being turned down–she had said yes. I made her a promise that day that I would never let her down again. I'd made myself a promise that day, too. I vowed to myself that I'd never let her go, not after coming so close to losing her.

Twice.

I almost lost her last Christmas when she miscarried one of our twins. It had nearly killed her. But the second time was so much worse. Lee had been the target of an unhinged woman intent on taking her life in her pursuit of *me.* I often wondered how she could stay with me. She had never–not fucking once since she'd opened her eyes in that hospital bed–blamed me for what had happened to her. I didn't understand the girl. Rachel Grayson had murdered her best friend Cam. She had very nearly cost my daughter her mother. And me? Rachel had almost taken my entire fucking world away from me. Lee had been shot in the stomach and kidney back in June and it was a goddamn miracle that she'd survived.

We both knew I was to blame. I'd known Rachel had a problem. I'd seen the warning signs and I'd ignored each and every one of them until it was too late. Yet, all Lee had done since she'd woken up was look up at me with those big, trusting gray eyes and thank me for being such a good father to Hope. If she'd been awake and had seen the way I behaved after the shooting, I doubt she'd thank me so much. My behavior had been disgraceful. The days that followed the shooting had been the first in my life that I had given up hope. Truly given up on living. It had taken my sharp-tongued hotel manager, Linda, to remind me of who the hell I was and how I didn't give up on anything, no matter how bleak things seemed.

Of course Linda had been right–she usually was–and our lives were slowly returning to normal. I was trying my best not to smother Lee, but it was difficult for me to let her go anywhere on her own. She was fragile and vulnerable, and dammit, the girl was too important to me. If I had my way I'd lock her away somewhere safe where no one could touch a hair on her head again. I got the fact that she needed her independence–her life back, but my blood pressure rose every time she went off on her own. Although, to be fair, I always knew where to find her.

The cemetery.

It was the only place Lee went without me and I felt like crap that I wasn't able to take her as often as she needed. Because it was a need for Lee–a comfort.

I was still pretty fucking annoyed about the whole bathroom incident yesterday. I had to meet with our lawyer to discuss Rachel's latest letter and had freaked out when Lee suggested going to visit Cam on her own. She went anyway and locked me in the bathroom so I couldn't stop her–for two fucking hours. When I'd eventually picked the lock and made it to my attorney's office, Derek had texted me to let me know where she was and why. I'd felt like the worst piece of shit on this planet for not remembering the date. October 06th: Cam's birthday. I'd seen the desperation in Lee's eyes–heard it in her voice when she'd begged me to let her go–and I'd refused to listen…

Personally, I didn't understand how she could sit in that place for hours on end chatting to a slab of marble. I missed Cam–thought about her every day–but I knew she was gone. I knew she wasn't under that earth and she couldn't hear my words.

I'd said my goodbyes when I'd pulled back that sheet and exposed her lifeless body. I'd prayed for her and cried for her and then I'd locked that shit up and kept on going. It wasn't about me being insensitive, because I fucking cared. I cared and I grieved like everyone else, maybe not in the same way, but I did. It was about me accepting the fact that death was death. It was final.

There was no phone signal or Wi-Fi wherever the hell Cam was now. She couldn't hear us and I couldn't change a damn thing. That might be a cold way of thinking, but it was my way. I lost my mom to suicide when I was three years old and I'd spent enough of my childhood praying to a black sky and getting no response. It helped Lee to talk to Cam though and I wanted to give her what she needed, but I didn't want her going anywhere without me. I knew that sounded selfish, but the girl was my heart. If anything else was to happen to her and I wasn't around...I'd lose my mind.

I fully acknowledged I was being a possessive asshole. There was no point in denying the truth, but my behavior was driven by love and fear. If it had been Lee sitting at my bedside for weeks–not knowing if I would live or die–I reckon she'd be a lot more understanding of my protective nature. I'd watched her struggle as she re-trained her body to do the things that had always come easily and it broke my fucking heart.

It scared the hell out of me that she may have to undergo another transplant in a few years. The doctors warned us that the average kidney transplant lasted between ten and twelve years. He'd also pointed out–since I'd lost my shit in his office–that others have been known to last for the lifetime of the recipient.

Because Tracy is Lee's biological mother, her chances are better than most. The doc had said that living donors are the best kind because the kidney's completely healthy, and blood relatives make the best donors because their tissues match or some shit. All I knew was Lee was healing and recuperating and I was living in a constant frenzy of fear, waiting for the next bad thing to strike us...

"Tell him there's an extra twenty grand if he's out by the end of the month."

Kelsie gaped at me. "But...today's the seventh, sir."

I smirked as I turned around and headed towards my car. "Fine, fifty grand," I said, throwing my hand in the air. "Just get me in that house as fast as possible, Kelsie."

It was a twenty-minute drive from South Peak Road to University Hill, and within ten my phone was ringing. "Kelsie," I said, putting the phone to my ear. "Tell me you have good news."

"Yes, Mr. Carter," I heard her say on the other line. "I offered twenty. He accepted. You'll have the keys by the twenty fifth."

I sighed in relief.

Thank fucking god.

"Good. Thanks, Kelsie, I owe you," I said before hanging up. Little Kelsie was going to be getting a bonus – that was for fucking sure. The girl had the temperament of a skittish foal, but she was a damn good lawyer.

Pulling into the driveway of my old house, I killed the engine and headed up the steps. My head hurt every time I came here. Pushing every fucked up mental image my mind was shoving to the surface aside, I turned the door knob. "Derek," I called out as I stepped inside. Jesus Christ, it was a good thing Lee couldn't deal with coming back here. Derek was living like a slob. "Derek," I shouted louder as I made my way through the rubble.

What a fucking pig sty.

I climbed over the piles of dirty laundry and empty beer cans, not stopping until I reached the kettle. Flicking it on, I busied myself with washing a couple of mugs and then grabbed some milk from the fridge. I opened the gallon and quickly closed it. Uh, I was sure I'd bought that very same gallon when I moved out, along with some groceries when I'd realized my dumb as fuck best friend wasn't feeding himself. Jesus.

Carrying the two mugs of black coffee, I made my way down the hall to Derek's room, opening the door, I looked inside and shook my head in disgust. "Get your ass up, douchebag," I growled. "It's seven in the evening."

Derek stirred from where he was lying face down on his bed. "Fuck off, Kyle," he mumbled, grabbing a pillow and covering the back of his head with it.

"I'll give you fuck off," I muttered. I'd tried everything with him these past few weeks. Talking didn't work. Pleading worked even less. Action was the only thing left. Setting the mugs down on the floor, I crossed the hall to the bathroom and filled a jug with water before heading back into his room and tossing it over his stupid ass. The blonde, who was sprawled out next to him, squealed and leapt up off the bed.

"Oh my god," she screamed, boobs out and pussy bare. She glared at me for a moment before her eyes took on a predatory gleam. "Divert your eyes, pretty boy, unless you feel like joining us?"

I snorted in disgust. "Divert your ass, Blondie, out of my fucking house. Now."

"Sorry, sweetheart," Derek grumbled as he sat up slowly. "The slumber party's over. *Daddy's* home."

"Say goodbye to your friend," I growled as I swung around to leave. "And take a damn shower."

"What's with the cock blocking?" Derek muttered as he strolled into the kitchen ten minutes later with a towel around his waist. "Not cool, Kyle. Not cool at all."

I had to use every ounce of my self-control to keep my ass in my chair and remind myself that Derek wasn't himself. The memory of how I'd found him a few weeks back came to the forefront of my mind–a constant reminder that Derek wasn't coping as well as he made out.

I'd met his first sleepover buddy–naked in my goddamn kitchen–five days before Lee was due home while my daughter was upstairs sleeping.

I'd gone downstairs to grab Hope's morning feed, in just my boxers, only to be violated by a big breasted brunette with a dirty fucking mouth. Needless to say I'd lost my shit, and after tossing her ass out of my house, I stormed into his bedroom and almost choked with fear…

His room reeked from the stench of whiskey and sex. He was sitting at the foot of his bed, fresh from a shower with a towel wrapped around his waist. "Is she gone?" Derek asked. I couldn't answer his question because my heart had stopped fucking beating when I saw what he was holding in his hand.

"What are you doing, Derek?" I managed to squeeze out, even though my lungs felt like they were about to burst inside of my body.

"I'm tired, Kyle," he slurred, obviously still drunk from the night before–if he'd even gone to bed. "It's like my mind is stuck on repeat.

Constantly playing out the same scenes over and over, until I feel like I'm going crazy. And then I welcome the insanity. Sometimes I want to fall into that dark hole in my head. Fall in there and stay in the black. Black is easy." He laughed, but it was forced. "I was fucking her and seeing Cam. How messed up does that make me? Visualizing myself with a dead girl who didn't even want me when she was alive…"

"No," I choked out, as I sank down on the bed next to him and grabbed the bottle of sleeping pills–I hadn't even known he'd been prescribed–out of his hand. "You don't fall into the black, the dark or any of that shit. You feel like falling, then you fall on me, you got it? You can always fall on me."

Derek slumped over. Resting his elbows on his knees, he covered his face with his hands. "This isn't me. I don't do this to women…I don't know who I am anymore. I don't have a fucking clue of what to do with myself. I've lost my job. I'm so screwed…I'm sorry, dude. I know you probably don't want Hope around me when I'm all fucked up like this. Shit, I don't want her around me when I'm like this."

"Stop talking crap, you know Hope loves you. You're fucking great with that girl and we all know it…Why does this conversation sound like you're saying goodbye?" I asked, fucking terrified. I'd never been in this position before, or at least not with someone I'd give my right arm for.

Derek didn't answer me, which caused my anxiety levels to hit the roof. "Look, Derek, I know this sucks. I don't ever want to feel what you're feeling right now. She tore your fucking heart out when she left with Mike and I know you said you were okay about it, but it's clear that you're not. It's okay to be angry, to be shredded. If Lee pulled that shit on me and died before I had a chance to get closure, I don't think I'd even function. But you have to get through this dude. I'm here for you. You need to know that, man. I am here for you."

Since that morning, I had tried everything to wake his ass up. Nothing worked. Even though he did seem a little more stable and smelled better. I found myself losing patience fast with the stranger walking around in my best friend's body. "You're an idiot, Derek. That chick was nasty. I could smell the STD's a mile off."

"I've been called worse," he grumbled plopping into the chair next to me. "And unlike your stupid ass, I always wrap it up. So are you here for an actual reason, or did you just stop by to berate me for my poor choice in women and drill me on my methods of birth control?"

"How much did you drink last night?" I asked, ignoring his smart remarks. I was starting to think that I was stuck inside some warped universe.

For the past four months, I'd put every ounce of my time and energy into getting Lee better and out of that damn hospital. And now she was home, Derek had gone and lost his damn mind. I knew he was hurting. I'd known that even when Lee was in her coma. He'd managed to keep it together for me even though his whole world had crumbled. I'd leaned on him too much. When I'd needed help with Hope, or with the business, I had turned to Derek and he'd supported me without clause or stipulation. I'd put too much on his shoulders. It was only a matter of time before he cracked.

Derek didn't answer, but the way his eyes flinched when I spoke too loud was answer enough. I hissed in frustration. "Jesus, man, you have to stop this. You're gonna put yourself in an early grave."

He looked at me with dead eyes. "Do I look like I care?"

"Don't," I warned. "Don't fucking say shit like that. Not after Cam..."

"Don't talk about her to me," he shouted, jumping up from his chair. "I'm dealing with this my way."

That was the problem. He wasn't dealing with it at all. He'd closed himself off. I think the shock and the adrenalin kept him functioning for the first few weeks after the shooting, but when that wore out the guy had just...slumped. Now he refused to speak about Cam, to me at least. "You're going to have to talk about her, preferably sooner than later."

"Preferably never," he shot back in annoyance.

Okay, change tactics...

"I bought the house on South Peak Road," I told him, watching for some glimmer of life. I saw nothing besides the slight flare of his nostrils. "The one I was telling you about with the apartment in the basement. I will get the keys in a few weeks. I want you to come with us and get out of this damn house."

He folded his arms and stared at me. "No thanks."

"This is not healthy, dude," I argued. "Living in this house after what..."

"I said I'm not moving out, Kyle," he shouted. "I don't want to. So you can either accept that or throw me out."

I sighed heavily. "You know I'm not going to throw you out, you idiot."

"Then let it go."

"Fine," I hissed as I stood up and made my way out of the kitchen. I wasn't getting anywhere with him and I was needed at the hotel. Lee got nervous if she was on her own too long and I'd been gone for hours. It was dark outside, she'd be worried by now. I never left her on her own. This was the first time we'd been apart in the twenty-two days she'd been home. Fuck. I needed to hire someone to keep an eye on her when I couldn't be there. It didn't do either of us any good to be constantly worrying. "Did you talk to Lee about meeting her mom yet?" I'd asked Derek to drop it into conversation whenever he saw Lee. I was hoping he could make her see sense...

"It's not happening, Kyle," Derek said with a sigh. "You need to let it go, man."

"Not happening," I snapped. "They need to speak to each other. It's going to happen. I can't just sit back and do nothing."

"That's your problem, Kyle," Derek growled. "You don't always have to *do* something in order to help a person. Sometimes you can help more by just listening and more by *hearing* what that person is telling you."

"Whatever, dude," I growled, as I gestured around at what used to be a respectable looking house. "Listening won't get shit done around here. Clean this mess up."

"Sure thing, dad."

"Dig deep, Derek," I said, when I reached the front door. "And keep digging until you find yourself. I know you're in there. Don't let it win. Fucking fight it, dude."

THREE

LEE

WHERE WAS HE?

He'd been gone for hours.

I paced the floor of our makeshift home in the honeymoon suite of the Henderson hotel. Anxiety was gnawing at my stomach. I didn't like feeling this way but it was impossible not to, all things considered. I checked on Hope, and then I checked on her again. She was sleeping soundly in her crib–had been for the past thirty minutes and I knew she was down for the night. I'd been blessed with a baby who slept right through since she was eight weeks old.

I peeked through the curtain once more. It was getting dark outside. I hated the darkness. You could never tell what was lurking in the shadows–or who. Grabbing my cell, I powered it up and dialed his number.

"Hey, you've reached Kyle. Leave a message."

"Kyle," I whispered into the phone. "Can you please call me when you get this?" I hung up and turned my phone off quickly. I needed to get a handle on these nerves. I needed to get rid of them. They were ruining my life. I was okay with being on my own, but it freaked me out when I was alone at night. The silence disturbed me–it unleashed my nightmares.

I couldn't turn on the television. My face was all over it. I couldn't turn on my phone, my parents were tormenting me. All

I could do was sit in this damn hotel room and stare at the four walls, while my mind stirred up every bad memory just to torment me.

"Your mother's alive."

Those were the same words I'd been battling with since I opened my eyes in that hospital room and looked into his blue eyes.

"She's a real nice lady," Kyle had said to me when I woke up from my coma. I couldn't say that I agreed. I was grateful for the kidney and I was incredibly lucky that it had worked right away. There was a girl down the corridor from my hospital room who had to have continued dialysis after her transplant. The type of kidney failure I'd suffered was called acute kidney injury (AKI). It happened to me because of the damage caused to my kidneys when Rachel shot me.

At the time, my body had shut down and had been running on less than eleven percent kidney function. Basically I was dying. I would have died if my mother hadn't come out of hiding and saved me. And while they had removed my left kidney–the one the bullet had penetrated–and replaced it with Tracy's one, Dr. Michaels, my nephrologist, had hope that my right kidney would eventually begin to function normally. I was afraid to get my hopes up too much. I didn't dare.

I knew I owed Tracy my life. Without her, I wouldn't be here. Lord knows I was grateful, but my gratitude didn't change the past. It didn't erase my memories, or lack of.

Twenty years' worth of memories that didn't include her. I didn't have one single recollection of the woman who called herself my mother.

The only mother I had known was the one I had prayed to every night of my childhood to come and take me in my sleep, because being an angel in heaven with my momma seemed more appealing than being a battered child at the hands of my daddy. The mother who I'd sent silent messages of misery to every time my father put his hands on me. The mother whose death I had spent my life feeling guilty for. The mother who I'd been told died giving birth to me. All lies…

The worst thing about this whole messed up situation was Kyle's lack of understanding. I loved that man with every fiber of my being, but his attitude hurt me. He was one hundred percent pro-Tracy.

Kyle didn't understand my animosity towards her. But then again, he had never been a six year old girl forced to hide in the woods all night because her daddy had beaten her on her backside with a bicycle chain for eating the last slice of bread and then hit her harder for crying. Nor had he been that ashamed little girl when she had to let her best friend put cream on the wounds. Or an eleven year old girl who'd thought she was dying when she got her first period because no one had explained to her a menstrual cycle.

I had been that girl.

And I would never forgive the fact that there was someone out there who could have protected me–should have protected me–and didn't. I didn't have any photographs to document my childhood. There were no knitted booties or boxes of treasures marked 'Delia' to show that I had been born, let alone loved. All I had from my childhood was nightmares and scars.

I had a daughter, and I knew in my heart that there wasn't a force on this earth that could stop me from protecting her. I understood what it meant to be a mother. I just didn't understand what it was like to have one. I had survived twenty years without one, I didn't need one now.

The door of our hotel room burst open and my heart almost climbed out of my throat. Call it survival instincts or call me being a coward, but I couldn't stop myself from crouching between the couch and my daughter's crib. Every loud noise I heard brought to the surface memories I tried so hard to stifle.

Blood pooling around her pale, sunken face. Seeping into her blonde hair…

Those evil green eyes dancing with malice as the sound of a gun being fired bellowed through my eardrums…

The sound of flesh ripping apart as the smell of burning skin infected my senses…

My life flashing before my eyes as the darkness of death loomed over me…

"Pack your shit, princess. I got us a house." My heart restarted at the sound of Kyle's familiar husky tone and I let out a quivering breath. "Lee, where are you, baby?"

Climbing awkwardly to my feet, I smiled sheepishly at my fiancé. "Hi," I mumbled.

Kyle, who had about half a dozen duffel bags hanging from his neck–and two suitcases in his hands–tipped his head to one side. He stared at me like he could see right through my skin, straight to the core of me, and knowing Kyle, he probably could.

Kyle Carter knew every inch of my body. Every fraction of my soul. He was the first man I'd ever been with intimately. The first to break my heart. The first to put it back together again. He was my first and my last, he was my everything that came in between. He was also the sexiest man I'd ever seen and I wasn't kidding. Seriously, the man was so beautiful it hurt to look at him. Tall and toned, he had a body worthy of an underwear model. His short brown hair had a naturally tousled appearance–it was the kind of hair that made a woman want to run her nails through it–soft and silky, with just enough length to grab hold of…And when he looked at me, really looked at me with those blazing blue eyes, the intensity was almost too much.

I still couldn't believe I'd gotten so lucky. This man was going to marry me. *Me.* Lee Bennett. The small town girl from Montgomery, Louisiana. We'd talked about setting a date but had decided to wait until the trial was over before making any plans. Well, I had decided to wait. Kyle had pouted for three days until he reluctantly gave in. If he had his way we would fly to Vegas tonight. He'd tried to take me the day I said yes, but I'd persuaded him to slow down before informing him that I didn't have a passport. *I did now.* The man worked fast. That was the thing about Kyle. He never sat still on anything. If he wanted something he got it.

Kyle was a force to be reckoned with. He was like a tornado blowing in and sweeping up everyone and everything in his path. Thankfully, he'd decided to take me along for the tumultuous ride and in a few months' time I would be his wife.

"What were you doing on the floor, baby?" he asked in his deep husky voice as he placed the cases at his feet. His eyes trailed over every inch of my body, causing the heat in my belly to rise to my face. I dropped my hand from where I'd been clutching my side.

"Um..." I racked my brain for something to say that wouldn't add to the unnecessary guilt he carried.

Kyle had absorbed so much guilt from the night of the shooting. I didn't want to add another layer by telling him I was scared to death when he wasn't close by. He didn't need to worry. He was a busy man. Sometimes I wondered how he was able to make so much time for us while running twenty hotels around the country. I knew he felt responsible for Cam's death and for what had happened to me. It wasn't true though. Not in the slightest.

There were things that had happened to us in the past that Kyle was responsible for. The lies and his constant hot and cold attitude towards me when we first met was something I had no problem with him taking responsibility for. The night I'd miscarried his child while he'd been with his ex was another. But his ex-girlfriend breaking into his house and shooting us down in cold blood was not.

I wished I could take some of the burden off his shoulders, but that was the type of person Kyle was. He internalized absolutely everything negative that happened to us until he found some reason to blame himself. But instead of moping and sulking he turned his fear and his guilt into something positive. He had a never say die attitude and he was a man of action. He got things done when they needed to be done. His mental strength and dominant protectiveness of the people he loved were some of the things I admired most about him. They were also the things that drove me freaking crazy.

Besides, if Kyle was blaming himself then I deserved to be blamed, too. Rachel had cornered me weeks before the shooting and I hadn't told anyone. She'd threatened to bury me and I had ignored it..."I was doing some...exercise," I muttered in an attempt to drag myself back to the present. Kyle's expression was one of disbelief and I knew he could smell the bullshit a mile away for two obvious reasons. One: my cheeks were as red as tomatoes. And two: I wasn't a fitness bunny and it showed. I had hips, thighs and a mommy ass. "You said you got us a house?" I asked as I crossed the room to close the space between us. "Where?"

Kyle nodded his head in the direction of our bedroom before stalking off. I checked Hope and fixed her blankets before following Kyle. He closed the door as soon as I stepped inside our bedroom. Pulling the straps of the duffle bags over his head, he dropped them on the floor before tugging on my hips gently. "I didn't think," he whispered as he trailed his hands up my sides to cup my face. "I should've knocked." He ducked his head and placed a soft lush kiss on my lips before pulling back quickly.

"Where is this house?" I asked, as I nuzzled my cheek against the warmth of his chest. I refused to let him dwell. We were moving forward. It was the only way we would survive our past.

KYLE

"South Peak Road," I grunted as I held her frail body in an attempt to calm myself down. "It's nice, baby. Secluded." An array of emotions ran through me. Hatred towards Rachel for causing all of this. Pity for the tiny woman in front of me, who seemed more afraid now than she'd ever been before. And pure fucking anger with myself for not having the common sense to knock on the damn door first. Jesus Christ, it had shredded me inside when I saw her hiding on the floor. What the hell was wrong with me?

"Did you sign the lease yet?" Lee asked in a soft tone as she snuggled against my chest. "I'd like to see it before you do."

"Lease?" I shook my head and looked down at her. Shit, was she going to be pissed? "Lee, I bought it. I will get the keys in a few weeks."

"You bought a house?" she gasped, stepping away from me. "Just like that?" She snapped her fingers to emphasize her statement and I couldn't help but laugh at her shocked expression.

"Took me long enough," I chuckled. "I should have had you moved into a house the day you came home, but I was waiting on the right one to come up" I shrugged and smiled down at her. "Happy birthday…well, consider it more of a sorry for fucking up your last two birthdays…birthday." I hoped like hell the house would make up for the disastrous birthday meal I'd thrown for her.

Lee turned twenty last week and I felt like the worst piece of shit in the world for making her celebrate it in the hotel restaurant. She deserved a big bash in a huge house and instead she'd had a cake, some candles and had been pooped on by Hope that day, and then puked on by Derek later on that night. It was a goddamn disaster right down to the stupid stuffed gorilla I'd bought her with the logo *'you blow my mind'* on it. I still couldn't explain why I hadn't realized how insensitive the words were. The only damn reason I'd chosen that gorilla in the first place was because he had fingers and I was able to slide the engagement ring I'd bought for her on one of them. Lee had grinned like a lunatic and thanked me repeatedly when I gave it to her, but when I'd discovered what was written on his chest I could have kicked myself in the balls. I'd tried to get rid of the gorilla, but she refused point blank to give him back. Now the damn thing was in a place of pride in our bed...But my crucial mistake had been the stupid fucking song I played on my iPod dock–and possibly the half dozen shots of tequila I'd done with Derek–when I got her back to our suite that night. I'd been fairly wasted and I'd dragged Lee out of bed to dance to *Foster the People's* song *'Pumped up kicks.'*

Yeah, I was an asshole.

"Sorry about your birthday, baby," I mumbled as I tried to block the mental image of my drunk ass singing the words *'you better run, better run, faster than my bullet,'* to my fiancée.

She stared up at me with those beautiful gray eyes and hit me with one of her killer smiles. "I had a great time," she beamed. "You were so funny. You're incredibly cute when you're drunk, Kyle."

I snorted and decided to ignore the *cute* comment before asking, "You're not pissed that I didn't ask for your input on the house?" I forgot these type of decisions were supposed to be made together. This was a learning process for me though. I never had a family before Lee and Hope. Everything I'd done before them I'd done on my own.

"Kyle, you just bought a home for us to live in," she said in a soft tone of voice. "Of course I'm not angry. I'm thrilled." Her eyes bore into mine with such intensity that my skin started to burn. She burned me with one look. Jesus, I was in deep... "Our own place," she added with a grin as she reached up and stroked my cheek with her small hand. "A fresh start...sounds pretty nice right about now."

A weight lifted off my shoulders. She was happy. I decided to take the plunge. "Your mom phoned me today." I paused to let that sink in before adding, "Lee, you need to speak to the woman. She keeps calling. Nonstop."

The light in Lee's eyes evaporated. I could see the shutters closing and I regretted opening my stupid mouth and ruining the moment. "I'm going to take a shower," she muttered as she backed away from me. "Don't forget to check on Hope. Oh, and turn on the baby monitor please."

I watched her stalk into the bathroom. The sound of the bathroom door locking confirmed to me that I was on her shit list. No surprises there. Most days I ranked first on that list. Sighing deeply, I went to check on the other woman in my life. At least Hope was too young to have shit lists.

FOUR

LEE

I STAYED under the hot stream of water until my skin was pruned and my anger had disintegrated. I wished my mother would stop phoning my fiancé. It was unsettling to think of what her motives could be. I didn't trust her. Not one bit. I often wondered if she would have come forward and helped me had Kyle not been in my life. Was it me who she sought to build a relationship with or was it the wallet of my million-dollar man in the bedroom next door?

Shutting the water off, I climbed out of the shower and wrapped a large fluffy towel around my body. I purposefully avoided looking in the mirror as I brushed my teeth and prepared for bed. There was nothing in my reflection that I wanted to see. Cursing myself for forgetting my pajamas, I made my way back into the bedroom.

Kyle was standing next to our bed when I opened the door. His hands paused on the waistband of his jeans as his eyes locked on mine. "You okay?" he asked in a gruff tone.

"Yeah," I whispered as I chewed on my lip and tried to keep my eyes on his face and off his bare chest. "I don't want to meet her yet, Kyle. I'm not ready. It's going to put more strain on us if you don't let this go."

Resting his hands on his hips, Kyle shook his head in frustration. "It's something that needs to happen, Lee. You can't spend the rest of your life ignoring the fact that she's alive. I can't live the rest of my life knowing more about your parents than you do. You will regret this so fucking much if you don't get some closure. I'm not asking you to be her best friend, Lee. One meeting. That's it."

"I need more time, Kyle," I growled. "I woke up three and a half months ago to find my whole life altered. I'm dealing with my injuries. I'm handling having our personal life splashed all over the newspapers. I am coping with the realization that my best friend is dead. I cannot deal with her as well. Please...just give me some time to wrap my head around this. I've spent my whole life believing she was dead. I need more time. *A lot* of it."

Kyle hissed loudly and threw his hands up in exasperation. "When the hell did you get so stubborn?" There was a smirk to his lips that told me he was dropping this, for now at least.

"It's a self-preservation tactic," I said with a small smile. "Did you check on Hope?"

"Three times," he sighed. "She's fine, baby. Stop worrying." I couldn't help it. It was probably a first time mom thing, but some nights I actually got out of bed and crept into her room to make sure she was breathing. Kyle caught me once, when she was a month old, with my ear about an inch from her chest. The following day he'd arrived home with one of those sensor mats to put under her mattress–the ones that sent out an alarm if the baby stopped breathing for longer than thirty seconds. She was only twenty-two weeks old and should be sleeping in our room with us, but we had to cordon off a section of the lounge area for her to sleep because I'd woken her up every night with my screaming. I felt terrible about it. The child was supposed to wake up the mother at night, not the other way around...

The guilt I felt for missing so much of my daughter's young life crushed me. I wasn't the one who had slowly coaxed Hope into her sleeping routine. I wasn't the one who had taught her to clap her hands or discovered she preferred to have a night-light on in her room when she slept. I wasn't there when she rolled on her belly for the first time. I hadn't held her little hand when she got her vaccination shots. I wasn't the one who weaned her from breast milk to formula, or stayed up all night with her when she cut her first tooth. Kyle was the one who did all of those things for our daughter. He'd been her father and mother when I couldn't. I'd been in hospital and had missed twelve crucial weeks of my daughter's life...

Hope was barely eight weeks old when I was shot and I had been in hospital six weeks before the doctors had cleared her to visit me. Kyle had been very insulted when the doctors had refused to let Hope visit me after I woke up. *"What the fuck do you think she has?"* he'd hissed at the doctor. *"Baby cooties?"* But my body was extremely weak at the time and they were worried about the possibility of infection. As it stood, I'd caught three infections–one in my bowel and the other two in my bladder–after my surgery. My recovery had been a slow and painful process – excruciatingly painful. I had some nerve damage in my lower back which required weeks of intense physiotherapy.

When she was finally allowed to see me, Kyle had brought her every day, but Hope had forgotten who I was. For weeks she would cry and scream whenever I held her, only stopping when Kyle cuddled her. It used to kill me. It hurt more than a hundred bullets. I couldn't soothe her or calm her down when she fretted. All she'd wanted was her daddy…This went on for weeks and I used to cry so hard when they left. Kyle always came back at night, but it devastated me to know my baby was so far away from me. Growing up without me…

"Lee, she's okay. I promise," Kyle said in a soft tone. "Nothing bad is going to happen to her. I won't let it. All right?"

"I know that. I'm sorry," I muttered. "I just worry about her."

"That's what mothers do…"

"Don't," I said in a weary tone. I knew full well where he was going with this. "Please, Kyle. Not tonight." A vein in his neck pulsed as he nodded his head.

I watched–more like gawked–as Kyle shrugged off his jeans and climbed into bed. He stared at the stuffed gorilla he bought me with a look of disgust before flinging it on the floor and focusing his gaze on me. I hovered at the foot of the bed nervously. He was staring and I didn't like it. "Come on, baby. Get your sexy ass over here," he purred as he patted a spot on the mattress next to him.

He wasn't fooling anyone with that 'sexy' remark. We hadn't made love since before the shooting and I wore a t-shirt and sweats in bed. He had enforced a no sex rule the day I came home from the hospital and I hadn't protested. I didn't want to embarrass either of us by having him tell me why. I knew Kyle loved me, but even I had to admit that I wouldn't be overly enthusiastic about getting me naked if I was him. He was gorgeous, painstakingly beautiful, and my body was a road map of scars. They were all over my skin. It was disgusting.

"Can you turn around please?" I asked him. I knew I sounded foolish but the light was on and it made me uncomfortable. "Or at least close your eyes?"

Kyle frowned and leaned on his elbows. "Why?"

"Kyle," I groaned, as I tightened my grip on the towel around my breasts. "I'm a blanket of scars. I don't want to sicken you." I wasn't ashamed of my nudity. I was ashamed of my body. There was a very big difference.

He'd seen my scars once in the hospital and that one time had been enough to confirm what I'd been secretly dreading. The distraught look on his face when he'd helped me into the shower stall in the hospital...The horrified look in his eyes as they'd roamed over my skin had hit me hard. I knew at that moment that it was too much. I had too many marks to be desirable. I was too deformed to be sexy.

Kyle sat straight up. The white bed sheets pooled around his waist. "Do you honestly think that I see you any differently tonight than I did the first night I saw you?" *Yeah, actually I do... You have eyes and you're not blind.*

I let out a sigh and walked over to the light switch. Flicking it off, I shrugged my towel off and felt around for the dresser where I kept my underwear while I mentally cursed myself for not bringing my clothes into the bathroom with me.

The light flicked back on and I tensed. Kyle stood in front of me with a pained look in his eyes. I moved to turn it off, but he captured my hand. Without a word, he dropped to his knees, placed his hands on my hips and started kissing my stomach. "Don't," I begged, closing my eyes.

"Beautiful," he murmured, as his lips traced the thick scar on my left side that curved around to my back–the scar from my kidney surgery. I had an identical scar on my right side. Kyle turned me around and continued to place kisses across my back. His fingers trailed over my rough uneven skin. His tongue caressed my damaged flesh. I whimpered and opened my eyes. He pulled back and lifted his face. "You are so fucking beautiful,

Lee Bennett," he husked as he looked me square in the eyes. "How the hell did I get so lucky?"

"Kyle, I..." I choked out. I wasn't sure how I felt about this. I didn't know if this was an act of pity or love. I knew it wasn't an act of desire because he couldn't...he just couldn't find this desirable. My body trembled.

"Do you love me, princess?" he asked as his lips touched on the bullet wound in the center of my belly and then the one below it that represented my bowel surgery.

"You know I love you," I breathed. His mouth slipped lower to the scar over my bikini line–the one from my ectopic pregnancy–and I felt him suck in a breath.

"Sometimes I wonder how you can," he whispered, stroking his nose against my skin. "I don't understand how you can love me when I caused this. I caused you all of this...pain."

"No," I said, shaking my head. My heart was hammering in my chest as if it was trying to burst its way through my ribcage to claim him. I'd given him my heart and every morning I woke, I thanked Jesus for giving me another day on this earth. I prayed to him–begged him– not to burst our bubble. I prayed Kyle wouldn't hurt me again. I knew he was a different man to the one I first met. He was older, more open and a hell of a lot less secretive. But loving Kyle Carter was like throwing my heart into a boxing ring and trusting that every punch, every blow I was dealt wouldn't kill me. That he would save me...that he could somehow build me back up. It was exhausting. *It was exhilarating.*

"You did not do this," I whispered, as I stroked his cheekbones with my thumbs.

"But I caused it," he replied, looking directly into my soul with those blue eyes. "There won't be any more." He ran the palms of his hands over my stomach. "Not one single scratch. I promise."

"We're going to be okay, aren't we?" I asked as I stroked his hair. When I felt vulnerable I depended on his strength. I drew courage from his assurance.

Kyle smirked. "You can bet your ass we're gonna be okay, princess." Climbing to his feet, he cupped the back of my neck and leaned down to press his forehead to mine. "We'll be better than okay. I made you a promise and I plan on keeping it."

KYLE

"I wish I was as strong as you," Lee whispered, as her small hands clung to my arms. "You have so much faith in us. So much confidence."

"I'm gonna marry you, princess," I told her. "It's a done deal. My confidence comes from seeing you wear my ring on that finger of yours." I didn't want to tell her that I was scared shitless she'd wake up some morning and realize I was more trouble than I was worth. I'd rocked her world and not in a good way. And the worst damn thing was I couldn't even attempt to rock her world the good fucking way because I was terrified I would break her. Jesus Christ, there were no words to express how badly I wanted her right now, but her body needed time to recover. She had surgery on her goddamn organs. I didn't want to...poke anything.

Whatever Lee saw when she looked at herself wasn't the same as what I saw. When I saw those marks on her skin, I saw life and felt relief. She was here. Alive and breathing.

Every scar, blemish and wound on her beautiful body was a mark of survival. She was a survivor and I'd lay down my heart and soul for her. And those silvery lines on her sides and lower belly made me want to beat my fucking fists off my chest. She was my woman. She'd grown my child inside of her body. I fucking loved looking at those silver lines. Those were the only marks a man was supposed to put on his woman's body.

I had a hell of a pain threshold to be able to put myself

through the torture of kneeling in front of this naked woman and not take it any further. I knew it was bothering her that I hadn't touched her since she'd come home, but she had to know I wanted her. How the hell could I not? Her body was insane. Lee had the tiniest little waist I'd ever seen, that spanned out into these beautiful deep curves. The wide set of her hips alone set my pulse racing and had my dick hardening. Her body was a dream.

"I can't wait to marry you," she admitted with a sigh. "I just hate what they're saying about me. It makes what we have seem...dirty. Fake." I knew what she meant and it made my blood boil. I wanted to personally kick the ass of anyone who believed the stories suggesting Lee was with me for my money. She'd spent the majority of her pregnancy proving she didn't need my money–or me. Their smart comments were the reason she kept putting off getting married. I was far from stupid. I knew the gold-digger references were *exactly* what was bothering her. I was leaving her alone about it because the girl was vulnerable as hell at the moment, but one of these days she was going to have to toughen her skin to other people's opinions. If she didn't we'd never make it up the aisle. I loved her. I loved her so fucking much that it was almost painful. Nothing anyone could ever say or do could change that. She was mine, finally with me, and I was never letting go.

"Don't listen to one word of that bullshit," I growled as I flicked off the light and guided her over to our bed. Switching on the lamp on her bedside table, I stared down at her lost little expression. *Jesus, the girl had the loneliest eyes I'd ever looked into...*"I don't. The way I see it we both know the truth. Do you think I like it when they write shit about me hurting you? Hell fucking no. But I don't let it get to me because we know the truth. Lee, all of this crap we're going through, it won't break us. The trial, the shit they're saying about us...we're gonna get through it."

"I know we will," she whispered as she leaned on her tip-toes and kissed my lips. "And you should probably know that I'm going to love you forever."

I smirked as my heart decided to do somersaults inside of my body. "Then I should tell you, I wouldn't have it any other way."

Pulling back the covers I watched as she reached for my shirt on the floor. "Don't even think about it," I warned as I slipped off my boxers. "No more cover-ups, baby. You're mine. I want to see you. I want to fucking hold you in my arms without any barriers."

She shook a little but nodded and climbed into bed. Climbing in behind her, I drew her to me and kissed her shoulder before flicking off the lamp. "Don't ever think I don't want you," I told her, as I pressed my erection against her peachy little ass.

She squirmed against me and twisted her head so she could see me. The moonlight was shining through the crack in the curtains and I could tell she was blushing. "Then why haven't you…"

"Why haven't I touched you?" I finished her question for her. "Why haven't I fucked that tight little pussy of yours?"

"Yeah," she breathed. "If it's not because of the scars, then what is it?"

I groaned and wished to god I hadn't thought about Lee's pussy. That's all I could think of now. She nudged herself against me. Shit… "Because you're not ready for me. You're gonna need every ounce of your strength, princess." I smirked when I heard her breathing hitch. "Because I've been without you for too long. And the next time I'm inside you it's gonna be hard, rough and all fucking night long. Now close your eyes and go to sleep before I cave in and we both end up in the ER."

"God," she muttered as she turned her body to face me. "You can't say things like that and expect me to just go to sleep."

"Lee," I warned, when I felt her small fingers brush against the trail of hair under my navel. "Behave."

"We could do other things," she whispered, as her hand moved lower until she had my dick in her hand. "You're hard," she purred.

"No shit," I groaned, as I closed my eyes and flexed into her touch. "Stop. Please…" *Control… Have some self-control, dumbass…*

"Do you want me to put it in my mouth, Kyle?" she whispered. "We've never done that before…"

Fuck me.

Jesus Fucking Christ.

"Is that a serious question?" I moaned, as her hand stroked the length of my shaft. My back arched off the bed when I felt her mouth close around the head of my dick. "I'm trying to be good,

Lee...no sex until you're better." Her hands cupped my balls and I dropped my hand down to fist her hair. My legs were shaking as she took me to the back of her throat. I didn't have a whole pile of self-control and, after more than three months of being without her, she was pushing me to my limit. "You're...breaking my rules, baby."

"I'm not breaking your rules," she purred, as her tongue lapped around the tip. "You're inside my mouth instead." I felt her slide her legs over mine. Sitting on my knees, she started sucking me as she was grinding her wet pussy against my legs. "Is this okay?" she asked in an unsure tone of voice. "Am I doing it right?"

"Are you doing it...what?" I shook my head and groaned as she took me to the back of her throat. "Yeah, Jesus...shit." I thrust myself upwards as my fingers tightened in her hair. "You're perfect."

She did something–something fucking amazing–with her tongue and I was sunk. "You're a dangerous woman," I growled unable to take this fucking torture a second longer. Raising my knees, I grabbed her under her arms and pulled her towards me. Rolling her onto her back, I pushed her legs apart and settled between them.

"What are you doing?" she asked wide eyed and breathless as she rested her hands on my chest.

"I warned you." I palmed my shaft and rubbed it against her wet folds. Releasing myself, I bent over the side of the bed and grabbed my wallet out of my jeans and pulled out a condom.

"Don't worry," she whispered quietly as I knelt between her legs with my junk in my hands. Rolling the condom on, I rested on my elbows as I hovered above her. "About what, baby?" I asked as I slid inside her. Oh sweet Jesus... The heat, the sensation of her clenching around me nearly set me off.

"Oh..." she moaned, clutching my shoulders as I moved inside her. "One tube...I won't get...pregnant again," she breathed as she rocked her hips up to meet my thrust. I stopped moving. I stopped fucking breathing. I'd only put one on because I thought that's what she wanted, not because I was worried about getting her pregnant.

"I'm not worried," I whispered, as I bent down and claimed

her lips with mine before pushing inside her again. "I'm not worried at all."

I felt her body relax as her breathing slowed. When I was sure she was asleep I lay on my back and waited. It wouldn't be long before the screaming started.

Her nightmares were the reason I didn't dare close my eyes. She needed me and I was never going to let her down again.

FIVE

LEE

"IT'S TRACY." Kyle stood in the doorway of our hotel bedroom, with his shirt half unbuttoned and his phone pressed to his chest. "She wants to talk to you."

Here we go again…

Resting Hope on my knee, I continued brushing her wild curls with a soft bristle baby hairbrush I had bought in the infants section of a baby boutique in town. She wriggled on my lap, not one bit happy about being groomed. I knew how she felt, but I also knew how tangled curls like hers could get. "You're getting so big, sweetie."

Hope was a sturdy baby and I felt every ounce of her in my arms. I swear my womb fluttered every time she looked at me with those big beautiful blue eyes. She was so cute and chubby. A feminine version of her father–minus the chubbiness. No one could accuse Kyle of being chubby. He was built like one of those swimsuit models–albeit the dirty, wild untamed kind.

I focused my attention on Hope, while I prayed that Kyle would take the hint and back off. I wasn't going to speak to her. I had hoped that we'd put this conversation to bed the other night. I most certainly had. I was nowhere near ready to talk to that woman. Kyle needed to drop it...

"Lee, she's still on the line," he said, holding the phone out towards me.

Ignoring Kyle, I stood up carefully and carried Hope out of the room. "Come on, let's get you some breakfast," I murmured quietly as we stepped into the corridor.

"Where are you going?" he demanded.

"Breakfast." I had to move away from Kyle and his phone call. My temper was rising which was funny because before I moved to the hill I would have never considered myself an angry person. I had darkness inside of me I didn't have when I was eighteen. I was actually surprised he let me pass without a fight. I usually wasn't allowed to leave the suite until Kyle did a sweep of the hotel for 'reporters.'

Thankfully, they seemed to be growing bored of us. I hadn't been ambushed in a couple of weeks. Hopefully Kyle would start relinquishing some control now that they were creeping back under the woodwork. I prayed he would because I was smothering in that room...

My back was really hurting this morning. It felt like I was being stabbed with a thousand tiny needles directly into my spine. It was a side effect of my screwed up body. *Bullets, spinal cords and kidneys did not mix well...*

The elevator was out of order and carrying Hope down the stairs exhausted me. The doctors said that it would get much easier but it would take time.

I had time.

Thanks to Cam, I had a whole life worth of time ahead of me. I planned on visiting her later if I could get away from the very angry CEO who was following me down the hotel stairway.

"Yeah, I know. Look, I have to go. Okay, you too," I heard Kyle mumble then felt his hand slip around my elbow, halting me mid-step.

I didn't bother saying anything when he took Hope from me and carried her down the rest of the steps with her polka dot changing bag hanging from his shoulder. There was little point. I knew he had my best interests at heart. Well, my best interests physically.

KYLE

"You're doing the wrong thing, princess," I said quietly as I sat Hope into her highchair at our table. I sat opposite her and watched as she fiddled with the cutlery in front of her, obviously ignoring me. Thankfully the restaurant was practically deserted this morning. From the look on Lee's face, I guessed I was talking my way into a storm.

I'd been trying my best not to hassle her about her mom, but when the woman started sobbing down the phone, begging me to get her daughter to meet her, my heart fucking squeezed in my chest. I was not good with criers. Especially the female kind with their crazy hormones. The only woman in my life whose tears I could handle was my daughter. Those tears I could fix with a cuddle, a bottle or a clean diaper. When Lee cried I morphed into a wild animal. Her tears brought out the beast in me and I wanted to tear whoever had upset her apart. Unfortunately, that person was usually me…

Lee waited until Theresa, our waitress, left after placing two mugs and a pot of coffee on our table before she spoke. "I love you, Kyle," she said in a tight voice. "But if you keep pushing me on this you're not going to like what I have to say." She picked up the pot of coffee and filled both mugs. "You promised you would let this go." *Actually, I'd promised no such thing…*

I leaned my elbows on the table and watched as she prepared our coffee. She was wearing one of my black t-shirts over her jeans and it swamped her tiny body. It was loose enough to camouflage every amazing curve I knew was hidden underneath it. She tucked then re-tucked her hair behind her ears–a sure sign she was anxious.

"You haven't given her a chance to explain," I said as I wrapped my fingers around her wrist and pried her hand away from her hair. Her hands were shaking, but I didn't comment on that fact. Lee had a continuous tremor since she woke up from her surgery. And those tremors worsened every day that we grew closer to the trial.

"Don't lecture me on parents," Lee warned as she swung her face up to glare at me. Her gray eyes narrowed to initiate a challenge; I narrowed mine with acceptance. "If you want to go around fixing families like Jerry freaking Springer, then maybe you should start with your own. You're hardly an expert on the matter." She was lashing out, trying to hurt me so I would back off. Well, if she wanted a fight she'd get one.

Lee had been as alive as a house plant for too long. She needed to get her claws back and if fighting with me brought her back to life then I'd fight all fucking day. I had no pressing engagements and my skin was tough.

"No, I'm not an expert," I said deadpan. "My mother's dead and my father denied me. I was dumped into a home when I was three. So you're right, princess, I don't have a clue what it feels like to have a living relative who would risk their life to save mine." Regret flickered in Lee's eyes and I felt like an asshole for making her feel guilty, but she needed to hear this. "You have a chance at having a mom. A real, honest to god decent parent, but you're judging her when you don't know the whole story."

"She had a choice, Kyle." Lee snapped, pulling her hand away from mine. "I didn't."

"What the hell is that supposed to mean?" I asked as I tore the lid off a yogurt and started to feed Hope. "What the fuck kind of choice did she have when her husband put his hands on her? What choice did you have when your father beat you? Baby, that man is a tyrant. You think she chose to be beaten?"

"I meant that she *chose* my father. She chose to date him, to marry him, to have a child with him." She balled her hands into fists and I knew she was forcing herself not to cry. "Where were my choices, Kyle?"

"It's not that simple, Lee," I sighed, as I plopped another

spoon of yogurt into Hope's waiting mouth. "You haven't heard her side of things. If you talked to her you'd see things clearer. Baby, I know you're hurt, but right now you're being very judgmental."

"No, you don't understand me, Kyle," Lee croaked out. "Of course I don't think she chose to be beaten. No one would choose that. I know what it feels like, so don't put that guilt trip on me. And I don't blame her for leaving him," she paused and inhaled deeply through her nose before continuing. "I blame her for leaving me behind. She ran away and left me to take her place. She left me in that house. With *him*." She yanked on the end of her ponytail, clearly distraught. "Eighteen years, Kyle. I spent eighteen years of my life hungry, hurt and terrified. She had eighteen years to come back for me…to take me away from that life–from him. But she didn't. Would you do that to your daughter?"

"Don't turn this on me," I argued, but she'd hit me hard with the daughter card. "This isn't about…"

"Would you leave Hope with a man you knew was capable of beating her to a pulp?" she demanded in a hushed tone. "Would you leave our baby daughter with Jimmy Bennett?"

"No," I admitted through clenched teeth. The thought alone made me want to put my fist through the fucking wall. I thought back to the day Jimmy showed up at the hospital, the day before Lee was discharged.

I'd been in the cafeteria getting Lee a coffee when he arrived. Lee swore to me that he'd only been there a couple of minutes before I came back, but I wasn't sure. She had an awful habit of covering up for that man. She couldn't help it; it was built into her psyche after spending years of her life covering up her bruises and burns. Jesus, I'd never felt anger like I had the moment I walked into that room and witnessed him slapping my fiancée across her face. I lost it. Completely fucking lost my mind. I would have put that child-beater out of commission if the damn security guards hadn't arrived. When I'd calmed down enough to make a phone call, I had Kelsie ship that piece of shit back to where he came from with a check. It had pained me to give him anything, but twenty thousand dollars was a small price to pay for his departure. I wanted him out of her life. Permanently. That piece of scum would never so much as stand too close to his daughter or my daughter again. *Not while I'm breathing…*

"Then why?" Lee begged in an exasperated tone as she sat back in her chair. "Why can't you support me on this? If you knew what my life was like because of that woman. The things he..."

"Then tell me." I dropped Hope's spoon down and gave Lee my full attention. I wanted her to talk about this. Maybe if she said the words out loud she'd realize it was her father who did all the damage. "Tell me."

"What's the point?" she said in a weary tone before pushing back her chair and standing. "You've already picked a team."

"Lee, don't run..." I started to say as she backed away from me. Frustrated as hell, I watched her rush out of the room.

My phone vibrated in my pocket and I groaned loudly. "Daddy's in trouble, Hope," I mumbled, pulling my phone out of my pocket as I fed Hope another spoon of yogurt. "Have you got room for daddy in your crib tonight? I think mommy needs a time out."

Hope answered me by spitting yogurt on my shirt. "Thanks for that, angel," I muttered, as I pressed the answer button on my phone and held it to my ear. "What's up?"

"Kyle?"

I sat straight up when I registered the voice on the other line. "What do you want?" I said coldly. I'd never liked that guy and after he sold me out to the papers I liked him even less. He'd better have a damn good reason for calling me.

Dixon sighed heavily before he spoke. "I need to talk to you."

"Forget it, asshole," I snarled. "Run along to the papers. Fill them up with more of your bullshit. I'm done."

"It's about Derek," he growled. "He arrived at my place last night and went on a rampage. Trashed the whole damn house."

I sagged in my chair. "How much damage?" I asked wearily. This shit had to stop. Derek needed to get a handle on himself. He couldn't keep behaving like this and I sure as hell couldn't keep chasing after him. All I seemed to be doing was running around after everyone.

"Two windows, the front door and I need to replace my TV," he said before adding, "He needs help, Kyle. That guy needs to be checked in for some serious fucking treatment. He's lost his grasp on reality."

"I'm dealing with it," I growled. I didn't need Dixon Jones

telling me what I already knew deep down. I knew Derek wasn't himself, but he wasn't fucking crazy. The man was torn apart. You couldn't stick plaster on a broken heart and expect it to heal overnight. It took time and patience. He was going through the stages. Right now I was guessing he was at the anger stage and to be honest, I'd rather clean up some broken glass than slit wrists–or worse.

"Yeah, well someone better go check on him," Dixon grumbled. "Wouldn't be surprised if the cops have picked him up. Fucking lunatic."

"Watch your mouth, dumbass," I snarled. "Keep your mouth shut about Derek and I'll pay for the damage…" My voice trailed off as my eyes took in a very flushed looking Lee stalking back to our table.

I hung up, slipped my phone in my pocket while keeping my eyes trained on my fiancée. Holy shit, she looked pissed. Her eyes were red-rimmed, her jaw tight with tension as she silently lifted Hope out of her highchair and held her to her chest. "What are you doing?" I asked cautiously.

Glaring down at me, she whispered, "I don't walk away from my children."

"Lee, she didn't walk away for no reason," I argued. "I'm not saying what she did was right…"

"Don't," she hissed as she clutched Hope to her chest. Tears filled her eyes and I watched as she blinked them away roughly. "Just leave it alone, Kyle."

I shook my head in defeat as I pushed my chair back and stood. "I have a meeting with Kelsie in a half hour," I said with a sigh. There was no point in fighting. She wasn't thinking clearly and I was too fucking stubborn to back down. "I need to go check on Derek afterwards. Will you be okay on your own?"

She nodded her head once before turning on her heel and hobbling out of the restaurant with Hope in her arms.

"Stay in the suite," I called after her.

Shit.

"Another one," I muttered as I strolled into Kelsie's office and dropped the letter on her desk. Sinking into the chair opposite

Kelsie, I drummed my fingers against the armrests of my chair in agitation. This day was going from bad to downright catastrophic. Lee was pissed with me. Derek was AWOL. I'd just spent the last two hours trying to convince Dixon fucking Jones not to press charges and when I finally got that mess cleaned up, I get another damn letter from Rachel... "When is she gonna get it through her thick fucking skull that I am not going to visit her."

"This is good, Mr. Carter," Kelsie mumbled, as she tore open the envelope and poured over the hand-written letter inside. "Do you want to read it?" she asked as she peered up at me through her overly large glasses. "It may be of interest to you."

"Hell no," I grumbled as I pulled at my tie. "I just want this nightmare to be over."

"April thirteenth," Kelsie muttered as she leveled her gaze on my face. "That gives us a little under four months. If we don't break her down, Lee goes to the stand on April thirteenth."

"Then crush her," I snarled. Leaning forward, I rested my elbows on her desk. "I want you to do everything in your power to obliterate that woman. Take her down, Kelsie, and I'll make sure you're set for life."

"We have to do this as above board as possible, Mr. Carter."

"No trial," I hissed as I pushed my chair back and stood. "Do whatever the hell you have to...just get her to change her plea. I don't want my girl on that stand." I fucking hated using my money as a bargaining tool, but we were on countdown and Lee...Jesus, I was not going to stand by and watch her be picked apart by Rachel's defense team or have her name dragged through the mud again.

"Any suggestions on how to...sway her?" Kelsie asked and I was pretty sure she was being sarcastic.

"Do you think I'm joking?" I demanded. "This is my goddamn reality Kelsie. It's not a game."

She paled and shook her head. "No, Mr. Carter..."

"Money," I said with a sigh. "Money is Rachel Grayson's god."

LEE

As I pushed Hope's stroller down the path towards Cam's grave, I could feel my anger dissipating. I knew I couldn't hide from Kyle forever, but I couldn't sit in that hotel room and wait for him to come home either. I'd said some pretty horrible things to him in the heat of the moment, but he just didn't get it.

I would *never* try to force David on him. I was on *his* side, not his father's. David probably had reasons of his own for doing what he did to Kyle, but I didn't want to hear them because they didn't matter to me. There was no excuse for abandoning Kyle. Not in my eyes and that's what hurt me so much. Kyle didn't seem to see my side-or else he didn't want to…

My step faltered when I noticed the familiar broad shaped man crouched in front of her headstone with his head bent. "Hello Mr. Frey," I said quietly. He swung around in surprise and I felt terrible for spooking him. "I didn't mean to startle you."

Ted Frey looked up at me with the saddest gray eyes I'd ever seen and all I wanted to do was hug him. "Lia," he whispered. He always called me that. I think he did it because my daddy hated it so much. They had never gotten along too well. Daddy hated it when anyone shortened my name. "I should have guessed you'd come here today," he said as a small smile tugged at his lips. "Old habits and all…"

"I come most Saturdays," I told him as I locked the brake on Hope's stroller and eased myself down on the grass next to him. I was grateful to be sitting. The ground was cold, but I welcomed the numbing sensation. My back felt like it was going to shatter into tiny pieces of bone. "I don't like her to be on her own for too long," I told him. "And Saturday was always our time together." I didn't add that I came here because his dead daughter was the only one who understood me.

"I remember," he said sadly. "I'm sorry we haven't been to see you." He shook his head. "We weren't sure you would want to see us after finding out..." His voice trailed off and I flinched. I understood what he was talking about.

My mother.

Mr. and Mrs. Frey had helped my mother leave my father. I hadn't wanted to know anything about the whole ordeal, but Kyle had blurted out some of the details one night when I was in hospital. "I'm not angry with you, Mr. Frey," I said quietly. "Or Mrs. Frey." I didn't judge Ted or Mora. They didn't abandon their child. They'd given Cam a wonderful life full of love and nurture and a clean, safe home. And through my friendship with Cam, I'd tasted the love of real parents.

Cam's parents had been good to me growing up. Especially Ted. I remembered overhearing a conversation when I was little between Ted and my father. He had come by late one night and had asked daddy to allow him and Mora to take me and raise me with Cam. I remembered being so excited as I sat on the top of the stairs. I'd been sure my daddy would accept Mr. Frey's offer. Even at four years old I'd known I wasn't wanted. Wasn't loved. Not like other children. Not like Cam. Of course I'd been wrong. Daddy had gone ballistic and after throwing Mr. Frey out of the house he'd come looking for me. I still had the burn marks on my bottom from that fire poker.

"I wish things could have been different," he whispered, as he patted my knee. "I have two regrets in this life, Lia," he told me. "Do you know what they are?"

"Camryn," I breathed. It was hard to hear this, to sit next to my best friend's father and hear the hurt in his voice as his pain radiated off him in waves. I ducked my head in shame. "I'm sorry. I know it should have been me."

"Don't say that." Gently clasping my chin with his fingers, he lifted my face. "I never want to hear those words come out of your mouth again, is that clear?"

"Yes sir," I mumbled, blinking back my tears.

He sighed heavily as he wrapped his arm around my shoulder. "I have two regrets in life, Lia," he repeated, tucking me into his side. "The first regret I have is failing through inability. My second regret is failing through ability."

"I don't understand," I told him. The man had always spoken in riddles.

"I hope you never do," was all he said.

DEREK

Kyle was sitting on the steps of the porch when I got home. "Where the hell have you been?" he demanded as he stood up, grabbed his grocery bags and followed me inside. "This is my third time coming here."

"Out," I muttered. There was no point in telling Kyle I'd spent half the day sitting at our old table in the coffee dock of the school campus. The guy had a heart of gold, but tact and sensitivity were not his strong points… He had as much empathy as a moose. Sometimes it was hard to be around him. He was an emotionally strong person…hell, he was virtually invulnerable and his strength exposed my weakness.

"I'm having a really shitty day, Der," he growled, as he stormed into the kitchen and started unloading the groceries I had come so used to receiving. I wasn't hungry anymore, and I didn't feel jack shit, but if I could, I think I would be warmed by his attempt at keeping me alive. "Hope was up half the night teething. Lee's on the warpath. Rachel won't back the fuck off, and you," Kyle continued as he pointed a bunch of bananas at me. "Running around the neighborhood, breaking and entering is something I could do without, dude."

"He deserved it," I snapped, feeling something for the first time today. Anger. I welcomed it. "He's a douchebag with a big mouth." I honestly couldn't remember why I went to Dixon's place last night, but I guessed the empty bottle of jack I found in my bed this morning had something to do with it…

"Yeah," Kyle sighed, as he closed the fridge door and started gathering up dirty glasses and mugs. "Well, now he's a douchebag who's seven thousand dollars richer."

"You paid him off?" I asked in disgust. "What the hell, Kyle."

"What the fuck else was I supposed to do?" Kyle asked defensively. "It was that or bail your ass out of jail and read all about it in tomorrow's paper."

"I was looking forward to seeing my face on the front page," I shot back, knowing I sounded like an asshole, but not caring enough to shut up. "It's been a while."

Turning on the water faucet, Kyle started washing the dishware as he continued his rant. "You could have been locked up, dude. Don't you get it? Dixon could have made life ten times worse for you."

"How much worse can it get?" I asked in an aggressive tone as I folded my arms across my chest and glowered at the back of his head. "My fucking girl…" I stopped, blanked her face out of my mind and inhaled deeply. "You said Lee was on the warpath?" I said, changing the subject. "I wonder fucking why…meddling again, Kyle?"

"She needs to talk to Tracy, man," Kyle growled as he dropped a plate in the sink and started pacing the floor. The guy couldn't stand still for a minute. The fucker gave me whiplash half the time. "Dammit, it needs to happen." He cracked his knuckles and let out a breath before stalking back to the sink.

I rolled my eyes in disgust. "You think she needs to talk to her. Lee obviously isn't ready."

"Fuck that," Kyle growled. "She needs to hear her mother's side of things. The things he put her through…" He shook his head, as he wrung a wet dishcloth and proceeded to wipe down the countertops. "She has so much compassion for Jimmy. Remember when he had his heart attack? She went running straight to Louisiana to sit by his side. The man that beat her for years, Derek. And then her mom gives her a kidney and she won't even hear the woman out. It's driving me crazy." I didn't bother speaking. I knew he wasn't finished. "He's scum," Kyle continued, as he grabbed some empty beer bottles and tossed them in the trash. "Jimmy Bennett is a serpent and I swear she would rather speak to him than her own mother. It's sick, Derek. It's disgusting."

I knew for a fact that Lee wouldn't *rather* talk to Jimmy. She was petrified of the creep. Broke out in a cold sweat when his name was brought up in conversation. My guess was the girl would rather erase both of her parents, or at least avoid them if she could. "Kyle, you need to calm your shit. It's her choice. You can't force her to want what you want."

"I love her," he shot back. "She's my woman. I'm supposed to take care of her. That's my fucking job, Derek."

"Yeah, Kyle, you're supposed to take care of her, not control her," I snapped. "Dude, you seriously need to cool off, and back off. You pulled this crap with her before and look where it got you. You need to give that girl space and stop breathing down her damn neck. It's not healthy for either of you."

"She nearly died," he hissed, running his hands through his hair. "I'm never going to let her out of my sight again."

"So what, you're gonna give up working so you can watch her twenty-four seven?" I said sarcastically. "Or hire a nanny to watch your fiancée?"

"You don't get…" he paused for a second before smirking. "Are you looking for a new job, Der?"

Oh Jesus…

"It's your funeral," I muttered, too tired to bother trying to reason with him. He'd do whatever the hell he wanted to do, whether I warned him or not. Might as well save my breath. "Keep pushing her and all you'll be left with is the dust from her shoes as she runs out on you..."

"Derek," Kyle snapped in an agitated tone as he swung around to face me. "Don't say shit like that," he said as he shuddered. "Don't even think about it…" His phone started to ring and I sighed in relief. I wasn't getting into this with him. I was exhausted and Kyle had enough energy to argue for a decade.

Pulling his phone out of his pocket, he pressed a button and held it to his ear. "Marcus, everything okay?" I watched as Kyle's face turned red, then white, then red again as he listened intently to whatever was being said on the other line. "She's back now?" he whispered. "She's okay?" His whole frame shuddered as he nodded his head. "Thanks, man. I'm on my way." He ended the call and stood motionless with his eyes closed and his hands balled into fists at his sides.

"Everything okay?" I asked cautiously. He wasn't moving. I

wasn't sure if he was even breathing. "Kyle?" I asked again. "Is everything okay?"

"One day," he hissed out through clenched teeth. His eyes flew open and he glared at me in barely contained rage. "All I want, Derek," he roared as he stalked past me into the hallway. "Is *one* day." Swinging the front door open, he turned and glared at me. "One fucking day where the people I love listen to me and do what I goddamn say. Is that too much to ask for?"

KYLE

She was going to be the death of me. If she didn't start listening to me soon, I was going to lose my shit. One argument. One goddamn disagreement and what did she do?

Run.

She was the victim of a shooting. A *shooting*. She didn't need to be going to any damn place on her own. I knew she didn't like being ordered around. I was being hard on her, but I was worried. I was more than worried, I was terrified something was going to happen to her. To Lee, I looked like a control freak, and maybe I was, but everything I did was for her.

To keep her safe.

To keep her *alive*.

I sat in my car until the sky darkened and I was certain I was calm enough to deal with her. *Vulnerable, vulnerable, vulnerable,* I chanted the word to myself in the elevator on my way up to our suite, in a bid to keep my cool. Taking a few deep breaths, I slipped inside and checked on Hope, who was sleeping soundly, before making my way into our bedroom. The sound of water running filled my ears and I opened the door of the bathroom and stepped inside. My panic started to recede the moment I set eyes on her standing under the steady flow of water coming from the shower head–naked.

Her eyes met mine and I watched as she sighed deeply before continuing to lather her hair with shampoo. "If you've come for a fight, Kyle, you'll have to wait."

"You left without telling me," I said in a much calmer tone than I thought I was capable of. "You didn't tell anyone where you were going, Lee. Do you have any idea how worried I was when Marcus called me?" I closed my eyes and forced away all the horrible what ifs and notions that were swimming around in my brain. "*Anything* could have happened to you."

"You cornered me this morning," she countered in an equally quiet tone. "You push and push, Kyle. I have a breaking point. I have my own views on the world–on my *mother*. You can't force your opinions on me and expect me to lie down to you just because you think yours is the right way."

"Where were you?" I asked quietly even though I knew full well where she'd been.

"With Cam," she replied softly, confirming what I'd already guessed.

Shaking my head, I shrugged my clothes off and went to her. "Jesus Lee," I hissed the second I stepped into the shower. "Have you no feeling in your body?" I asked as I hopped around, trying to dodge the spray until my body grew accustomed to it. "The water is scalding."

"I like it hot," she murmured, as she tipped her head back to rinse her hair. "It helps with the stiffness."

I couldn't agree more with her. I was as stiff as a board from just watching her, but her words sobered my arousal. "You're sore today?" I asked in a gruff tone. The fight I had in me earlier was fading fast. Now, all I wanted to do was hold her. Lock her away. Keep her safe…

"Yeah," she whispered, as she massaged her hands through her hair and my chest ached. Her one word omission cut me deep. "I pushed myself too far today," she admitted quietly. "I feel like an old lady…I'm exhausted just trying to stand up."

Stepping behind her, I suffered the oven-hot temperature of the water as I gently brushed her hands aside and started to rinse her hair. "You never listen to me," I whispered. Brushing her hair to one side, I dropped my head and placed a kiss on her shoulder before lowering my hands to rest on her hips. She sagged against me, allowing me to take her weight for her. "You need to start listening to me."

"I do listen to you, Kyle," she replied softly. "But that doesn't mean that I have to agree with you or do what you say all the time."

"I'm trying to keep you safe," I growled. "I'm not sorry for that, Lee."

"I'm capable of making up my mind about my own mother," she shot back. "And I'm not sorry for that either, Kyle."

"Do you still…are we okay?" I asked, feeling like a needy asshole for craving reassurance, but her response freaked me out.

She turned around and looked up at me with those big gray eyes. "I'm really mad at you," she said, her eyes wide, her voice weary. "But I'm really in love with you, too." Her lips tipped upwards in what looked like a reluctant smile. "So, I guess love overrules anger."

"So, where do we go from here?" I asked, feeling at a total loss as to where this was going. We weren't agreeing, but we weren't fighting either. It was…weird as fuck. "How come you're not screaming and shouting at me?"

Lee laughed–*fucking loved that sound*–stretched her hand up and turned off the water. She stepped out of the shower and grabbed a towel before answering me. "It's my new technique when dealing with your antics," she mused as she wrapped a towel around her body and another around her hair. "I call it being a grown up."

The weight on my shoulders and pressure around my chest lightened the moment she smiled at me. *We were okay…*"Antics?" I teased as I stepped out and prowled towards her. The night could be salvaged…

LEE

I was finding it really hard to hold onto my anger with Kyle prowling towards me–stark naked–with that playful glint in his eyes. "Antics?" he purred as he grabbed my waist and pulled me flush against him. "I thought you liked my antics?" His face dipped to my neck, his lips snaked out, trailing hot kisses from my collarbone to my jaw. "Don't be mad at me," he whispered between kisses. "I just wanna fix everything for you."

I groaned loudly–a combination of arousal and despair. "Kyle…I don't want to have a relationship with her. You need to stop…"

"Stop this?" he purred, as his hands slipped between the openings of my towel and began a gentle onslaught on my breasts. *Stroking, kneading, tweaking…* "Or stop this?" He trailed his fingers down my stomach until he had me cupped in his palm with his finger pushing inside…

"I can't talk to you…when you…we need to…sort this…" My words trailed off and I grabbed his shoulders in a bid to keep my balance. He was wrecking me. I had so many emotions coursing through me and he was annihilating every one of them with his fingers and lips. "You're…cunning," I managed to choke out before his mouth found mine, cutting off whatever the hell it was I was trying to say, and to be honest, I couldn't remember, nor did I care. His hands cupped my butt, lifting me easily, and I was lost.

"Let's call a truce for tonight," he whispered, as his hands slid up my back and dragged my towel away so that we were skin to skin. "Are you too sore?" he murmured softly as he walked forward until the cool, moist wall-tiles could be felt against my back.

I shook my head, panting when I felt his erection probing my entrance. My body had obtained a new lease of life…His hands on me made everything tingle, and the energy sources inside of me were replenishing at an alarming rate. Kyle smirked before slowly sinking inside me, so deep it felt like he was penetrating my womb. "I'm still mad," I gasped as I rocked against his thrust.

Holding me captive with his hips, he rested his arms on either side of my face, his fingers stroking the hair on the top of my head. "Lee," he moaned as he looked into my eyes with the rawest of passion pooling in his. "I've had a really bad day." He rolled his hips and whispered, "I don't wanna fight, baby. I wanna fuck." He kissed me softly and I was gone... A traitor to my own entreaty.

"Do you think we fight more than we're supposed to?" I asked Kyle as we settled into bed. I grabbed my gorilla–who Kyle had aptly named *King Kong*–out of his hands before he had a chance to throw him off the bed, and held him tightly to my chest.

"Can't we throw him out?" Kyle grumbled as he flicked off the light and climbed into bed. "It's like a constant reminder of how stupid I was."

"No, we can't," I cackled as I tucked him behind my back before moving over to snuggle into Kyle. "I love him."

"You have read what's on his chest, right?" he asked, his voice full of self-loathing. "'You blow my mind.' Jesus…"

"Consider me sentimental, but you are the first person who bought me a stuffed-animal," I told him. It was the truth and it meant a hell of a lot to me. "So, I don't care what's written on his chest, I love him. I'm keeping him."

"Lee…"

"Kyle…" I countered. "Let it go. King Kong is staying."

"Fine. Keep the damn monkey," he huffed as he turned onto his side and pulled me into his arms. Leaning his arm over my body, he grabbed King Kong from where he was tucked behind my back and threw him off the bed. "But not in our bed," he added smugly. Resting his hand on the curve of my hip, he smirked. "And back to your earlier question, 'do I think we fight more than we're supposed to?'" He raised his hand and tucked my hair behind my ear before resting it once again on my hip. "I don't know," he answered with a grin. "What's the recommended daily allowance?"

"I'm serious," I said, nudging his leg with my toe. "I just don't know if it's normal to argue as much as we do."

He snorted and ducked his head for a kiss before pulling back and fixing me with a crooked smile. "We fight because you're fucking crazy sometimes."

I stiffened, my earlier anger returning with a vengeance. "You're the one who's..."

"Relax, princess," he said softly. "We fight because we care. I'd be worried if we didn't."

"It's exhausting isn't it?" I whispered.

Kyle frowned at me. "What is?"

"Finding a common line," I admitted. "Knowing when to argue, when to back off...trying to figure out what exactly is worth fighting about, and what's worth fighting for...?"

"You're worth fighting for," he murmured. Turning me over, he shifted his body so that the front of his body was aligned with the back of mine. "That's all I need to know. That's my common line." Kissing my shoulder, he wrapped a strong, comforting arm around me before yawning. "Now, go to sleep, princess."

"Kyle?" I whispered a few minutes later.

"Yeah?" His tone was gruff–sleepy.

"I'm sorry for calling you Jerry Springer...You're nothing like him."

He chuckled and squeezed me tighter. "Turn your brain off, woman."

SIX

KYLE

"ARE YOU OKAY?" She wasn't and I was stupid to even ask that question. Lee just shoved me off her in the middle of sex and ran like a lunatic into the bathroom. This was a first for us...She usually didn't run when I had my dick inside her. I scratched my head in confusion because I honestly didn't have a clue what I'd done. "Did I hurt you?"

"No, you didn't," I heard her call out in a high pitched tone from behind the bathroom door. "I'm fine. Just go to work, okay?"

"What are you doing in there?" I asked. I probably looked like a tool, standing outside the bathroom, balls naked, with a hard-on that wouldn't lie the fuck down. Glancing back at the bed, I noticed the sheets before looking down at my junk. I sagged in relief.

Got it.

I didn't have a clue why she was so embarrassed. It wasn't a big deal. Not to me. It was a woman thing. It was a good thing. It was a fucking great thing. Her body was starting to regulate again. *Finally.* "Baby, it's not a big deal. Can I come in?"

"No," she called out. "I'm peeing. Go to work, Kyle. I'm fine."

"Are you sure?" I wasn't sure. I wasn't one bit sure about this. She was being weird as fuck about this. This was beyond my comprehension. Did I go in anyway? Would I be breaking some weird girl code? I didn't care if she peed in front of me...

Fuck it, I needed to check.

Opening the door slowly, I peeked my head through the opening. "Lee, don't be embarrassed. It's just me…Ouch, what the fuck." My hand shot up to my nose. I staggered back as my eyes watered. I looked around for the source of the pain in my nose and my eyes locked on the weapon. Bending down, I grabbed the shampoo bottle and slammed the door open. "Did you just hit me with a fucking shampoo bottle?"

"Get out," she screamed as she scrambled to cover herself up. "For the love of god, get out now. Close the door."

"For fuck sake, Lee," I hissed, throwing the bottle on the floor. "I've seen you naked. I've seen you give birth. Christ, I looked up your v…"

"Oh my god, will you just get out," she screamed. "Some things are private, Kyle."

"Fine," I huffed, backing away. "But just so you know, you're on my shit list for this." I had no idea why I was saying this, but I was feeling wounded. Damn, my nose was stinging. "That's right, Lee. I have a shit list, too."

"Fine by me," she snapped. "Close the door after you, asshat."

Slamming the door closed, I took a few deep calming breaths. I grabbed my clothes. "Fuck this, I'm going downstairs to the pool room for a shower."

What a perfect start to the day.

Crazy fucking woman…

LEE

"That sounds normal," Dr. Bromwick said, after I told him all my symptoms and I felt anything but relief. My hand tightened around my phone as I listened to him roll off an explanation I knew in my gut was wrong. "Intercourse can be painful after childbirth alone and given the circumstances I'm not surprised you're feeling some discomfort."

I'd scrambled out from underneath Kyle before rushing into the bathroom and confirming what I'd thought I felt while we were having sex. I was bleeding. Not heavily, but enough to be worried.

Oh god, I shouldn't have thrown that shampoo bottle at Kyle…but I'd been mortified. He stuck his head round the door and stared straight at me while I was peeing. What the hell?

I wasn't used to men or relationships, but I was pretty sure that wasn't normal. Husband-to-be or not, we needed boundaries. But I deserved everything he would say to me when he came home. I knew I was in trouble. He couldn't hate me more than I hated myself right now…I hit him. Again.

I'd phoned Dr. Michael's office the moment Kyle had stalked out. Dr. Michaels wasn't available and I'd been put through to his much younger, much grumpier, registrar. "But what about the blood?" I asked Dr. Bromwick, feeling incredibly embarrassed. "Do you think I could come in for a checkup? Just to be safe?" The blood terrified me. It wasn't the sex. Kyle was gentle. I was burning and bleeding and everything ached.

"How old are you Miss Bennett?" Dr. Bromwick asked impatiently.

"Twenty," I whispered as my cheeks reddened.

"And what do you think, at your age, is supposed to happen to your body on a monthly basis?"

Shame engulfed me. I was glad Hope was the only one who was in the room because I was sure I was about to burst into tears. "A menstrual cycle," I muttered in humiliation. "But that's not what this..."

"Very good," he said, interrupting me in a sarcastic tone before sighing. "Look, take some Advil for the cramps and put a hot compression against your back. You'll be fine in a few hours."

I bit down on my lip as the burning intensified. I didn't feel right. Something was very wrong. My body had been quite literally torn apart and pieced back together in the past year. The doctors reckoned that the injuries my body had endured, along with stress, was the reason why I didn't ovulate anymore. And even if this was a period, I shouldn't be burning. I was in agony. This wasn't right. "Dr. Bromwick, I really think I need to be examined. Dr. Michaels said to call him immediately if I had a problem..."

"And I really think I need to examine patients who have an actual ailment, Miss Bennett," he snapped. "Not stupid little girls with period pains. If young ladies such as yourself are old enough to have babies, then surely you're old enough to understand your own body. There's no cure that I can prescribe for imprudence."

"Okay, I'm sorry for bothering you," I whispered before hanging up. I sank down on the couch and buried my head in my hands. I'd been sure what was happening to me was an *actual* ailment...but then again he was the doctor and I was the uneducated house-keeper. He knew more than I did. I knew nothing really. Nothing at all. Oh god, I wasn't sure what to think. Maybe I was overreacting?

KYLE

"Open the damn door, Derek," I growled as I tried my key in the lock for the fifth fucking time. He'd locked it on the inside and I was getting agitated. I had a hell of a lot to do today, but I needed to check in on him. His phone call earlier had freaked me out. "Come on, dude. Just let me in," I said in a softer tone. I could hear banging coming from the other side of the door and it was scaring the shit out of me. I knew exactly where the noise was coming from and I hoped like hell he'd answer the door instead of putting his head through it.

"Do you think she was hiding something from me?" he blurted out the second I'd answered his call and for a moment I hadn't a clue who he was talking about. I'd quickly realized who when he added, *"She fucking hated Mike. It makes no sense, Kyle. I can't accept this shit…"*

He never brought Cam up in conversation with me and I was hoping this was a break-through. His behavior was unpredictable as hell lately, and Lee's behavior had been even more unpredictable. Jesus Christ. I rubbed my nose and made a mental note to never walk in on her peeing again…

"You on your own?" I heard him ask and I sagged in relief.

"Yeah. It's just me." I pressed my forehead against the door and waited. After a couple of minutes I heard the sound of the lock clicking and I stepped back. When he opened the door I had to force my features to remain impassive. Inside I was burning. He looked like a mess and I knew in my heart of hearts that the guy drank himself stupid last night. So much for doing better...*Goddammit.*

"Sorry," Derek mumbled as he held the door open for me.

Picking up the bags of groceries I'd bought, I stepped through the doorway and was hit with the nastiest stench I'd smelt since Hope's bout of diarrhea last week. "What the hell, dude?" Dropping the bags of food on the kitchen table, I covered my nose with my hand. "What's that smell?"

"I got a puppy," he mumbled. Strolling out of the kitchen, he returned a few minutes later with the ugliest fucking creature I'd ever seen in his hands.

"What the fuck is that?" I pointed at the ball of matted fur in his hands. I wasn't sure if I was looking at a dog or a gremlin.

"His name is Kevin," Derek said deadpan. "And I think he's a shiatsu. I found him last night on my way home from Bobby's. The poor guy was huddled behind the dumpster at the back of the bar."

"Kevin?" I shook my head and stepped forward to get a closer look. "Hate to tell you, dude, but he's not a puppy. Did you see the size of his...?"

"He was dumped, Kyle," Derek said in a tone which implied I should shut the fuck up. "He was freezing cold and starving. What the hell was I supposed to do, leave him there? Abandon him? Get a newer version instead? Some things are worth fixing. Sometimes people should fix the shit they have instead of running off and getting an upgrade."

What the hell was he talking about? I held my hands up in defense. "I didn't say you had..."

"I'm keeping him," Derek growled in a warning tone as he held the *dog* to his chest. "So don't even suggest an animal shelter."

"Fine," I said wearily as I started unpacking the groceries. "Keep the damn dog. Just give him a bath. He smells like ass."

"See, Kevin," Derek crooned. "He's just a big softie deep down."

Jesus, he was as moody as a woman.

"And for god's sake, don't tell Lee about *Kevin,*" I growled. "The last thing I need right now is a dog. I have enough responsibilities."

"You liked Bruno," Derek said and I flinched. "Be honest, Kyle. You were attached to that old guy."

Yeah, I liked Lee's old Labrador, Bruno. I liked him a lot until he was poisoned last May. "He was different," I mumbled. "He smelled a hell of a lot better than Gismo over there."

"He'll grow on you," Derek chuckled as Kevin licked his face.

"Hey, Der," I said as I flicked on the kettle. "Did you ever walk in on a girl when she's…using the bathroom?"

"Ha," Derek laughed and it was a rare sound. "You fucking idiot." Placing the dog on the floor, he folded his arms across his chest and grinned at me. "What was her weapon of choice?"

"Shampoo bottle," I muttered.

"Could have been worse," he chuckled. "I walked in on Cam once. She threatened to castrate me in my sleep with a blunt scissors – after she cracked me over the head with the toilet paper holder."

"That's nothing," I chuckled.

"It was a *metal* toilet paper holder, Kyle," he added in a serious tone. "I ended up with two stitches." I laughed out loud when he ducked his head and showed me the small scar on the back of his head. "You need to be careful, dude," he warned. "Women are really weird about shit like that."

"That's what I don't understand," I said in exasperation. "What's the big deal?"

"I have no clue," he replied. "But here are my words of wisdom from past experience. Steer clear of the three P's."

I shook my head. "Three P's?"

"Pee, poop and period," he said solemnly. "Never, and I mean *never*, walk in during, or bring into conversation any of those three bodily functions and you'll remain unscathed...hopefully."

"God, they're so fucking weird," I sighed.

"Tell me about it," he agreed.

"Are you still coming to dinner on Saturday?" I asked. "You haven't stopped by in a while, and the girls…they're missing you, man."

"Yeah," Derek sighed. "I'll be there. I wanna be the first person to say I told you so when it blows up in your face. Because it will blow up in your face, Kyle."

"I know what I'm doing," I snapped, really irritated as hell that he didn't agree with me. "It's happening, Derek, and I would appreciate your support on this."

"*You* have my support," he grumbled. "But your stupid fucking plan sure as hell doesn’t. But then again, you don't need my approval. You're gonna do it anyway, aren't you, dumbass?"

"Yep," I muttered as I poured another carton of sour milk down the drain. *Black coffee again today…*"By the way, your room in the new house is pretty cool, Derek…well, your own floor actually. It's really sweet, man." When he didn't answer I swung around and realized he was gone.

The mutt was sitting where Derek had stood and was staring directly at me. "You don't know what you're getting yourself into, Kevin," I muttered, as I knelt down to pet him. His bottom teeth jutted out over his top ones as he wagged his tail, and I had to admit he was kind of cute–if I didn't breathe through my nose. "I'd take my chances on the streets if I were you, man," I told him. "Derek's worse than any bitch you'll ever meet."

LEE

The second Kyle walked through the door of our suite, I scrambled off the couch and rushed towards him. "I'm sorry," I blurted out as I rushed over to him. He stood, frozen to the spot, staring down at my face with a look of confusion on his own. "I am so, so sorry," I whispered as I wrapped my arms around his waist. "I will never throw a shampoo bottle at you again. Ever."

After a few moments he sighed heavily, wrapped his arms around me and kissed my hair. "Or an apple."

I cringed in shame. "Or an apple."

"You know, princess," he mused as he lifted my chin up with his fingers. "You would have made a fine pitcher. Your aim is pretty damn perfect."

"It's not funny," I mumbled, burying my face in his shirt. "Don't let me off the hook so easily. You should be really mad at me. I'm a horrible person. I'm not good, Kyle. You should…you should…"

"I should what, baby?" he said in a soft tone, lifting my face again. "I should punish you?" He shook his head. "I'm not him, Lee. There's nothing you could ever do to make me want to hurt you. I'm never gonna hurt you. I'm never gonna leave you." Leaning down, he pressed his lips to mine before pulling back and smirking. "Even when you're behaving like a hormonal anti-Christ."

"Kyle," I choked out. "I've slapped you twice. Thrown an apple at your head and now a shampoo bottle. I am a disgusting person. I know how it feels. I don't want you to feel like that. I don't want to make anyone feel like that. Not you...Never you."

He frowned deeply as his eyes studied my face. "Baby, every time you've reacted like that you've been provoked. By me."

"Provocation is no excuse," I urged. "In any situation. I did wrong. This is all on me, Kyle."

"Lee, I'm a major douchebag sometimes and you're only human." He clasped my face in between his hands and grinned. "Did you know that Cam went all *Bruce Lee* on Derek with a toilet paper holder once? I got off lightly with a shampoo bottle..."

"What?" I shook my head and stifled a laugh. "She didn't..."

"She did," Kyle grinned. A sadness crept into his eyes, but he blinked it away quickly. Taking my hand, he led me back to the couch before sinking onto it and pulling me down on his lap. "I never know what to say to you," he said quietly. "You need to let me know if I bring stuff up that's hard for you to talk about."

"I'd like to hear more," I whispered as I snuggled against him. My back was throbbing, but I ignored the pain as I rested against Kyle. "Please tell me more."

"About Derek and Cam?" he asked quietly.

I nodded. "About anything you can remember about Cam."

"Well, she tramp-stamped Derek when we were in college," he mused.

"What's a tramp stamp?" I asked in confusion. I wasn't sure what that was code for.

"It's a tattoo, baby," Kyle chuckled before bending down and kissing my hair. "Sometimes I forget how sheltered your life was before moving to the hill."

"How come you're not tramp stamped?" I asked.

"I hate needles," he whispered with a shudder. "Besides, it's not my thing."

"I'm glad," I whispered. "Your body is beautiful. You don't need to be scarring it."

"Cam could drink a beer faster than most guys I know," Kyle said, veering the conversation away from scars before laughing softly. "And I don't know if you ever noticed, but she used to do this weird thing with cereals."

I smiled and turned my face up so I could see him. "She would scoop the cereal up with a spoon, but tip it sideways and let the milk spill out before she ate them."

"Yeah," Kyle said eagerly as his eyes lit up. "It used to drive me fucking crazy."

"Me too," I chuckled. "She always did that. Since as long as I can remember."

"Such a waste of milk," he mused.

"I used to drink her leftover milk when I was small," I admitted, red faced.

"Uh..." Kyle groaned. "That's fucking gross, baby."

"What," I shrugged. "It was a waste and I was hungry. And in my defense I was like four or something."

"Were you hungry a lot as a child?" he asked in a soft voice.

"Not really," I mumbled, arching my back to ease the throbbing. "I mean, I was never full, but I wouldn't say I was starving…although I probably would've starved if Ted and Mora weren't so good to me." I frowned as I thought about it. "I'm still confused as to how he kept me alive as a baby…he was always drunk, Kyle. Like every single day. It's a miracle he remembered to feed me."

"Jesus," Kyle muttered as he tightened his arms around me and kissed my shoulder. "You have to stop. I can't hear this... I can't."

"Okay, I'm sorry," I muttered. We sat in silence until I couldn't take it anymore. "I'm sorry for today, Kyle."

"Lee," he sighed. "Please stop apologizing."

"What if I'm like him?" I whispered in mortification. "What if I'm going to turn out like him? Do you think behavior like that is genetic?"

"You're not now, nor will you ever be anything like him," he spat. "I'm still trying to figure out how that bastard's blood is running through your veins."

I sat up and turned to look at him. He was so sure I was good. He was wrong. "I'm not perfect, Kyle."

"No, you're not," he said with a smirk. "And I'm glad for that because I'm so fucking far from perfect it gives our relationship a little balance when you drop your halo and show you're human. You're so far above me, Lee, I feel like I'm hanging on to your ankles just to keep you on the ground with me."

"What?" I asked in confusion. "Kyle, that makes no sense."

"It does to me," he said simply. "We're both fucked up, Lee. It's nice to know that. It's lonely being the only screw-up."

Huh...I stroked his cheek with my palm and smiled sheepishly. "I guess we're both a little broken, aren't we?"

"That's an understatement." Kyle laughed and squeezed me tightly. "At least we can be each other's glue. You fix me and I'll fix you. Deal?"

I smiled. "Deal."

"And by the way," Kyle whispered, several hours later as we were lying in bed facing each other. "Don't ever leave me hanging like you did this morning. Trust me, my dick hurt ten times worse than my nose."

"Kyle," I whispered, completely mortified. "I was b..."

"I don't care," he said before I could finish. "I don't care about that and neither should you." He yawned loudly as his eyelids fluttered closed. "I'm not some adolescent asshole who doesn't understand how a woman's body works," he muttered, his voice drowsy. "I wanna be inside you...no matter what's going on inside of you."

"I was worried," I confessed. "I'm still worried..." My voice trailed off as the sound of Kyle's heavy breathing filled my ears. I stared at his peaceful face. He looked so much younger when he was asleep. "I love you," I whispered before climbing out of bed and into the shower.

SEVEN

LEE

"LEE, COME ON, GET DRESSED," Kyle grumbled as he pulled my shoes out of our wardrobe and dropped them on the bed next to me. Rachel's gun hadn't killed me, but I had a feeling the pain I'd woken up with would. Getting out of bed this morning and taking care of Hope was hard enough. I was sore and didn't feel up to going out for dinner, but telling Kyle this would only result in a humiliating trip to the ER.

I woke up again this morning with horrible back pain. I was aching all over and every time I peed I felt like diving into a bathtub full of boiling hot water to stop the burning sensation. I actually had to do that twice this afternoon. I was used to the pain in my back but the pee-burn sucked. I wasn't completely sure if I was on my period or not, but it had been five days since I called Dr. Bromwick and I was still spotting. I'd called Dr. Michaels again yesterday, but the secretary I'd spoken to informed me that he was out of the office for another two weeks and the only doctor available was Dr. Bromwick…

I spent an unhealthy amount of time on my phone last night googling my symptoms and after a dozen heart-stopping, terrifying possible causes for the bleeding, I'd come to the conclusion that Dr. Bromwick was right about two things. I was on my period and I was stupid. Incredibly stupid…

I'd also woken up in the middle of the night screaming my

head off. Every time I'd tried to close my eyes I'd been haunted with memories of Cam. Last night's nightmare had been more disturbing than others. As usual I was back in the kitchen at Thirteenth Street, holding Cam's lifeless body in my arms, except last night she'd spoken to me...

"I don't want to die, Lee."

"Don't make me die for you."

"Why are you letting her hurt me?"

"It's you she wants."

She had chanted the same four sentences over and over until her eyes started to roll back in her head. Then she started to cry. That had been the worst part. Her tears were blood and they'd soaked my body. When I woke the guilt had been so smothering that I'd felt like I was going to suffocate from the pain. Kyle hadn't spoken a word when he held me in his arms. He hadn't tried to shush me or tell me it would be okay. He let me cry it out and I was grateful for that. He couldn't say anything to make it better or make the nightmares stop. He couldn't do anything to change the past. But sleep hadn't come and this morning I couldn't eat.

"This isn't a setup, is it?" I asked as I watched Kyle button his blue shirt and tucked the tails of his shirt into his black pants.

"There's no set up, baby," he said grinning and for a brief moment I wished he had a vagina just so he could understand what it felt like to pee razor-blades. "I just want us to have a nice family meal. Is that so hard to believe?"

Quite frankly it was and I smelled a rat. His obsession with playing happy families with my mother was upsetting me. I'd been forgiven for the whole shampoo bottle incident. I was sorry. I shouldn't have done it, but my actions seemed to have kick started his fixation with repairing my relationship with my mom. He re-started the 'talk to your mother' conversation the moment I opened my eyes this morning and had continued with it on and off throughout the day. I was fairly certain I would explode if I heard the words 'that poor woman' come out of his mouth one more time.

"Come on, princess. Hope's all dressed up and looking adorable...let's go show her off to Theresa and the girls in the restaurant." *Hit me with the daughter card why don't you...*

"Fine," I muttered as I grabbed a plain black dress out of the closet. Easing my string top off, I pulled my dress over my head. Stretching hurt my back and I winced when a stab of pain hit me.

Kyle looked at me for a moment with an odd expression...a saddened expression before masking his features and walking over to me. I felt his hands skim my sides and then move around to my lower back. "I love you," he whispered before placing a kiss on my shoulder.

My anger evaporated and I sagged against him. "I'm sorry. I'm just lonely today. Last night Cam..." I stopped. There was no point dragging up the past or my screwed up dreams. "I shouldn't take my bad mood out on you."

He slid the fabric of my dress down my body before moving his hands around to my back to zip me up. "I just want you to be happy, Lee."

"I know," I breathed.

Sometimes it was too much.

The feelings I had for Kyle...sometimes they threatened to drown me.

KYLE

I had an infallible talent for making things worse. Seriously, it was a gift. I seemed to make every situation twenty times worse by just opening my mouth. I knew the moment I walked Lee into the hotel restaurant I'd made a huge mistake. She'd been so down on herself all day, missing Cam…I should have called this dinner off. Derek had tried to warn me, but I'd thought…No, I hadn't thought. I should have fucking thought. I was in serious trouble.

"How could you, Kyle?" Lee whimpered and I couldn't stop my ears from reddening, or my cheeks.

Yeah, I was an asshole.

I'd thought by inviting Tracy to dinner it would give Lee the push she needed to break the ice. But I'd obviously thought wrong. I had a pair of very angry gray eyes boring into my skull and I didn't feel so smart now. Derek, who was lounging in his seat at the table, with a half dozen empty shot glasses in front of him, gave me two sarcastic thumbs up. Asshole…

"Should I go?" Tracy mumbled from her seat beside Derek and I swear my heart strings tightened.

That poor woman…

"No," I said at the same time Lee said, "yes."

Tracy worried her lip, clearly unsure of what to do.

"Fine," Lee sighed as she dragged her chair out roughly and sat down. It didn't slip my attention that she winced when she sat. She was in pain… "If you want her here so badly, Kyle, then you can talk to her. I have nothing to say..."

"I have," Tracy said quietly, halting Lee mid-sentence. Lee glared across the table at her and Tracy seemed to straighten her spine a little. "You don't have to say anything," Tracy urged in a desperate tone. "Not one word if you don't want to. All you have to do is stay."

Lee frowned and wiped her eyes with the back of her hands. "There's nothing...."

"Kyle told me how forgiving you are. Well, I'm not asking for forgiveness. All I want is to spend some time with you."

Lee stiffened for a moment before her shoulders sagged slightly and her head nodded. "It's a good thing you're not asking for forgiveness," she said quietly. "Because that's something you will never get from me."

I released a breath when I saw Lee wasn't leaving. Placing Hope's car seat on the floor, I sank my ass into the chair next to hers, though I slid mine as far away as I could. I had a feeling I would need the space. She had high fucking heels on and I wanted to keep my toes.

LEE

With deep reluctance I lowered myself onto my seat, inhaled steadily and fought the urge to run. Looking up, my eyes immediately sought and found Tracy. She sat less than two feet away from me. I felt myself stiffen, my ankles locked together, and my eyes roamed over the woman who claimed to be my mother. She was looking at me with this...yearning look and I wanted to vomit. Her yearning should have happened twenty years ago. Not now. My eyes traveled over her face seeking a memory. One single memory.

I came up empty.

"You have a beautiful daughter," she told me.

"I do," I replied, bowing my head. Her stare was too much.

"And a good man," Tracy mused in a dreamy tone.

"*Good* wouldn't be a phrase I would use for him right now," I managed to grind out through clenched teeth as I glanced at Kyle. The side of his face–that I could see–was red. He seemed to be extremely interested in his fingernails all of a sudden. I turned to look at Derek, who was sitting opposite me at the table. *'Chin up'* he mouthed as he gave me a reassuring smile.

A waiter was dispatched to our table within minutes of us sitting down and took our order. Kyle made small talk with Tracy while we waited for our food. I didn't hear a word of it. I was too anxious and I couldn't sit still. I squirmed in my seat but no position helped with my discomfort. It was more than discomfort. I was in agony. Biting down on my fist, I pushed the pain to the back of mind. I was such a wimp. I usually had a much higher pain threshold. I was disgusted with myself for whimpering over menstrual cramps. Every nerve ending in my body was on high alert. I looked around at their faces in a bid to occupy my mind and distract myself.

Kyle looked guilty. Derek looked bored. Hope *was* bored because she'd fallen asleep in her car seat, between Kyle's chair and mine. And Tracy looked nervous. Her brown eyes were wide as she chewed on her lip with her teeth.

Brown eyes.

I'd never known what color my mother's eyes were. I guess I got my gray eyes from my daddy. Her hair was the same as mine though. Wild brown curls that she held back from her face with a single clip and I wore mine flowing free. "So, Kyle, where did you grow up?" she asked, setting down her glass of water.

Kyle shifted uncomfortably in his seat and cleared his throat. "Uh…I grew up in care. I moved around a lot as a kid."

My eyes snapped up and I glared at Tracy before softening my gaze when I looked at Kyle. "You don't have to talk about this," I said protectively. His past bothered him and I wasn't going to sit back and watch his old wounds open. Besides, all she had to do was open a newspaper and she could read all about it. We'd been slaughtered in the press. The only thing about our lives that hadn't been written about, funnily enough, was her. "This is your business," I told him before glancing at her. "Nobody else's."

"Oh, I'm sorry," Tracy blushed. "I wasn't trying to pry…"

Kyle clasped my knee with his hand to reassure me. "Its fine, princess," he said in a gentle tone before turning to Tracy. "As far as I know I was born in a small town close to Colorado Springs. My mother was young when she had me and from what my case workers could gather we moved around a lot. The only place they're certain we lived, is Aspen..."

Our waiter returned with our order and I breathed a sigh of relief. I felt raw pain in my chest every time Kyle spoke of his childhood. We ate in silence although I had no appetite for my steak. I messed around with the food on my plate, slicing up pieces of meat aimlessly while I prayed this night would end soon. I needed a shower and some pain relief. *I needed a tranquilizer.*

"Why Aspen?" Tracy asked and I wanted to throw my fork at her.

Kyle sighed heavily and lowered his fork from his mouth. "That's where she died. That's where they found me."

"Oh, I'm sorry," Tracy gasped. "What happened to her?"

"Look," I said through clenched teeth, interrupting both of them. "I am grateful for the kidney, truly I am. So thank you for saving my life." I inhaled a deep breath before continuing. "But you should know that there is only one reason I am sitting at this table, sharing a meal with you." I covered Kyle's hand with mine. "And it is because of this man. He is my world and for some strange reason he has a soft spot for you. Don't mistake his feelings for mine and don't throw his kindness in his face. I won't sit back and allow you to make him feel uncomfortable. His private life is exactly that. Private. Are we clear?"

"Lee…" Kyle started, but Tracy interrupted him.

"No, Kyle, I'm sorry," she said quickly. "Lia is right. I shouldn't be asking you such personal things." She lowered her face. "I haven't had much company over the years. I've been alone for a very long time."

"Whose choice was that?" I couldn't help but ask. "And my name isn't Lia."

"Lee," Kyle said in a warning tone, but I ignored him. I was sick of sitting here and playing happy families with the woman who abandoned me to a life of mental and physical torture.

"Mine," Tracy said, staring directly at me. "It was my choice."

"At least you admit it," I whispered, unsure of what else to say. She was confusing me with her honesty. I didn't understand her.

Tracy sighed and wiped her forehead. "I admit that my will to live caused me to make the biggest mistake of my life. I can't change what happened to you when I left. But I can tell you that I didn't think he'd harm you. He loved you. We both did."

"Just not enough," I whispered under my breath, though I was sure all three of them heard me.

"Phew," Derek said as he blew out a breath and stretched. "It's hot in here tonight. I might just grab some fresh air." He smiled apologetically. "Won't be long." I watched as the traitor stood up and retreated from the table.

Two on one…

"I need the bathroom," I mumbled as I tossed my napkin on my plate and pushed my chair back. I needed to get away from this woman. I wasn't ready for this and I was done with being forced into things.

I felt Kyle's hand take mine. His fingers threaded through mine. "No running," he whispered as he leaned into my ear. "I'm not going to let anything bad happen to you," he added before pressing a kiss to my temple.

I pulled my hand from his. "You already have," I muttered as I stood up and left.

KYLE

My girl was like a tiger tonight. Protective as hell over me...and in a weird way I loved it. I wasn't used to having people stick up for me. It always shocked the hell out of me when Lee stepped out of her comfort zone. She was usually so mild-mannered and timid. It never ceased to amaze me when her claws came out.

The morning she stood her ground against Rachel in my kitchen, defending my honor, was one of the most surreal moments of my life. I was pretty sure I'd stood there with the biggest smile on my face as I watched this tiny ball of curls punch over her weight.

She'd shocked me again tonight. When Tracy had asked about my childhood, for a moment I'd thought Lee was going to explode. There was a dominant look in her eyes as she stared her mother down, an almost feral wildness in those fiery gray depths. Princess was coming back to life. Thank fucking god.

Now all she had to do was come back to the table...

"This was a bad idea," Tracy said as she pushed her chair back to stand. "I should go."

"No," I said, leaning forward and grabbing her hand. Tracy flinched and I released her hand immediately while I battled down a surge of anger I had directed solely at Jimmy Bennett. Was he proud of himself? Did it make him feel good to know he was the cause of his wife and daughter shrinking and shying away from a man's touch? *Bastard...* "Just give her a minute," I choked out. "She'll calm down."

Tracy reluctantly sat back down. "You're very optimistic, Kyle," she said with a small smile. "But this is wrong. I shouldn't have put you in this position."

LEE

My anger had simmered down by the time I found Derek perched on top of a bench table in the beer garden at the back of the hotel. *It had been replaced with pain.*

"Sorry, ice," he chuckled. "I love you, sweetheart, but that was one hell of a drama overload in there."

When I saw what he had in his hand my step faltered. "Derek," I asked. Even my voice sounded confused. "Why are you smoking?"

He dropped his head and stared at the ground. "Calms me," he breathed as he exhaled a puff of smoke. "I promised Cam I'd quit when we met," he added as he took another drag and exhaled. "Seems kind of pointless keeping that promise now, don't you think?"

"No, I don't think that," I urged as I stepped closer to him. "I feel her around me every day. Looking down on us. I bet she can see you now." I patted his knee. "She'd be sad to see you hurting your body like this Derek."

"If," he said as he put his cigarette between his fingers and picked up a small tumbler that was resting on the bench next to him. I watched him toss the golden liquid back his throat and shivered. I hated that golden liquid. Whiskey did dangerous things to a man. "*If* she is watching us," he continued as he wiped his bottom lip. "It's not my body she's concerned about."

I had no answer for that.

I racked my brain and came up empty. Everything I wanted

to say wouldn't do any good..."I'm sad to see you hurting yourself," I told him as I climbed awkwardly onto the bench and sat alongside him–not an easy task in heels. "I'm concerned about you. I love you and I care." It probably didn't help, but he needed to know he was loved.

"If I had a baby sister," he chuckled as he nudged my shoulder. "Then I would want her to be you."

"You're the only brother I'd ever want, too," I replied, nudging him back. The pain in my back was getting worse and I was burning inside. I had to force a smile, but I was sure it looked more like a grimace.

"Don't be too hard on him, Lee," Derek said after a moment, I knew he was talking about Kyle ambushing me with Tracy. "As fucked up as it looks, he does all these stupid things because he loves you. Trying to get you to make up with your mother is his way of trying to repair some of your childhood. He wants to fix you because he loves you and he fucks it all up because he's never done any of this before. He's never had to because you're the first person he's let in, Lee. Ever."

"He let you in..." I started to say, but Derek shook his head and smiled.

"He's never been in love before you," he said in a serious tone. "He's never *been loved* before you. Not in the way he needs. You give him that. This is his way of showing you he loves you, too. He doesn't know any other way to express himself because he's never been shown. He runs around thinking he can fix everyone because he's spent his whole life trying to make up for the things that he couldn't change. The things he's had no control over."

"His mom," I whispered.

"Bingo," Derek said. "Kyle's a problem solver. That's the way his mind works. He wasn't raised, Lee, he was dragged up. Spent his whole life on his own, pushing people away, not trusting a soul until he met you. You cracked him open. Exposed his weaknesses, revealed his secrets and loved him regardless. He's never had that before. You're his biggest risk, his deepest fear and his greatest accomplishment all rolled into one. So, just think about that before you chew him out over this."

"I love him too, Derek," I whispered. "So much."

"So much," he mused before chuckling softly. "You don't have a clue what you've done to him, do you?"

I shook my head. "What do you mean?"

"It's a scary thing, Lee," Derek replied. "When a man falls so hard for a woman that he can't figure out if she is his salvation or his downfall."

"That doesn't sound very appealing," I muttered.

"No," he smiled. "It's not the most comforting feeling to have your heart walking around in someone else's body. It makes you feel incredibly exposed and vulnerable."

"Which one was Cam?" I asked.

"Which one was Cam what?"

"Was she your salvation or your downfall?" I blushed and mentally slapped myself on the head. *Stupid Lee. Stupid!*

Derek sighed heavily. "That's the really fucked up thing about love," he said. "When it's real. When it is really honest to god love, you'll know that she's both. She's gonna ruin you and save you all in one breath."

"I..." I trailed off because I had no words. I was stunned. Nothing had ever been so confusing yet made more sense to my ears. I'd never heard a man explain feelings quite like that. It was humbling to think that Kyle could feel like this for me. It was absolutely heartbreaking to know that Derek felt like this for Cam. He would never get over her. If this was how he felt, how in god's name could he ever move on?

"Here, I have something for you," he mumbled as he shoved his hand into his pocket. "I meant to give it to you the night of your birthday, but...well, we both know how that went down."

"Ah, yes. The vomit," I mused. Derek and Kyle both got rip-roaring drunk the night of my birthday. Kyle had sang me a song about chasing me around with a gun. Derek had puked on my lap... "I have to say Der, it was definitely a birthday I'll remember."

He smiled sheepishly. "Yeah...uh, sorry again. Well, your gift is second hand, but I think you'll like it."

"Derek," I breathed when he handed me the gold locket wrapped in tissue paper. A gold locket I'd seen more than once. I shook my head as I tried to make sense of why he would have this. I'd thought they'd taken everything. "Where..."

"Did I get it?" he said with a small smile. "I stole it from her bag of things that Ted collected from the morgue. He left it on the kitchen table, and I...I just thought I needed it at the time I guess." He threw his head back and exhaled loudly. "Except that's not what I needed." Opening the locket my legs wobbled as I looked at the two tiny cut out photos of Cam and Derek. *Oh Derek...* "Besides," he said with a forced smile. "I bought it for her so technically I didn't steal it."

"Derek, I can't take this," I whispered as I pushed it into his hand. I didn't want to have this in my hands.*This was on her neck the night she died...Why was she wearing a locket with Derek's photo when she was with Mike?*

"Please take it, Lee," he choked out. "Please. Just take it away for me."

"She loved you," I sobbed as I wiped my nose. "She did, Derek. I know she did. Cam loved you."

"Just not enough," he whispered, throwing my earlier words back at me.

Helping me down from the bench, Derek opened the clasp and I held my hair up for him. The tremendous weight I felt when he tied the clasp and stepped back wasn't from the weight of the gold around my neck, it was from the incalculable amount of heartbreak it carried.

If it were possible for a human heart to float into another body it would be at this moment. I felt like I was bleeding for him. I'd never wanted to take another person's pain away like I wanted to take Derek's. It was physically painful to be so utterly useless. His problems put mine into perspective...

"Hey," he said softly as he grabbed my arm. "You okay?" His eyes were full of concern that I wanted to cry. "Lee, you're wobbling a little, sweetheart."

"I'll be fine," I whispered and I hoped I was telling the truth, but the pain in my back was calling me a liar. "I need to...go," I muttered as I stepped away from Derek. "Will you tell Kyle I'm going to bed?"

"You are going to bed. Right?" Derek asked in a sharp tone.

"Yes, Derek," I managed to squeeze out. I bit down on the inside of my cheek and waved limply before hobbling off in the direction of the elevators. I managed to make it into the shower in our suite before crumpling to the floor.

God, I hated bathrooms.

DEREK

"She's gone upstairs," I growled as I staggered over to the table and sank into my seat. I glared at the two idiots sitting at the table. I actually felt sick to my stomach looking at either of them…well, maybe the alcohol was causing the pain in my stomach. I'd made a small pit-stop at the bar before coming back to the table. I needed all eight shots. This was the cruelest thing I'd witnessed Kyle do in a long time. I'd warned him. He needed to start listening. That girl was heartbroken and he didn't fucking get it. He had the woman he loved. Why the fuck was he messing it up? "She's not coming back. I hope the two of you are happy with yourselves."

Kyle glared at me in warning before turning to Tracy. "I'm sorry about this," he muttered.

"Don't be." Tracy smiled and I nearly hurled when I saw the crocodile tears in her eyes. This shit was a joke. No, I decided it wasn't the whiskey. That woman's face was making my stomach turn. "I'm not expecting miracles," she said. "Lia has every right to feel the way she does."

"Damn straight," I sneered. "An organ won't erase eighteen years of having the shit kicked out of her or starving on the side of the road, while sleeping in a house that's not fit for a dog to piss in." She blanched at my words. Well, good. About time someone gave her some home truths. I didn't have an ounce of sympathy for her. My sympathy was bone dry.

"Derek," Kyle hissed. "Jesus Christ." He looked mortified and

I debated keeping my mouth shut. Kyle was my best friend and anything I had to say was going to fuck things up between us, but then I thought of Lee...Cam wasn't here to knock some sense into the dumbass. She was completely defenseless...

"Fuck it," I snapped unable to sit back and stay silent. Drunk or not, they were going to hear my opinion on the matter. "I'm sorry, but you both need to hear this." I leaned forward and grabbed a glass of whiskey, tipped it back my throat before slamming the glass on the table and continuing. "I've known Lee just as long as you have, Kyle," I told him. "She's like a sister to me. I lived with her for a year and I'm not fucking blind." I turned to glare at Tracy. "Have you seen your daughter's body?" I asked, my voice full of sarcasm. "Well, if you ever do, you'll see that she wasn't just beaten. She was fucking tortured." My voice was laced with disgust because I was disgusted. I was repulsed. I'd seen the scars on Lee. She had more burns, stitch scars and dents on her body than I'd ever seen on a human body.

Kyle seemed to forget that I was the one who held that girl in my arms as her life, and the life of their baby, bled out of her last Christmas. I was the one with her in the ambulance after she was shot. I was the one who watched the paramedics work franticly to bring her back to life when her heart stopped beating–three fucking times–on the ride to the hospital. I had lost the love of my life and Kyle was pushing his love away...

"Tortured," I hissed. "Because some spineless woman decided to give birth to a baby and play house with an alcoholic bully." I laughed dryly before pointing a finger at her in a seemingly casual gesture. "And *then*, to add insult to injury, one day that woman decides she doesn't want to be a punching bag and says to herself 'hmm, I better leave the baby with him, maybe he won't look for me if he can knock her around instead.'"

"That's enough, douchebag," Kyle snarled when Tracy burst into tears. "No one is saying what Tracy did was right, but have a heart, Derek. Some fucking compassion. She saved Lee's life."

"*Cam* saved Lee's life," I roared as I shoved my chair back and stood up. "I happen to have compassion, Kyle. And it's not for *her*." I leaned my fists on the table and glowered at him. "You," I spat. "Need to pick a fucking team. And you." I pointed at Tracy, who was out of her chair and backing away from the table. "Need to crawl back under the rock you came from."

Kyle waited until Tracy had bolted from the restaurant before speaking to me. "You," he said calmly as he lifted his, now wide awake and terrified, baby from her seat and cuddled her to his chest. "Are lucky my daughter is here." I felt like a piece of shit as I watched Kyle trying to calm Hope down. I'd scared her...He stroked Hope's face and tried to soothe her. "Shh, baby," he murmured. "Daddy's here. It's alright. I'm here, baby girl."

My shoulders sagged as I sighed heavily. "I'm sorry for raising my voice, but I'm not sorry for what I said. She needed to hear that."

"Go home and sober up, Derek," Kyle said wearily as he pushed back his chair and stood. "Before I say something *you* need to hear."

"I don't understand you, Kyle," I said sadly. "Look at that baby." I pointed at Hope and shuddered. "Lee was like that once and instead of having a father like you, she had him." Grabbing the bottle of wine that was on the table, I turned around and walked away from the table. "Think about that, dude."

KYLE

Jesus, my intervention went down about as smoothly as a ton of bricks.

I was setting a record for the number of times I could screw up in a week. Last week, Lee ran away to the cemetery to avoid me. This week I'd pissed her off so much she locked herself away in the bathroom. At least I was consistent in my assholeness.

"Lee," I said for the hundredth fucking time. "Open up, baby."

I listened and waited. Nothing.

"Lee, open the door. You don't have to talk to me. I know I fucked up. You don't even have to look at me…just let me see you're okay." I wasn't sure how long she'd been in there. I'd waited for over an hour in the restaurant with Hope and Tracy before Derek came back. Yeah, my mind was still reeling over what he'd said. Jesus, his words had hit me hard.

He had a point, but so had I…

I'd put Hope to bed an hour ago and had been sitting on this fucking bed, staring at the bathroom door since. I wasn't in the mood to be attacked with flying objects, but I was worried sick. I needed to fix this. "Open the goddamn door, Lee," I growled, anxiety tearing at my gut. "You have two fucking seconds to open this door or I'm kicking it in."

Losing my patience, I got up and stormed over to the door. Slamming my hand down on the handle, I felt like the world's biggest tool when it opened inwards.

I was sure I felt my heart crack when I saw her curled up in a ball on the floor of the shower. Rushing over I swung the shower door open. Steam hit me square in the face. Jesus, she was going to burn her skin off. I moved to turn off the shower. "Don't," she cried.

"What are you doing?" I whispered as I crouched down in front of her. Her skin was flushed. Her face was scrunched up.

"I'm in pain," she whispered as she clutched herself.

"Down there?" I asked as I knelt in front of her and brushed her hair out of her eyes. She nodded as she bit her lip and winced.

I knew it. I fucking knew she wasn't ready to have sex. Jesus Christ, I needed to start listening to the head on my shoulders and stop listening to the head on my shaft. "Come here, baby," I whispered as I leaned into the shower to pick her up.

"No, no," she cried, pushing my hands away. "The heat helps. Please let me be. It stops the burning."

"Lee, I think you have a kidney infection," I told her, remembering the list of signs the doctor had told us to look out for. "I'm gonna call the doctor, okay?"

"There's no point," she mumbled. "It's normal."

"What?" I shook my head and stood before pulling my phone out of my pocket. "Don't be stupid, of course there's a point. There's a very big point, baby. You've had a kidney transplant. You have pain and you need to get it checked out. This is not normal."

I must have said the wrong thing because her whole face caved and she burst into tears. "Yeah," she squeezed out before clenching her eyes shut. "Okay, thanks."

I was right. Lee had a nasty urinary tract infection and the muscles in her back were in spasm. Dr. Bromwick gave her a shot for the back pain, prescribed some antibiotics for the infection and a prophylaxis to prevent any future recurrences.

He'd been more than helpful, coming straight to the hotel when I called. I was grateful as hell because I hadn't been sure how I was going to get her out of the room and into the car if I had to take her to the hospital. I had to coax her out of the shower with a heating pad just so I could get her dressed before he came. "Thanks for coming so quickly, doc," I said as I opened the door for him.

"No problem," he mumbled with red cheeks. "Glad to help. Call anytime, Mr. Carter."

Locking the door of our suite, I checked on Hope before going to our room. "Why didn't you tell me you were sick?" I said in a weary tone. I was fucking weary. I was sick to death of not being told shit. The argument I was sure we would have about her mom had been put on the back burner. She hadn't brought it up yet. I guessed she realized how fucking serious this was. "Lee, I need to know these things. How long has this been going on?"

"A few days," she muttered as she climbed into bed achingly slowly. I shrugged off my clothes and slid in next to her. She curled into a ball on her side and I slid in behind her. "I didn't want to worry you," she whispered. "You have enough problems…"

"Princess," I groaned as I rubbed her back in slow steady circles. Her skin was damp and I wasn't sure if it was from the shower or the pain. If I could take this pain from her I would. It fucking killed me to watch her hurting. "You're not a problem for me, goddammit. A problem for me is when you're sick and don't tell me and we end up like tonight or worse…"

"I'm sorry," she whispered as she pressed herself against my touch. I rubbed her a little harder and she moaned in relief. At least I was doing something right. "He said it was normal. I googled it…I'm sorry."

"You googled it?" I asked in disgust. I brushed her long curls to one side and started rubbing her shoulders. "You self-diagnosed yourself on Google? What the hell. You could have had a relapse, Lee. Or septicemia or any number of things. Baby, you can't Google your goddamn health…" My words trailed off as her words registered in my head. I sat up and looked down at her. "Hold up, who the fuck told you it was normal?"

She slowly rolled onto her back and looked up at me with tear-filled eyes. "Him," she sobbed. Tears slid down her cheeks, landing on the pillow under her head. "Dr. Bromwick. I called him the other day to get an appointment. He said it was menstrual cramps. That's why I freaked out on you when we were…"

"What?" I shook my head as I tried to contemplate what the fuck I was hearing. "What?"

"He was horrible," she whispered. Her lip wobbled as she spoke. "I knew something was wrong, but he said…he convinced me it was nothing. I felt so stupid for even calling. He made me feel so stupid, Kyle. I *knew* it wasn't my period…"

"You're not stupid," I snarled as I climbed out of bed and grabbed my pants. "He's stupid. He's a dead man walking."

"Kyle," Lee said in an anxious tone as she struggled to sit up. "Where are you going?"

"To find him," I hissed as I slipped on my shoes and grabbed my keys off the bedside table. "Let's see how he likes it when he's pissing blood. I'm gonna give that piece of shit a period of his own."

"Don't you dare," she warned as she scrambled out of bed and hobbled over to me. I couldn't look at her face. I wanted to break something. I *was* going to break something. Him. "Do not make this worse. You can't just hit a doctor, Kyle," she begged as she wrapped her hands around my wrists. "There are rules about that kind of thing."

"Where were the fucking rules when he refused to see you?" I roared as I pulled my hands away from hers quickly. Too quickly.

Shit.

She flinched and backed away from me. My anger turned inwards. Guilt swamped me. "I'm sorry," I whispered as I reached out slowly and stroked her arm, giving her a chance to relax. "It's okay, baby."

Her nervous eyes studied me for a moment before she stepped forward slowly. I wrapped her up in my arms while I mentally kicked the shit out of myself for being so stupid. I would *never* hurt her. Jesus, it cut me when she looked so afraid of me. My anger evaporated as shame and fucking guilt took its place. "Please calm down, Kyle," she whispered. "Breathe. Count to ten."

"I'm not five, baby," I mumbled. "Just…just go lie down. I'll sort this out."

"I don't want you to go," she begged as she gripped the sides of my pants with her fists. "Please don't go. I'm sorry for not telling you, okay?"

"He's not getting away with this, Lee," I whispered, my anger re-filling to the point I felt I would burst if I didn't get it out. "He could have killed you. That's neglect. I am not paying those goddamn doctors a fortune to talk shit to you." I shook my head in pure rage. "No one is going to dismiss you like that and get away with it."

"He probably didn't check my file," she said, obviously trying to comfort me. "He may not have known about my kidneys, Kyle."

"He's a goddamn nephrologist," I spat as I desperately tried to rein in my temper. "You were hardly calling him for a friendly chat. It's his job to check your file, Lee. He is *paid* to know about *your* kidneys."

"Are you going to leave me, Kyle?" she asked in a soft tone.

"Leave you?" I shook my head and gaped at her. "No. Jesus, Lee, what the hell are you talking about?"

Stepping back from me, she looked into my eyes. "People mess up all the time, Kyle," she told me before climbing onto the bed and crawling over to her side. "I'm hurt over what you did tonight too you know, but you don't see me running out looking for a fight." She curled into a ball on her side before whispering, "You don't always have to use your fists to prove a point…"

"Lee," I sighed as I climbed into bed and curled my body around hers. "I'm sorry, okay? For ambushing you with Tracy… for fucking up...I won't do it again."

"Please don't," was all she said and I wasn't sure if I'd gotten off lightly or if I was in deeper shit than I'd originally thought.

EIGHT

LEE

I WAS HAVING A BAD DAY. Every inch of my body ached as I made my way down to the lobby with Hope in my arms. My limbs felt like noodles and my mind was stuck in the past. I hadn't touched the prescription of sleeping pills I'd been prescribed, but last night I'd woken up from a nightmare in such a panic that I staggered into the shower at 5am and scrubbed my skin raw. It hadn't helped. I still felt dirty. I could still feel her blood on my hands. *All over my body…*

The elevator pinged as the doors slid open. I was glad I'd tucked a muslin cloth over my shoulder. Hope was a bad traveler when it came to elevators. Stepping out of the elevator, I stood to one side and cleaned us up as best I could. Thankfully, she hadn't eaten lunch yet and I had my hair tied back. Otherwise this would have been a code red puke-fest.

Kyle would probably kill me if he knew I was wandering around the hotel, but I had to get out of that room. I needed to integrate myself back into society again and he needed to let me. I planned on doing this by having lunch in the hotel restaurant.

We had been doing really well, but things were tense between us now. I was mad at him for forcing my mother on me–although, to be fair, he did seem to have dropped it. He was mad at me for not telling him I was sick. I'd suffered for my omission. Kyle had been methodical in having me test my urine every morning since. He had also re-enforced his sex ban. He hadn't actually told me that, since we weren't really speaking, but I guessed sex was off the menu when he started wearing sweatpants and a t-shirt to bed. Although, apparently it was absolutely fine for him to have sex with himself. He hadn't even blushed when I walked in on him jerking off in the shower this morning. I'd almost died of embarrassment while Kyle had just grinned and carried on. To be honest, I could have sworn he enjoyed my eyes on him. But he really didn't have to bother wrapping himself up at night. The only thing I was tempted to get on top of right now was my bed, and the only thing I was getting under was my duvet.

I was so exhausted from lack of sleep. My nightmares had been plaguing me lately, and even though Kyle was mad at me, he still held me when I woke at night and comforted me until I fell back to sleep. Being in love helped when we drove each other crazy, and trusting him helped even more. There was a structure to our relationship that hadn't been there in the beginning. A security. But sometimes it was hard to find a steady medium when we'd lived the past couple of years in a state of constant drama. I was working on not running when things upset me. And Kyle was working on not losing his temper with me when I pissed him off. I thought we were doing a good job until my mother had jostled her way between us. Now all I wanted to do was run and all Kyle wanted to do was shout.

Stupid damn woman…

"Miss Bennett."

I groaned internally when I saw Kyle's henchman approach me with a frustrated look on his face. "You're not supposed to be down here," Marcus stated as he stood in front of me with his hands on his hips. He – like most others – towered above me, which made me wonder how tall my daughter would grow to be with Kyle's giant genes in her. She was a long baby–had weighed eight pounds when she was born. I had a feeling I was going to be the shortest member of our little family. *Maybe if we got a dog…*

"Mr. Carter said…"

"I know, I know," I mumbled as I cradled Hope to my chest. I couldn't rest her on my hips because my scars were feeling tender. I felt like a child being told off by a grownup, which was absurd considering I was holding my own child in my arms. "I just felt like stretching my legs and grabbing a bite to eat."

I hated explaining myself to every tom, dick and harry he had watching me. I found it especially embarrassing since I'd worked alongside the majority of the staff in this place when I first moved to The Hill. I was totally paranoid that they believed what was written in the papers about me. I hoped they didn't believe it, but I wasn't a fool either. I'd made it to the top of the gossip pile when I fell pregnant with the boss's babies, but we'd kept the details within our small circle of friends. Now they could read all about it. It felt like light-years ago. It was a simpler time. Hurtful, but less complicated. I never knew where I stood with Kyle back then, but I had Cam back then...

"Mr. Carter gave you implicit instructions not to come down here, Lee," Marcus said in an embarrassed tone. I was glad he felt embarrassed. This was ridiculous. At least he called me Lee today. I was getting tired of this Miss Bennett trick. I wasn't posh. I was simple. I was one of them. I wished they would remember that. "You would be doing me a huge favor if you went back to your room."

"Where is Kyle?" I asked as I shifted around, trying to keep my grizzly baby content. I guessed she didn't like her mommy being interrogated either. Sometimes I felt like I was the one who had committed a crime instead of being the victim of one. "Is he here?"

"Who knows," Marcus grumbled and I didn't miss the 'as usual' he added under his breath. "Linda isn't here either, which leaves me in charge. And no offense, Lee, but I value my job a little more than you value your appetite."

"Leave her alone, Marcus. She needs to come out of that room sooner or later," I heard a male voice say from behind me and I wanted to run back into the elevator and hide. I'd been avoiding him for months. I didn't have anything to say to him and there really wasn't anything I wanted to hear from his mouth either, unless it was an apology to Derek.

"Well, you can explain this to the boss," Marcus grunted as Kyle's half-brother, Mike, came to stand beside me.

"I will," Mike said in a firm tone. Marcus glanced at me in annoyance before storming off.

"How have you been?" Mike asked, turning to face me. I

wished I was quick tongued like Kyle so that I could toss out a sharp retort, but sadly when it came to uncomfortable situations, nine out of ten times, I became a mute. "Lee…"

"Fine," I managed to squeeze out. My face was burning, but I wasn't blushing, I was anxious. I didn't want Kyle to find me talking to him. He would freak out and I'd put him through enough last year. I hadn't seen it at the time, probably due to the pregnancy hormones, but I had been a bitch. I had a lot of time to think when I was lying in that hospital bed. I'd thought through all of our behaviors and I'd come to terms with the fact that I'd pushed Kyle's buttons on purpose. Cam had been right when she said I was being deliberately cruel to Kyle. I had been. I was actually pretty mortified about my behavior and anytime I saw Mike my shame intensified.

Mike had been to almost every doctor appointment when it should have been Kyle. He was such an amazing dad and I felt sick with guilt over the way I'd forced him out. I felt even worse when I thought back to the night when Cam had tried to force me into the bathroom. *"I was there, too, Cam. Every fucking night. I never left,"* Kyle had said. I hadn't thought about it much at the time, but I've thought about it now. I thought about it every time he held his daughter and every time he smiled at me...

"She's getting big," Mike crooned as he shook Hope's tiny hand. Hope gave Mike a wide smile and scrunched her little hands out for him to pick her up. I stepped away quickly and rushed for the restaurant. I needed to teach my daughter not to smile at snakes. It would be a good lesson for her to learn. She needed to know that some of the most dangerous people came in beautiful packaging. "Lee," Mike called out as he stepped around me and blocked the restaurant doorway. His brown eyes were sunken in his face. His blonde curls were limp on his head and I would bank money on the fact that the clothes he wore hadn't been ironed. He looked awful and I had to slap away the worry that was seeping into my heart. He was deceitful. He was the same as his father. I needed to remember that. "I know this is probably bad timing, but do you think I could come with you and talk?" He sighed and shook his head. "Please…I could use a friend right now."

"I have a friend," I said quietly as I held Hope tightly. "His name is Derek Porter, and because of your selfish actions he's living in hell. In hell, Mike. I don't think he'll ever pull himself out of it. So no. I'm sorry, but we can't be friends. I won't risk my relationship with Kyle and my friendship with Derek for you. I made too many bad choices when it came to you in the past. I won't make another."

I forced myself to step around him. The look of hurt on his face was something I refused to feel bad for. Mike was a risk, one I wasn't willing to take.

I swung the door of the restaurant open and came face to chest with the most dangerous person I'd ever come into contact with, wrapped in beautiful packaging. "You need to get your hearing tested, princess." Kyle glared down at me and I could feel the anger emanating off him. It was thick. It was directed at me. "I could have sworn I told you to stay …"

"Back off," I snapped. "I am hungry, I am tired and I am not in the mood for your caveman antics. I'm not breaking your rules, Kyle. You said stay in the hotel. I am. Now, I *am* going to eat here." Meeting his stare with a glare of my own, I mentally patted myself on the back for not whimpering under his hard stare before saying, "If you want to join us, you're more than welcome, but if you want to continue glaring at me like that, then maybe you should go take a time out."

Kyle's eyes moved from my face to behind me. The anger I felt coming from him multiplied in waves. "You need something?" he growled. I craned my neck around to see who it was, even though I already knew whose face I would see. *Oh yeah, I was having a swell day.* Mike stepped closer to us and I groaned loudly. I swear I had enough of today and it wasn't even ten o' clock. I didn't need this crap.

"Just a word with Lee." Mike inclined his head in my direction and Kyle's spine straightened. "It won't take long." Good god almighty, this was uncomfortable.

"Not happening," Kyle hissed as he took Hope out of my arms.

"I already told him no," I told Kyle. If I was about to be thrown to the wolves, I wanted my name cleared first.

"My office. Now." Kyle looked between the both of us when he spoke and for a moment I wasn't sure who he was talking to.

"Me?" I asked in a squeaky tone. I cleared my throat and

straightened my stance. I had nothing to be nervous about. He wasn't my boss anymore.

Kyle glanced down at me and his expression visibly softened. "No princess," he said in a softer tone. "Go eat. Just...just stay inside."

"But what about Hope..." I started to say, but my words fell on deaf ears. I watched in dismay as Kyle stalked off with our daughter in his arms and his brother reluctantly trailing after him. I secretly wondered if I should slip Kyle some of those sleeping pills I'd been prescribed. Maybe they would calm him down a little...

KYLE

"You've got one hell of a nerve to even approach her," I said in a low tone as I sat at my desk and propped Hope on my knee. I hated when she talked to him. I fucking hated it. He'd wanted Lee for as long as I had. I didn't blame him for being attracted to her, I could understand the attraction, but he needed to back the hell off. She was mine. For Christ's sake, even when she was pregnant with *my* baby he had sniffed after her like a dog.

Mike had a problem with crossing lines. He screwed Derek over. He wasn't going to get a chance to do that to me. Never again. "You know why I can't fire you," I told him because it was true. It was in writing. A stipulation of my inheritance. "But don't push me, Mike. I'll break all my rules for her. Upset her again and you're out."

Sighing heavily, Mike moved away from the door and walked over to my desk. As he sat in the chair in front of me, I couldn't help but notice he didn't have the usual air of assholeness around him. His shoulders were slumped. His face was full of some emotion, I couldn't put a name on. He looked...vulnerable. Fuck, now where did that come from?

Mike slumped in the chair in front of me and sighed. "I'm sorry."

He was sorry?

Had I heard that right?

"You should be," I muttered as I tried to summon my anger. It wasn't coming. He wasn't baiting me and I had no fucking clue how to handle this version of my brother. Was this guy the same brother I despised? He didn't look the same. He definitely didn't sound the same. "What the hell is wrong with you?" I blurted out, confused as fuck. "You're never sorry. I've never heard you apologize for anything in your spoiled, entitled life."

"She didn't love me," he whispered. "She played me, Kyle. I need to know why she would do that."

Who? "Rachel?" He should feel glad Rachel didn't love him. She *loved* me and look how she showed it. The both of us had gotten tangled up with a bad fucking woman and as far as I was concerned, Mike had a lucky escape. That girl was bat shit crazy and if Mike was still pining for her after all these years then he was just as crazy as she was.

Goddammit, if Frank had just left everything to Mike or David we wouldn't even be having this discussion. Mike would be all loved up with the crazy one, and my girl wouldn't have holes in half her body or that god awful limp when she walked. Cam would still be alive and Derek would still have his sanity.

I would have met Lee whether I inherited the hotels or not. She was always going to come running to Cam–to Thirteenth Street–and I was always going to be the one to break her fall. I was snared the second I laid eyes on her and if I had been free back then, I wouldn't have made half the mistakes I made with her. It would have been easy for us. Like other people's relationships. Instead, I had to fight every day I woke up just to keep us together. She was mad as hell with me right now and it fucking sucked. It had been a week since the disaster of my try hard intervention and I was still silently simmering with rage.

That asshole, Bromwick, had gotten off lightly with a three month suspension. And Lee, she'd gotten off lightly, too. I knew she wasn't very confident, but Christ, she'd been bleeding. *Bleeding.* She needed to learn to trust her own instincts. Just because some asswipe doctor told her she was wrong, she rolled over like a dog. It fucking made my blood boil. She was smart. I knew she was. She needed to use her brain. Seriously, the girl was hopeless when it came to taking care of her body. Sometimes I wondered if she even cared about herself. She didn't act like it. She didn't fucking tell me anything…

Yesterday, she swanned off when I was working without telling me where she was going. I'd nearly lost my mind with worry when I realized she was gone. I hadn't been able to concentrate until she came back. Yeah, she had only taken Hope out for a walk, but still… Running off to the cemetery was pointless. Cam was dead. She couldn't keep her safe. That was my fucking job and she was making it hard on me. She didn't seem to understand how dangerous it was to be wandering around on her own. She was the sole survivor, and main witness to a murder. She didn't seem to have a clue of the trouble that could be lurking around the damn corner. I didn't want to unnecessarily frighten her, but Jesus Christ, Rachel's letters worried me. *Terrified me…*

We hadn't resolved anything about her mom. I knew I messed that up by cornering her, but Lee wouldn't talk about it and I was afraid to broach the subject. We were just covering up our problems and trudging on, and the worst damn thing was I didn't even know if that was what we were supposed to do or not. This was my first relationship…like a real honest to god have-to-make-this-work-or-die-trying relationship and it wasn't like I had a father who I could turn to for advice. All I had was Derek, and the mood he was in lately meant I couldn't exactly drop my problems on him. And Lee…she had about as much worldly experience as a goldfish and was as fragile as a butterfly – *as flighty as one, too.* I was her first everything. The pressure I felt to keep us both afloat was weighing heavily on me. Jesus, it felt like we were fumbling around in the dark. We were both as clueless as each other…

"Mike," I said with a sigh. "Rachel played everyone. You're not an exception here. Be glad you're not me."

He shook his head and exhaled a shaky breath. "I'm talking about Cam."

Oh sweet Jesus. Pushing back my chair, I stood up and bounced around with Hope in my arms. I had enough problems. I had enough people leaning on me. When the hell had I become everybody's agony aunt? I shook my head and looked down at my daughter. *I hope you never have these problems, angel…If you do, then tell mommy. Daddy needs a break. He's not good with drama…*

"I'm not trying to get in between you and Lee," he continued. "That's not my intention. I know my previous actions make it look that way, but I'm not Kyle. I swear. I just have to know if Cam told her anything about me. I need answers…"

"No," I said firmly, not asking what answers he needed because frankly I didn't have enough room left to worry. I didn't have that kind of relationship with my brother. We didn't have deep conversations. Hell, we didn't have conversations, period.

We'd gotten along well enough as teenagers–hung out whenever he visited Frank's house, but that ship had long sailed. Our grandfather had forced us together in the beginning. Personally, I hadn't given two shits that I had a long lost brother, but Mike had been curious about me. Apparently, he'd been lonely and needed a friend...*Must have been hard growing up in his daddy's million dollar mansion. Must have really sucked to have a maid and a driver. Oh, and private school, a warm bed at night and home cooked meals, it must have been just torture for the poor little guy.*

I'd gone along with the whole 'bond with your brother' idea more out of boredom than anything else. I was only three months older than Mike so we ended up doing a lot of shit together. Guitar lessons, learning to drive and the importance of wrapping it up ...all the crap that our dad couldn't be bothered teaching us, Frank had either taught us or hired someone to show us. I'd almost pissed myself laughing throughout the 'sex talk' with our seventy-two year old grandfather.

"Now boys," Frank had told us when he sat us down for 'the talk' at seventeen. *"Women are gonna stick to both of you like flies. You have money and they love shiny things. You're gonna have to watch out for the one's with that glint in their eyes. You're both gonna have to learn how to weave around the jezebels with your dicks securely in your pants."* The virgin Mike had lapped up every word, nodding enthusiastically. I'd merely smirked my way throughout the whole thing. Frank's sex talk had come about two years too late for me. I was fairly certain I knew more about a woman's body at seventeen than good old Frankie. God, I was a dick back then...I dropped my eyes to look at my daughter. Jesus, I hoped there weren't any baby boys being born that were anything like me.

I'd never be able to let her outside the front door.

"Please Kyle," Mike begged, pulling me out of my daydream. "I need to know why she played me like this..."

I shook my head. Whatever was going on in his head, he needed to keep it away from my fiancée. She didn't need him dragging up the past and cutting open old wounds. "Don't even think about putting any of your problems on her shoulders," I warned him. "She has enough to deal with." *'Like me'* I mentally added.

I waited for his smug grin and snide comment. It didn't come. He merely nodded and fiddled with his thumbs. "You're right," he mumbled in a dejected tone. "And for what it's worth, I am sorry."

"I'm right?" I shook my head in confusion. "You're sorry? Mike, what the hell is going on here? You hate me..."

"I don't hate you, Kyle," he said quietly as he stood up. "I've never hated you. I was jealous of you. But I've grown up. I've woken up."

"What am I supposed to say?" I asked.

"You're a good father, Kyle." Mike shrugged and smiled at Hope. "You should be proud of yourself. God knows, you didn't learn how from our father." He lifted his chin and stared directly at me. I caught a glimpse of pain in his eyes and an unfamiliar feeling settled in the pit of my stomach.

Worry.

I was worried about Mike and it didn't sit well with me.

I stood with my mouth hanging open as Mike turned around and walked out of my office. "What just happened here?" I whispered.

Hope grinned and I had a feeling that my six month old daughter was more clued in than I was. I would have been more prepared for Miss Piggy to walk through the door than I was for this...shit bomb.

LEE

When Kyle came back to the restaurant with Hope, he was in a weird mood. I'd been expecting to be told off for leaving the suite. I had my entire speech rehearsed and ready to throw at him. I hadn't expected the contemplative look he wore on his face, or the question he asked me.

"How was...Cam?" he asked as he sat in the chair opposite mine, with Hope on his lap. "You know, before the...how was she? Was she acting strangely? Say anything out of the ordinary?" He looked at me apologetically–like he thought it hurt me to talk about her. He couldn't be more wrong. I wanted to talk about Cam all of the time. Derek was the one who wanted to erase her from his mind. I needed to keep her fresh. It helped. She needed to be remembered.

"What do you mean?" I asked him as I rested my elbows on the table and leaned closer to him. I watched as he stroked Hope's little fist with his thumb and brushed a kiss to her head. I could tell that he was thinking of how to phrase his next sentence. "Do you mean the night of the shooting?" I offered.

"No," he said quickly. Pushing a butter knife out of Hope's reach, he scratched his clean-shaven jaw. "Mike said something to me...but it's probably nothing. I don't want you worrying about this shit..."

"What?" I prayed Mike hadn't been stirring up trouble. "Kyle, what did he say?"

His eyes locked on mine and I could feel his confusion. "He

said she didn't love him," he whispered. He shrugged his shoulders, clearly uncomfortable. "He thinks she played him. Why would he say that, Lee? It makes no sense."

"Cam?" I asked and Kyle nodded. Mike had told Kyle that Cam didn't love him? That she played him? "I don't know why he would say that," I muttered. I didn't know why she would tell him that either. This was so confusing. Cam had walked away from Derek for Mike. Of course she'd loved Mike. There was no other explanation for her actions. She told me she loved him. They were going on a trip…

"Forget it," Kyle said, breaking through my thoughts. I blinked over at his face. "We don't need to worry about this," he continued. "We have our own troubles."

"Yeah," I whispered, but I wasn't going to forget it. I needed to know. What was going on with Cam before she died? Why was this coming out now? None of this made any sense to me. I couldn't get my head around it…My breath caught in my throat as my mind clicked. "Oh my god," I yelled as I slammed my palm on the table.

My outburst startled Kyle because he jerked back from the table. "What?" he asked, eyes wide and unblinking. "You nearly gave me a goddamn heart-attack." He let out a breath. "Jesus Christ, Lee."

"I need your help," I said with a grin as I pushed my chair back and stood. "It's in the house. Oh my god, I just know it, Kyle. I can feel it in my bones."

"What house?" he asked as he stood up with Hope in his arms. "What the hell are you talking about, baby?"

"Cam's journal," I practically sang. "She *always* kept a journal. If we read it…then maybe we'll know what was going on in her head and find out why she…."

"Whoa," Kyle said in a stern tone of voice. "We are not doing that. No fucking way, princess. It's none of our business…"

"Kyle," I snapped. "Don't you want to know what was going on in her head? Why she did what she did?"

"No." He shook his head and glared at me. "I am perfectly content to never know."

"Please?" I begged. "Please Kyle?"

"No way, Lee," he growled. "No goddamn way."

KYLE

I should have known Lee wouldn't let this drop. My stupid questions were the reason I was parked in the driveway of my house on Thirteenth Street, with my fiancée trembling in the seat next to me and my daughter cooing in the back seat. If I wasn't so worried about her frame of mind right now, I'd be seriously impressed with her progress. This was the closest she'd been to the house since the shooting. "Lee, baby, everything is gone. Her parents took everything." I had a bad feeling about this. It didn't feel right and I usually trusted my gut feeling. It was nearly always right.

I watched with my heart in my mouth as Lee inhaled a shaky breath and turned her face towards me. "Please Kyle," she begged, eyes wide with fear and hope. "There has to be something, some clue that could help? I need to know."

"It's empty," I told her. "Lee, there is nothing there. All that's left is her bed."

Her eyes widened as she jerked towards me and grabbed my arm with her small hand. "Did you flip it?" she said with excitement.

I shook my head and sighed. "Did I flip what?" I was about to flip something alright…I was about to flip out on my stupid fuck of a brother for worrying me, and me in turn for worrying Lee. God, I was so stupid sometimes. She rolled her eyes at me and sighed that way women do when they know something you don't, but think you should. "What?" I asked defensively.

"The mattress," she squealed. "Did you check under her mattress? She always kept a journal. I think she used to keep it in the drawer of her vanity table, but maybe she moved it when they broke up...Oh my god, Kyle." She paused and looked up at the house before turning back to face me. Her gaze met mine and the excitement I saw glittering in her eyes was something I hadn't seen in months. "What if her journal really is in there? We could find out what she was thinking…"

"No," I said in a firm tone. She didn't need to be building her hopes up. That room held nothing that could help anyone. Cam was dead. Her stuff was gone. She'd moved out weeks before she died. There was nothing in there. It was over.

"Kyle," Lee said desperately as she pulled her legs underneath herself and knelt on her seat facing me. "Please. Please just check for me. I am begging you to check under the mattress. Just this once, please?" Lee batted her big, gray eyes at me and I knew I was screwed. Aw shit…

"Fine," I grumbled as I opened the door and climbed out. "But you have to promise me that you won't let this drag you down." I rested my arm on the car door and leaned down so I could see her face. She looked entirely too excited about this and I didn't want to be the one to break her spirits. What good could come from Cam's journal, even if we did find it?

Why did it matter to her?

It meant nothing to me.

Whatever was written inside of it was her own private thoughts. I didn't want to go messing with that. No way. I had a hard enough time cracking the thought process of my living fiancée. My dead friend's mind wasn't a place I ever wanted to visit.

"I'll do it this once, Lee," I said in a firm tone. "But just once. It's not fair to you, me or Derek to drag this shit back up. We need to move on, princess."

"Okay," she agreed quickly, too quickly, which meant she hadn't listened to a word I said.

Closing the door of the car, I had the biggest urge to kick something as I made my way up the steps to the porch. This was a bad idea. A really bad fucking idea. I knocked a couple of times before trying the door handle. It creaked open. Derek hadn't even locked the door.

Jesus.

I made my way down the hallway and paused at her door. I didn't want to do this, I didn't want to go in there. It felt wrong. I felt like I was breaking the law. "Cam, if you can hear me, then you already know that *none* of this was my idea," I muttered into thin air before putting my hand on the door knob. "So, just don't go haunting my ass, okay?"

Twisting the door knob, I slowly opened her door and stood in her doorway for a moment. It was exactly as I knew it would be. Empty, with the exception of her bed, bedside table, dresser and a couple of boxes thrown on top of her bed. The neon pink walls of her bedroom were devoid of the numerous photographs that used to clutter them. Her window sill, which once held more beauty products than a pharmacy, was now empty.

She was gone.

I worked quickly and quietly as I deposited the boxes on her floor before lifting her heavy assed mattress. I'd barely glanced underneath when a voice drilled in my ears, freezing me to the spot.

"What are you doing here?"

Shit.

Turning my head, I came face to face with a very pissed looking Derek. Dropping the mattress back down, I scratched my head and attempted to look confused. It wasn't a hard look considering I was confused as hell right now. "Hey Derek," I said sheepishly. "How's...Kevin?"

"You're selling the house, aren't you?" he demanded as he stood in the doorway with arms at his sides and his hands fisted.

What? "What makes you say that?" I asked as my brain went into overdrive, I strived to find a good enough lie to get my ass out of this mess. He'd crack if he thought there was a journal of Cam's hanging around the place. I didn't want him going frantic on me. Jesus, he was only starting to talk again. This could put him back fifty paces.

"You're in her room," he snarled, stepping forward. "Touching her stuff." He stepped closer until there was less than two feet between us. "Tossing her things around like they're worthless. You can't sell it, Kyle. You promised. You fucking promised me."

"Calm down," I coaxed as I placed my hand on his shoulder. "I'm not selling the h..."

His fist came up before I had a chance to block it and landed on my jaw. I turned my head and spat out the blood that was pooling in my mouth on the floor. "You good?" I snapped. "Or do you need to do it again?"

He hit me again, harder this time. "Hit me back, Kyle," he roared. "Hit me. Fucking hit me."

"No," I said calmly as he slammed my back against the bedroom wall. I kept my hands by my sides. I wasn't going to react. I wasn't going to fight him. If he burst my skull open, I wasn't going to lay a hand on him. Everyone needed a scapegoat at one time or another. He'd been mine on enough occasions. It was my turn to be his.

"Hit me," he roared as his voice broke. I didn't. I just took his beating. "Please…just fucking hit me, Kyle," he begged as he slammed my shoulders against the wall.

"Get it out, buddy," I coaxed. "Get it all out."

Derek dropped his hands from my throat and staggered backwards, shaking violently. "I'm sorry," he whispered in a shocked tone of voice. "I'm so fucking sorry, dude." He sank to the floor and wrapped his arms around his knees.

"Derek," I whispered as I knelt down beside him. "Der, it's okay man."

"I hit you," he hissed as he rocked back and forth, pulling at his hair. "I could've broken your jaw."

"Dude, I have a head like a rock," I joked, in an attempt to console him. "It's gonna take more than a few bitch slaps from you to break me." I was lying. My jaw was killing me and I was pretty sure he'd loosened some teeth.

"He ran away," he whispered.

"Who did?" I asked.

"Kevin." He looked at me with tear-filled eyes. "He left me…" Staggering to his feet, he backed away from me slowly. "You need to stay away from me, too," he whispered. "I'm a fucking trainwreck." With that he turned on his heel and bolted from the room.

"See what you did to him, Cam?" I muttered as I pulled myself to my feet. "You really did a number on him, pretty girl."

"Was it there?" Lee called out as I stalked back to the car.

"No," I growled as I swung the car door open. "Like I said. Everything's gone."

"What happened to your face?" she cried out the minute I sat into the car. Scrambling across the seat, she climbed onto my lap and started stroking my face gently. "Your lip is bleeding…Kyle, what happened to you?" Her fingers froze on my cheek and she blanched. "Oh my god, is your jaw swelling…"

"Relax baby. I'm fine," I coaxed as I pried her hands from my face and held them in between our bodies. "A loose bedspring popped up and cracked me in the face." The image of Derek crumpled on the floor invaded my mind. What the hell was I going to do with him…?

"A loose bedspring?" She furrowed her brow and fixed her incredulous gaze on me. "A bedspring just happened to jump off the bed and attack you?"

"That's what I said happened, so that's what fucking happened," I snapped. Lee flinched and I was filled with self-loathing. "Sorry princess," I whispered as I patted her thigh.

She blinked a few times before exhaling heavily. "Does it hurt?" she asked, as she gingerly cupped my cheek. "Are you sore?"

"I'll be fine," I told her.

I only wished I could say the same for Derek.

NINE

DEREK

MY COPING SKILLS SUCKED.

Whiskey, sleeping pills and grief weren't the best recovery aid for a man in my position.

I didn't know why I was still sitting in the bar of the hotel. Well no, that was a barefaced lie. I knew exactly what I was doing here and exactly who I was looking for. I wasn't going home. Not until I got this fucking notion out of my system. I knew she would be here. All I had to do was wait. It wouldn't take much. She'd offered before. Tonight I would be accepting.

My conscience started to pipe up and I shut that fucker down with the image of Cam naked in his arms.

I spotted the familiar face I had been waiting for and tossed my drink back.

Showtime…

Sliding off the stool I was sitting on, I pushed past a couple of drunks until I was standing behind her. She swung her face around and when her eyes met mine I knew it was a done deal. "Hey sweetheart," I purred as I pressed myself against her. "I've been looking for you."

I probably should have chosen someplace other than Kyle's hotel to do this. If he knew what I was about to do it could destroy our friendship. Then again, he might just clap me on the back. My plan was genius and revenge was a dish best served with a blonde.

LEE

"I got a call earlier," Kyle mumbled as we were lying in bed. He was twisting one of my curls around his finger as I snuggled into his chest. He was also void of clothes and I had a feeling his no-sex rule was about to come to an end…"The house is ready. We can move in the day after tomorrow."

"Already?" I asked excitedly as I stretched up to look at him. "But you only got the keys the other day?" Kyle didn't say anything, but the smug grin on his face was enough of an answer.

Money was power…

I rested my cheek in the crook of his arm and sighed in gratification. "Thank you for taking such good care of us, Kyle." I was really excited about getting out of the hotel and the bustle and noise of the city. It would be really nice to get some fresh air into my lungs again. I'd been inside for so long I was feeling sticky. I was also really excited about raising Hope away from the city. I wanted her to have nature at her back door and space to run and play. The freedom of living in the countryside had been the best part of my childhood.

Growing up in Montgomery, I'd always enjoyed the peace and quiet when I sat in the woods at the back of our house or took a walk down to Benny's bridge to throw rocks in the creek with Cam. I used to love being outside. I hoped she would, too.

The only thing that dampened my excitement was the fact that Derek was still refusing to come with us. Kyle kept telling me he would be okay, but I knew he was saying this so I wouldn't worry. Derek was in a bad place. A blind man could see that. I wished I could do more for him, but stepping foot inside that house was not an option. I couldn't…My mind reverted back to our wild goose chase the other day and I flinched. I'd been so convinced Kyle would find her journal. The tiny spark of hope I had in my heart had deflated when he stormed back to the car, in a horrible mood, with his face all cut up. Kyle was a fast healer, he didn't have a mark left, but I still wasn't sure if I believed the whole bedspring line he'd fed me. It sounded as realistic as a pig flying, but I wasn't going to push him. He just about tore my head off the last time I questioned him…I shouldn't have forced him to go in there. I was such a selfish person. This was hard for Kyle, too. I needed to remember that. Cam was his friend, too…

"Are you happy, Lee?" Kyle asked me quietly and I didn't miss the nervousness in his voice, or the way his fingers trailed over the scars on my back when he whispered, "Am I making you happy?"

"Yes Kyle, you are," I reassured him. "Are you? Do I make you…?"

"Yeah, baby, you make me happy," Kyle murmured as he stretched out underneath me. "Lee," he said in a serious tone. "I know you feel smothered being stuck inside all the time, but it's only until the trial is over and it won't be so bad in the new place. I know you think I'm being a dick, and maybe I am, but I need to keep you safe. There's a lot of bad stuff out there. Things I need you protected from…"

"I don't," I interrupted him as I stroked his chest. "I don't think you're a…well, maybe I do, but I'm starting to understand why you react the way you do, or least I'm trying to."

"Yeah?" he murmured as he trailed his fingers over the dip in my back. Everywhere his fingers touched left a trail of goose bumps on my body.

"Sometimes I forget about how things were for you in our relationship before…" I paused to think of how to phrase my words best. "You're so strong and self-assured and well, I'm…I tend to be a little flighty."

Kyle laughed and it was a deep throaty sound. "Understatement of the century, princess."

"Hey," I admonished gently. "If you're referring to my

behavior when I was pregnant, then I'd like to plead hormonal insanity."

"Is that even a medical condition?" he asked, his voice laced with amusement, as he stroked my back. "Being honest, you scared the shit out of me half the time, princess."

"Listen," I said in a serious tone of voice. "Every morning you get ready for work, all I want to do is barricade the door and keep you with me." I felt guilty for worrying him so badly last week. I wasn't sorry for walking away from the conversation–he needed to drop it–but I didn't think about how he'd feel when he found me gone. I needed to put myself in his shoes more often…"I want to keep you safe, too, Kyle," I admitted.

"I can take care of myself," he said and I could tell that he was smiling as he spoke. "You're the one who seems to need round the clock surveillance."

"I'm not an invalid, Kyle," I snapped. I knew he was referring to my kidneys. "I did call the doctor, you know. I didn’t ignore my health. I was misinformed."

"No, Lee, you're not an invalid," he said in a serious tone. "But you are a target with a very high price tag around your neck. Baby, walking around the place on your own right now, after everything that's been written about our wealth. It makes you as vulnerable as a lamb walking with wolves."

"No one wants…" I began to say, but he interrupted me.

"People want money," he snapped and I could feel the tension seeping into his body. "I have money and I have one very obvious weakness. One guaranteed way of getting my money. What is it?"

Me…"Okay, Kyle, but it's a very small risk."

"One I'm not prepared to take," he said with a sigh. "I'm not taking any more risks. Not when it comes to you..."

"Fine, so how about a compromise?" I asked quietly. "I promise not to run off without telling you and you promise not to push me to meet her?"

"You're gonna use your safety as a bargaining tool against me?" he asked, his voice laced with disgust.

"Try and see it from my point of view, Kyle," I muttered, equally disgusted. "We're both doing things that are hurting each other, so let's just stop doing those things. No more lying to each other…*Both* of us."

"The things I do, I do with your best interests at heart," he countered. "The things you do could potentially…"

"Did you see Derek today?" I asked, changing the subject before we had a full on fight. I was too tired to argue and he was too adamant. Kyle's body tensed and his arm tightened around my back.

"He phoned me this morning ranting and raving, but when I went to the house he wouldn't answer the door," he mumbled in a gruff tone. "He sent me a text earlier, so at least I know he's conscious, but I haven't seen him since Thursday. He's still refusing to come with us."

"Kyle, you know this isn't your fault, right?" I whispered. "Derek's suffering from depression. Unfortunately that's not an illness that has a quick fix. You can't save the world, baby."

"I don't want to save the world," he replied. "I want to save the ones I love who have to endure this world. That's a pretty small list, Lee. One that seems to keep getting smaller no matter what the hell I do."

I flinched at his words. *Cam.* My heart ached. "You couldn't save her, Kyle. You weren't there. There wasn't a thing you could have done…"

"I'm not just talking about Cam, princess," he hissed. Releasing my hair, he rubbed his face with his palm and groaned. "There's our baby. My grandfather. My mom…fuck, I couldn't even save your damn dog. And Derek? He's so screwed up that I don't know what the hell to say to him half the time. And now Mike's all fucked up, too. I shouldn't even care about Mike…I shouldn't give a damn about him."

"But you do," I whispered. I watched Kyle nod his head from under his arm. "You're not superman, Kyle. No one expects you to fix everything." I pulled myself onto my knees and looked down at him. He was thrown on his back with his arm tossed over his face. Covering his eyes with his arm was something I had discovered Kyle did when he was upset.

"Don't hide from me," I whispered, as I moved his arm away from his face. He looked up at me with the most lonesome expression and my heart broke. It was a rare thing to see his vulnerability. He hid it well.

"I'm just tired, Lee," he admitted. "Some days I feel like I'm slamming my head against a brick wall. No matter what I do, everything keeps going to shit, baby. It makes me sick to my stomach to know that my daughter is going to grow up in a world like this. With all of this…suffering."

"Kyle," I said quietly. "Sometimes, no matter how much you try and plan and pray, things just go to hell. Life is full of heartbreak and the world is cruel, but it's still a beautiful place to be." I stroked his chest, right over his heart. "It's beautiful because we have the ability to love. We love harder than death. We love fiercer than we hate. A human heart has more power than any nuclear weapon. It is impenetrable, even when it stops beating. You can break it, tear it to pieces, put a hole in it, but you can't erase the feelings, and those feelings are contagious. The contents can never be wiped clean. They spread in our thoughts, words, actions and our memories. So don't lose hope, baby." I stretched forward and pressed my lips to his. "Because yours is the biggest heart I've ever felt." I rubbed my nose against his cheek. "We'll figure this out together, okay. You're not on your own in this. I'm by your side. I'm on your side."

"Where the hell did you come from, Lee Bennett?" Kyle shook his head as he pulled me onto his lap. "Seriously, how the hell did you turn out so pure?"

"I'm not pure, Kyle," I giggled. "You saw to that, remember?"

"Baby, you're like snow to me," he purred. Sitting up he tugged on my hips and pulled me forward until our chests were touching. "I love that you were a virgin. It's sexy as hell knowing the only thing that's been inside you is me."

"You're always holding me up, Kyle," I said in a serious tone, wrapping my arms around his neck. "Let me hold you up, too. You don't always have to be the strong one. You don't have to carry all the weight. Let me help you."

He stared into my eyes with such intensity that I could feel the atmosphere in the room changing. "Jesus, you pull on my goddamn heart like a guitar string," he said with a shudder. "When we first met, I knew you would be my downfall," he said in a hoarse tone, as he cupped my neck and pressed his forehead to mine. "I'm glad I was right," he whispered before sealing my mouth to his.

"I love you," I said against his mouth as he rolled me onto my back. My legs fell open of their own accord and Kyle slipped between them, his body in sync with mine. My whole body trembled from the feel of him on me. The size of him, the sheer strength of him...I never felt safer than I did when I was in his arms. He was my addiction. My utter absolution. I wanted to climb inside of him. There wasn't a physical interaction powerful enough to portray how I felt for him. He coaxed my mouth open and slid his tongue inside at the same time he pushed inside me.

"I love you, too," he breathed.

KYLE

"Do you believe in god, Kyle?"

Derek's question caught me unaware. We were sitting in the living room of my old house. Well, I was sitting. Derek was sprawled out on a mattress on the floor with an empty case of beer–and a woman's bra–at his feet. It was beyond me as to why he was camped out here when there were four perfectly good bedrooms in the place, but the guy was acting so strange lately I didn't ask. *I was afraid of the answer.* I'd dragged myself out of bed at three in the morning and rushed straight here when I read the text message he'd sent me.

Cupid's gonna kick my ass, dude.

I was as confused about the meaning of that text, as I was about the question he'd just tossed at me. At least he was docile tonight. I never knew what version of Derek I was going to get when I came here. His mood swings were impressive to say the least.

Derek's suffering from depression, Kyle….

Lee told me she thought Derek had depression and, to be honest, the word alone scared the hell out of me. She said there wasn't an overnight cure for what he was going through and even contemplating agreeing with that statement went against my natural disposition. I couldn't just sit back and do nothing. No way. There was no way in hell I was going to leave him here alone with his demons…

"I don't know," I told him while I thought about his question. I wasn't an overly religious person. I'd lived with families from various religious backgrounds over the years and nothing had appealed to me. My grandfather's religion was money. Hell, money had been his god and he'd been damn good at making it. Worst grandparent ever for keeping tabs on a kid, but Frank Henderson had the golden touch when it came to doubling profit. "I believe there's something out there," I told him. "We'll all know someday I guess."

"I do," he replied as he sat up and reached for his beer. "I went to mass every Sunday when I lived at home."

"Uh…good for you, man." What the hell was I supposed to say to that?

"You mind?" he asked as he waved a box of cigarettes in the air before taking a sip of his beer. I shook my head and watched guiltily as he lit up a cigarette. I hadn't realized he'd started smoking again. Derek smoking was something else that I was responsible for...

I was fresh out of high school and flat broke when I first met Derek Porter. I'd moved out of Frank's swanky pad in Denver the day after my high school graduation and into University Hill in Boulder. To be fair, it had been my choice to move out. Frank had gone along with it knowing that place had never been my home.

Frank Henderson had taken me out of the system before my thirteenth birthday. He'd provided me with a roof over my head and a college education, but I never forgot. I never let myself forget where I came from and who shared the blood that ran in his veins. The five and half years I'd lived with him had been a stopping gate for me and we'd both known it. I was never going to be Frank's golden grandson–he had Mike for that–and he was never going to hang my fucking moon. We'd both known he'd taken me in over guilt and I'd stayed out of desperation.

I'd worked my ass off the summer before starting college, but the rent on Thirteenth Street had crippled me, so after about a month of living on toast, I'd placed an ad for a roommate online. At the time, I hadn't known the place was mine and the rent I was paying was going into a bank account my grandfather had set up for me. If I had known, I would have packed my bags and left. I'd appreciated his help, but I never planned to fall at his feet for it, or take handouts. My future had been the one thing that I had control over. The one thing I'd clung to when I was a kid. I'd never intended to follow him into the *family* business. I hadn't wanted that life. *I still didn't want that life.* Before Frank died, and I inherited his fortune, I had plans and goals of my own…

The day Derek moved in with me I remembered thinking *this is a mistake* as I watched him saunter through my front door, six weeks before our first semester at C.U, his baseball cap was turned backwards on his head and his football shirt was stretching over his muscles.

I'd answered the door with a cigarette hanging out of my mouth, a towel wrapped around my hips and a hangover from hell. I remembered feeling amused as hell when I watched his mommy kiss him on the cheek and then cry all over my kitchen table as she came to terms with the reality that her precious baby boy was moving in with *Mick Jagger*–her words not mine.

I hadn't made the best impression on Mrs. Porter that day. The first black mark against me was when I handed her–*lord forbid*–underage son a beer from the fridge. The second was when she met my houseguest from the night before when she sauntered into the kitchen in nothing but a G-string. I'd almost choked on my beer when Derek muttered, *"Dude, I think I love you already,"* and Mrs. Porter pulled out her rosary beads and started blessing herself.

I was wary of Derek in the beginning, but then again I'd never been into the whole trusting people deal. I was used to being let down, but Derek was different. For starters, the guy never shut the fuck up, and second, he never let me down. He used to yap on and on and he was so full of life and positivity that I got infected with it. His word was his word and he stood by–and up for–whatever he believed in. *And apparently he'd believed in me….* Everyone loved the guy, my grandfather included. Frank gave him a job working with me in the bar at the hotel over the summer. We'd gotten along okay, but what had really bonded us was when Derek discovered he hated my father as much as I did.

The day Derek punched my dad in the nose, in the middle of the bar, after being caught hitting on my stepmom was the day that sealed our friendship for life. I'd been so impressed. David had thrown some smart comments and Derek had flipped out and punched him. Then Mike had punched Derek for hitting his *daddy* and I had punched Mike for hitting my…Derek.

We were both fired and thrown out of the hotel and I'd coaxed

Derek to the dark side with booze, house parties and girls. I gave him his first cigarette that night. I also filled him up with a wagon load of Jacky D before setting him up for the most memorable night of his life with the Sullivan twins from down the street. At the time I'd thought it was hilarious to hear the jock hack up a lung and watch him morph from a focused athlete into a horned up teenager who had just figured out he was in a parental free zone.

We ended up spending the rest of the summer getting drunk and getting laid until we realized we couldn't take care of ourselves or the bills…Cam moved in a month later and whipped both our asses into shape.

I lost my wingman the second she walked through our front door with those horrible pink suitcases. I swear I'd never seen so much pink in my life until Camryn Frey walked into our lives. She snared Derek that very first day with a flick of her blonde hair and had enforced a no-smoking-in-the-house rule within a week of moving in. I'd protested but it was pointless and ended up quitting a few months later. The queen had taken residence and had confiscated our balls in the process. Within a month she had the house under order. I'd learned more shit about pores and female beauty products, too much for it to be ever deemed acceptable for a man to know about.

It might have been my name over the door, but Cam had always been in charge and I'd indulged her bossy nature. I'd also banished myself to the upstairs of the house because there were only so many times a man could walk into a bathroom and have to stare at the scraps of lingerie drying in the bathtub. It wouldn't have been so bad, but she was like a baby sister to me. I didn't want to even think of that shit on her body. It was…wrong.

Cam cared about us and had mothered us to the point where one night she sat me down to talk about my *habit.* I laughed into her face the night she handed me a pamphlet for a treatment center in Denver. Yeah, I might have been a screw up and a slut when I was younger, but I had never put so much as a joint past my lips. I was only three when my mom died, but I remembered exactly what that stuff did to her when it was cocktailed with cocaine and heroin. Even growing up the way I did, and seeing what I had, I knew I wasn't going *there.* I was never going to walk *that* line...

"Do you think I'll be forgiven for the things I've done…for the things I'm thinking of doing?" Derek asked, stirring me from my reverie.

"What have you been thinking, Derek?" I choked out.

"Just about past mistakes I've made."

"We've all made mistakes dude," I told him as I slipped my phone out of my pocket to check the time. "I've fucked up way more than you," I said as I typed out a quick message to Lee, to let her know where I was in case she woke up again. She'd already woken up with a nightmare and usually slept through once I got her back to sleep. "So don't worry about any of the shit you've done," I said with a smirk. "I bet I've trumped you."

"But you always redeem yourself, Kyle." Derek smirked but his eyes were lifeless. He took another slug of his beer before speaking. "There's no coming back for me."

"What have you done that you can't fix?" I asked nervously. This was a conversation I wasn't entirely comfortable with. In fact, I was about two seconds away from phoning his parents or his brother and having him signed in for treatment. I wasn't losing him as well. No fucking way.

"There's this guy from back home," he said as he took a drag of his cigarette. "I have a lot of history with him. We were…close in high school. He's here in Boulder. Showed up at the house today."

"Yeah…" I tried to coax.

Was he about to tell me he was gay?

Because I have to be honest, right about now that would be a huge fucking relief.

"Does that make you…happy?" I asked. *Shit, I was not good at this.*

"I guess I'm happy to see him," Derek replied. "I've got a lot of love for him and his family, but what I did isn't something I want broadcasted, you know? I took off afterwards and haven't seen him in over four years."

Be tactful Carter.

Be fucking tactful.

Ah, screw it.

"So you had sex with a dude," I blurted out, losing all tact in my bid to comfort him. "Big deal. You've nothing to be ashamed of. Love is love, bro, it doesn't matter if it comes in the form of a pussy or a penis."

"What the fuck?" Derek shouted in a shocked tone as he jumped off the mattress. "I'm not gay, Kyle."

"There's nothing to be embarrassed about, Der," I coaxed. Standing up, I walked over to him. "So you're bi-sexual." I shook my head. "It's not a big deal. Don't be ashamed about how you feel," I told him as I clasped his shoulders. "Embrace it and screw any narrow minded asshole who tells you otherwise. You have my full support."

"I fucked his sister, dude," Derek snapped as he jumped away from me. "Jesus."

His sister?

"Oops," I laughed. "Oh man, I totally thought you were coming out on me."

"Yeah," Derek grumbled. "I guessed that."

"I'd be cool with it if you were..."

"I'm not," he said before sighing. "But thanks for the love. Appreciate it."

"So, who owns the lace?" I pointed at the red bra next to the mattress. "Or do I want to know?"

"You really don't." Derek sighed heavily before adding, "Kyle, about the other day...I'm sorry for hitting you. I was having a..."

"Forget it," I said in a stern tone. "I have." He didn't need to bring that shit up. My face was fine. Not even a bruise. Guess I really did have a head like a rock..."So, have you thought any more about moving in with us?" I asked in a coaxing tone. "We're moving in a couple of days."

Derek didn't answer me.

Instead, he turned around and walked out of the room.

Lovely.

TEN

DEREK

I SAW things in my dreams sometimes. Her hair floating over my chest. The scent of her shampoo poisoned my senses. Her blue eyes bored into my soul.

It seemed that even in death she was intent on haunting me. On tormenting me.

I kept finding myself at her grave. I couldn't keep away. Every memory, every touch, every breath she'd taken in my presence was replaying inside my head.

Would I ever get over it? I didn't think so. Six months later and I was still as devastated as I was the day I read that text.

* It's over. I don't love you anymore, Derek. I'm sorry. C x.*

If she'd been unhappy for a while I could understand, but we were solid. Kyle and Lee were the ones with the screwed up relationship, not me and Cam. We'd been fucking strong. Closer than ever after Lee's miscarriage.

Finding Lee hemorrhaging on the bathroom floor had messed Cam's head up. Mine, too. She'd been extra clingy in the days after Lee's surgery. She'd talked a lot of babies and how what Lee had gone through scared the life out of her. I couldn't have agreed more with her. It terrified me, too. All I could think about when I was holding Lee in my arms on that bathroom floor was what if this was Cam? How would I feel if the love of my life was losing our child? It shook me up and I felt Kyle's pain. I'd put myself in his shoes and it was somewhere I never wanted to be again. Not even hypothetically.

I remembered the morning everything changed. I remembered the exact moment I'd lost Camryn Frey and it wasn't that day in April when I'd received that text. She'd been all fucked up since that morning back in January when she ran out of my room crying. To this day I still didn't know why. We'd woken up as normal and had some amazing morning sex before I slipped across the hall to take a shower. Cam always used to join me. That morning she didn't. I hadn't thought much of it at the time, but when I'd walked into my room ten minutes later she'd thrown my phone at my head and ran out crying. That day was the beginning of the end for us. She didn't come home for three days and when she did she had closed herself off from me. Three months later I lost her. Two months after that I buried her.

It wasn't right. I'd known it then and I knew it now. Something must have happened to her. I'd gone over and over it in my brain. What had I done? What the hell had I done to make her stop loving me? I'd checked every call and text in my phone even though I knew I had nothing to hide. There were no other girls. I'd been faithful to that girl from our very first day to our very last. There had been no secrets between us…

Dammit, I should have done more. Fought harder for her. I could have kept her safe. She sure as hell wouldn't have been in that house if she had been with me. I looked down at the plane tickets in my hand before tucking them into my back pocket.

Ireland.

Cam had always wanted to go. I'd worked in a shitty kitchen, for twelve hour days, all summer to pay for us to go. It was supposed to be her graduation gift. I had it all arranged. We were supposed to fly out the morning after graduation, but she'd left me before I had a chance to tell her. Walked the fuck away from me for Kyle's asshole brother.

At the time I'd been too proud to fight for her. Too heartbroken and angry to say another word to her. I hadn't told her what she meant to me. She didn't know the plans I'd made for us. She'd never know about the engagement ring I planned to give her after we kissed the Blarney Stone in Cork. Or the cruise I'd booked for us to take on the river Shannon. That ring and those dreams were in the same place as her now. Dead and under the ground.

The day she was buried, when Kyle had chased after Ted and Mora, I'd gone back to her grave with Hope and tossed the ring into the ground with Cam's casket before they covered it over. It had been for her. It would never be for anyone else. I would never be anyone else's. Jesus Christ, the regret was killing me. I felt like I was choking on bitterness. Most days I could barely breathe.

Just the other day I found her hairbrush under my bed. Yeah, that's about all I can remember from that day. I'd seen her golden hair on the bristles and I'd lost my shit. I had ended up at a bar and had tried my very best to drink myself into oblivion. It didn't help. I'd woken up still tormented and with another girl in my bed.

I hated myself. I wasn't me anymore. I'd never been a big drinker, not really, and I wasn't a whore. But lately it was all that helped.

And believe me it helped.

Maybe Kyle was right. Maybe I did need to leave Thirteenth Street. But I knew what he'd do the minute I left. He'd sell the house and I couldn't let that happen. I wasn't ready to let her go. There was also a very high chance that he'd torch the place. Therefore, I considered it my civic duty to remain there until I was ready to let go and until my best friend got over his new favored notion of arson. He said he'd do it on enough occasions and he was an impulsive guy… I didn't want him to come near me, but I didn't want him to give up on me either. I knew that didn't make any sense, but I wasn't making sense. Nothing fucking clicked in my brain anymore. I wasn't sure if there was a way out of this darkness, but if there was, then Kyle would find it. He was good at fixing things. He'd get me out of this…

The sound of footsteps approaching stirred me from my daydream. I swung around and was faced with my worst fucking nightmare. "Derek," Mike said, nodding his head in my direction as he moved to stand beside me at Cam's graveside. I watched as he placed a bunch of flowers on her grave next to mine. Roses. What an idiot. Cam's favorites were lilies.

Showed what he knew...

"Have you been here long?" he asked as he straightened his spine and wrapped his coat around himself. Clenching my jaw, I shoved my hands into my jean pockets. He'd some fucking nerve. I'd give him that. "Derek?" he repeated.

"Don't talk to me," I ground out as I concentrated really hard on not tackling the creep. "Don't ever speak to me, you got it?"

"I didn't mean any harm," Mike muttered, stepping away slightly. Wise move. "But you're soaking wet and shaking, man," he added.

I looked down at myself and realized he was right. I was drenched. When did it start to rain? I hadn't noticed. I also hadn't worn a coat. All I was wearing was a black t-shirt and jeans. In October.

"I don't remember," I mumbled more to myself than to him. Come to think of it, I couldn't remember how I came here. Fuck, I was confused.

"Do you want a ride home?" he asked as he placed a hand on my shoulder. That was the wrong fucking thing to do.

"Don't touch me," I growled as I swung around and caught him by the back of the neck. Kicking him in the back of his knees, I pushed him to the ground and forced his face into the earth.

"You fucking did this," I roared as I forced his face into the wet mud. "You took her from me and you couldn't keep her safe." Pushing him forward, I released his head and backed away from her grave. "I hope your conscience chokes you."

I kept walking until the graveyard was out of sight and my heartbeat returned to its normal rhythm. The rain hammered down on me but I trudged on. I walked for hours through the rain. I didn't have a clue where I was or where I was going. I didn't care and it didn't help. I couldn't walk away from my memories. I couldn't shake her off. Not one single building looked familiar to me, so I guessed I was lost. Good. I wanted to lose myself.

I hated him.

I fucking hated him.

How could Mike walk up to me and talk like nothing had happened, like we were friends? It was his fault.

He'd ripped my heart out of my chest.

He'd taken my whole world away from me and then he let her die...

LEE

"Are you sure this is what you want?" I asked Kyle, as we pulled up in front of the huge wrought iron gated entrance. My fingertips hovered over my name on the paperwork on my lap that I'd–rather reluctantly–signed this morning. A home. A fresh start for the three of us…

"This is a big decision, Kyle," I told him. "It's your money and it's not like I'm bringing anything to the table. I want you to be sure about this."

"Am I sure?" he scoffed as he keyed the password into the small handset on the wall. "Of course I'm fucking sure." I could tell he was excited because he was more restless than usual. His knee was bobbing at a furious pace as he tapped his fingers against it while we waited for the gates to open. "I have no doubts when it comes to you, Lee."

"Okay," I whispered in relief. It felt good to hear him say that. "I just don't want you to feel like you have to put my name on the house just because we're engaged."

I just didn't want Kyle to feel like he had to give me half of his house–or feel like I wanted his money. I also didn't want to kill his buzz by telling him that I'd live in a tent just as long as it was with him. I'd follow him anywhere…except back to Thirteenth Street.

I didn't know what kind of strings he'd pulled to get the keys so quickly, nor did I want to know. Sometimes the less I knew about Kyle the better. He'd been up since the crack of dawn and had been on the phone for half of the day arranging for our things to be moved from the hotel and ordering furniture. We had left everything at the house on Thirteenth Street and when Kyle had asked me if I wanted him to get any of my possessions from my room I'd told him no and fought the urge to vomit.

This was our fresh start and I didn't want it tainted with death, miscarriage and heartbreak. I needed to let go and stop trying to dig into the past. Kyle was right. Cam's journal–even if it had been there–was private. I would have never even contemplated breaking her trust and reading it when she was alive....so what gave me the right to do so now? Nothing. I had no right to violate her privacy...I was going to let it go. I had to. We all needed to start anew.

The gates opened inwards, revealing a narrow wooded driveway. My breath caught in my throat as I took in our surroundings. Everything was ...green and orange. Huge evergreen fir trees were lined like soldiers on either side of the lane, orange leaves that had fallen from the deciduous trees covered the lane ahead of us, as the car ascended the hilly drive. The car crunched to a stop on the gravel in front of the property and my heart stopped in my chest. The house–if you could even call a property of that enormity a house–was breathtaking. It was wooden, warm and welcoming, with huge glass windows gleaming in the watery October sunshine. There was a balcony, a deck and... everything. This house had *everything*.

Kyle turned in his seat. His blue eyes locked on mine with such an intensity I squirmed in the passenger seat. "Our house. This is *ours*. And believe me, princess," he purred. "You've brought more to my table than you think." Unfastening his seatbelt, he leaned towards me and cupped my cheek. "And here's a little heads up." His mouth grazed my ear before moving to within an inch of my lips. "I plan on tasting what you've brought to my table." His lips touched mine. "In every room of this house."

"Kyle," I whispered against his lips as I pulled him towards me.

"Patience, baby," Kyle chuckled before pulling away and climbing out of the car. "All good things come to those who wait."

Opening my door, he helped me out before getting Hope

from the back seat where she was sleeping soundly. She stirred slightly before snuggling into her father's chest. I didn't know why but I always found it incredibly sexy to see a man take care of his children. The loving way Kyle held Hope, the gentle way he stroked the back of her tiny head. It made my insides clench up.

Kyle unlocked the front door and I felt like a kid being shown around Disney World. I wriggled in excitement with each step I took further into the house. "Go on, princess. Go investigate."

The smell of fresh paint hung in the air as I wandered through the house. There were six rooms on the main level and every room had warm wooden flooring with the exception of the tiled kitchen and bathroom. It reminded me of a cabin. The biggest, most luxurious cabin I'd ever stepped foot inside. The floor to ceiling windows...the view of the mountains. Wow. Just...wow.

The kitchen was enormous and completely fitted with dozens of cupboards, a center island with stools and a separate area with a dining table and chairs. It had every appliance a person could possibly wish for and the light coming from the huge bay windows was incredible. The lounge was even bigger with a real open fireplace. A downstairs bathroom and separate laundry room were situated in the hallway closest to the kitchen and there was an office equipped with more technology than I'd ever seen, in the last room in the hallway.

There was a fully furnished nursery, painted in a soft pink, with about a hundred stuffed animals lined on shelves. "She has a bedroom upstairs, too," Kyle said from behind me as I stood in the doorway of the nursery. "I thought it might be easier for you during the daytime...until you're better." His thoughtfulness caused my heart to swell. He knew me too well. Stairs crippled me. Since the shooting, my muscles were like noodles. I had a lot of work ahead of me to build back some muscle strength, especially in my stomach and back. Lying in a bed for twelve weeks had caused havoc on my body. I was improving every day, but I was nowhere near my old form. The fact that I was shot eight weeks after giving birth, when my body was still healing, made my recovery ten times more complicated. Adding my ectopic pregnancy and surgery last Christmas to the list made the fact that I was breathing, walking and talking a pretty huge miracle.

God works in mysterious ways...

I turned around and smiled at his eager face. "I still can't believe you bought this place. How many levels are there?" I asked as my eyes roamed over everything. I'd expected the house to be empty and unfurnished. I'd obviously underestimated my fiancé. Every wall was painted. Every room was filled with furniture. It was a home waiting for us to live in.

"Four," he said proudly. My jaw dropped open which made him laugh. "There's an apartment in the basement for Derek." Kyle grinned and closed my mouth with his finger. "It's so fucking cool Lee," he grinned. "If he doesn't decide to move in, I'm calling dibs."

"You need a man cave, do you?" I joked, but it was a weak attempt. My heart sank when I thought of Derek alone in that house with his ghosts. I'd hoped he would change his mind. I still hoped he would. Kyle and I both knew why he refused to move out of that place. He wanted to be close to Cam.

So did I, but I preferred to do that at the cemetery, where I could pretend the things that had happened to her hadn't. There was no way I could sit and drink coffee every morning in the kitchen where I watched life seep from her body.

If Kyle had his way he would drag Derek out of there and lock him in the basement, and for once he had my full support. Derek needed to get out of that place. That house was toxic and his home was with us.

"Let's have a look upstairs," Kyle said, tactfully changing the subject. This was a bittersweet moment and I knew he felt it, too. Our lives changed so drastically in the past eighteen months. What had started as four of us living together in Kyle's house on Thirteenth Street, had grown to five with the arrival of our daughter. Now for the first time in our relationship we were on our own, having buried one friend and living in a constant fear of losing the other to his grief.

Tucking Hope into the crook of one of his arms, Kyle wrapped the other around my shoulder and led me towards the staircase. "The bedrooms are on the first floor and there's a converted attic on the top floor with a couple more rooms. I've left those empty. I figured we could use them for storage until we decide what to do with them."

The staircase had about thirty steps and when I reached the

top I was out of breath. I was breathless because I was faced with more doors than I could think up rooms for.

"There are five bedrooms up here," Kyle said as we walked down the hall. "All fitted with their own bathroom, though I'm not sure how that will work for us when Hope starts walking. Toddlers like toilet water…"

Five bedrooms... I was going to have my work cut out for me. I would never complain of boredom again.

"This is my favorite room in the house," he murmured as he opened the last door on the right. When I looked inside I was in complete agreement with him. "Master bedroom…" he announced in a husky tone, letting his words trail off and curl around me, igniting my imagination, lighting a fire in my belly. "Do you like it?"

"Do I like it?" I whispered, shaking my head. There wasn't anything *not* to like. The walls of our new bedroom were painted a soft green. The walnut timber-framed sleigh bed was the size of a boat–and I wasn't joking. You could easily fit five fully grown men on it with their arms spread out and still have plenty of room. The wall opposite the door was made entirely of glass with a door opening onto a balcony. The closets, bedside tables, the dressing table…every piece of furniture in the room was made of thick walnut with an intricately carved finish.

"I tried to imagine what you'd like…You can change anything you don't like, princess. Colors or furniture…"

I held my hand up to make him stop talking. "Kyle, stop talking. It's perfect." Kicking off my sneakers, I threaded my toes through the thick white luxurious carpet. "Oh god. I think I'm in love." The whole house was beautiful. So homely. I shook my head and turned to face him. "How did you do this? I mean…thank you so much, but how in god's name did you organize everything so quickly?"

He snorted as he rocked Hope in his arms. "When you want something badly enough you move heaven and hell to get it." He shrugged his shoulders. "I want you happy. I need you safe. There's not much I wouldn't do when it comes to you."

"You make me happy," I whispered, grinning from ear to ear. Stretching up on my tip-toes, I planted a kiss on his lips. "You make me feel safe. Every day."

Kyle smiled fondly. His eyes gleamed with mischief as his lips tipped up in a smirk, revealing that edible dimple. "You make me hard. Every day."

I gasped when I noticed the built-in bookshelf in the corner of the room. I darted over to it with my mouth hanging open. "Oh my god," I breathed as I stood in front of shelf after shelf full of books. "I'm definitely in love."

Kyle chuckled from behind me. "I thought you'd like that little addition best."

"You were so right," I murmured as I trailed my finger down the spine of one of the *many* books.

"You should have seen the look on the old lady's face in the store," he mused as he pulled out a book and showed me the cover of a half-naked man. "I looked like a fucking douchebag walking up to the counter and asking for girly porn with a pink stroller and a polka dot bag on my shoulder."

I covered my mouth to stifle a laugh as I looked up at his bemused expression. "You didn't."

Kyle raised his brow and smirked. "How the fuck was I supposed to know they're called *contemporary romance…*"

My cheeks reddened and I felt oddly defensive. "Because that's what they're called, Kyle…"

"Sure they are," he snorted as he rocked Hope gently in his arms. "Keep lying to yourself, princess, but I know the truth. It's porn." He grinned and winked down at me. "Plain ole girl porn. I just can't understand why you girls don't put pictures on the pages…" His voice trailed off as he frowned in what looked like confusion. "Just seems like a hell of a lot of work to have an org…"

"It's not porn, Kyle," I snapped, annoyed and a little turned on. "It's literature."

"Oh yeah," he snickered in a mimicking tone. "He seared me with his manly touch…" Kyle pressed the back of his hand to his forehead as he made the worst attempt at imitating a woman I'd ever heard. "Oh dear, my nipples hardened from the sight of his huge cock. His rippling abs caused my womanhood to flutter and clench…" he snorted *again*. "Literature. Good one, baby."

"That's rich coming from the man who cried like a baby when we watched *The Notebook*." His smirk faded and my smile widened. "I have to say, I was more than surprised with how in touch you are with your sensitive side, Kyle."

"Thought you were asleep," he muttered.

"That's pretty pathetic, *baby,*" I teased. "I thought you were going to need some valium when the old lady died."

"You're heartless," he said deadpan. "That was a great fucking movie."

"And these are great books," I countered. "So, if you plan to make fun of me in the future, just remember that I'll have something up my sleeve."

"Something up your sleeve," he said in a sarcastic tone of voice. "Could it be the vibrator to go with your book boyfriend? I know paper is made from trees baby, but I'm pretty sure you'd prefer my wood."

"You are a douchebag," I mumbled red-faced. "I can't believe you actually said that out loud."

"Are we having our first fight in our new home?" he asked with a smile. "Over porn of all things."

"Yeah," I laughed. "I guess we are." Shrugging my shoulders, I nudged him softly as I walked past in the direction of the bathroom. "Start as we mean to go on and all that..."

We headed downstairs to test Hope out in her new nursery. "I'll put her down," Kyle said quietly as he slipped past me. I nodded happily as I wandered back to the lounge. The cream leather U-shaped couch was beautiful as were the matching armchairs that sat either side of the fireplace. A lone silver photo frame on top of the ledge of the fireplace caught my attention and I had to cover my mouth with my hand to hold in a sob when I realized why.

"That girl is something else," Kyle chuckled as he strolled into the lounge not a minute later. "Nothing fazes her. She didn't even stir when I put her in the crib."

I couldn't answer him. I was in shock. "Where did you find this?" I whispered as I stared in disbelief at the photograph of the two little girls. One of the girl's was blonde and beautiful. Dressed immaculately in a white sundress, she had her arm wrapped around the other girl's shoulders and was smiling broadly for the camera. The other girl was younger and smaller with dark messy curls and nervous eyes. She was dressed in a worn pair of jeans that swamped her little frame and a dirty gray t-shirt. The smaller girl was tucked under the blonde girl's arm and my heart broke in two as the memory of that day flooded me.

"It was in her room," I heard Kyle say from behind me. "Stuck to her vanity mirror. Ted gave it to me when he was packing up her things. She left a lot of stuff in her room when she moved in with Mike." I watched as Kyle picked up the frame and gazed down at it. "Lee, if it's too much I can put it away..."

"No," I whispered as I took the frame from his hands and returned it to the ledge. "She needs to be remembered. We should never forget why we're here together."

"Come here," he said in a gruff tone as he cupped my neck and pulled my face to his chest. "No one's gonna forget her, baby." I felt his lips brush my hair. "Heroes are never forgotten."

KYLE

There were no words to express how relieved I was to finally have Lee moved out of the city and into this place. Maybe my heart would stop trying to jump into my throat now that I knew she was protected and miles away from trouble. She was safe now. They both were…But I should have known that photo would fuck with her head. We'd been having a good day–enjoying our first day in our new home–until she looked at the photo over the fireplace and the light in her eyes faded. I hadn't gotten one word out of her during dinner and I was worried. She'd cooked in silence while I fed Hope and settled her down for the night...

"Do you wanna check out the hot tub?" I asked her, more out of desperation than anything. "There's an enclosed glass porch out back, so it's warm…heated floors?" Lee handled her grief with gracious dignity, but she was hurting deeply and I felt useless. Her mood had plummeted and nothing I seemed to say was pulling her back up. She had this horrible habit of retracting into that shell of hers and I knew she was slipping into the past. I needed to pull her out of there and fast. Our past didn't exactly paint me as a gentleman… "Or we could watch a movie?"

"I think I'm going to go lie down if that's okay," she mumbled. She just sat staring at me for ages until I realized why. She was waiting for permission. Fuck. I nodded my head and clenched my jaw as I forced a small smile. Pushing back her chair, it scraped over the kitchen tiles as she slowly stood up. "Do you mind if I clean this up in the morning?" she asked, pointing to the dinner plates.

"No, I don't mind," I said in an emphatic tone. "You don't need my permission if you don't want to wash dishes baby. This is your house." I fucking hated when she became docile and pliant. It didn't happen often anymore, but when it did, it hurt. It made me wonder if a small part of her still lived in that house in Montgomery.

Jimmy Bennett left his mark on her…

Besides, she didn't have to ask my permission to do anything in this place. This really was her house. I had the property contracted solely to Lee. She thought it was in both of our names and I let her think that. She'd freak out otherwise and I needed to know that she had some security to fall back on. This was my reasoning when I deposited one hundred thousand dollars into her personal account this morning–the one I'd made her open after Hope was born. I needed her taken care of.

No matter what.

Cam's death had fucked my head up, too. Lee dealt with it by hiding her pain with a smile. Derek, by shouting and getting angry and I dealt with it by making a plan. That was my thing. Cam's death had made me see how fickle life could be. I needed to know Lee would be taken care of if anything was to happen to me. Call it being morbid, but I hated the thought of her being dragged through the courts by my father if I was to die before I got her up that aisle. We weren't married yet and I knew he would. Hope had security, she was my flesh and blood, but Lee…God, she wasn't strong enough to fight him.

According to my father, David Henderson, my inheritance was undeserving. That fucker would do just about anything to get his hands on the hotel chain his father–my grandfather–had left me. I couldn't underestimate him. He was a shrewd opponent… "You make the rules around here," I told Lee, as I pushed all thoughts of my father–and hers– to the back of my mind. "In this house *you* are the boss."

My words got a small smile out of her. "And what are you?" she mused as she leaned against her chair. "In this house, I mean."

"Well," I said with a grin as I stretched my arms over my

head. "You're the queen of this house. You can order me around all you like…but in our bedroom, I'm your motherfucking king."

I must have said the right thing again because she awarded me with a megawatt smile. "King," she said in a teasing tone. "Do you want me to make you a crown? I'm sure we have some paper and glue somewhere."

"I'm serious," I told her even though I was thrilled that she was smiling.

"So am I." Lee smiled. "Now, do you want me to use the blue crayon or the green one for your crown?"

"Red," I chuckled as I stood up and grabbed our plates from the table.

"Why red?" she asked quietly as she hovered behind me.

"I don't know." I shrugged as I scraped the remainder of Lee's burnt chicken casserole into the trash before loading the dishwasher. The *girl couldn't cook for shit…*"I like red. Red's a good color for a crown."

She was silent for so long that I thought she had left the room. Then I heard her whisper, "I didn't know that."

"Hey," I said softly as I closed the door on the dishwasher and turned around to face her. "You okay?"

"Yeah," she sighed as she fiddled with the hem of her t-shirt. She looked deep in thought as she frowned at the floor before looking up at me. "It's just that night I was…" She stopped mid-sentence. Her eyes flickered to the ground and then to the fridge. She shook her head and shivered.

"You were…" I coaxed as I walked over to her. Tipping her chin up with my fingers I stared down at her lonesome expression. "You were what, baby?"

"I was wearing red the night she shot me," she blurted out before shuddering. "It's probably stupid, but I really don't like red anymore. The color makes me nauseous…Reminds me of the blood."

Thank fuck I hadn't painted any of the rooms in the house red…

"Lee," I sighed, pulling her body into mine. "It's over, baby. She's never gonna hurt you again." I pulled back to clasp her face in my hands. "In a couple of months, she'll be locked away forever."

"I know that," she whispered. "It's just going to take me some time, you know? Some things stick in a person's mind. I can't help it, but I am trying to move forward. I promise I am."

"I know you are," I said in a gruff tone as I stroked her back gently. "God, you're doing so well. I'm so proud of you for handling all of this with such dignity."

"That's because of you," she replied in a soft tone as she tightened her arms around my waist. "Being with you makes it easier to breathe, Kyle. When I'm with you I feel like I am wrapped up in a protective blanket and nothing can harm me...but it's also a scary feeling because I should be able to take care of myself, you know?"

"No," I replied as I looked down at her. "No. I don't know, princess. You're mine and I'm gonna take care of you. There's nothing scary about that."

Lee squeezed me tighter. "Kyle, people who try to protect me get hurt," she whispered. "Bruno...Cam...oh god, if anything ever happened to you..."

"Shh," I crooned as I held her face to my chest. "You're safe. Hope's safe. I'm safe," I said softly. "I promise you. I fucking promise you things will be better for us here. I'm not gonna let a damn thing happen to you. Never again, Lee. I swear to you."

"We'll survive together," she whispered, squeezing me once more before stepping away from me and walking towards the door. "Night Kyle."

"Night princess." I watched her tiny frame retreating with a heavy heart. It was only seven pm. "I'll be up soon."

"Take your time," I heard her say as my eyes followed her until she slipped out of my vision.

I was feeling jittery and had an unusual amount of excess energy thrumming in my veins that I needed to burn off before I could even think about lying down.

Sometimes I had a really hard time just trying to sit still and relax my brain. It didn't bother me too much since I'd always been like this, but every now and then I thought back to my childhood and something I once overheard one of my foster-parents discussing with my case-worker when I was ten. I'd heard them talking about my mother and how she'd taken drugs throughout her pregnancy with me. They had come to the conclusion that my tetchy, volatile behavior was a result of being exposed to the intravenous drugs my mother had taken. After a lengthy discussion with my case worker about my aggressive nature, the Osborne family had come to the conclusion that I was too much of a *high-risk* to be around their other children. The following day my bags were packed and I was shipped on to the next family. Of course, my *volatile* behavior had nothing to do with their asshole fifteen year old son who'd kicked me in the balls for using the shower before him and I, in turn, had retaliated by breaking his nose. *Assholes…*

Pushing those memories to the back of my mind, I tidied up the kitchen, went through the quarterly financial report for the hotel in Denver, called Derek to check in, and then spent about thirty minutes admiring the alarm system before conceding to exhaustion.

"The alarm system in this place is awesome," I said in a hushed tone as I climbed into bed next to Lee. "A fly couldn't get into this place unnoticed…" I poked her in the ribs gently. "Hey Lee, you awake?"

"Yeah," she whispered as she rolled onto her back and looked up at me. Her eyes were puffy and swollen. "Did you remember that it's Halloween tomorrow, Kyle?" she asked, her voice thick with emotion.

"Yeah," I mumbled. "I know." I had hoped she wouldn't remember. The thought of taking her out in the dark, with idiots running around the place wearing masks and setting off fireworks made my blood run cold.

"I don't…" she paused, closing her eyes and exhaling heavily. "I know it's Hope's first Halloween, but can we stay at home this year?"

I felt like sagging in relief. Stretching out on my back, I pulled her body closer to mine and wrapped my arm around her. "That sounds like a pretty good plan to me, princess."

"Are you sure?" she asked as she snuggled into my side.

"Yeah baby," I whispered. We had enough monsters lurking in the shadows. No need to go out looking for more. "I'm sure."

ELEVEN

KYLE

HALLOWEEN HAD PASSED IN A–MOSTLY–DRAMA-FREE blur. Hope had woken up with two new teeth and an upset tummy, and Lee and I had been too elbows-deep in baby poop and vomit to even think about the date. Her tummy had settled by evening, and when we got her down for the night we'd both collapsed from exhaustion and worry. I hadn't been too stressed about Hope's diarrhea–it always happened when she cut a new tooth, but Lee had been frantic.

The following morning Lee asked me to take her to the cemetery–and every day since–and I took her there, no questions asked. I wasn't happy about her going there so much, but I was just grateful she was asking me instead of sneaking out behind my back. I was trying to pull her out of her sadness and Lee was trying, too, but she went to bed early since we moved in, and even though she tried to be quiet about it, I heard her crying into her pillow in the middle of the night when she thought I was asleep. Her nightmares were just as vicious as before and it tore my goddamn heart up that I couldn't fix it. All I wanted was for her to be happy again.

This was the seventh night in our new home and I was relieved as hell that Lee was in better spirits tonight. Cam's photo had messed with her head, and to be honest, I had a feeling it still was messing with her head. Every now and then I caught her looking up at it and discretely wiping her eyes. I debated whether I should take it away, but I didn't want to upset her further.

"How was it?" Lee asked as she snuggled into my side. We'd bathed Hope and put her down for the night and crashed out on the couch watching some shitty chick flick in front of the fire. This was the first night in a week that I'd persuaded her to stay up later than nine o clock, and I hated to admit it, but Lee's taste of movies was growing on me. She'd chosen Dirty Dancing for us to watch and I was feeling a little put out that I couldn't dance like that. *Jesus, what the hell was this woman turning me into?*

"How was what?" I asked turning down the volume of the TV with the remote.

"Your childhood," she replied, breaking me out of my reverie. "You never say much about it. I know you were in the system, but you don't say anything else about it."

"It was what it was, princess." I really didn't know what she wanted me to say. Yeah, I'd been dealt a crappy hand, but it paled in comparison to what she'd gone through with her father. I had been one of the luckier kids. As a child I was like an alley cat–more than capable of fighting my own corner. "I was tall for my age," I told her as I stretched my legs out next to hers. "And I had a mouth that got me out of as much trouble as it got me into."

"That sounds like you," she chuckled as she played with the hem of my t-shirt. "Did you get into many fights?"

"Define many," I teased as I looked down at her smiling face. *Keep talking Carter. Keep her smiling...* "I was a horrible kid," I laughed.

"Where did you see yourself when you were older?" she asked.

"In one place," I told her. "I never had a clear idea of what I wanted to do. I just knew whatever it was, it would be in one place with my own house, not moving every six months."

"Was it hard?" she whispered.

"It was fine." I didn't want to bum her out. She needed to smile. "What about you?" I asked her. "What did you want to be when you grew up?"

"Alive," she said and her honesty took the breath out of me.

"Okay," Lee grinned as she pulled herself up to sit cross-legged. "Let's play a game."

I raised my brow in amusement. "A naked game?"

She rolled her eyes. "A 'getting to know each other better' game."

Laughing, I sat up and mirrored her body language. "Uh, engaged with a kid here, princess…"

"Don't spoil it," she growled as she leaned over and pinched my nipple.

"Shit baby," I groaned. "That hurt." It didn't. I just wanted to be petted a little. Her raised eyebrow was a sign that there would be no petting. "Fine." I sighed. "Let's play your game, brat."

LEE

"Tell me a secret?" I asked Kyle as we sat facing each other on the couch. Kyle had forced me to watch a movie with him and I had to admit that I was feeling the best I had in days. It was nice to do one of the normal things that couples were supposed to do. Maybe we could make it a regular thing…Movie night. Kyle complained throughout the entire film, but it hadn't slipped my attention that he'd tapped his feet during every dance scene. At one point I'd actually thought he was going to jump off the couch and start dancing to the mambo…

Leaning forward, Kyle placed his beer bottle on the floor before sitting cross-legged facing me. "When I was nine, I went through a phase of thinking I was a power ranger."

"No way," I spluttered as a mouthful of coke spilled from my lips.

He shook his head and laughed. "Way. I was obsessed. One of my foster moms bought me a black power ranger costume for my birthday. I thought I was the shit," he chuckled as he wiped my lip with his thumb. "I slept in that suit every night for a month."

"When I was nine I used to peek down Cam's Ken dolls pants," I admitted before covering my mouth with my hand to stifle a laugh.

Kyle grinned and tipped his head sideways. "You little pervert."

"What?" I said defensively. "I didn't have a clue back then. I thought that's what *it* looked like."

"Ha," he snorted. "You must have been surprised when you saw my...*it*."

"Um..." I pretended to think about it and Kyle narrowed his eyes.

"Shut up," he growled, nudging my knee with his hand.

"I'm kidding," I told him. "I really should've been looking at the black power ranger figurine. What was it again? Morphy nine?"

"Morphing Time," he stated in a serious tone. I had to hold in a laugh at his serious expression. "It's morphin time, princess."

"Rats make my skin crawl," I confessed. "Our house got infested once. It was terrifying. They were huge."

"Turtles freak me out," Kyle said deadpan.

"Oh my god. Are you serious?"

"Come on," he argued, using his hands to shape a turtle. "You don't think it's creepy when they look at you with those...beady little eyes." He shuddered. "No, fuck it they freak the hell out of me."

I had to hold my side. I laughed so hard. "That's the funniest thing I've ever heard."

"Not as funny as you and your Ken fetish." He waggled his eyebrows. "I better tell Hope to lock up her dolls around you."

"I think I prefer the real thing," I chuckled, loving every moment of this conversation.

He smirked. "Good to know, baby," he purred. "If you're a good girl, I'll let you look down my pants later."

"What's the weirdest thing you love but you'd never admit?" I blurted out, trying to veer the topic of conversation away from sex. If I didn't, we would be naked...

"What the fuck kind of question is that?" Kyle shook his head and chuckled. "If I'll never admit to it then why are you asking me?"

"Because I'm going to be your wife," I teased. "And it is my eternal right to know all things Kyle Carter."

He smiled fondly at me. "You're a pain in my ass."

"So, you secretly love that I'm a pain in your ass?"

"What can I say?" Yawning loudly he stretched his arms over his head. "I'm a glutton for punishment."

"Have you..."

"Wait," he said grinning. "Do I get to ask a question?" The way his eyes danced with mischief worried me.

"All right." I rolled my shoulders and sighed. "Give me your worst, Carter."

"If you could have something," he said grinning. "Right now. What would it be?"

I narrowed my eyes. "Is this a trick question?" I thought Kyle would use his question to ask something…worse.

"No," he grinned. "If you could have something just for you–something realistic–what would it be?"

"My driving license," I replied honestly. I didn't have to think about it, I was dying to get behind the wheel of Kyle's beast of a car.

"Huh…" he mused as he scratched his chin. "You want me to teach you?"

"Oh my god! Yes," I squealed. "Will you? You're not just saying this? Will you really teach me?"

"Of course I will," he said with a smirk. "But only if you call me Master…no, wait. Call me Sensei."

"I thought you were afraid of turtles," I teased. "Now you want me to call you Sensei?" My comment backfired on me because I visualized that ugly cartoon rat and shivered.

"I'm not afraid of them," he growled. "I just happen to believe they are creepy little fuckers. There's nothing normal about their eyes, Lee."

"Okay," I crooned. "I'm sorry, Sensei."

"Favorite breakfast food?" he asked grinning.

"Eggs."

His eyes twinkled. "How do you like your eggs in the morning princess?" His grin widened as he asked, "Fertilized or not?"

"You're sick," I groaned.

Kyle laughed. "Sorry baby. I always wanted to say that."

"What does it feel like to have a penis?"

Kyle gaped at me in feigned horror. "Should I be worried?"

"No…" I blushed. "I always thought it must be uncomfortable for you to have something that big hanging around the place."

"Jesus Christ," he muttered. "You're getting weirder by the minute."

"This is me," I teased. "Warts and all…"

Kyle's phone decided to choose this moment to ring and I immediately jumped. "Relax," he said softly as he fished it out of his pocket and frowned at the screen before glancing briefly at me.

Holding his phone to his ear, he maneuvered himself off the couch and held his fingers up to me before walking out of the room. "Hey, you okay?" I heard him say before he closed the door, obviously not wanting me to hear.

I sat on the couch feeling unnecessarily wounded by his evasive behavior.

It shouldn't bother me that he had to take a call.

It *didn't* bother me that he had to take a call.

What bothered me was the fact that he was hiding something.

It was obvious and it was going to drive me insane...Climbing to my feet, I slipped out of the lounge and followed the sound of his voice until I was standing outside the door of his office. Pressing my ear to the door, I listened intently as Kyle's voice filled my ears.

"She's doing much better…yeah, it's all set….no, and it won't. Trust me on that….I haven't had a chance to speak to her about it yet….how are you feeling....Tracy, if you're sore..."

My blood turned to ice at the sound of her name coming from his mouth. Turning on my heel, I dashed towards the stairs, not stopping until I was inside my bedroom with my heart hammering in my chest and my pulse drumming in my ears. "Traitor," I whispered into thin air as I stripped off my clothes and climbed into bed. "Goddamn turncoat."

Reaching into my night stand, I carefully avoided touching Cam's gold locket–*I still couldn't wear it*– as I retrieved my phone from the drawer and powered it up. When I looked at the wall-paper on my screen, I felt like screaming in agony. It was a picture of Cam holding Hope. I'd taken it the day before she died. She'd wanted a picture of her and Hope together, but she forgot her phone in her car. I'd forwarded her all three pictures I'd taken to her phone, and I thanked god that I had the good sense to save them on mine. "I miss you," I whispered as the tears trickled down my cheeks. "I miss you so much." I closed my eyes for a few moments and breathed slowly and deeply in a bid to get a handle on my grief before I had a meltdown.

When I felt a little bit more in-control of my emotions, I began to scroll through the various folders in my photos in an aimless attempt to distract myself from Kyle and his phone call. I scrolled through at least a dozen in my Bluetooth folder until my eyes landed on one that stumped me. What the heck…

Sitting up, I folded my legs beneath myself and studied the picture. "Good lord," I gasped as I stared at the picture of Cam in a tender embrace with…Derek?

They were lying in bed and one of Cam's hands was cupping Derek's cheek as she used the other to hold the phone. She was tucked under his arm, and he had his face turned into her cheek. His eyes were closed, his lips turned up in a smile of pure contentment. Her blonde hair was pillowing his chest and his hand was resting on her breastbone.

Why was this on my phone? I checked the date it was sent, June twenty-seventh, and then I looked at the photo again. I felt like squirming. It was such an intense, intimate picture. Did she send me this on purpose?

Scrolling through my contacts list, I clicked Derek's number and held my phone shakily to my ear.

"Hello," he said in a lifeless tone of voice.

"Hey Der," I whispered nervously. I didn't expect him to pick up, and now he had, I wasn't sure what to say…I could hardly ask him about the photo…could I?

There was a pause and then his voice filled my ear. "Lee," he said in a soft tone. "You okay?"

"No," I admitted. "Are you?"

"No," he whispered. Neither of us spoke for a long time, but the sound of his breathing was, in a strange way, comforting to me.

"Bad day?" I asked eventually when the silence became too much.

"Bad life." He laughed once, but it was a humorless sound. "You?"

"Same," I agreed as I rubbed my palm against my forehead. "I miss you."

"Yeah," he said in a gruff tone. "Miss you, too, ice."

"Will you come home Der?" I pleaded as the tears I thought I'd stemmed pooled in my eyes. "I can't stand the thought of you being all alone in that house…please, please come home…"

"Lee," he said in a heavy tone. "It's not that…I can't just…" His voice broke off and I heard him inhaling deeply. "I'm not ready to let her go," he confessed, his voice ravaged with grief and pain.

"I'm sorry," I sobbed. "I wish I could come visit you, but it's that house..."

"I'll come see you soon, I promise," he said in a gentle tone. "You don't need to be here...you're too...this house is cursed...it's tainted."

"It burns," I choked out as my tears scalded my cheeks. "Oh god, it cuts so deep..."

"Right through the heart," he added shakily and I knew he was crying, too.

KYLE

I should have turned my phone off. If I had I would still be enjoying the goddamn movie night with Lee, instead of spending the last hour trying to coax her mom into calming the fuck down. She was a nervous wreck and fully convinced that Jimmy was coming for her. He wasn't coming for her, but telling her that over and over again had depleted my limited source of patience. I was at breaking point and damn glad the conversation was over.

"Sorry again for calling you so late, Kyle," Tracy said in a much calmer tone of voice than earlier. "I hope I haven't ruined your evening."

"No, not at all," I mumbled. "Call anytime." Ending the call, I made sure I switched my phone off before heading back to the lounge with a heavy heart.

When I saw the couch was devoid of Lee, I wasn't surprised. I'd bailed on her and wasn't expecting her to sit and wait for me. Climbing the stairs, I checked on Hope before heading down the hallway to our room. When I opened the door of our room and saw her with her knees tucked against her chest, I was filled with panic. She was crying. She was crying so hard, she didn't even notice I was in the room. She didn't even flinch when I climbed into bed next to her.

Jesus...

"I'm sorry," Lee sobbed as she held her phone to her ear and clenched her eyes shut. "I wish I could come visit you, but it's that house..." Her voice broke off as a fit of crying enveloped her. "It burns...oh god, it cuts so deep..."

Who the fuck was upsetting her?

One name to my mind – *Jimmy* – and I reacted instantly. Moving quickly, I reached over and snatched the phone out of her hand. "Who the fuck is this?" I snarled, chest heaving.

"Calm down, asshole."

Derek's familiar voice filled my ear and I sagged in relief for a moment before worry replaced my fury. "Why is she crying?" I asked in a confused tone. I heard him sniffle loudly and I shook my head as my eyes flickered from Lee's face to the fist I was forming on my lap. "Derek, are you crying, too?" What the hell was going on? Had I missed something...?

"Go comfort your woman," he choked out. "She needs you." With that he ended the call and I was left clueless. Clueless and staring at Lee's phone like a dumbass.

Twisting my body around to look at Lee, I asked, "What's wrong? Did he...was he drunk or something?"

"No," she sniffed as she threw herself back on the bed and curled into a tiny ball.

"Lee," I coaxed as I shook her shoulder gently. "Baby, what's wrong?"

"Everything," she whispered.

"Tell me what's wrong and I'll fix it." Pulling on her shoulder, I pushed her gently onto her back and brushed her hair off her face. She closed her eyes in an obvious attempt at blocking me out. I sighed heavily. "Lee, I can't help you if I don't know what's wrong. Talk to me, princess."

"I heard you talking to her," she hissed, eyes still closed, her whole body tense. "I don't want you to talk to her, Kyle."

"Lee..." I let my voice trail off as I tried to think up something to say that wouldn't result in a battle. Lee had issues with her mom and I got that. I understood her reasons for wanting to keep Tracy at arm's length. But I also understood why Tracy had left Lee as a baby. Why she ran away and left her three month old daughter in the hands of an abusive fucking bully.

I wasn't happy about it and by no means did I agree with her actions, but I'd heard her side of the story. The man had made her life a living hell. Lee's dad had broken more than just bones in her mom's body...he'd crushed her spirit and ruined her life. She lost more than her baby daughter the day she escaped Louisiana. She lost her identity, her friends and everything she'd ever known. Tracy Gibbons had spent the last nineteen years locked away in a cottage, with only her flowers and potpourri for company, while living in a constant state of terror, fearing that at any moment that bastard would show up and drag her back to Montgomery…

God, I felt so fucking sorry for the woman. I couldn't turn my back on her, no matter how mad it made Lee. I owed the woman. I owed her everything I had. During the darkest hours of my life, Lee's mother had stepped in and saved my girl and I'd made her a promise to protect her from her husband. I didn't make promises easily and this was one I wasn't prepared to break. Lee was going to have to deal with it. She needed to see that she was putting a lifetime of blame on the wrong parent. She needed to hate her father. Her mother was as much a victim to Jimmy Bennett's abuse as she was.

"I don't wanna fight with you about this, princess," I said quietly. "But I won't back down either. She saved your life. We owe her."

"You never back down," she mumbled as she turned onto her side. "That's the problem."

TWELVE

DEREK

I LIVED in a world that made no sense. Colors and light. People and places. All of it meant nothing to me anymore. The world was a cruel and torturous place. I wanted out.

"Derek, will you do this for me?" Kyle asked me and I wanted to puke. It was easy for him. He hadn't lost what I had. He didn't sleep with his regrets. He slept in a warm bed with his woman in his arms. He didn't live with his ghosts because his world was still breathing.

My life was a warped and cruel fucking existence and I was sick to death of pretending, of carrying on. I didn't see the point and I didn't want to. It meant nothing to me. Clothes, food, work, breathing, it all meant nothing. I hadn't realized the only thing that had ever meant anything to me was dead. I hadn't fucking realized and I hadn't told her. Jesus.

"I don't know, Kyle," I told him as I held the phone to my ear. "Seems kind of pointless." I could hear him growl and I knew he was close to losing that infamous temper of his. It actually made me smile.

"That's bullshit," he growled before adding in a much softer tone, "It's good to talk about your feelings."

Ha. "You're something else," I chuckled. "Telling me it's good to talk about feelings. When have you ever talked about your feelings, asshole?"

"Whatever douchebag," he retorted and I could tell he was smiling. "Just think about it, okay? Lee said that Dr. Roberts really helped her when she was in hospital. I figured she might be good for you, too. For all of us."

"Kyle, are you suggesting we take couples counseling? Because I gotta tell you, dude, I don't think we're *there* yet." I used sarcasm as a self-preservation tactic for when shit got too heavy. Like now for example…

"Yeah," Kyle snapped. "Well, if you don't get a handle on this I might just divorce your ugly ass. Think about Dr. Roberts. I'll text you her phone number. Make an appointment."

"Does your fiancée know about us?"

"Ha fucking ha, dude. I gotta go. I'm heading over to see Kelsie. I'll come by after."

"Whatever." Hanging up, I tossed my phone on the bed and resumed my numbness. If Kyle would just fuck off and leave me to rot I would be dead by now. I didn't know whether to thank him or resent him.

LEE

"I'll only be an hour. Two at the very most," Kyle muttered as I watched him make the worst tie knot I'd ever seen. If I could have helped him I would, but fancy suits weren't something I'd ever come into contact with before him. Kyle looked beautiful in everything he wore, but when he wore tailored black pants, a crisp white shirt and vest I struggled to keep my concentration.

"We'll be fine here," I said in a thick tone of voice. I knew where Kyle was going and it wasn't to work. He was going to our attorney's office to see if there was any new development with the case. He did this every week and every week I either refused to go or pretended not to know where he was going. Ignorance was bliss. She was locked up and we were safe. *For now*. I didn't want to hear about her latest request for Kyle to visit her, or how her *treatment* was going. I knew she was writing to him. He tried to hide the letters from me, but I wasn't blind and I had never expected her to go away easily. A mental health facility hadn't stopped her from pursuing him. I just prayed that a jail cell could…

Last month we found out that Rachel's trial had been pushed forward to April. It was due to the hype and speculation surrounding the case. That was the only positive thing about having our lives ripped apart by the media. At least she would be locked away much quicker than we'd anticipated.

I'd spent the first month after waking up from my coma being questioned and giving evidence. During some of that time I'd felt like I was being groomed, but mostly I'd just felt like I was being judged. Everyone wanted to know why Rachel did it and since she wasn't telling anyone the bucket had fallen at my feet. No one ever seemed to be satisfied with my answer, probably because I knew why she did it as much as they did.

"Come on Miss Bennett," I'd been asked by several exasperated officials. *"There has to be something. Some incident or altercation you're forgetting that could have provoked Ms. Grayson. It makes no sense."*That was about the only thing they'd said that I agreed with. It made no sense. None of it.

Kyle, who had demanded to be with me when I was being questioned, had lost his cool on more than one occasion. I think it upset him more than me. He got truly distressed whenever anybody suggested I did something to provoke Rachel. Whenever an officer or a suit had insinuated such a thing, Kyle reminded me of a wild animal being backed into a corner and getting ready to fight. *All snarls and growls.*

I tried to put on a brave face for him, but I was terrified. The prosecution team had warned me that I would be portrayed as the other woman. I'd been forewarned that I *would* hear a lot of ugly things about myself. According to Kyle's lawyer, Kelsie Mayfield, Rachel's lawyers were leaning heavily on the defense that I was a homewrecker. They were going to claim I had broken up a two year relationship between a couple who had intended to marry. I'd taken her fiancé and future away from her and in a temporary moment of madness she'd snapped. I felt physically sick every time I thought about how I would have to stand in a courtroom in a few short months and tell the world what I didn't want to remember. I would be judged and ridiculed, and have to face that woman again. The thought of seeing her face again caused my blood pressure to rise and my body to break out in a cold sweat…

Content with his haphazard tie knot, Kyle dropped his hands to rest on his hips and frowned at me. "Maybe you should come with me?"

"Kyle, we will be fine here. I promise," I said with a forced smile as I bounced Hope on my lap. I'd been shocked to the core when he agreed to let me stay on my own today. Things had been frosty between us since Wednesday night and I wished to god that we could just agree to disagree on my mother. No. Actually, I wished he would agree with me for once in our lives... "What trouble could we possibly get into?" I added in my lame attempt at making a joke. I wasn't feeling it though, and neither was he by the look of apprehension on his face.

"That's what I'm worried about," he grumbled. Walking over to me, he lifted Hope off my lap. "You're in charge, baby girl," he crooned as he lifted her over his head and made airplane noises. Hope grinned madly, splaying her little hands and legs out in excitement. Bringing her back down to rest on his chest, he kissed her cheek before casting a smirking glance at me. "Daddy's counting on you to keep mommy in hand." I just rolled my eyes at him. I wasn't good with quick retorts. Usually I either made no sense or just made a fool of myself. "Stay inside, princess," he said in a stern voice, as he sat Hope in her bouncer. "Do not, for one minute, go outside those gates until I'm back. Are we clear?"

"Crystal," I muttered as I looked away, purposely avoiding eye contact with him. I hated when he spoke to me like this. Whenever Kyle talked down to me I tried to remember what Derek had told me. *"His intentions are good. It's his execution he needs to work on."* Kyle was paranoid that someone was going to run off with me. And all I wanted to tell him was before him no one had wanted me so the likelihood of being kidnapped was slim.

Kyle saw me through some strange dysmorphic lens. I was no Scarlett O'Hara. I had severe scarring on pretty much every slither of my skin from my thighs to my breasts. Front *and* back. I'd lost a lot of weight when I was in hospital, and weighed less now than when we'd first met, but my skin felt loose. That's a weird explanation for it, but that's how it felt. I hadn't toned up since I gave birth. I just kind of wobbled...

"Do you remember how to work the alarm system?" he asked as he slid his laptop into his messenger bag, frowning when several pieces of paper – and another *letter* – fell out and scattered around our bedroom floor. "You remember the access codes?" he asked as he bent to pick up the papers.

"Yes," I nodded eagerly and a little flushed. Truth was I didn't remember a word of what Kyle had said to me yesterday when he stood me in front of the complicated array of buttons and touch screens in our hallway, and he had proceeded to ramble on for fifteen minutes about this switch and that code. Hope had managed to stick her foot in her mouth around the same time and my attention had been on how cute she looked as she rolled around on the play mat, battling her chubby little leg into submission.

"Do not open those gates for anyone," he ordered in a stern voice.

"What if it's someone important…?" I started to protest, but the weight of Kyle's disapproving glare caused me to shut my mouth quickly. A ball of nerves settled in my stomach as I watched him prowl towards me, tension emanating from every pore in his body.

"I don't give a shit if the pope, the queen of England and the goddamn Easter bunny all swing by. You do not open those gates to anyone. You got it?"

"I got it," I muttered in a petulant tone, biting down hard on the inside of my cheek in anger. I felt his thumb stroke my cheek and I clenched my eyes shut.

"Don't be mad at me for needing to keep you safe," he whispered into my ear before brushing my lips with his. "I love you."

I caved.

Totally and completely caved.

Whatever spark of anger I was feeling over his bossiness, and his phone call with my mother, disintegrated the moment he whispered those words. My heart swelled to the point where I was nervous it would burst whenever he told me loved me. I'd waited almost a year to hear him say it and relished every time since. "I love you, too," I breathed as I wrapped my arms around his neck and dragged him down to me. Losing his balance, he fell forward causing me to land on the flat of my back on our bed with him resting on his elbows above me.

"Just do this for me, Lee," he murmured, as he pushed my hair back and cupped my face in his hands. "It's not forever. Just until the trial is over. I need you out of trouble. It keeps my mind at ease."

"Is there something you're not telling me, Kyle?" I asked softly, as I looked up at his face. I worried about his intentions. He was always trying to shelter me and it was hard to know whether there was a serious concern or if he was just being paranoid. "Should I be afraid?"

"No, I'm just being cautious." Kissing me softly, he rubbed my nose with his before smiling. "You know you could ease my mind in another way if you actually did what you agreed to do..." He kissed me again before pulling back to look at me. "I don't wanna wait anymore, princess."

"Go to work," I grinned as I stared up at his playful expression. I knew what he was doing and it wasn't going to work. I also knew that we needed to resolve our issues before we stepped foot near a church. "We have an agreement."

"Yeah, so did we," he purred. "You said yes. Usually after a proposal, people follow it up with a dress and some vows." He kissed me once more before climbing off me. "Maybe even some cake and lingerie..."

"Really?" I asked in a playful tone. "I had no idea."

Shaking his head, he grabbed his keys and smiled at me ruefully. "You drive me fucking crazy with your indecisiveness."

"Just so you know," I said as Kyle opened our bedroom door. "I was never undecided about you."

He raised his brow as he smirked at me. "Oh yeah?"

"Yeah." I nodded, returning his smile. "You had me at *'you wanna take a shot with me, sweetheart'*."

His face broke out in a huge smile. It was a rare smile. It was an awesome smile. "Well, you sure fooled me." He shook his head in amusement as he opened the door. "Be good, princess."

"Come on, sweetie," I said to Hope when I heard the front door slam. Bending down, I picked her up and winced when a sharp stab of pain ricocheted through my back and hips. "Mommy's very unfit, Hope," I groaned, as I carried her out of our room and down the stairs. The heat that flared through my joints intensified with every step I took on the staircase. "Maybe we should make a slide for mommy," I mumbled when I reached the bottom step. "Or buy a Zimmer frame." Hope beamed up at me with such an innocent expression that I felt a twinge of remorse for feeling sorry for myself.

"So, what's our plan of action while daddy's away?" I cooed as I carried her into the lounge and lowered myself onto the couch before sitting Hope on the floor between my legs. The house was eerily quiet without Kyle's larger than life presence. This was the first time he had left us on our own in the new house and I was already having a weak moment, wishing we'd gone with him when he asked. I'd wanted some freedom and Kyle was giving it to me. I should be happy. I shouldn't feel so…lost.

"Grow up, Lee. You can do this," I muttered to myself in a bid to calm my flailing nerves. If I couldn't handle a couple of hours on my own without him, what hope did I have?

I was too dependent on Kyle and that worried the life out of me because…well, because a potent part of my mind was convinced Kyle would change his mind about me–and an even bigger part of my mind wondered why he hadn't already…He was successful, strong and driven. I was needy, plain and boring. We were arguing all of the time again. Nothing went smoothly for us. We never seemed to get anything right. We had fallen into this relationship head first and eyes closed. He didn't know much about relationships and I knew even less. His response to fear was to control me. My response was to run…

That picture of Derek and Cam popped into my mind and I cringed. They were so in love. Their relationship–before it went to hell–had been one of unambiguous equality. Just thinking about how in sync Cam and Derek used to be, it made the fears and doubts I had about me and Kyle rise to nerve wracking levels. I would never admit it out loud, especially not to Kyle, but in my eyes I could only see one reason for him loving me, and that reason was sitting on the floor, babbling happily. He was so young, had so much on his plate and I was another weight on his shoulders. A burden.

No, you know he loves you. Stop freaking yourself out.

But how long would he love me? If we weren't able to move past the obstacle that was my mother, would Kyle leave me? I knew he was disappointed in me. I saw it in his eyes the other night. He couldn't understand why I didn't want to have anything to do with Tracy…and I was awful at trying to explain my feelings. I loved him. Oh god, I loved him so much, but if he left me…if it became too much from him, where would I be?

Pulling my phone out of my jeans pocket, I sent Kyle a quick text before sliding off the couch to sit on the floor with Hope.

Faith.

I needed to have some faith…

KYLE

"How did it go?" Derek asked me as he opened the front door in his boxers. I'd come straight from my attorney's office to check on him. This trial was hanging over us like a goddamn raincloud. It was a messy ordeal. One I wished we could get the hell away from. I'd be happy if they dumped her ass in a jail cell for the next sixty years. That would suit me just fine. I only wished they took away her letter privileges. She kept fucking writing to me. I received another one this morning. She sent me one a week, but I'd only read the first letter. It came about three weeks after her arrest and the crazy shit she had spurted had been enough to make the blood in my veins turn to ice. I remembered one specific line in the third paragraph.

'He's going to get her, Kyle. You won't be able to save her this time. It's already happening and you have no idea…'

Logically I knew Rachel was just trying to mess with my head. She was the only one who held a grudge on Lee, but I still hired a private investigator to ease my nerves. After weeks of digging he'd found nothing. Not one piece of evidence to back up Rachel's claims. Since then I brought all of her letters to Kelsie unopened. I didn't want Lee knowing Rachel was in contact with me and getting any notions. She was insecure enough and I was the one who had made her that way. She didn't need the unnecessary worry, certainly not about where my loyalties lay. I had my heart set on her. I had my whole future banked on her…

My attorneys had advised me to say nothing to the cops and

let her write as many as she wanted. She wasn't sending anything to Lee, so I was able to handle this without her knowing. Rachel was pleading not guilty to all charges–based on the grounds of diminished responsibility– and with every letter she sent me, she was becoming more frantic and closer to confessing.

I couldn't be more relieved that she'd decided not to plead guilty on the grounds of insanity. It had been a major concern for me. It would have been a fucking crime in itself to abuse the system by allowing that woman to use insanity as her excuse. She wasn't insane. She was evil. Mental health wasn't something that should be mocked. It wasn't fair to the people who truly suffered and it wasn't fucking fair to the families of victims who were seeking justice from the judicial system.

Kelsie was sure Rachel was cracking and it was only a matter of time before it all spilled out. If we could break her down, we might get a full admission out of her and avoid a trial. We were playing dirty, but she'd started it and I was taking her down. I wasn't depending on anyone else to do it for me. As it stood I was sick to my stomach over the fact that she was getting a trial. She fucking did it! Why the hell anyone had to sit in a courtroom and discuss her reasons was beyond me. There was no reason, NONE, that made it okay for her to take away another person's life. It didn't matter that she *didn't mean* to kill Cam. She fucking meant to kill *Lee*. That should be enough…

"Same," I muttered, walking past him to the kitchen. The only good piece of news I'd received today was the text message Lee had sent me this morning.

I love you Kyle Carter.

I'd sagged in relief when I read it and thanked god she was over the whole mother thing. I'd texted her back a smiley face and couldn't fucking wait to get home…

"You fix things with Lee?" Derek asked, stirring me from my thoughts. "I assume that you had something to do with her calling me at twelve-thirty at night. Crying again, Kyle. Upset *again*."

"It's sorted," I snapped in annoyance.

"Hope so," he mumbled. "That girl doesn't need any more stress in her life."

"She's fine Derek," I said in a warning tone, as I glared at him.

"Fine," he answered as he raised his hands in defense. "Only tryna help you out here, dude."

I stared long and hard at him for a moment and had to force my hands to stay by my sides. He was fading away in front of my eyes. It made me sick to my stomach to have to watch it. Derek had always been a muscular guy. He'd built up his form by slaving away at the gym for years and eating well. Hell, he'd played more sports in high school than I'd known existed and kicked my ass at just about every sport we'd ever played. The only advantage I had was that I could run faster and hit harder. I figured that was down to how we were raised. Derek had decent parents, a stable home life and after school activities growing up. I had my fists and myself.

I'd been to his hometown of Addyston for winter break of freshman year. I'd seen the photos, awards and trophies draped around his bedroom. The guy was as close to a physical machine you could get. It seemed hard to believe that the lean framed guy standing in front of me was the same Derek...

Opening the fridge, I started to unload the groceries I'd bought for him. He looked like death warmed up and if he didn't get rid of that wild animal look he was sporting on his face soon, I was going to break in when he was asleep and do it for him. "Here," I muttered as I tossed a packet of disposable razors in his direction. "I can't talk to you when your face looks like an old lady's vagina."

Catching the packet mid-air, Derek smirked. "How would you know what an old lady's –"

"Go shave," I ordered as I handed him the bag of clothes I'd brought over. "Shower and put some clean clothes on. I'll cook something and then we're both gonna sit down and eat a meal."

"Jesus Christ," he snapped. "Why the fuck can't you just leave me alone and go order Lee around instead? I'm not your problem, Kyle. I want to be on my own."

"Sorry dude," I said, as I turned on the gas and grabbed a skillet. "I've already reached my *piss Lee off* quota for today. It's your turn."

"Pain in my ass," he growled as he retreated with his bags.

"Don't forget to wash behind your ears, sunshine."

Twenty minutes later, Derek returned to the kitchen looking more himself. He still looked like a bag of bones, but at least I could see his face again. "Sit down," I told him as I placed two bowls of mac and cheese on the table.

"Comfort food," he mused as he slumped in his usual chair, closest to the door. "That cooking class during the summer served you well, man," he muttered as he took a bite of pasta. "Your roux is getting better." He licked his lips and stabbed his food with his fork. I sagged in relief at seeing him eat. *Thank god…* "A little less flour next time should thin it out."

"Yeah," I chuckled, as I sat in my spot and grabbed a fork. My dish was a poor substitute for Derek's. None of us could cook like him. Seriously, the guy could serve up food worthy of a five star restaurant. "Why didn't you go further with it, Der?"

"Further with what?" he asked as he hoofed another forkful of food into his mouth.

"Cooking," I replied. "You're awesome, man. Better than most of the chef's I have on my books."

He lowered his fork and stared straight ahead for a moment before shrugging his shoulders. "The family business is construction." He said it as if that was an answer in itself.

"So?" I muttered as I pushed my chair back and went in search of a clean glass. "Isn't your brother…what's his name again…Jake?"

"Jackson," Derek mumbled as he swallowed some food.

"Yeah, isn't Jackson helping your dad with the business?" Rinsing two glasses, I filled them with water before heading back to the table. "Is construction something you're even interested in? You've never talked much about it."

"Is the hotel business something you're interested in?" he countered as he took the glass from me, his eyes boring into mine.

"Fair point," I mumbled, feeling a little burned. The hotel business was definitely not something I was interested in. It was something I was *in*. I didn't have a choice…

"Look, Kyle," Derek said wearily. "Sometimes we gotta do what we gotta do." He stood up and moved to the fridge. "What I did for a living was never going to be what I was–who I was. It was just a means to have a good life…"

"And now?" I asked as I watched him open a can of beer and chug it back.

Derek sighed heavily. "And now...." He stopped speaking. His eyes flickered to the floor and I watched as he flinched and scrunched his eyes shut. "There's no now. There's only then. Now, is full of regrets."

"Derek." I shook my head and made to stand up, but he held his hand out to ward me off.

"No," he whispered as he backed out of the kitchen. "Just... just go away, Kyle. Please."

I dropped my head in my hands as I listened to the sound of his footsteps retreating down the hallway and then the sound of the front door slamming.

What the hell was I going to do with him?

How could you help someone who not only didn't want your help, but they didn't want to help themselves?

Standing slowly, I grabbed the hoover and set about cleaning the dump that once upon a time had been my house.

LEE

I was closing out Hope's bedroom door, after putting her down for the night, when I heard the sound of a car engine revving outside. I made my way down the stairs cautiously, freezing on the bottom step when the front door opened inwards.

"I'm so fucking sorry I'm late, princess," Kyle grumbled as he stalked into the hallway, his hair drenched from rain. Dropping his messenger bag on the floor, he proceeded to strip off his jacket and tie. "I know I said I'd only be a couple of hours, but I stopped by to see Derek, and he…and time got away from me." I watched him undo the top two buttons of his shirt as he prowled towards me with a look of hunger in his eyes. "I missed you," he purred, coming close enough to wrap his hands around my waist, even though I was standing on the step above him, my forehead barely reached his nose.

"I missed you, too," I whispered, wrapping my arms around his neck tightly. "I made dinner," I added as I breathed in the faded scent of his aftershave. His neck was wet from the droplets of water that were trickling from his hair. "It's probably still warm."

"I know what I'm hungry for," he said in a gruff tone as his hands dropped to cup my butt. "And it's not on a plate in the kitchen."

"I'm not a piece of meat, you know," I joked, feeling right for the first time since he left this morning. He was home. All was good again. The nervous butterflies were caged again. Blocking out all my earlier doubts and fears, I allowed myself to bask in his comforting presence–in the palpable heat that was burning in his eyes and melting my heart.

Kyle smirked and shrugged his shoulders before dipping his face to my neck. "On the contrary, princess, you're my favorite cut, taste and flavor." I felt the wet heat of his tongue against my skin and my legs weakened.

"Seriously?" I breathed as I sagged against him. "Dirty talk revolving around a meat product?"

"What can I say," he teased as he hoisted me into his arms and began climbing the stairs, eyes dark and full of sensual promises. "I'm a red blooded male in the prime of my youth."

———

"I've always wanted to ask you something," I confessed as I rested my head against Kyle's chest. "But I've been too afraid."

I felt his finger tip my chin up to meet his face. "You can ask me whatever the hell you like, princess," he said in a gruff tone as he brushed his thumb over my cheekbone. "You know this."

"Okay," I said. "But it's not an accusatory question. It's more curiosity than anything. So don't get mad, okay?"

"Okay..."

"The night I miscarried," I whispered, pausing to gauge his reaction. Apart from the skin around his eyes tightening, his face remained impassive. "Where did you sleep?"

My question must have surprised Kyle because his eyes widened, his forehead creased. Gently rolling me off his chest, Kyle sat up and rubbed his forehead with his hand. "Lee..."

"I'm not angry, Kyle," I quickly told him as I sat up. "I just want to know. You told me you went to Rachel's and had words with her. But you didn't arrive to the hospital until the next day. Where did you go?"

He shook his head. His body tensed. "I really don't see what this has to do with anything," he hissed. "None of that matters now. It's in the past."

"Where did you go, Kyle?" I asked in a firmer voice, suddenly nervous. What was he hiding? Oh god, what did he do?

"Why don't you ask what you really want to know, princess?" he said in a cold tone of voice. "You think I stayed with her."

I didn't think that, or at least I hadn't thought that. Until now. "I'm not going to argue with you," I told him as I shook my head. "I would just like to know."

We stared at one another, my gray eyes welded to his blue ones, waiting to see who would hesitate and who would back down. Surprisingly, it was Kyle who looked away first. "I did stay at Rachel's," he muttered in defeat. "But not for the reasons you're thinking."

Ice ran through my veins, but I forced my body to stay firmly on this bed and hear him out. Closing my eyes, I inhaled a steadying breath through my nose as I tried to push every painful thought, notion and sickening image out of my mind.

"I had a lot to drink that night, Lee," he whispered. "Rachel drove us to her apartment."

When I felt I was ready for him to continue, I opened my eyes and made a point of keeping my features blank. I didn't want the 'make Lee feel better' truth. I deserved the god honest truth, warts and all. "You could have called a cab." The words spilled out of my mouth without my brain's approval. "You could have walked."

Calm, deep breaths.

"I know that," he sighed. "Christ, don't you think I know that?" His shoulders sagged as he hissed out a sharp breath. "She went fucking nuclear that night, baby. I know that doesn't excuse my actions, or the fact that I wasn't with you when you were losing our baby, but I had an honest to god fear of her harming herself. The shit that spurred out of her mouth was insane…If I knew then what I know now, and could go back to that night, I would hand her the bottle of pills she was threatening to take and tell her to go fuck herself. "

"Don't say that, Kyle," I choked out as I reached over and grabbed his hand. "You did the right thing." The words tasted sour in my mouth. I was fighting an internal battle. Half of me was happy that he wished he'd let her die. I wanted Rachel to burn. Not for what she had done to me, but for what she had done to the people I loved.

I wanted justice for Cam; for Derek's depression.

For the nightmare's that stalked me.

But mostly for Kyle. He was no angel, but he was a good man who hid that huge heart of his well. Thoughts like that did no favors for good people. Thoughts like that blackened a person's soul. She'd tainted me. I was scarred, but I'd be damned if she marked my man.

THIRTEEN

DEREK

THE SUNLIGHT BEAMED through the crack between my bedroom curtains, illuminating the short golden hair of the woman asleep beside me. I groaned and threw my hand over my face.

I had to stop doing this.

The first night had been revenge. The second was loneliness. And the third...I wasn't sure what this was, but it had gone too far. She wasn't supposed to stay the night. She had a goddamn family waiting for her at home. "Come on, sweetheart," I whispered, nudging her arm. She didn't stir. "Wake up." She opened her brown eyes and gave me a smile of pure female satisfaction. Well, I was glad she was content. I, on the other hand, was a fucking mess.

"Morning," she purred as she stretched her arms over her head and twisted her body into mine. I pulled away and climbed out of bed. I didn't fucking snuggle and she should have left last night.

"You need to go," I said coldly as I pulled on my jeans and rooted around for my shirt. Kyle was right. I needed to clean this house up. I needed to clean my act up. I couldn't keep living like this. I'd sworn after the last time never again. Yet here I was. What had started as revenge was now just sick and twisted. I looked down at her naked body, sprawled out on my bed, and disgust chewed at my gut. She was a beautiful woman for her age, but this was so wrong. "Anna," I snapped when she didn't move. "You need to go home. Now."

"He doesn't care," she said in her soft British accent. "He never has."

Fuck, I didn't need this.

LEE

"Did you take your meds today?" Kyle stood in the doorway between our bathroom and bedroom, with his arms folded, legs apart. A white towel hung low on his narrow hips. Droplets of water dripped from his hair, falling to his chest before slithering down his toned stomach. *Sweet Lord Almighty…*

Forcing my face to meet his, I rolled my eyes, picked up my hairbrush and resumed my task of un-knotting my curls. If he didn't look so hot, and I hadn't lost my train of thought from ogling him, I'd be pretty annoyed he was bringing this up again. "Of course I did. I also took it yesterday and the day before that, too. You know this." He was referring to the anti-rejection medication I had been prescribed and needed to take daily.

For the rest of my life.

The meds were to prevent my body from rejecting my new kidney. I knew all this, but Kyle seemed to enjoy lecturing me on every rule and regulation of my new lifestyle when he felt inclined. "Did you…" he began, but I interrupted him quickly, knowing full well what he was about to ask. The man was methodical.

"Yes, I remember what the doctor said. I've been very thorough in my application of SPF 50. And look, I even did my nose," I teased, leaning my hip against the bed frame. It was pouring with rain outside, but according to Kyle, a person in my *condition* could burn through rain clouds – in November. What a crock…

"So, have I been a good girl, Mr. Carter, or should I go sit on the naughty step?"

The tension around his eyes eased and his lips rose in a reluctant smile as he prowled towards me. "Hmm," he purred as he wrapped his arms around my waist. Grabbing my ass, he hoisted me into his arms. "Maybe I need to take a closer inspection."

Wrapping my legs around his waist, I groaned when I felt his hardness press against me. Capturing my lips with his, Kyle kissed me so deeply and with such intensity that every inch of my body vibrated with desire. "I think you need to check here," I whispered against his mouth as I rubbed myself against his erection. I needed this. I needed to be with him. I needed him to be inside me. It was the only time things felt worthwhile. I felt worthwhile when I was in his arms. When everything became too much I clung to our connection as my lifeline. He always pulled me back from the darkness. He could fix everything broken in me as quickly as he could break me. I belonged to him and I'd give him anything he wanted…

"Christ Lee," he groaned as his lips dropped to my neck. Guiding us to the bed, Kyle laid me on my back before lowering himself on top of me. He didn't put his full weight on me and I wished he would. I needed all of him. Every ounce and every touch. He was my anchor. I'd been haunted with nightmares last night and needed him to ground me.

Sliding up my night-shirt, his tongue lapped over my bare breasts. "You can't say shit like that to me," he grunted as he flicked one of my nipples with his tongue. "I'm gonna explode and you're not…"

I didn't let him finish speaking. I couldn't. Grabbing his face between my hands, I pulled his lips up to meet mine as I rocked my pelvis upwards. I felt him harden with each thrust of my hips. Slipping a hand between us, Kyle pulled his towel away and shoved my t-shirt up my body. "You're soaking, baby," he purred as he rolled my clit between his fingers. Oh god… He knew just the right amount of pressure to apply, the speed I needed him to use.

"Kyle," I moaned, spreading my legs wider for him. "Please..."

"Please what, princess?" he crooned as his fingers worked me into a frenzy. Every vibrating touch of his thumb to my clit caused my body to shake violently. I was a quivering mess underneath this sex god of a man and he'd barely touched me. "You want me to stop?"

Shaking my head, I reached for his erection. I couldn't speak. Words were beyond me. I needed the physicality of our relationship. "Fuck," he hissed as he bit down on his lower lip, losing his expert rhythm on my clit when I stroked his length.

Wriggling myself further down the bed, I had to bite back a moan when I found what I was looking for. The head of his shaft against my entrance was almost enough to set me off. I was throbbing and clenching in anticipation as I guided his erection inside of me.

"Princess…" he moaned as he sank fully into me. His weight came down on me and I relished his temporary loss of control. Wrapping my legs around his hips, I rocked upwards as he filled me. The feel of him inside of me was both agonizing and mind-blowing. I'd never been with anyone but Kyle, and I couldn't be certain, but I guessed he was bigger than the average man. When he was fully erect and inside of me, stretching and filling me to the brim, the sensation was so overwhelming it was close to painful. Painfully amazing…

"Easy baby," he whispered as he slid in and out slowly. "You're not ready for the hard stuff…"

"I want the hard stuff," I moaned as I quickened the pace of my hips. I was frantic in my search for release. My orgasm was building inside of me and I was desperate to come…

"Wah…Wah…"

My desire abandoned me the instant I heard the soft cries coming from the baby monitor next to our bed. Dropping my hands from around his neck to his chest, I let my legs fall away from his hips as I gently pushed him off me as I attempted to stifle a giggle.

"Fuck," Kyle groaned as he dropped his head to my neck. Growling in frustration, he pulled out slowly and rolled onto his back. "Goddammit to hell," he muttered as he covered his face with his arm.

Sitting up, I fixed my night-shirt before climbing off the bed. "Sorry." I grinned. "Duty calls."

KYLE

Christ, I thought I'd explode this morning when Lee climbed off me–mid-sex. Yeah, it was a little awkward when Hope started crying, but, Jesus, I was *this* close. Didn't she understand a man's body? She could have killed me. Seriously, I had a genuine concern for my dick. It wouldn't lie the fuck down. I'd been walking around with wood half the goddamn day. I needed to get my ass home and have her finish what she started…

I looked up when I heard the sound of my office door open. A young girl with cropped blonde hair stood in the doorway with a cleaning cart. "Shit," she mumbled. "I mean, sorry, Mr. Carter. I thought your office was empty."

"It's fine," I said wearily as I grabbed my jacket and laptop. I wasn't getting anything done around here today. I was pissed off and horny as hell.

Bad combination.

"Will I come back later?" the blonde asked.

Jesus, I'd been so distracted with the past few months that I couldn't even remember hiring this one. She looked familiar. I knew I'd seen her head around the place–not many girls wore their hair so short–but I couldn't place her. "What's your name?" I asked, embarrassed at not knowing.

"Karen," she replied. The light bulb in my brain started flashing.

Code fucking red.

She was the one who'd let Rachel into the honeymoon suite a

few months ago. The day she'd tried to seduce me. The event that had screwed Lee's head up and mine with it. I would never forget the look of betrayal in Lee's eyes when Rachel handed me my wallet. I would never forget the feeling of disgust I had when I realized she didn't trust me. It hurt then. It hurt now...

"Karen Vale?" I asked in a pissy tone. "Good thing you're here. We need to talk." Her cheeks reddened but she straightened her spine and nodded.

"Karen Valentine," she corrected as she met my gaze with hard brown eyes. *Tough little cookie.* "And I know what you want to talk about, so here's my input on the matter," she said before taking a deep breath. "I watch TV and I read the papers. I know what happened to your wife and her friend and I'm sorry for your troubles. But you have to know that I had absolutely no idea that woman was a basket case when I let her upstairs. She told me she was your girlfriend. I know I messed up, but I was new and green to the job. I sympathize with your family, Mr. Carter, I do. I have a family of my own who are my world. So, if you're about to fire me because of one mistake then just get it over with. But if you do fire me, then you should know that makes you a total dickhead."

I was pretty fucking impressed in that moment. I'd never heard a woman speak so many words without taking a breath. I also liked the fact that she'd called Lee my wife. I was mentally calculating how many words she'd spoken when she piped up again in a much softer tone.

"I am sorry about your wife, Mr. Carter, and I'm not saying that to save my job. Her picture was in the paper. She was very beautiful before that woman butchered her. I can't imagine what you must be feeling. Knowing that you used to date..."

"Two things, sweetheart," I snapped as I loosened my tie. "First, don't ever, and I mean ever, speculate about the shit they write in the papers about my family. Most of it is bullshit and any little truth has been fabricated to sell stories. My *wife* is beautiful. Very fucking beautiful. Past, present and future tense, got it?"

Karen nodded stiffly. "I'm sorry, Mr. Carter. I wasn't gossiping. I just feel bad for her. But yeah, I get it. Loud and clear." My heart hurt to think people were talking about Lee like that. She was self-conscious enough without having that kind of shit said about her.

"And second, I'm not firing you." I surprised myself with that one, but a plan was forming in my head. "I'm relocating you." This girl could be the answer to a lot of my problems. "Or at least I'm hoping that you will accept the new job I'm offering. It will have better pay and less stress."

"What kind of job?" She looked dubious. I didn't blame her. This conversation had taken a U-turn. I was going with my gut on this one though.

Walking over to my filing cabinet, I started digging around for her résumé. "You're young, right?" I asked as I grabbed her file and opened it.

"I'm twenty-seven," she said as she rubbed her brow.

Bullshit. "Try again," I muttered as my eyes trailed over her paperwork. Yeah, her employee file had her down as twenty-seven. *Linda.* She had a soft spot for the ones with sob stories. I wondered what this one's story was...

"I am twenty-seven," she repeated nervously. She was no more twenty-seven than Lee was. The girl had the face of a teenager. She was twenty at the very most. I raised my brow and her gaze faltered. "Fine," she admitted, folding her arms across her chest in a defensive stance. "I'm twenty-one. The blonde guy who works downstairs in the bar told me you have an issue with hiring young girls. Linda's fine with my age." Of course Linda was fine about it. She loved the strays–I was her favorite mongrel. I also had no doubt in my mind that the blonde guy she was talking about was Mike. I was going to have to talk to that dumbass, too.

"Yeah, he's right," I said. "I do."

During my first few months running the hotels I'd been hit with a huge scandal involving one of my underage employee's sexual antics with a hotel guest–a fucking senator of all people. Mindy Simmons had put me off hiring young women for life.

"I've only ever hired two girls under twenty-five and both were in housekeeping," I told her. "The first girl I hired damaged the hotel's reputation. The second one ruined me."

"What did you do with them?" she asked nervously. "The girls, I mean."

I smirked and leaned against my desk. "I fired the first one." Picking up the frame on my desk I walked over to where Karen was standing and handed it to her. Karen's fingers hovered over the picture of the three of us. It was my favorite photo. Derek had taken it a few minutes after Hope was born–in the back seat of my car.

In the photo Lee was leaning against my chest, holding Hope tightly and gazing down at her with so much love that it was spilling from the picture. Both of us were smiling. Lee was smiling at our daughter. I was smiling at Lee. That was the best day of my life. I never wanted to forget it. We had so many bad days. I kept this on my desk to always remind myself of our best day.

"Your wife," she whispered. Her eyes flicked up to meet mine. "You fell in love with your housekeeper."

I shook my head and looked down at Lee's smiling face. "I fell in love with my best friend."

"That's…wow," Karen breathed.

Prying the frame from her fingers, I returned it to its spot on my desk. "I'm going to be straight with you, Karen," I told her. "Lee, she has some medical issues. I've been thinking about hiring someone who could help out around the house. Someone to keep her company when I'm not at home. Is that something you might be interested in?"

"I'm not a nanny," she blurted out, suddenly looking very nervous. What the hell…

"I'm not looking for a nanny," I said evenly. I wasn't too fucking sure of the job I was offering let alone the job title, but it definitely wasn't a nanny.

"And as you can see, I'm also not very tactful," she added sheepishly. "I know you don't want me to bring it up, but believe me, Mr. Carter, I am the last person you'd want around your wife at this time."

"But you're young," I countered feeling more sure by the second that this girl was exactly who I needed to hire. She would be good for Lee. I could practically smell the victory. Perfect. "If it's your safety that concerns you, I can assure you our home is completely secure."

"It's not," she said nervously. Her cheeks were flushed as she rubbed her forehead. "I can't do it."

"Karen," I said almost pleadingly. "I'm not looking for a nanny or a babysitter..."

"Then what are you…"

"Jesus, will you let me finish," I sighed as a reluctant smile spread across my face. "You'll be good for her–for all of them actually."

"I really don't think I can take the job Mr. Carter," she whispered. Shit, she looked sick. Her face was pale. Her brow was sweating. "I have a..."

My phone started to ring causing Karen to halt mid-sentence. Glancing down at the screen, I was anxious as hell when I saw Derek's name appear. "I have to take this," I told her. "Think it over. Come see me when you've made your decision."

"I already have," she said firmly. "The answer is no."

"Just...just think about it, Karen," I growled as I rushed out of my office with my phone in my hand.

"Hey man. You okay?" I asked, answering the moment I closed my office door. "Derek, are you all right?" I asked again when he didn't respond.

"I'm..." His voice was slurred and I held my phone tighter in my hand as a million different emotions coursed through me. "I'm...lost."

"Lost?" I asked softly as I made my way down to the lobby. "Why do you think you're lost, buddy?"

"I went for a walk," I heard him say. "But I don't remember my way home..."

"I'm coming, bud," I told him, emotion thick in my voice, as I stepped into the elevator and made my way down to the underground parking lot. "I'll find you. Just...just sit tight and wait for me, okay?"

"Yeah," he whispered. "I'm sorry, Kyle."

"You're fine," I assured him as I cranked the engine and pulled out of the parking lot. "You're gonna be just fine. I'm on my way."

DEREK

I felt like a world class idiot as I sat on the edge of a sidewalk, in a street I should know, but I couldn't remember. I was losing my mind. I couldn't remember why I walked in this direction. I couldn't fucking remember which direction *this direction* was. The only thing that had been on my mind when I left the house this morning, was to get as fast and as far away from that woman as possible.

Jesus Christ. If I wasn't so numb, I'd be worried. I should be worried, but I couldn't feel it. I couldn't feel anything. I looked down at my hands. They were shaking, literally shaking violently, and if I hadn't looked down at them I wouldn't have known.

I pinched the skin over my knuckles hard.

Nothing.

I slammed my fist against my forehead.

Nothing.

Was I in my body anymore? I felt like I had floated out of it and was looking down at this worthless piece of shit, curled up on the side of the road, waiting on his best friend to come and bail him out. *Again.*

My phone started to ring on the ground next to me and it was like I had a ten second delay or something because it took me that amount of time to register the fact that I needed to pick it up and talk.

"Hello," I mumbled.

"Derek, sweetheart, it's mom. Don't hang..." I flinched and hung up. I felt that. Shame. It came in abundance when I thought of my parents. They were worried, but it wasn't enough. It didn't change anything. Fuck.

I registered footsteps approaching a few seconds before a tall figure slumped down on the sidewalk next to me. His arm came around my shoulders and I shuddered.

I started to cry.

KYLE

"Come on, buddy," I said softly as I squeezed Derek's shoulder. "Let me take you home."

"I can't go anywhere," he said in a panicked tone as he tried to push me away. "Kyle, don't…I need to go back. I'm not leaving the hill."

"All right," I crooned as I pulled him to his feet and led him over to the car. "I'll take you back to the hill. I promise…just get in the car for me." It killed me to promise him I'd take him back to the source of his pain, but I knew if I tried to take him anywhere else he'd run.

He slumped in the passenger seat and I watched him from the driver's seat as he tried to fasten his seatbelt. He couldn't. His hands were shaking too badly.

Leaning over, I silently fastened his seatbelt before cranking the engine and willing my own hands to calm the fuck down. I was shredded. I was ripped clean open watching him falling apart. "Thanks, Kyle," he whispered.

"For what, man?" I managed to squeeze out.

"For keeping me alive."

My lungs squeezed so tight in my chest I struggled to breathe. "Always, Derek," I whispered. "Always."

We drove in silence back to Thirteenth Street and I spent every second of the drive plotting. I was going to have to call his parents. He would freak, but I couldn't do this on my own. What if he died? Jesus, what if he fucking died? I would be responsible.

He needed help…He needed help and I couldn't give it to him. I wasn't good enough for this…

Pulling into the driveway of my old house, I braced myself for battle. "Der," I said as I opened the passenger door for him. "I think it's time to call your folks."

"No," he growled as he stormed up the porch steps.

Taking his keys from his hand, I unlocked the front door and led him inside. "I'm calling them, Derek," I said in a stern tone of voice. "I'm sorry, but I can't do this anymore…" My voice broke and I closed my eyes, inhaling slowly in a bid to calm myself. The image of my mother's body, slumped over the steering wheel of our car flooded my mind. I shook my head and focused on my best friend. "I can't watch you do this to yourself." I stared straight into his lifeless green eyes. "I will not be the one who opens this door one morning and finds you dead. I've been there," I whispered. "I won't sit back and wait for you to kill yourself."

DEREK

"I'm not going to kill myself, Kyle," I said quietly as I stepped past him and went into the kitchen. "I wouldn't do that."

He followed me into the kitchen and grabbed my shoulder, swinging me around to face him. "Are you sure about that?" he demanded and I could hear the anguish in his voice. His blue eyes were glassy and I knew I was hurting him. "You've been doing a fucking fantastic job at proving me right so far," he hissed as he ran his hands through his hair in frustration. "Drinking yourself into oblivion. Whoring your body to every piece of skirt who looks twice at you…"

"You're calling me a whore?" I roared, shoving him in the chest hard. He didn't even stagger so I shoved him again. "You're one to talk, Kyle. Just because you've turned into Brad fucking Pitt now, doesn't mean I don't remember your life pre-Angie."

"Brad Pitt?" Kyle shook his head as stepped away around me. "Pre-Angie? What the fuck are you talking about, dumbass?"

"You're a family man now," I snapped as I moved to the kettle and flicked it on. "And I'm happy for you. I am. But don't you dare criticize me for doing the very things you used to do before you met Lee." Shaking my head in disgust, I leaned against the kitchen counter and stared out the window. "I've supported you through thick and thin, Kyle," I growled. "When Frank died. When you had a car accident with Rachel. When your girl lost her baby…When you needed help with Hope…Everything. I've had your back through *everything*. Don't even think about selling me out to my parents now."

"It's not about selling you out. It's about keeping you alive... Goddammit, Derek," Kyle growled as he slammed the door of the refrigerator shut. I swung around to meet his glare. "You think you could buy some fucking milk?" He looked me up and down and winced. "Or maybe some food? You are starving yourself. Don't you look in the goddamn mirror anymore?" he hissed. "Your bones are jutting out...everywhere."

"Sorry mister fucking money bags," I snapped as I poured some water into a mug along with a spoon of instant coffee. "We're not all flush with cash, asshole. We normal folk don't have a spare couple million in our change jar." Handing him a cup of black coffee, I glared at him. "Guess you're gonna have to slum it with me today. It's this or go back to your mansion, trust fund baby." I felt like an asshole the minute the words had slipped out of my mouth.

It was below the belt and I knew it.

Kyle froze, his face remained impassive, but the hurt in his eyes made me want to slam my head against the wall. He clicked his tongue as he stared at me. "Trust fund baby," he mused in a quiet voice–in an eerily quiet voice. He tilted his head to one side and folded his arms over his chest. "You can throw whatever shit you want at me," he said in a soft tone of voice. "Blame me. Take all your goddamn issues out on me. Punch my face in and hate me for everything if it makes you feel better," he said, his voice growing thicker, huskier. "But don't ever call me *that* again."

I shook my head. I was disgusted with myself. "Dude, I'm..."

"You don't have the slightest clue of what it feels like to *slum* it, Derek," Kyle choked out. He was right. I didn't. I didn't know what it felt like because he was carrying me. "You have no clue," was all he said before turning around and walking out of the room. The front door slammed and I sagged against the counter.

Well, I'd done it this time.

I'd pushed away the only friend I had left...The only friend who mattered to me.

Rubbing my hands over my face, I willed myself to calm down and breathe, but it wasn't happening.

I was screwed...

The front door slammed again and Kyle stormed back into

the kitchen. "Goddammit to hell," he roared, kicking the refrigerator door on his way over to where I was standing.

Grabbing me by the shirt, he glared down at me, his eyes full of trepidation. "I won't call them. But if you even think about hurting yourself," he whispered. "I will personally drive you to the closest hospital and sign you in. Is that clear?"

"Clear," I whispered as I shoved his hands away and pushed him back. We both stood frozen, chests heaving, eyes locked on one another, until both of us lunged forward simultaneously and hugged it out quickly.

"You good?" Kyle asked gruffly as he pushed me away and stepped back.

I sighed heavily. "I will be. Are you?"

"I will be," he said with a smirk as he sauntered off in the direction of the living room. "When I kick your ass on FIFA."

"Oh, man," I chuckled as I trailed after him. Kyle couldn't play Xbox to save his life. "Lead the way."

FOURTEEN

LEE

I OFTEN THOUGHT back to the days when I didn't have a cell phone. Those were simpler times. If someone wanted to speak to me they could seek me out, and if I didn't want to speak to them, I could close my front door. I glared at the screen of my phone as it flashed the word *Home* over and over. My heart felt like it was being squeezed inside of my chest. It was almost as if the man could put his fist through the phone and into my rib cage. The fear, even from a phone call, caused my hands to sweat and I held the phone a little tighter for fear of dropping it.

The way I saw it I had two choices. Answer my father and listen to his demands and threats, or ignore him and wait in fear until his patience runs out and he comes looking for me. It was easier to ignore my mother. She wouldn't come for me, not like daddy would.

I knew he would.

There had been an altercation between Kyle and my father when I was in hospital. Kyle told me that he arrived into my hospital room, while I was in theater, drunk as a skunk and slurring abusive threats and demands. Kyle had him sent on his way with a return ticket to Louisiana, but I figured that was more for Tracy's benefit than mine. She didn't want my father to know where she was and Kyle was more than obliging when it came to her…

However, Daddy had returned the day before I was discharged and demanded that I come back home to Montgomery with Hope. When I refused and told him I wasn't leaving Kyle, he had flipped out and accused me of abandoning him. I had quickly figured out he'd read the papers and discovered the vastness of Kyle's wealth. I think daddy always knew Kyle had money, but when we had spoken on the phone I never mentioned anything about his wealth–or the fact that I was having his baby.

Daddy discovered my new family when Kyle had flown him to Colorado to be tested for a kidney. I was pretty ashamed to admit, even to myself, that I was glad I was in a coma and in the safety of a hospital when Kyle dropped that bombshell…

When I refused to go home with him, he had plenty to say on the matter. I couldn't count the number of times he had called me a slut before slapping my face. It wasn't a hard slap, but Kyle happened to walk into the room as it happened and went berserk. I'd never seen him lose control like that. He was spitting and snarling and the speed of his fists had been a blur in my vision. Both of them had ended up being escorted from the hospital grounds.

When Kyle finally coaxed his way back in, four hours later, he had a black eye and a busted lip. Kyle had promised me that daddy was out of our lives. He told me daddy wouldn't be back, but I wasn't that naïve. Kyle had money, *a lot* of money, and my father was an opportunist. He would be back. I had no doubt about it. I could feel trouble brewing and I was quickly learning that things never sailed smoothly for us.

"You gonna answer that, Hun?" Linda asked, startling me from my reverie. Hope and I were sitting in Kyle's office with Linda, having been dragged out of bed at six o' clock in the morning by a very agitated Kyle, and driven to the hotel to 'hang out with' a very unwell looking Linda. Seriously, the woman looked like death warmed up. I actually thought she needed a doctor more than company. Kyle hadn't seemed to notice, but I had. I'd asked her several times in the past few hours if she was feeling okay, but she kept avoiding answering my question so I dropped it. I knew what it felt like when people nagged and I didn't want to make her feel uncomfortable…

Kyle had some important meetings in Denver with his father

and according to Kyle, I distracted him from business... I didn't understand him. Not one bit. I'd been doing well, spending a few hours every day for the past couple of weeks on my own at the house with Hope. I hadn't broken any of his rules and I never went outside. If he didn't want us to be in the house without him then he should have kept us in the hotel. It made no sense…or maybe it made too much sense and I was afraid to delve into the reasons why Kyle was keeping us tucked away. Every time I thought about his possible motives, one name popped into my head.

Rachel…

"No," I mumbled as I sent the call to voicemail before switching it off and forcing my fear to the back of my mind. "It's not important."

"She's getting so big, Lee," Linda cooed as she gazed lovingly at Hope, who was sleeping in her stroller next to my chair. "It's frightening how much she looks like Kyle."

"Yeah," I said as I smiled down at my daughter. "Just as long as she doesn't get his attitude. I don't think I'm ready for a female version of Kyle. Can you imagine trying to make her listen to me when she's a teenager?"

"You have no idea," Linda chuckled as she sat back in her chair. "Boy's like a wrecking ball. You'll have your work cut out for you if she has his pigheadedness. I went gray within the first month of knowing him."

"What was he like when he was younger?" I asked, curious to hear more about Kyle as a teenager. Linda had been the one who'd taken care of him when he moved in with his grandfather. Kyle adored her.

"He was horrible." Linda smiled fondly which was a contradiction to her words. "Rude, hormonal, wild and headstrong. He never listened to a word Frank or I said. A typical moody teenager."

"Wow," I muttered, unsure of what to say. I wasn't like that as a teenager. I wouldn't have dared. Oh god…I glanced nervously down at Hope which caused Linda to laugh.

"Relax, Hun," she laughed. "If she has a tenth of Kyle's determination running through her veins she'll be okay. Why do you think Frank left everything to Kyle?"

"Kyle told me his grandfather left him the hotel chain out of guilt," I mumbled. "You know…because of how his father abandoned him."

"And you believe that?" Linda shook her head and laughed. "Lee, if Frank wanted to stem his guilt he would have given Kyle what he gave Mike. A nice little apartment and a few thousand dollars to start him off in life. Frank left everything to Kyle because he knew Kyle was the best man for the job. Frank wasn't a fool, Lee. He always knew that David didn't have the head for business. His mind has always been focused on spending money, not earning it. Mike didn't have the drive or determination. Kyle had every single quality Frank felt was needed in his successor. He was damn proud of that boy."

I gaped in confusion. "But Kyle said…"

"Kyle says a lot of things," Linda said with a smirk. "A lot of which is bullshit. He sees the world in his own peculiar way. He drums to his own beat. He always has. That's what makes him so successful. He's ruthless and soft-hearted all in one. Do you know in the three years he's been in charge, the annual turnover for sixteen of the hotels has increased by twenty-eight percent? And thirty seven percent for the other four?"

"No," I whispered and I felt like an idiot for not knowing any of this. This was the man I was going to marry and I knew nothing about his professional life.

"He has the same golden touch his grandfather had," she said in a soft tone. "Frank adored Kyle. We both did."

"Were you in love with Frank?" I covered my mouth with my hand in mortification. I shouldn't have asked that, but I'd always been curious. Kyle had told me that Linda and his grandfather had raised him together–that his grandfather had been very fond of his hotel manager. I'd always wondered if they had been romantically involved.

"I was," Linda said with a fond smile. "You're the first person to ask me outright."

"But…he was old," I blurted out. *Jeez, could you be any more blunt, Lee?*

Linda laughed. "Just how young do you think I am?" she asked through a fit of coughing.

"I don't know…" I mumbled as I studied her face. "Forty-eight. Forty-nine?"

"Ah," Linda grinned. "I knew there was a reason I like you, Lee Bennett. I'm sixty four years old."

"Wow," I mumbled. "I hope I look like you when I'm your age." Linda was beautiful. I would have never guessed she was a day over fifty. Well, maybe today I would. She looked…below par.

She grinned at me before folding her arms and resting in the chair. "I first met Frank when I was twenty-five years old." She smiled at nothing in particular as she carried on. "I remember the first time I laid eyes on him I was crushed. He was breathtaking." She smiled knowingly at me. "He was all wild hair, blue eyes and dimples, hot-tempered…so handsome."

I blushed, feeling a little awkward thinking about how *hot* Kyle's grandpa was. I squirmed in my chair and watched as Linda's smile faltered. She sighed heavily. "Frank was a mess when we first met," she said heavily. "He was grieving his wife Lucy, and struggling to deal with their son's erratic behavior while running the hotel. It was just this hotel back then." She leaned forward and stared at me steadily. "And if you think Kyle is hard work, you should have met his father when he was a teenager." She shuddered. "David was impossible. Spoilt, entitled and deliberately cruel. He used to play on the fact that his mother was dead to get what he wanted."

"So, pretty much the same as he is now?" I said with a smirk. I couldn't stand Kyle's father. He was horrible. Even if he hadn't offered me money when I was pregnant to disappear–something I'd never told Kyle–the way he had treated Kyle was enough for me to hate him forever…The man made my skin crawl.

"Pretty much," Linda agreed. "I don't know where he came from. If you had met Frank when he was alive, you'd understand what I mean. He was an incredible person, Lee." Linda smiled dreamily. "The only thing Frank passed down to David was his looks," she confessed. "Sometimes I wonder how David fathered Kyle and Michael. They're nothing like him…thank god for that."

"I beg to differ," I muttered. Mike was just as bad as his father. Derek's face flashed in my mind and I felt like growling. "Mike is a chip off the old block."

"No," Linda said in a stern tone of voice. "No Lee, he's not. He's made a few poor choices, but the boy is good at heart. You're blinded by loyalty. Michael had it hard–nothing compared to Kyle–but growing up with David wasn't exactly a picnic for him," she said. "Kyle had a horrific introduction to life, but I am so incredibly grateful that David didn't raise him. He didn't have a chance to sink his claws into him…David did Kyle a favor by staying away from him."

I didn't have an answer for her.

"Things would be very different for you and Hope if Kyle had been raised by his father, Lee," Linda said softly and I immediately tensed and looked down at my daughter. I knew what she meant. If Kyle had been raised by his father, there was a very high possibility that I would be a single mom right about now…"Although, if Frank had lived he would have loved that little girl," she mused. "His gene pool is still strong," she gushed. "Just look at those blue eyes…"

"Didn't Frank love you back?" I asked in confusion. "How come you never married or lived together?"

Linda smiled sadly. "Yes, in his own way he loved me, but Frank was fiercely loyal to his wife's memory–very much like Kyle is to you. He never loved me the way he loved her." Linda sighed heavily. "I stood faithfully by his side for nearly thirty six years, gave up my dreams of having children of my own, and in all those years he was never truly mine. She was the love of his life and he was the love of mine."

"That's…so sad, Linda," I whispered as I wiped a tear from my cheek. "I'm so sad for you."

"Don't feel sad for me," she said as she reached over and grasped my hand gently. "I had thirty-six wonderful years with the man I loved. He may not have loved me the way I wanted, but he gave me the world, Lee." Her eyes gleamed with mischief as she smiled at me knowingly. "And the sex was out of this world. The man was gifted."

Uh…I barely managed to restrain my hands from covering my ears. "That's very…nice," I mumbled, red-faced and mortified. "Sounds like he was very, uh…generous."

"He was," Linda agreed dreamily. "Except when it came to giving his heart. He only gave it away once, and when his wife died, she took it with her."

"So, she got the best of him," I stated as I tried to make sense of what she was telling me. I was finding it really hard to understand why Linda wasn't bitter. I know I would be. I'd been in her shoes once, when I suffered months of being second best to Rachel. It was one of the most hurtful things I'd ever endured and I couldn't imagine spending the best years of my life feeling that pain. That constant feeling of worthlessness-of not being good enough–it could break a person. It had broken me... "And you..." I looked up at her face and frowned. "What did he give you, Linda–besides a job and a generous sex life?"

She looked down at Hope and smiled. "He gave me Kyle."

"You really love him, don't you?" I said, my voice thick with emotion.

"It's impossible not to love Kyle," Linda chuckled. "You should know that better than anyone, Lee. He has something inside of him, something special. Given the chance, he's gonna show the world what he's made of. The boy's gonna shine. Just you see."

"No wonder Kyle worships you," I whispered, more to myself than to Linda. She was an incredible person and would have been a wonderful mother...No, she was a wonderful mother. She was a mother to Kyle.

Linda stood up slowly, achingly slowly, and moved towards the mini bar in the corner of the room. For a moment I thought she was going to pour herself a drink until she knelt on the floor and pulled a set of keys out of her jacket pocket. "Kyle's a top shelf drinker," she joked as she unlocked the drawer that was embedded in the bottom of the bar. "I doubt he's ever looked close enough to know there's a drawer down here." I watched in fascination as she removed a thick brown folder from the drawer before closing it and locking it.

"What is that?" I asked, my curiosity getting the better of me as I stood up and walked over to her.

"Kyle's life," Linda said. "Or at least his life from the age of twelve." She placed the folder into my hands and smiled. "Take care of this for him, Lee. He doesn't know it exists and he's not ready to handle what's inside yet. Keep it in a safe place until the time comes. You'll know when he's ready. Give it to him then."

"I am so confused right now, Linda," I confessed. "Why are you giving this to me? Why can't you give it to him?"

"He's yours now. This falls on you," she whispered. "There's no more I can do for him." I could have sworn I saw a deep pain in her eyes, but when she blinked it was gone, replaced with her usual crinkled kindness. "Protect him, Lee, and stand by him. He's going to need you."

"What's going on...?" My question was interrupted by the sound of the office door swinging open.

"That fucking man," Kyle hissed as he stormed into the room with his jacket thrown over his arm and his tie hanging loosely around his neck. I leaped in surprise and Linda placed a gentle hand on my arm to calm me. "Linda, you're gonna have to go through that will, word for fucking word. I *cannot* work with him anymore. I can't."

"Calm yourself, Kyle" she chuckled as she winked at me before walking over to my fiancé. I stood with my mouth hanging open, holding god knows what in my hands. What the heck just happened?

"Don't let him antagonize you," she crooned as she patted Kyle's slumped shoulders as he leaned over his desk. "That's what he wants, Kyle. You know this. Your father wants you to screw up. Don't give him the satisfaction."

'He doesn't know it exists and he's not ready to handle what's inside yet.'

With Linda's words of weirdness drumming in my ears, I slipped the folder behind my back before moving over to my daughter's stroller. Kneeling down, I tucked the folder into the basket underneath her seat and covered it with some diapers.

"You okay, princess?" I heard Kyle ask. Peeking up, I nodded and smiled as reassuringly as I could.

I was okay.

I hoped he was, too.

KYLE

"Have you been taking your meds?" I asked Lee as she stepped out of the bathroom. She had to take a tablet every day to make sure her body didn't reject her new kidney. The doctors had also warned us that her skin would burn more easily because of the anti-rejection meds. I'd bought a truck load of sun-cream the day I brought her home from the hospital. I was so nervous about messing this up. It wasn't like making a normal mistake where I had a chance to fix it. This was her life. Any more mistakes could kill her...

"Yes Kyle," she replied, as she swept her hair back from her face before securing it with a hair tie. She was walking slower than her normal snail pace and it was bothering the hell out of me. If she didn't feel well she needed to tell me. I hated feeling powerless and Lee's health made me feel that way. She was so fucking fragile and she didn't even know it. I knew for a fact that was her second shower today and she'd been moving around like an old lady. If she thought she could hide the fact that she was in pain from me with a smile, then she was wrong.

I watched as she climbed onto our bed and crawled over the bed to where I was resting against the headboard. "Kyle, I'm okay," she assured me as she kissed my cheek. "I promise. I'm just tired and Hope is getting heavy. She actually pulled herself along on her belly today. It was just for like two minutes," she gushed as she sighed happily. "But it was amazing."

"You need help," I muttered. Christ, I couldn't turn my back on the woman for a minute. Maybe I should have kept her in the hotel. At least I had staff to do the things she shouldn't be doing. I knew she was upset that I made her stay with Linda when I went to Denver, but I'd needed to be focused when dealing with my father and worrying about whether Lee was okay or not, was something I couldn't afford. I trusted Linda. I trusted the woman with my life. She was the only person I would entrust the safety of my girls to and if she would come with us, I would move her into the house with us this very minute, but the woman was set in her ways.

Knowing the girls were safe with Linda was the only thing that kept me calm during my meeting with David. If I could fire him I would, but I'd be going against my grandfather's wishes. David and Mike were to have employment in the hotel chain for as long as they desired and there wasn't a damn thing I could do about it. The only positive thing was the fact that David was based in our hotel in Denver and I used the hotel in Boulder as my headquarters. I was stuck with Mike working here, but I'd take him any day over his daddy.

David Henderson was a fucking snake. He was watching every move I made, especially since the shooting. I knew he was waiting for me to screw up and I knew he wouldn't think twice about swooping in and trying to take over. There wasn't much he could do with regards to a takeover. I didn't answer the board. I didn't answer to anyone – well, with the exception of Linda. All of this was mine. Solely and completely on my shoulders. But David wanted this particular hotel. There was nineteen others besides this one, and I could relocate him to any one of them, but it wouldn't appease the fucker. Frank had started here. This was where it all began. He'd built his empire from the ground up, and this place had been his pride and joy–his most prized creation. I wasn't a sentimental person, but I guessed that was what was driving David. He wanted the reins of his father's centerpiece. That was the impression I got when he started sprouting shit during our quarterly meeting this morning…I was distracted and he was lurking in the shadows waiting to pounce. I couldn't afford to make a mistake. I couldn't take my eye off the ball. Not around him. *Asshole…*

I'd been expecting a battle when I brought Lee home, but she'd surprised me by being all cuddly and clingy instead. I wasn't complaining. I loved a cuddly, clingy Lee. I'd take that version any day over a silently seething Lee. But, Jesus, I definitely needed someone here to keep an eye on her. I couldn't take her everywhere with me and I didn't want her on her own. Rubbing my face with the palm of my hand, I sat forward and pulled her gently onto my lap. "Is this place too much for you? Is it the stairs? What do you need, princess?"

"Kyle," she said in a firm voice as she cupped my cheek. "I am fine. I'm going to get tired sometimes and yes, there will be days when I will have some pain. But that doesn't mean I'm dying. I need you to relax. And no, I don't need help, okay?" She focused her stare on me. "I'm doing better. I'm getting stronger."

I heard what she was saying, but my fear was overruling her logic. "You heard the doctor," I muttered. "No heavy lifting or strenuous activity for six months."

"And I'm not," Lee coaxed as she stroked my chest with her hand. "I haven't been doing any of those things. Calm down. I unpacked a few cases and bathed our daughter. Nothing hardcore I swear."

"No contact sports." I listed off another rule as my brain went into overdrive.

"You forgot to add no babies for the first year," she said sarcastically, as she used her fingers to list off each rule. "Which isn't likely since I only have one tube and haven't had a period in a year," she muttered before adding, "or no breastfeeding." I flinched with guilt.

All your fault asshole…

"Princess…"

"Take my temperature daily," she growled, adding another finger as she climbed off my lap. "Weigh myself daily. Take a weekly urine sample. Maintain a healthy diet. Have a low salt intake." She stared meaningfully at me. "Do you want to scare us both to death by going on and on about something we can't change?"

"No," I mumbled awkwardly.

"Then stop worrying about something we can't change," she said as she climbed under the covers. "You are going to give yourself high blood pressure."

"Check blood pressure…" I blurted out before wisely shutting my mouth.

Lee rolled her eyes at me before turning on her side–away from me. "Stop talking, Kyle," she said with a sigh.

After a few minutes of me keeping my mouth shut, Lee rolled onto her back and grinned up at me. "Wow, you actually listened to me," she teased. "I'm shocked."

"I have been known to listen on occasions," I smirked. "But you might wanna memorize this moment because it probably won't happen too often."

"Oh no," she squealed as she sat up quickly. "I forgot the turkey, Kyle."

What the hell…"The turkey for what?" I asked her, confused as fuck. *Talk about a conversation turner…*

"For thanksgiving tomorrow," she said quietly, eyes wide and lonesome. Her brows furrowed for a moment, her expression pensive and I knew she was thinking about thanksgiving last year… God, I was such an asshole to her. She'd been pregnant with the twins–neither of us had known–and sick all day. She'd stayed in her room all day and every time I'd worked up the nerve to go upstairs and talk to her, she'd been locked inside that god-awful bathroom, vomiting her heart out. Jesus, thinking back to those days made me feel sick. The suffering she'd endured…Even now, a year later, I was still mad as hell at myself for not recognizing the signs. "Did you forget it was tomorrow, too?" she asked in a soft tone as she looked down at me.

"No baby, I remembered," I said in a gruff tone. I knew thanksgiving was tomorrow and I also knew that we had an unlucky streak when it came to the holidays. The way I was feeling right now, all I wanted to do was boycott every damn occasion and wrap her up in my arms. "Screw the turkey," I told her. "And forget about Thanksgiving. Let's do it during Halloween and pretend it's just another day."

Lee worried her lip as she looked up at me with wide gray eyes. "You're sure you don't mind?"

"Positive," I murmured as I settled down on my back and pulled her on top of me so that we were chest to chest. "So, did you have fun with Linda?" I sighed heavily and stroked her back. "I know you're pissed that I dragged you out of bed so early, but I can't concentrate worth a damn when I'm not with you."

"Yeah…" Lee frowned for a moment and chewed on her lip. I was instantly suspicious.

"What happened?" I asked. "You know something, don't you?"

Her eyes widened to the point that I thought they would fall out of her head. "How do you do that?" she demanded.

"Do what?" I asked with a smirk. "Know when you're hiding shit from me?" She nodded eagerly and I burst out laughing. She was so innocent. "You do realize that you've just admitted you're hiding something from me?"

Her brow furrowed for a moment before her lips curled up in a smug little grin. "That's blatant trickery," she teased as she sat up and straddled my hips. "Do you want to hear a little bedtime story, Kyle?"

Fuck, I didn't want to hear a story. I wanted her to keep wiggling.

"It's really juicy," she purred as she rocked back and forth on my junk. *Jesus…*

She beamed down at me and I shook my head in amusement. "What did you do, princess?"

"Not me," she sniggered. "It's something your grandfather did." She frowned for a moment before smiling. "Well, it's more like *who* he did."

"Uh," I groaned. "Sweet Jesus, no, of course I don't wanna know who my grandfather did." Especially since I had a fair idea of *who* she was talking about. I'd walked in on a 'moment' between the pair when I was fourteen. I tried to keep the image locked in a box in the darkest fucking corner of my mind. No way was I opening that can of worms…

"He was with Linda," she blurted out with a laugh, clearly enjoying my discomfort. "For years, Kyle. They were a couple…" she whispered as she waggled her eyebrows. "Sexually."

"Ahhh," I shouted, closing my eyes. My brain was screaming *'la la la.'* "Please stop, princess. I can't hear this shit."

"What's wrong, Kyle?" Lee purred as she stroked my chest. "Old people have sex, too."

"Lee," I warned, all notions of fun-time fading fast as my dick went into hiding.

"Sexual Intercourse, Kyle," she squealed. "Your grandpa and Linda, doing it…maybe even on your desk."

"Fuck," I groaned as I sat up and tossed her off my lap. "You really know how to ruin the mood, don't you?"

She flopped onto her back and cackled. "Your face," she laughed. "Oh god, your face was priceless." Her shirt rode up as she squirmed on the bed laughing, revealing the lace white panties she had on, and my dick perked up once again.

"You wanna talk about sex," I grinned as I leaned over her. "You wanna make me squirm?"

She nodded her head as she grinned up at me. "Correction. I made you squirm."

"Funny," I purred, as I sat back on my heels and grabbed the edges of her panties. "Well, I should probably return the favor then, shouldn't I?" Her eyes widened as I dragged her panties down her legs before pushing her thighs apart.

"I'm sorry," she breathed, eyes wide and cheeks pink.

I grinned and shook my head slowly. "No you're not," I teased as I settled between her legs. "But you will be."

LEE

"Sorry about this, baby," Kyle mumbled, as he pulled on a pair of gray sweats and grabbed a hoodie from the dresser drawer. Kyle received a frantic phone call from Marcus about twenty minutes ago, who had demanded he come straight to the hotel. "I know it's late, but he's freaking the fuck out."

"Its fine," I coaxed as I sat on our bed and watched him dress quickly. "What's his problem anyway?"

"Fuck if I know, baby," he grumbled as he slipped his feet into his sneakers and knelt to tie his laces. I grinned in amusement as I took in Kyle's attire. I'd never seen him wear sweats to work before, but he looked so stressed that I decided not to comment on the fact. "Someone called in sick or something," he growled as he stood up and stretched his arms over his head. "And he can't find anyone to cover." Stalking over to where I was sitting, he bent down, grabbed my neck and kissed me deeply. "Stay inside," he whispered against my lips. "Don't answer…"

"The door," I finished for him and gently pushed him away with a smile. "I know. I won't." He looked at me longingly for a moment before nodding and rushing out of our bedroom.

As soon as the door was closed, I climbed off the bed and dropped to my knees. Pulling the folder Linda had given me out from under the bed, I sat on my heels and rubbed my fingers over the paper. I shouldn't look at this…Should I?

I glanced nervously at the door and then down at my hands. What if there was something in this that I wasn't supposed to see? What if I read something and *had* to tell Kyle? Linda said he wasn't ready for what was inside of this. I looked down at Hope, who was sitting on the floor next to me, and got the distinct impression that she was frowning at me.

She *was* frowning.

God, even my baby knew I was doing the wrong thing.

I slid my finger under the opening and paused. No, this was wrong. I would be betraying Linda. She trusted me to take care of this for Kyle. It wasn't my privilege to go snooping in his private things. I should respect that. I shouldn't read it.

It wasn't mine to read…

Climbing to my feet, I held the folder to my chest and walked over to my chest of drawers. Tucking the folder into a drawer, I covered it with some underwear and forced myself to step away from it. I would not open it. I would do the right thing.

I would wait.

FIFTEEN

LEE

"SO, what the hell does that mean for us?" Kyle asked, his tone agitated, his posture frantic. His knees were bobbing, his hands were drumming on the desk in front of us and if he didn't calm down soon, I was going to ask the doctor for a tranquilizer–for Kyle. We were sitting in Dr. Michael's office, receiving the results of my last kidney biopsy test and I was growing agitated. I hadn't gotten a word in edgeways with Kyle–and neither had Dr. Michaels. "Is this good or bad? In lay-man's terms," Kyle continued, not one bit mindful of the fact that it was *my* body he was talking about. He had already embarrassed the hell out of me, threatening to surgically remove Dr. Bromwick's…nether regions if he so much as looked in my direction again. Dr. Michael had spent twenty long – and painfully boring – minutes reassuring Kyle that he would be the only doctor to treat me from now on.

"Calm down," I hissed as I pressed my palm on his knee to stop him from shaking. "Let the man speak." Good grief, his anxiety levels must be through the roof…

Kyle looked down at me, his expression apologetic. "Sorry baby," he murmured, covering my hand with his. His fingers threaded through mine and he gave my hand a little squeeze. "Go ahead, doc," Kyle said, as he took a deep breath. "Lay it on me." Dr. Michaels smirked at both of us and I rolled my eyes in exasperation.

'Lay it on me…'

"The results of your biopsy are positive," the doctor told us. I sagged in relief and Kyle groaned–literally groaned like the doctor had just removed an unbearably painful stick from his butt. He stopped fidgeting and actually sat still to listen to the doctor. "Everything looks good. No signs of infection or obstructions." He gazed down at his notes before looking at me. "Unfortunately, there is still no sign of reversal in the right kidney, but it's very early days. Have you menstruated this month, Lee?" Dr. Michaels asked and the blood drained from my face as the fidgeting coming from the big ape beside me started up again.

"No," I whispered, feeling acutely embarrassed at having this conversation with two men. "Nothing has happened in over a year," I added, red-faced.

Dr. Michaels frowned for a moment before masking his features and smiling once again. "Well, you're very young," he said in a kind voice. "Plenty time for things to correct themselves," he paused before adding in a much softer tone, "I can refer you to a specialist if that's what you wish, a doctor who specializes in fertility, but I'm not overly concerned for now. I feel time is the best healer for that particular issue."

"No, no," I mumbled as I clasped my trembling hands together. "I'd rather not, doctor." The thought alone made me want to crawl under the desk in front of me and cower.

"What about sex?" Kyle blurted out and I thought I was going to die on the spot. My eyes darted to Hope, who was sitting in her stroller next to my chair wide awake. I had a moment where I contemplated reaching over and covering her ears.

"Your daddy has a problem with his mouth, Hope," I mumbled, trying to change the topic at hand as I stared down at Hope in embarrassment. "He doesn't know when to keep it shut." Hope's eyes fixed on mine and I cringed. I hoped like hell she wouldn't remember this. For all I knew Kyle could be scarring our daughter for life. I heard things like this really affected kids. She was seven months old, but she was smart. Oh no…

"Can we fuck? Is it safe or does she need more time?" he asked deadpan. Oh sweet Jesus, did he just ask the doctor about *fucking*? Oh my god. I sent a small prayer up to baby Jesus and begged him to retract Kyle's powers of speech for the duration of this appointment.

"Kyle," I growled, my face flamed with embarrassment. "For the love of god, stop talking."

Dr. Michaels grinned at us and I secretly questioned my religion when Kyle continued rambling with no shame. "Shh baby, we're all adults here," he said, patting my knee.

I stiffened and inclined my head towards Hope. "No, we're not..."

"Hope doesn't understand," Kyle snorted, dismissing me. "We've been having sex with..." his voice trailed off as he looked down at his fingers for a moment. "About nine weeks," he continued, staring at the doctor in earnest. "Nothing hardcore... mostly missionary..." He paused for a brief moment before adding, "Some nights Lee goes on top, too, but I wasn't sure if it's okay. Is there a certain position we're supposed to be doing? I don't wanna break her, doc."

"God," I muttered and covered my face with my hands. I made a mental note to *never* allow him to come with me *ever* again for the rest of our lives. I wasn't sure if I could ever look Dr. Michael in the eyes again.

"Mr. Carter," the doctor chuckled as he folded his arms over his chest and gazed at us in amusement. "I can assure you that you won't 'break' her."

Ahhh. I couldn't hear this. My eyes flicked towards the exit and Kyle clamped a strong hand down on my denim clad thigh, clearly reading where my thoughts were going before smirking down at me. "You're an adult," he mouthed as his lips curled up in an annoyingly sexy way.

"You're an asshole," I mouthed back at him which caused both men to laugh.

"You two are quite comical," the doctor joked, his smile falling when he noticed my glare. Clearing his throat, he assumed the usual doctor tone when he said, "Intercourse is perfectly safe, Mr. Carter. It's been almost five months since Lee's surgery. You're both young and a healthy sexual relationship can be quite beneficial..." He cleared his throat and dropped his gaze to his file once again before glancing up at me with a look of concern. "You haven't been taking the contraceptive pill, have you?"

"What?" My eyes widened, my face mirroring his look of concern. "No, why? Am I supposed to?" I wasn't on anything because I didn't need anything. The doctors had told me as much when they confirmed what I already knew. I was broken.

"Absolutely not," Dr. Michaels said in a relieved tone. "I've had a few female patients over the years who have shown signs of relapse. Studies have shown the ethinylestradiol in the contraceptive pill significantly reduces the function of the particular anti-rejection medication you've been prescribed."

"Oh," I mumbled, not having the slightest clue of what he'd just said to me. "Well, it's not a major concern for us, is it?" Dr. Michaels looked at me baffled and I sighed. "I'm not ovulating," I clarified.

"No," he said sadly. "The tests you were given before you were discharged from hospital verify that. Gynecology is not my specialized field, but like I said earlier, things can change, Lee."

"What the fuck is that supposed to mean?" Kyle interrupted and I wanted to gag him. Most of the time I liked the fact that he spoke his mind, but in certain circumstances the man needed to put a filter on his tongue. Leaning forward, he rested his elbows on the desk and concentrated on Dr. Michaels face. "Are you saying she can get pregnant again?"

"Kyle," I begged as I rubbed my brow. "Please stop. You know I can't."

"Who said you can't?" he countered, eyes locked on mine. "No one told me," he growled, answering his own question before turning his gaze back to the doctor. "Things can change how, doc?"

"Well," Dr. Michaels said as he stretched and relaxed in his chair. "At the moment, the chances of Lee conceiving naturally are slim to none, but once her body starts to ovulate regularly, and perhaps with some I.V.F treatment, there may be a possibility she could conceive and carry a pregnancy to full term."

"How long could it take?" Kyle asked quietly. "Are we talking months?"

"Months, maybe years, and quite possibly never," Dr. Michaels replied before adding, "The trauma to her body was substantial. Making an accurate call on your chances of conceiving again would be unprofessional on my behalf. I don't want to give you false hope."

"You're not," I interrupted quickly and Kyle swung around to face me. His questions were causing all kinds of red flags to fly up in my brain. "We're not having another baby, Dr. Michael," I said quietly, keeping my eyes locked on Kyle's. "So this conversation is pointless."

Kyle held my gaze for many moments, giving nothing away, until his lips tipped up in a smile. "We could have fun trying, baby." I paled, Dr. Michaels laughed and Kyle's grin widened. "I do enjoy a challenge, princess," he teased.

He was joking.

He better be joking…

"You're supposed to be a professional," I snapped, turning to glare at my doctor who was cackling in his chair like a schoolboy. "It's not funny and you shouldn't encourage him." I glanced at Kyle's smug, self-satisfied face. "He's cocky enough."

"I apologize, Lee," Dr. Michaels choked out before snickering. "If it helps, you could consider it as part of your physiotherapy..."

"I'm leaving," I growled, leaping out of my chair, grabbing the handles of Hope's stroller. He was a middle-aged doctor. A freaking specialist and he laughing and joking like a teenager with my overgrown fiancé. "You two are disgraceful."

Kyle burst out laughing, clearly enjoying the joke, as he rose from his chair and shook Dr. Michael's hand. "See you in three months doc," he said, pleased as punch with himself.

"Princess," Kyle choked out through fits of laughter as he followed me into the parking lot of the hospital. "Slow down, will you?"

"No," I snapped. The car lit up as I approached and I opened the back door. "You humiliated me back there. I have never been so embarrassed in my life, Kyle."

"You're over-reacting," he chuckled as he moved in front of me. "He's a doctor, Lee. They hear all types of shit daily."

I glared at the back of Kyle's head as he strapped Hope into her car seat. "You said *fuck* to the doctor," I hissed and then shuddered in mortification. "Kyle, you told him we *fuck*." I felt like howling in frustration as I stole a peek at Kyle and saw he was laughing at me.

"We do," he said in an innocent tone of voice as he tried to stifle a chuckle. "And I think he figured it out when he saw our daughter."

"You jackass. We do not f..."

Straightening his back, he turned around and snared me with a broad, dimpled smile. "I'm good, baby, but I'm not that good. I need to get in your pants in order to reproduce. So yeah, we have fucked, we do fuck and I can guarantee you that we will fuck..."

"Oh yeah?" I huffed, butting him out of the way so I could tighten Hope's restraints. Kyle had an awful habit of leaving them way too loose. He was afraid she would squash. I was afraid she would slip out if we had to brake. "Well, you can be rest assured that the only pants you'll be getting into from now on will be your own."

His hands grabbed my hips, pulling me backwards into his arms. He stretched an arm out in front of me and closed Hope's door gently before turning me in his arms and backing me up against the car. "On a scale of one to ten," he purred. "How mad are you right now?"

"Eleven," I muttered in a petulant tone. "Couldn't you have said lovemaking, or intercourse or...sleeping together?"

"You're serious, aren't you?" he said in a confused tone of voice. "You're really embarrassed about this?"

"Yeah Kyle, I am," I told him, straight faced. "I don't like our private affairs discussed. Especially not *that*."

"But you talk dirty when we..."

"That's different," I snapped, my face reddening. "That's when we're alone and in private – which won't be happening any time in the near future."

Kyle tried to keep a straight face, but failed epically. "Don't you like it when we...make love?" he sniggered. "I'm sorry, princess, but I hate that term...It's not me." He shook his head and smiled tenderly, his blue eyes locked on mine, snaring me, softening me. His hand came up to cup my cheek and my skin tingled from that small fragment of contact. "Just because I say I fuck you, doesn't mean I don't make love to you," he confessed softly. "Because I do. Every single time."

"And what the hell was with all the questions?" I asked, as I tried to hold onto my outrage–which was fading fast. The damn man had a way of influencing me with his words–and his mouth, which was currently teasing my earlobe. "You need to think before you speak, Kyle..." I didn't get a chance to finish what I was saying because Kyle's mouth covered mine. He nibbled on my lower lip, his tongue probing me softly, looking for access and I was lost.

Every nerve in my body came to life when his tongue slipped inside my mouth, massaging mine with slow skillful thrusts, causing the hairs on the back of my neck to rise, and the muscles in my pelvis to clench. I sagged against the car, reveling in the feel of his body flush against mine, his mouth possessing mine.

Kyle pressed one last spine-tingling peck to my lips before stepping back and brushing his thumb over my lower lip. I opened my eyes, feeling dazed and highly aroused.

"So, have I cheered you up?" Kyle asked, his eyes alight with humor. "Or do I need to take you home and make sweet, *discreet* love to you?"

"Jerk," I growled as I pushed him away and opened my car door. He had to ruin it...

"Cranky," he countered with a snort as he rounded the car and opened his door. "You know princess..." He grinned at me from across the hood. "I could always penetrate you."

"Don't push me, Carter," I grumbled.

Kyle raised a brow in challenge. "Don't tempt me, princess."

KYLE

I wasn't sure if Lee was actually pissed with me, or just trying to be. She sat stiffly in her seat the whole drive back to the hotel, but every now and then–when she thought I wasn't watching–she peeked at the side of my face and chewed on her lip. Yeah, I was fairly confident I was getting some tonight. I had the green light from Dr. Michaels…Things were looking up for us.

Pulling into my parking spot, I couldn't keep the smile from my face. "Stop," Lee said with a smile.

"Stop what?" I asked as I unfastened my seatbelt and climbed out. I was hoping Lee wouldn't notice I hadn't packed the monkey, but of course, the minute we unpacked the last box of our stuff the other day, she looked for King-Kong. I'd tried to persuade her to leave him behind, but she was determined to get him back. *Stupid fucking gorilla…*

"Stop grinning like that," she replied. "It's contagious."

"Good," I chuckled as I lifted Hope out and snuggled her to my chest. She yawned widely, giving me a good look into her mouth. "Oh angel," I crooned as I turned her in my arms to get a better look. "You have another tooth coming up." I looked down at Lee and frowned. "Should they be coming so fast? She's only seven months old."

"Apparently it's fine," she said in an anxious tone as she tugged on my arm until I lowered Hope enough for Lee to see. "She's such a good baby," she murmured as she stroked Hope's little curls and then her face. "She's good with pain."

Hope stretched her little chubby arms out for her mom and my heart inflated as I watched my woman hold my daughter. She was convinced she couldn't get pregnant and I was secretly determined to prove her wrong. I knew there was a possibility it wouldn't happen for us again and I had my own theory on the matter: fuck science. She was going to be my wife. I was going to make babies with her. She still had one tube and I had strong swimmers...

"I fucking love you, Lee Bennett," I whispered in my head. "Put me out of my misery…"

"Hmm?" Lee looked up at me with a perplexed expression. "Did you say something?"

"Nothing important, baby," I said, as I wrapped my arm around her shoulder and led her to the elevator.

"What the hell are you doing in here?" I demanded the second my eyes fell on my father. He was lounging on our couch, in our goddamn suite, without a care in the world.

"Well, hello to you, too, son," he said in his usual condescending tone of voice. He inclined his head to where Lee was standing, looking extremely baffled, holding Hope tightly in her arms. "How's the little family?"

"I'm not your son," I snarled, taking a step closer to the couch.

"Kyle," Lee said in a soft tone. "Calm down. Hope can hear you."

The knowledge sobered me and I lowered my tone. "What do you want, David?"

"Oh, you know," he waffled as he tossed a hand aimlessly in the air. "To check in. See how you three were doing. I heard you moved out. Bought a place in the mountains. How are you settling in?"

"I'm going to put Hope down for a nap," Lee mumbled as she hurried off in the direction of our old bedroom.

The minute the bedroom door closed, I was moving towards him. "Up," I hissed. "Get the fuck out of here."

"Kyle," David said in a weary tone. "For once can we not argue, and at least try to have a civil conversation?"

"I'm sorry," I spat, my tone sarcastic. "My civility went out the window around the same time I realized I had your fucked up genes in my body. So yeah, about eleven years ago."

"Will you just get over it," David said in a reprimanding tone. "Move on. I'd like to put the past behind us." His eyes flicked to our bedroom door. "I've been making some…changes and I would like the opportunity to have a relationship with my grandchild."

"Get over what exactly?" I whispered. "Get over the death of my mother? Or the almost ten years I spent being shipped around the state, living out of a fucking duffel bag? As for a relationship with my daughter: are you serious?" I shook my head and walked over to the door of our suite. "There's nothing here for you, David. Go."

"Listen," he placated, holding his hands up in defense. "I'm trying here. I am trying to make amends."

"You're twenty-three years too late to play daddy with me." I tilted my head in the direction of the doorway. "And breaking into my suite sure as hell isn't the way to affirm my sentimental side."

"I assumed having a child of your own would incite you to grow up and lose that chip you carry on your shoulder," he hissed. "But I see you're still the same hot-tempered little shit who stood on my doorstep…"

"Please leave, Mr. Henderson." My head swung around and my eyes nearly fell out of my head as I watched Lee stride towards where I was standing. Slipping her hand into mine, she stroked her thumb over my knuckles soothingly as she fixed her steady gaze on my father. "I want you to leave. Now."

"Delia Bennett." David smiled at Lee and it freaked the hell out of me. *Uh…* "Good to see you on your feet again," he said, not unkindly. "How's your mother?" Lee paled and David's grin widened. "Hope she's back on her feet. Big surgery you both had."

Lee blanched "How do you…"

"How do I know about your surgery?" David smiled knowingly. "Or how do I know about your mother's surgery?"

Lee didn't respond, but it was obvious she was wondering about the latter. It was the same question I was wondering about. I'd managed to keep Lee's mom out of the papers. It helped that she had changed her name from Delia Bennett to

Tracy Gibbons. The reporters hadn't made the connection...how the hell had he?

"Well, you were front page news for quite some time," he chuckled. "And I happened to visit you–on several occasions. We all did."

"What's your point, David?" I growled. Trouble and pain. That's all that man brought with him. I knew what his game was and I didn't need his assistance in driving a wedge between myself and Lee. I was more than capable of fucking things up all on my own.

"You didn't tell her, did you?" David asked me before focusing on Lee. "Both Michael and Anna visited you every day for a month." He shook his head in distaste. "But your overprotective boyfriend wouldn't allow anyone to see you...with the exception of the Porter boy."

"Why would you visit me?" Lee asked, her eyes focused on David. "The last time we spoke, you made it clear how you felt."

"What are you talking about?" I asked, bristling with anger. "When did you two talk?"

"When I was pregnant with Hope," Lee said coldly as she pointed a finger directly at my father. "When he tried to pay me off."

"Did he now?" I snarled. My mind reverted to the day my father arrived in my office, talking shit and trying to give me advice. *'One day you'll find yourself looking at your biggest regret. Like I am now,'* he'd said to me. The anger that was building in my body roared to the surface.

"I was trying to protect you, Kyle," David argued. "That's all. Obviously, I know now that I was wrong." Standing up slowly, he checked the time on his watch before smiling at us. "Well, I seem to have overstayed my welcome." He brushed past me as he stepped into the hallway. "Think about what I said. Talk soon, son."

LEE

In the hour since David's departure, Kyle's mood had switched from frustrated to livid. He bundled us into his car and drove us back to the house in an unnerving silence before stalking off the minute we stepped foot inside the front door. I wasn't sure what to say to him. I wasn't sure there was anything I could say to calm him down. He was terrifying when his mood darkened to this degree. So instead of a confrontation, or pointless coaxing on my behalf, I left him alone in his office and set about feeding and bathing Hope, before settling her down for the night.

When she was asleep, I refolded the laundry I had already folded this morning, and then I checked on the folder Linda had given me. It was exactly where I had left it–at the bottom of my underwear drawer, covered with bras and panties. Another hour passed and I knew I had to face him.

"Are you okay?" I asked quietly as I stood in the doorway of his home office, fingers braced on the door knob, ready to bolt.

Kyle, who was stalking around the room like a mad man, froze and spun around to face me. I watched his whole body stiffen as he clenched his eyes shut. His hair was sticking up in forty different directions, and when he finally did open his eyes and look at me, I was stunned at the wild, untamed fury staring back at me. "I hate him Lee," he whispered softly as he sank down on his black leather chair, resting his elbows on his legs and his head in his hands. "I fucking hate him, baby."

"Me, too," I told him as I cautiously moved towards him.

Kyle looked up at me with a lost expression. "Why now?" he asked, his voice barely more than a whisper. "Why is he doing this to me now?"

"Kyle..." I rushed towards him and climbed onto his lap. "Don't let him get to you," I whispered as I wrapped my arms around his neck. "He's not worth worrying about. He is a very bad man."

His arms wrapped around me so tightly I could barely breathe, but I didn't dare move. He needed the grounding and I needed the feel of him. "I can't..." He stopped and inhaled deeply, his breath hot against my neck. "I lose control around him, Lee," he admitted. "I fucking hate that he can do that to me, and I hate myself for giving him the power to do it."

"It's okay to lose control, Kyle," I told him as I clung to his strong body. "I spend most of my life not in control."

I felt him smile against my neck. "Yeah princess, you may not be in control sometimes, but you still have your self-control..." He shuddered and squeezed me tightly. "Mine just...snaps."

His words sent chills through my body and turned the blood in my veins to ice. I had lived with a man who had the very same problem...but this was Kyle. He would never hurt anyone.

'Mine just snaps.'

My heart vehemently squashed those red-flags.

"I love you," I whispered because, quite frankly, there wasn't anything else I could say. I could hardly deny he was hot-tempered. Whether it was right or wrong, the blistering fierceness Kyle possessed–the virile intensity that emanated from him–was a terrifyingly addictive enticement.

"I know you do," he whispered. "It's what keeps me sane."

"Kyle," I said as I pushed back so I could look at his face. "There's a difference between being in control and being in charge."

"I'm not following you, princess," he said as he frowned at me. I wasn't sure I was following myself, but the words had popped into my head and I was desperate to comfort him.

"You don't have to live your life being in control of everything," I said as gently as I could as I tried to verbalize what I meant. "Being in charge of something is just as effective. It just means that you can step back a little. Give yourself a little breathing space and be okay with it if things don't go to plan.

Life is unpredictable. You can't plan, plot and execute everything. Life is full of uncontrollable elements. Take charge of yourself and accept that it is enough. Let David Henderson, and whoever else that upsets you, go to hell. You can't change them, so why waste your energy on trying."

"Lee." He shuddered and tightened his grip on me. "It's not that easy," he admitted. "He gets under my skin. I'm so fucking angry right now. My body is literally burning with rage."

"Come on," I said, covering my anxiety with an upbeat tone of voice, as I climbed off his lap and crossed the room. I needed to get his mind off his father fast and I knew just the trick. "Let's go check out that hot-tub."

Kyle's whole frame relaxed immediately and I felt like sagging in relief. "So, I'm forgiven for earlier, am I?" he asked sheepishly as he stood up slowly and prowled towards me.

I'd forgive him for just about anything right now. I needed him to be happy. It crushed me to see him so lost. I hated David Henderson for doing this to him. For making my self-assured man feel so damaged. "That depends," I teased, feeling more relaxed now that I could see he was relaxing.

"Oh yeah?" Kyle grinned as he stalked towards me. "On what?"

"On how many times you can make it up to me," I said boldly as I pulled my t-shirt over my head and threw it at him before stepping out of his reach and unsnapping the front clasp of my bra. "If I remember correctly, you said you like a challenge..." Opening my jeans, I slowly peeled down the zip and exposed the front of my black lace panties. "Think you can take me on, tough guy?"

Kyle growled and it was a deep, guttural sound. "You wanna play, princess?" he asked as his eyes roamed over my body before landing on my flushed face.

He smirked and stepped towards me. I backed up again and shook my head playfully. "You'll have to be faster than that to catch me, Carter," I taunted, as I shimmied out of my jeans and used my toe to fling them towards him. He caught my jeans mid-air and tilted his head to one side in amusement. "Maybe I'm too fast for you," I added.

His eyes darkened and my heart hammered against my ribcage in anticipation. What had started as a distraction technique had backfired in the most delicious way. I was so turned on I was practically panting. "You're teasing me?" he purred. I practically drooled when he pulled his t-shirt off–that really sexy way men do when they grab the piece of fabric behind their neck and yank it over their head–before dropping his shirt to the floor and his fingers to his belt buckle. "You better run, baby."

"Make me," I breathed. The muscles in his stomach rippled as he stalked towards me and I was a goner…

The sound of Kyle's hushed whispers woke me from my first nightmare-free sleep in what felt like forever. Stretching lazily, I blinked my eyes open and sighed in contentment. My bones felt like jelly from our earlier antics in the hot-tub and I'd never felt more sated…more rested. I was actually kind of proud of myself and my female powers of persuasion. I'd talked Kyle down. I'd calmed him down. I'd brought him back to me…

"I'm on my way," I heard him whisper seconds before he threw the covers off himself and climbed out of bed.

I rolled onto my back and stared up at him. "What's wrong?" I asked quietly. "Who was that?" Kyle turned his face away from me, not looking me in the eye. "Kyle," I said nervously as I sat up and watched him dress quickly. Fear filled me. "What's going on?"

"Will you be okay if I head out for a little while, baby?" he asked me as he grabbed his keys off the bedside table. "There's a problem at the hotel."

Liar. "What kind of problem?" I asked in a flat tone of voice. I knew by the guilty expression he wore on his face, as he stood at the side of our bed looking down at me, he was lying. It was the same expression he used to wear early on in our relationship – right before he lied to me.

"Nothing for you to worry about," he muttered, staring at a point on the headboard next to my face. "Will you be okay here?"

If I thought it would make him stay I would scream *no*. There was little point in that though. He would either wait until I was asleep and sneak out then, or have Linda come over and sit with me.

Either way, I lost.

Either way he was going to run after her.

There was no emergency at the hotel.

He was going to see my mother.

"Yes," I replied while my mind was screaming 'bastard.' The betrayal I felt was heady–suffocating. After everything he'd been through with David…I backed him up. I freaking stood by him. And when I needed his support he wouldn't give it. How could he justify this? It wasn't fair. He was breaking my heart.

"I'll be back before you know it." He leaned down and kissed my forehead before rushing out the room.

I sat in a state of shock and disgust as my mind tossed up every horrific moment of my life. Everything she could have stopped. She did nothing. She left me on my own with *him*. And now, after everything we'd been through today, he was leaving me for *her*. On my own. In the middle of nowhere. Frantic fear settled inside of me. What if David showed up? What if daddy showed up? What if Rachel broke out and came looking for me… My mind knew I was overreacting, but my survival instincts were on code red…

It's dark. It is pitch black and I have no clue of how to protect us. What if someone breaks in? It's not like the hotel. No one is here. No one will hear me...

I waited until I heard the front door slam before climbing out of bed and rushing down the hallway to Hope's bedroom. Slipping inside, I locked the bedroom door and, as quietly as I could, I dragged the rocking chair over to fit behind the door. Hope snored softly in her crib, not even stirring from the soft scraping noise of the timber chair being dragged over the wooden floor. I didn't have a blanket so I grabbed one of the huge stuffed animals from her shelf and used it to keep warm as I settled down on the chair. I kept my eyes on the window directly in front of me.

I needed to be prepared.

I wasn't going to be anyone's victim again.

KYLE

I hit every red light on the way to Tracy's house and by the time I arrived it had been over an hour since her call. Unlocking the little wooden gate at the entrance to her garden, I walked up the path and knocked on the front door.

"Who is it?" I heard her ask from behind the door and I rolled my eyes. She knew I was coming.

"It's Santa," I muttered, rolling my eyes. "Let me in." The sound of a deadbolt sliding and numerous other clanging noises broke the silence. The door opened about a foot inwards and I slipped through the gap. "You know," I mused. "I'm gonna have to lose weight if you expect me to fit through here again."

"I'm sorry," Tracy mumbled as she held her cheeks in her hands. "I have to be cautious."

Tracy's hair, so similar to Lee's, was shooting out in all directions and I felt my heart squeeze. Everything about the woman made me want to tuck her away and keep her safe. She had such a horrific life. She'd suffered both physical and mental abuse at the hands of Lee's father. He'd broken Tracy down until she'd cracked and left–without Lee. She had redeemed herself in my eyes when saved my girl's life and she was still being punished for something that I was fully convinced was Jimmy Bennett's entire fault.

The thought of Lee standing up to my father flooded my conscience and I immediately batted it away. This was different. Tracy was a good person. David was scum…

"I think he's back, Kyle," she blurted out. "I think Jimmy is back in Colorado and I think he knows I'm here."

I sighed heavily. *This shit just kept getting better.* "He's not here, Tracy," I told her firmly. "Let's just calm down for a second and tell me why you think that." Walking into the kitchen, I switched on the light, grabbed the kettle and filled it with water before switching it on. I needed a truck load of coffee in order to deal with this calmly.

I knew for a fact Jimmy wasn't in Colorado. The fucker was back home in Louisiana living it up with my goddamn money and with any hope drinking himself to death...

"I saw him," Tracy whispered. "At least I think I saw him…"

"Okay," I said calmly as I turned around to face her. "Let's see if you're right." She was wrong, but telling her that wouldn't go down well and I wasn't in the mood to chase her flighty ass around the city. There was only one way I could convince her she was safe.

Leaning against the countertop behind me, I pulled my phone out of my pocket and dialed his home number before putting my phone on loudspeaker. I focused on her face while we both listened to the phone ringing.

"Who's there?" Jimmy's slurred southern drawl filled the room. I raised my brow at Tracy and turned the screen around so she could see it was his home phone number I was calling. She sagged in relief and covered her mouth with her hands as if she was afraid to make a sound. "You got nothing to say to me?" he demanded.

"Hang up," Tracy mouthed as she shook her head, eyes wide and fearful.

"Is that you, Delia?" he growled and Tracy whimpered loudly. Jimmy laughed roughly having clearly heard Tracy's startled cry. "What's wrong, darling?" he sneered. "City boy kicked you to the curb already? You wanna come crawling home to…"

"It's me, asshole," I snarled, taking my phone off the loudspeaker before putting it to my ear. "And the only person who will be crawling is you if you step foot in Boulder again." Tracy's eyes were bulging and fixated on my face in what looked like adoration. I turned around, feeling uncomfortable with being gawked at.

"Don't threaten me, boy," Jimmy said menacingly. "I've been

keeping to my side of my deal...although I could use a little top-up."

"You won't get another penny from me," I hissed. "Be fucking grateful you got anything in the first place."

"Is twenty grand all she's worth to you?" Jimmy taunted. "Then again, I can't really blame you. She's used goods. Why buy the cow if you can get the milk for free, isn't that the saying, boy?"

"Are you for fucking real?" I roared as I ran my hand through my hair before yanking on it in a bid to keep my free hand busy and stop myself from breaking something. As it stood I was fairly certain I'd cracked the cover of my phone. "That's your daughter you're talking about. What the hell is wrong with you?"

"Pity she doesn't remember that," he mused. "Spent eighteen damn years raising that little bitch and how does she repay me?" he snarled. "By running off to the city and getting herself knocked up, that's how. You know, she ain't gonna stay with you," he growled. "She'll be back. Girl's as dumb as a stack of bricks," he laughed. "All I gotta do is snap my fingers and she'll come running, boy…" My phone was pulled out of my hand before I had a chance to respond.

Ending the call, Tracy placed my phone on the counter before patting me on the shoulder. "You were right," she said in a soft tone. "Don't listen to his poison. It won't do any good."

I inhaled a few deep breaths before I found my voice. "I need to go." Jimmy's words were swarming my mind. I needed to check on Lee. I shouldn't have come here in the first place. I shouldn't have left her on her own.

"My daughter is a very lucky woman," was all she replied.

Our bed was empty.

Our bed was fucking empty and I couldn't find her. Jesus Christ. "Lee?" I called out as I rushed out of our room and into the hallway. "*Princess*?"

I heard the sound of furniture scraping and then the sound of a key unlocking before Hope's bedroom door opened and Lee peeked her head around the door. "Keep it down," she growled when her eyes met mine. I felt like collapsing on the floor in relief. I watched her as she crept out of Hope's room and closed the door quietly before walking straight past me, into our room.

"What were you doing?" I asked as I trailed after her.

"Sleeping," she snapped as she threw back the covers and climbed into bed. "What were *you* doing? And don't lie to me, Kyle."

"I was…" Shit, how was I going to explain this to her without upsetting her… "Your mother called me," I confessed. "She was worried."

"Make a list, Kyle," Lee hissed as she curled into a ball on her side.

"A list?" I shook my head in confusion as I shrugged off my clothes and climbed into bed beside her. When I tried to wrap my arm around her she flinched and batted my arm away with her elbow. "A shit list?" I asked feeling totally fucking confused.

"No," she whispered as she wiggled further away from me. "A list of priorities. But yeah, as far as shit lists go, you're topping mine."

"Nothing new there then." I sighed as I rolled onto my back. "And I happen to have my priorities in order, Lee."

"Are you sure about that?" she snapped as she sat up straight and rolled the sleeves of my long-sleeved t-shirt up to her elbows. "You lock me away in the hotel for weeks," she hissed. "Frighten me half to death about the dangers of being on my own, only to move us into a house in the middle of nowhere and leave me on my own at night to chase after…that woman. You know how I feel about her, Kyle."

I flinched. It sounded fucking terrible when she said it like that. "Princess…"

"Do you want my list of priorities, Kyle?" she asked as she stared down at me, her gray eyes full of hurt. "It consists of two people." She turned her face away and stared straight ahead. "You and Hope, Kyle," she whispered. "That's my list."

"That's my list, too, Lee," I said quietly. "But your mom…she's had a very hard life."

"Shut up, Kyle," Lee hissed and the venom in her tone stunned me. "I hate that woman. I hate her. You hate your father. Well, I hate *her*." Her voice broke and she sprang out of bed, clutching her back. I moved to follow her, but the look of hatred in Lee's eyes nailed me to the bed. "And I don't care what you think of me for feeling like that," she added as she flinched and clutched her side. "I was starved. Locked up and beaten with more objects than I can bear to remember," she cried, tears streaming down her face. "I was slapped for speaking, kicked for breathing too heavily, burned with irons and pokers..."

"Stop," I choked out as I covered my face with my hands.

"No," she screamed. "You wanted me to tell you, so here it is." She inhaled deeply and wiped her eyes with the back of her hands before glaring at me. "When I was six years old, I came down with a stomach bug." She backed up until she was pressing against the wall and then she lowered herself to the floor. "I was so sick..." she whispered. "And instead of having a mom, I had him," she spat. "Do you k-know what he d-did to me when I vomited in the sink instead of the toilet ..." Her voice cracked as she held the sides of her face and stared into nothing. "He filled the sink and held my face under the water and vomit until I passed out..."

"Lee," I begged. "Please, I can't hear this, baby. It fucking rips me open..."

"Well, join the club," she hissed as she stalked back to our bed and wrapped herself under the covers. "Because you are ripping my heart open every time you speak to her. How would you feel if I went running to David..."

"It's not the same," I snapped. "It is a totally different situation, Lee."

"To you maybe," she whispered. "But not to me."

DEREK

I spotted the maternity Merc pull into the driveway and groaned. I didn't want to get involved in their drama. And I just knew there was drama. It seemed to walk hand in hand with those two…

Besides, I had enough problems of my own. One very big problem I had was sitting on the couch right now, grinning at me like I was a good person. If he knew what I'd done he wouldn't be smiling at me. He'd be handing my ass to me.

"So," Danny grinned as he took a swig of his beer. "Is it cool if I crash here for the night?"

"Uh…" *No. No. Hell fucking no…*"Sure," I mumbled. "But I have to run it by Kyle first. It's his house."

The front door slammed and Kyle's voice rang through my ears. "She's driving me fucking crazy," he snarled as he stormed into the living room. "I swear to god, Der, I am going to lose my …" His voice trailed off as his eyes landed on Danny. "Who the hell are you?" Kyle asked in confusion.

Nice dude, way to be diplomatic…

"Kyle," I said with a sigh. "This is Danny, my *friend* from Addyston I was telling you about."

Kyle's eyes widened as he looked back and forth between the two of us. A slow smile crept across his face and I tensed. "Hey," he grinned as he stepped forward. "Sorry about the abruptness. Derek's told me a lot about you, man. Told me you guys were *close* growing up?"

"I've heard a lot about you, too, man," Danny said in a friendly tone as he stood and shook Kyle's outstretched hand. "Nice place you've got here."

"Yeah," Kyle replied. "Some people think so." His eyes flickered to me and I shook my head. "So, Danny…" Kyle said with a smirk as he sank down on the couch and propped his feet up on the coffee table. "Got any sisters?"

Bastard.

KYLE

My mood considerably lightened the moment I'd walked through the front door in the house on Thirteenth Street and realized Derek had bigger problems than me.

"Dad said to say hey, Der," Danny chuckled as he slid his phone into his back pocket and took a slug of his beer. "I swear that man loves you more than he loves me."

Ha fucking ha…

Derek squirmed in his seat and I had to bite down on my fist to stop myself from laughing out loud. Derek glared at me. "So, Kyle," he said with a smirk. "How's Lee doing? Made her cry lately?" He turned to look at Danny and waggled his brow. "Woman troubles."

Asshole.

If he knew just how bad my woman troubles were I doubt he'd make jokes. Lee wasn't speaking to me over her mom and I was growing agitated. The silent treatment was wearing me down and I'd come here to offload, but obviously, Derek was in one of his moods…

Danny laughed and slapped my knee. "Let her loose, Kyle," he chuckled. "That's my motto. You gotta throw the clingy ones back into the pond. Plenty more fish and all that…"

"And here's my motto." I turned my face to glare at the imp's stupid fucking face. Who the hell did this guy think he was? Jesus, my bad mood was back with a vengeance. "Don't talk about something you have no understanding of."

"Ooh," Danny smirked. "Hit a nerve, have I?" He shook his head and chuckled. "Girl must have you sunk like a stone. Who is she? The mother of your kid or something?"

"Yeah," I said through clenched teeth. "As a matter of fact she is."

The smirk fell from his face. "Dude," he muttered. "Sorry. I respect the hell out of that. Good for you. Fucking hate seeing women being screwed over by assholes who don't man up."

I reasonably relaxed and nodded. Danny had just saved himself from a guaranteed fist in the face. "Yeah, me, too." There wasn't a hope in hell I would ever be one of those guys. I was the son of one of those guys…

"Girl or boy?" Danny asked with a genuine mile.

I couldn't stop the smile from creeping across my face. "Girl," I told him as I pulled my wallet out of my pocket. "Hope. She's seven months old." Flicking it open, I pulled out a small photo and handed it to him.

"Cute stage," he said knowingly as he dropped his gaze to the photo. "Holy shit…she's beautiful." He looked up at me and then back down at the photo. "Seriously man, she's gorgeous."

"Thanks," I grinned, pride swelling inside of me. Hope was gorgeous. "And she's really advanced. She's started crawling a little and sleeps through the night."

"No," Danny muttered. "The kid's adorable, but I was talking about her." He pointed to Lee's face and I stiffened. "I can see why you're sunk. Holy hell, I have a semi from looking at her." He looked over at Derek and glared. "You've been living it up here, haven't you, jackass? Never thought to tell your oldest friend you had *her* living in your house for a year?"

Derek lunged for me and tackled me to the floor before I had a chance to take a good swing at the creep. "Calm down," Derek said slowly.

Danny laughed. "Hey Kyle, do you share around here?" He waved the photo in the air. 'Cause unless you have a wedding ring on her finger she's fair game."

"I'm gonna kill you," I roared as I glowered at Danny, who was still ogling my fucking woman. "Get the fuck off me, douchebag." I tried to buck Derek off, but the fucker was sitting on my chest with my hands locked under his legs.

"Are you stupid?" Derek hissed as he glared at Danny's smug face. "She's the mother of his child."

"What?" Danny asked innocently.

Yep, I hated him.

I fucking hated him already.

I was going to tear his throat out.

"You should take it as a compliment, Kyle," he smirked as he stood up and stretched slowly. "Not too many women have that effect on me. She looks damn fine for a woman who has a baby."

"Get out," Derek shouted. "Or I'm gonna personally kick your ass."

"Fine," Danny mused as he dropped the photo on the couch before sauntering over to the door. "Catch you later, Derek." He grinned down at me. "Kyle, tell your baby momma I said hi…"

"Out," Derek roared.

The front door slammed and Derek stared down at me. "You cool?" he asked as he slapped my cheeks with his hands, not hard, but enough to make me want to draw blood. "You good?" I nodded my head and he sat back and sighed.

Swinging my legs up. I wrapped them around his neck and dragged him backwards before climbing on top of him. "Yeah, I'm good, asshole," I growled, bitch slapping his cheeks. "But if I ever see that prick again and you try to stop me, I'm gonna take you out. Got it?"

"Yeah," Derek panted as I helped him to his feet.

"God, I hope you got his sister good," I snarled.

"Three times," Derek said with a smirk.

I clapped him on the back. "Nice dude."

He nodded his head. "Thanks man."

SIXTEEN

DEREK

I WAS A LIAR AND APPARENTLY, a mighty fine one at that. I'd mastered my new skill to a fine art. I could look my best friend in the eye, lie right to his face and not even flinch. "How are you doing, man?" Kyle asked me as he lifted Hope out of her crib, in the pinkest room I'd ever stepped foot inside. *No, it's not…*

"Nice room, dude," I said from the doorway gesturing at all the pink – and mentally blocking out the image of her face from my mind. "This is yours?" They'd moved in weeks ago and I'd finally dragged my ass out of bed to check it out.

"Funny," Kyle grumbled as he placed Hope on her changing table and unbuttoned her onesie.

"Don't hide behind Hope," I joked. "We both know about that pink feather boa in your old room. What was that chick's name again? Mia…Tia?"

"Fuck if I can remember." Kyle shook his head before adding, "And keep your voice down. I'm already in the dog house."

I shook my head and glared at him. "What did you do now?"

"Pass me that blue tube of cream from her diaper bag will you?" he asked, ignoring my question. "I think she's cutting another tooth. Her butt's a little red."

"Who are you?" Shaking my head, I passed him the cream.

"Good girl," he crooned as he pinned on the sticky tags of her fresh diaper before dressing her in an outfit I presumed had been laid out by Lee. If not, he needed to get his masculinity reevaluated.

"If the hotel business ever fails you'd make a killing as a nanny," I told him. "I can see it now. Carter's Crèche. Butt cream extraordinaire."

"Wait until it's your turn, douchebag," he retorted as he picked up his baby. "You'll see."

I followed Kyle into the lounge and stopped dead in my tracks and let out a whistle. "Oh man," I whispered. "She's beautiful."

Kyle grinned as he sat Hope into her baby-walker and turned on some cartoons. "Sixty inches of pure pleasure, complete with the latest Xbox just waiting to entertain you…if you move in that is…"

He was a manipulative son of a bitch. Shaking my head, I forced my eyes away from the most beautiful television I'd ever seen and sank my ass down on the most uncomfortable couch in the history of cream leather furnishings. "So, how are you doing, man?" he asked, taking the armchair opposite me.

Fiddling with my thumbs, I concentrated on *not* looking at the photo frame sitting in the middle of the fireplace. "Great," I replied, adding a little enthusiasm into my voice. "I'm doing really well, dude. Much better." See, I was a fucking fantastic liar.

Kyle fixed his blue eyes on me for a moment before grinning. "Good," he sighed in relief. "I was worried how you were handling…"

"It's all good," I said, interrupting him. I couldn't talk about it, not to Kyle. "How's Lee doing?" I asked tactfully, veering the conversation away from me. "You said you were in the dog house?" Kyle's face did that stupid glazed over gaze before he sighed and rubbed his face with his hands. "What did you do?" I asked, my tone laced with disgust. He'd screwed up. I knew it and by the look of it he knew it, too. "Tell me you didn't…"

"Don't start," Kyle grumbled. I watched him mutter something incoherent before standing quickly and stalking out of the room. I rolled my eyes and followed after him. He stood frozen at the kitchen door. "Brace yourself," he muttered, eyes locked on Lee, who was sitting on a stool at their kitchen island, with her head in her hands. "I fucked up the other night. Went to see her mom. This could get ugly."

"Jesus Kyle," I groaned. "You're amazing at fucking things up. You should take it up as a sport. You'd be guaranteed a gold medal." Pushing past him, I strolled over to where Lee was sitting and perched myself on the stool beside her. "How are you doing, ice?"

Lee's head snapped up and she looked at me with the biggest smile. A real, honest to god, I'm-happy-to-see-you, megawatt smile that touched something deep down in my heart. I couldn't remember the last time someone had smiled at me like that. Like they were happy to see me…It felt strange. "Hey you," she said as her big gray eyes searched mine. "Have you changed your mind? Are you coming home?"

"Nah. I'm enjoying my own company." I had to turn my face away. She was too perceptive. She saw right through my bullshit the same way she saw through Kyle's. I didn't know what it was about that girl–maybe it was the purity that bounced off of her–but it made it too hard to lie to her. You just couldn't. "So, how are you doing?" I mumbled as I stirred some sugar into the cup of coffee Kyle had placed in front of me.

"I'm doing," she replied quietly.

"Did you think about meeting Tracy?" Kyle asked. Lee glared at him and I personally wanted to kick him in the balls.

Fucking idiot.

"Kyle," she said in a warning tone and I knew the shit was about to hit the fan. "Let it go." She hopped down from the stool and stormed into the lounge.

I stood up quickly. I was getting my ass out of the line of fire. The last time I'd been around them during one of their arguments, I'd gotten an apple in the balls. Shit, for all I knew Lee had neutered me. "Keep pushing and she'll run," I muttered before leaving quickly.

LEE

"Just go to work, Kyle," I said wearily. I was close to breaking point. I needed to stop this conversation. It was the same one we'd been having for three freaking days. He didn't get it, and refused to see my point of view. The man had zero empathy and if he didn't back the hell off this was going to end badly. "I really don't want to have this same argument with you over and over. I've told you how I feel...I have explained to you. You need to respect that. Respect my choices. Respect me."

"You think I don't respect you?" He asked in a disgusted tone of voice as he stalked towards me. Grabbing my elbow, he led me back into the kitchen before closing the door behind us. A small part of my mind appreciated the fact that he was caring enough not to let Hope see us like this. "Where the hell did you get that notion from?" he hissed. "If I didn't respect you, do you think I'd be standing here listening to this?" He shook his head. "Hell no. I would have put your ass in my car and driven you to Denver months ago."

"Don't you dare threaten me." I knew he wasn't being serious. I knew it was an empty threat. But the thought of being physically forced to do something–even by Kyle–made me sick to my stomach. "Don't even joke about it."

Regret flickered in his eyes and he ran his hand through his untamed hair. "Princess..."

"Just trust my choices and stop trying to force me into doing what you want," I hissed as I shook his hand off my elbow. "I don't force you to do anything you don't want to do, so stop trying to force me. I'm a grown woman, Kyle. I have my own mind."

He released me immediately and ran his hands through his hair. "She's your mother, princess."

"Oh my god." I threw my hands in the air. "I can't talk to you." He didn't get it. Stepping around him, I moved towards the door. I needed to remove myself from this situation before I said something I'd regret.

"Dammit, will you just hear me out," Kyle growled as he pushed past me to block the doorway. He towered over me. His height and muscular build intimidated me. But there was no way in hell I was backing down on this one. I squared my shoulders and forced my eyes to meet his. "Don't even think about running, princess," he warned me. "There's nowhere you can hide that I won't find you."

"Nice choice of words, asshat," I growled even though my heart was in my mouth. "Do you plan to bully me for the rest of our lives, or only when I don't do what you want me to do?"

"Not if you stop behaving like a spoiled little brat for two damn minutes and fucking listen to me," he tossed back at me.

His words took the air out of my lungs. I felt physically winded. "Spoiled brat." I whispered. "Good to know that's what you really think of me."

Kyle hissed in frustration. He threw his hands in the air. "You know I didn't mean that...Fuck, you ruin my thought process." He was breathing hard as he pinched the bridge of his nose. I wanted to pinch his nose. I wanted to pull his stupid nose right off his face.

"And you are ruining our relationship," I snarled.

"I'm doing this for you, Lee," he growled, eyes full of hurt. "Every damn thing I do is for you… to make you happy."

"You're making me miserable," I spat. "And be honest, Kyle, the only person you're doing this for is yourself. If you're so damn desperate to have a '*mommy*' you don't need to use me as your excuse to play happy families. Take my one. She's flighty and probably won't stick around for more than five minutes. But hey, she's all yours."

I regretted the words the moment they slipped out of my mouth. The look of disgust on his face tore me. "Kyle…" I started to say, but he held his hand up and shook his head.

I didn't need to walk out.

Kyle beat me to it.

KYLE

I was regretting getting out of bed this morning. If Marcus hadn't called me–about some stupid emergency I was yet to be briefed on–I would still be at home trying to talk some sense into Lee. Jesus Christ, what she'd said hit a nerve. Worse than a nerve... She'd severed a damn artery with those words. I never spoke much about my mom to anyone besides her and she'd thrown it in my face.

Pacing the length of my office, I attempted to calm myself down. Calmness wasn't coming though. I was too riled up.

'If you're so damn desperate to have a 'mommy' you don't need to use me as your excuse to play happy families. Take my one.'

I knew she didn't mean it. I'd seen the regret in her eyes. If I'd stayed I had no doubt she would have apologized. It didn't matter much though. The fact that she'd thought it and said it out loud was enough. It was out there now. It was between us. She thought I was substituting my dead mother with hers...

My phone vibrated in my pocket. Sliding it out, I glanced at the screen and quickly sent the call to voicemail. That was the seventh time Lee had called in the past hour. Ignoring her was a shitty thing to do, but I couldn't deal with her right now. She was fragile and I was furious. Bad fucking combination. I needed to cool down first.

The door of my office swung open.

"She's called in sick again, Mr. Carter," Marcus, my weekend manager complained, as he came and sat in the chair in front of my desk. Scrolling through his iPad, Marcus continued to ramble like a lunatic. "I'm going to have to bring in a temp to help run this place. She's not dependable. I'm down two waitresses in the front bar and I can't man the desk while I'm doing double my workload."

"Who?" I asked, not one bit interested in what he was rambling on about.

"Linda," Marcus growled and he had my full attention immediately. "This is the eighth sick day she's taken this month, Mr. Carter," he grumbled. "Christmas is only around the damn corner and I'm sinking in paperwork."

I wasn't bothered about Linda taking time off. She could have as much time as she wanted. God knows, the woman had done enough for me. She could have whatever the hell she wanted. But I was worried. She was never sick. I couldn't think of a single day in the past eleven years where I'd seen her come down with anything worse than a cold. I hadn't phoned her in a few weeks. I'd been too self-absorbed with my own life…

Shit.

"Who were you thinking of?" I asked, stretching my legs out under my desk. I couldn't concentrate. I was agitated as hell. I was worried…

"I think you should promote Mike to temporary manager." That got my attention. Marcus looked at me with nervous eyes and wiped his brow. He was in his late forties and a loyal employee hired by my grandfather. I respected the man but he was pushing my buttons today. "I know there's some tension between you two, but he knows this place inside out. I can't think of anyone more suitable. It will take weeks to find, hire and train someone new."

He got that fucking right. Tension was an understatement. "No," I snapped. I felt sorry for Mike over the whole Cam thing, but I wasn't naïve enough to trust him…He could be playing me. It could all be a game… "No way. Find someone else."

"Fine," Marcus muttered. "But I'm gonna need you here until I can get someone else. Linda has been flaking on her duties and things have been slipping for a while."

*

hadn't realized the place had gone to shit so much. Walking around the hotel I was stunned to realize that Marcus was right. The damn bar was understaffed. There was only one waitress on the restaurant floor with thirty tables full with customers and, like he'd said, the front desk was empty.

Shit.

Pulling my phone out, I dialed Linda's number. She answered on the fifth ring. "Hey kiddo." Damn, she really did sound sick.

"What's wrong with you," I asked in a quiet tone as anxiety clawed at my gut. "You're never sick."

"I'm sixty-four years old, Kyle," she chuckled, but her voice was weak and raspy. "I'm getting old. I'm gonna get sick sometimes."

"What's wrong with you?" I repeated as I rubbed my brow. "Tell me Linda." The line went quiet and I knew it was bad. Fuck. I knew it. Something was wrong.

"Just an infection I can't seem to shake off," she finally said in a placating tone of voice.

"Bullshit," I growled as I ran my free hand through my hair. "You're lying to me. I can hear it in your voice."

"Don't be so dramatic, Kyle," she warned before coughing. "You'll give yourself wrinkles with all your damn worrying. I'm fine. But I'm gonna need some more time off."

"You know you don't have to ask me for that," I whispered. She was lying. Something wasn't right. This was bad. I fucking knew it. "Can I come see you?"

"Not today," she said quickly. Too quickly. "I'm going away for a couple of days. I need rest and recuperation. I'm gonna go visit my sister Patty for the weekend. You remember Patty, don't you? The lady who used to tease you for that Mohawk phase you went through."

"Yeah," I sighed. "I remember Patty." I couldn't forget her if I tried. The woman was bat shit crazy. "Don't try and change the subject."

"I'm not," she assured me. "You're overthinking things."

"What am I gonna do around here?" I mumbled.

"You're going to have Michael do my job until I'm back to

work," she said before adding, "Calm your temper, Kyle." I bit down on my lip in an attempt to keep my mouth shut. She knew me too well. "He's the right person for the job," she coaxed. "And to be honest, the boy's been a mess since the shooting. Help your brother. Be the bigger man Kyle, and make me proud."

LEE

I was a horrible human being. My brain was like a broken record, playing out every nasty word I'd said to Kyle this morning until I felt I would burst if I didn't apologize to him. The anxiety building inside of me quadrupled when he sent my calls to voice-mail–all seven of them.

I was sitting on the floor in the lounge watching Hope bounce in her jumperoo when the intercom for the front gate alarm starting buzzing. My first reaction was to crouch low to the floor until my lungs filled and my heart returned to its normal rhythm, which was a bad move since it gave my daughter ample opportunity to grab a fistful of my hair.

Freeing my hair from her chubby little fingers, I climbed to my feet and went into the hall only to stare in dismay at the keypad. "Which button did daddy tell momma to push, Hope?" I mumbled as my eyes roamed over the dozen or so buttons–all identical–all flashing.

Taking a gamble I pressed the one on the bottom of the keypad. The noise stopped and I sagged in relief, until I realized I hadn't checked who I was buzzing in. Dammit…

Rushing into the lounge to look out the bay window, I sighed in both relief and disgust when the familiar silver Lexus pulled up in front of the house.

"Oh boy, Hope." I muttered as I watched David Henderson climb out of the driver's side door and stare up at the house. "Daddy's gonna be mad."

David shook his head slightly as he tucked his hands into his tailored slacks. He was a handsome looking man–an older looking version of Kyle, but I didn't trust him. There was something very wrong about that man...

He was a jackass.

The passenger door opened next and out stepped his wife Anna. Anna Henderson was a different story altogether. The woman had a kind nature, the same kindness I'd seen in Mike–before he went and screwed Derek over. After I discovered Mike and Cam's affair I'd decided Mike had more of his father in him. Kyle never said much about Anna and I'd only met her a handful of times, but I liked her. She'd visited me in the hospital when I had Hope, and a couple of times before I was shot…

"Wish me luck, baby girl," I murmured to Hope. Sliding my phone out of my pocket, I sent Kyle a quick text before making my way to the door.

KYLE

"You wanted to see me?" Mike said as he stood in the doorway of my office.

"Yeah," I said, trying my best not to growl. "Come in." I was going against every instinct in my body. Red flags were shooting up in my brain as I fought the very strong urge to stick my foot up my half-brother's ass.

"I'm promoting you," I told him reluctantly. "It's Linda's idea," I added in a petulant tone.

"I won't let you down," he mumbled and I shook my head in confusion.

"You haven't even heard what job I'm promoting you to," I snapped.

"I don't need to," Mike said in a weary tone as he leaned against the doorframe of my office door. "I won't be letting you down again, Kyle."

Shit…I leaned back in my chair and studied his face for several minutes before coming to the conclusion that Mike wasn't faking this. The guy was…desolate. Standing up, I slowly made my way over to where he was leaning against the door. He looked up at me with the loneliest expression and my chest ached. "I'm taking a huge leap of faith with you," I told him. "Don't make me regret this, Mike."

"I won't," he replied, his voice full of honesty.

Shaking my head, I ran my hand through my hair and chuckled in disbelief. "What the hell am I doing?" I smirked at

Mike's nervous expression. "I'm fucking promoting my enemy…I may as well stick a knife through my own back."

"I'm not your enemy, Kyle," Mike said in a firm tone, straightening his back. "Don't confuse me with him."

"You screwed me over before," I shot back as the memory of Rachel and Mike flooded my mind, followed swiftly by the image of him and Lee…

"Rachel was mine before she was yours," he stated calmly. "You just didn't know it."

"No," I admitted reluctantly. He was telling the truth…"No, I didn't know she was yours, but Lee was mine and you knew it."

"Actually, I didn't," he countered. I raised my brow and he met my stare head on, unflinching. "I didn't know you were with Lee until the day you showed up at the hotel and tried to drag her off. I had lunch with her every day for months before I realized she was yours. She never mentioned you."

"You didn't back off," I retorted, feeling relieved that we were finally getting all of this out in the open, and even more relieved that we were managing to do it civilly.

"She needed a friend," Mike shot back. "She was pregnant with your baby. I'm a lot of things, Kyle, but I'm not *that*. She was pregnant with my niece…Besides, you never had a thing to worry about. With anyone. No one else stood a chance in hell with her. She only ever saw you." He shrugged his shoulders and leveled his gaze on me. "Pity you didn't treat her better in the beginning."

"Pity you didn't inherit this place and have Rachel blackmail you instead," I snapped.

"I don't want this place," he said softly. "I never have, and I thank my lucky stars grandpa left it all to you." I blanched at his response and was about to ask him what he meant, when my phone vibrated in my pocket. Glancing down at the screen, I froze when I read Lee's message.

Your dad is here.

Goddammit.

LEE

"Thank you, Lee," Anna said with a smile, as I placed a cup of coffee on the table in front of her. "Your home is beautiful." I loved her voice. I hadn't met many British people. When Anna spoke it was a novelty for me. "Hope has grown so much." She continued to bounce my daughter on her knee. I secretly hoped she wouldn't bounce her too much. Hope had just eaten lunch and Anna's clothes were designer. "Is she sleeping through the night yet?"

"Thank you," I said, returning her smile. "And yes, actually. She's been sleeping through since she was eight weeks old."

"She is the image of Kyle," Anna cooed as she gazed at Hope. "You're just like your daddy, aren't you, little one?" I didn't miss the snort that came from David.

"Can I get you something to eat or drink, Mr. Henderson?" I said through clenched teeth. What I really wanted to ask was why he was here. He wasn't fooling me with his *'I want to make amends with Kyle'* crap. He was a liar and the man made my skin crawl.

He turned around slowly from where he'd been standing looking out the kitchen window. "No," he said with a tight smile. "I've lost my appetite, Delia." I wished Kyle would hurry up and respond to my text. He needed to come home. That man gave me the creeps. "How's your father?" David asked with a smirk. "Have you spoken to him lately?"

His question caught me completely unaware. "Uh...." The front door slammed and I almost leapt out of my skin.

"Where is he?" The sound of Kyle's deep voice was like music to my ears. He was angry, but I didn't care about that. He was here. Angry or not, I needed him.

"We're in here," I called out. Kyle walked into the kitchen and I paled when I saw his expression. His jaw was strained, his eyes wild and completely focused on his dad. Oh god, he wasn't just angry. He was livid.

"Hello Kyle," Anna said in a nervous tone. Kyle swung around to look at her and I thought his eyeballs were going to pop out of his head.

Storming past me, he stalked towards Anna, swept Hope out of her arms without a word, before turning and fixing his glare on his father. "Out," he hissed. "Now."

"Kyle, your father wants to make it up to you..." Anna started to say but quickly closed her mouth when Kyle swung his head around and glared at her.

"Come on, darling," David said in a weary tone as he held his hand out for his wife. "He's a lost cause. Not one compassionate bone in his body."

"Now, wait just a damn minute..." I started to say, but Kyle interrupted me.

"That's right," Kyle snarled. "Not a single one." With that, he silently handed me our daughter before walking into the hallway and opening the front door. "You're not welcome here. Either of you. Get the fuck out."

"You need to grow up, Kyle," David said with a smirk as he guided Anna out of the house. "This 'poor me' act is getting old."

"Eat shit, asshole," Kyle countered. "Is that grown up enough for you?" He didn't give David a chance to reply. Instead, he slammed the front door shut.

"You do that on purpose, princess?" he asked in a quiet tone of voice, eyes locked on mine in pure fury. "You let him in here to teach me a lesson?"

"What?" I shook my head in confusion. "N-no, of course not," I stuttered. "He just showed up."

Kyle gave me one long hard glance and nodded his head. "I need to go out for a while," he said before turning around and opening the door.

The sound of the front door slamming was all the proof I needed.

I was in deep trouble.

Kyle was in a horrible mood when he came home. He barely spared me a passing glance as he stormed through the kitchen with his phone welded to his ear. A few moments later the sound of the back door slamming drummed in my ears. I deserved his silence. I'd been a bitch to him. The things I said to him this morning made me feel sick with guilt. I wasn't sure whether I should follow him out there so I could apologize, or give him space to calm down.

Deciding on the latter, I bathed Hope and changed her into her jammies. Tucking her bottle into my back pocket, I struggled up the staircase with her in my arms. These steps were a killer on my back and I was aching by the time I reached her bedroom. Slipping her bottle out of my pocket, I settled into the rocking chair by her bedroom window and started to feed her.

"Love you," I whispered as I kissed her brow. "Love you so much."

I watched as her eyelids fluttered and her breathing slowed. If I could hold her like this forever I would. The love I felt for her was so overwhelming. I never wanted her to be exposed to this cruel world. She'd always have me. I would always protect her.

KYLE

"Don't give me that crap, Patty. I know something's wrong with her." Linda's sister was as stubborn as she was. Jesus, trying to get information from her was like pulling teeth. I'd gone to Linda's apartment as soon as I'd gotten my sneaky fuck of a father out of my goddamn house. Linda worked fast. By the time I got to her place she was gone. "Put her on the phone," I demanded.

"Kyle," she sighed. "I've told you this three times. It's not my place to tell you anything. It's up to Linda and right now she's busy. Has she ever lied to you before?"

"No," I muttered reluctantly. Linda had always been honest with me which was why I was so irritated. Why the hell was I being kept in the dark? "I'm not being nosey. I'm worried, dammit."

"She has her own family to worry about her," Patty said in a kind tone of voice, but I got her meaning. I got it loud and fucking clear. Her own family. I wasn't included in that statement.

"Fine. If she needs me she knows where I am," I whispered before ending the call. They could try and block me out all they wanted, but I'd be damned if I was letting this go. I was not going to be kept in the dark. No fucking way. Dropping my phone on the wooden deck, I gripped my hair and fought the urge to roar. Jesus.

"Are you okay?"

I swung around from where I was standing on the deck to see Lee hovering in the doorway. "I'm sorry, I wasn't listening on purpose," she mumbled. "I could hear you from inside. I can go away if you want me to. I just need to apologize to you first."

Shaking my head, I let my shoulders sag. The sight of her in front of me–still with me–was enough to drain the tension from my body. "Come here," I said in a gruff tone.

She walked straight into my arms. "I'm sorry, Kyle," she whispered. "I didn't mean what I said."

Jesus, I needed her right now. I needed her to ground me. I was fucking electricity and she was my earth. Lifting her chin so I could see her face, I whispered, "The only place I want you to be is with me. And the only place I want to be is moving inside you."

LEE

Something was bothering him.

He was hurting. I knew he was. I could see it in his eyes when he was tearing the clothes from my body. I could feel it in the almost frantic way he crushed his body against mine. "What's wrong?" I murmured against his lips. Kyle didn't answer me as he carried me from the kitchen to the hallway. My back slammed against the back of the door as he crushed his lips to mine. His fingers dug into my hips as he filled my mouth with hot swipes of his tongue. Every nerve in my body was alive and tingling. My back was aching, but the throbbing in my core needed the attention much more.

"Jesus," he groaned as he dropped his mouth to my breasts. "The fucking taste of you. Even the taste of you drives me insane."

I pressed myself into his touch. "Oh god…don't stop." I needed him everywhere. His teeth grazed my nipple and I had to bite back a moan as his fingers trailed over the cusp of my panties. "Open up baby," he ordered, as he tore them away. His hands moved to free himself from his pants. "Let me in. I need in right fucking now." He could have me anyway he wanted. I was so worked up, I was about to come apart.

"You want me, princess?" he crooned, as he rubbed the head of his rock hard erection over my folds. I swear if he didn't stop teasing me I would scream. My legs shook every time he rubbed my clit with his shaft. "Yes," I begged. "Please, Kyle…I want you."

Fisting my hair in one hand, he dragged my face to his with the other and kissed me almost savagely. "No more fucking fighting," he snarled as he bent his knees. "We stick together..." Dropping his hands to my ass, he hoisted me onto his hips and slid inside me. "No more lies…"

"No more lies…" I cried out. He was so big it was almost painful to take him to the hilt. Grinding his hips against me, his erection stroked my g-spot as his used his hands to hold my hips in place "Yes…" I cried out as my thighs began to spasm around him. "That's it."

"I know exactly where your little spot is, baby," he crooned. He pressed deeper and I shuddered in pleasure. "You drive me crazier than any fucking woman I've ever met."

"I'm sorry for what I said," I moaned. My head fell back against the door. He moved faster inside me, heightening the pulsing waves and shocks of pleasure until they joined together in a wave of ecstasy.

"Me, too," Kyle mumbled. He stopped suddenly and I felt like screaming in frustration. "I'm gonna fuck up sometimes," he said in a gruff tone, his blue eyes locked on mine, his forehead pressed to mine. "You know it and I know it. Just…just don't give up on me." Taking my hand, he placed my palm on his chest. I could feel his heart pounding against my hand. "Can you feel this?" I nodded and he smiled, as he brushed his lips to mine. "This starts and ends with you," he whispered. "I start and end with you. You got it?"

I nodded my head and pulled his lips to mine.

"I got it," I breathed.

SEVENTEEN

LEE

KYLE RECEIVED another letter from Rachel this morning. I'd recognized the handwriting on the envelope the second I saw it lying on the coffee table in the lounge–along with all his other mail, Christmas cards and newspapers. It was identical to the one's I'd spied him slipping into his messenger bag when he thought I wasn't looking. Like the other letters she sent him, this one was unopened. The fact that it was lying out in the open surprised me. He usually hid them from me. He thought I didn't know about them. Curiosity burned inside of me.

"Are you going to open it?" I asked as I leaned against the doorframe and watched Kyle. He was standing at the sink in our kitchen, dressed in gray sweatpants and a black vest, holding a baby-formula scoop and a knife in his hands. Hope never woke up before eight am, but Kyle hated being unprepared, so he always got up early and made a bottle. He'd told me about how hard it was settling Hope when I'd been in hospital. I'd been breastfeeding Hope, and rarely expressed for bottle feeds. Linda had helped him to wean her onto formula, but it had been a tough stage. *One I had missed*. Even though I'd been home almost three months, Kyle sometimes forgot that he wasn't on his own anymore. I was home. I would share the load.

"Nope," was all he grunted, not even turning around to look at me as he measured the scoops of formula, shaving the extra formula off with the flat side of the knife, before plopping them into Hope's bottle. He looked deep in concentration as he frowned at the can of formula perched on the sink in front of him like it was a dangerous animal ready to attack him. I watched his lips move silently as he added scoop after meticulous scoop.

"Why?" I asked. "Kyle, maybe you should at least..."

"Dammit," he hissed and tossed the bottle into the sink before turning around and smiling sheepishly at me. "I lost my count."

"You were on five," I muttered as I fetched a clean bottle from the sterilizer and handed it to him. "And I think you should at least read one of those letters."

"One, two, three, four," he muttered as he refilled the bottle. "Five."

He wasn't even listening to me...

Rolling my eyes, I left him alone to continue the *tedious* task of preparing a baby bottle. On my way out of the kitchen, I grabbed the letter from the coffee table in the lounge and rushed upstairs. I only had so much self-control. I had resisted reading that folder–and looking for Cam's journal. I had a feeling that these letters were going to drive me insane if I didn't find out what she wanted from him.

KYLE

"You know, opening other peoples mail is a federal offense," I said with a smirk, while inside I was fucking quaking. This could blow the hell up in my face.

Lee's head jerked up from where she was engrossed in my letter. She stared at me with a guilty assed expression as she attempted to hide what I'd already seen her doing. "I'm sorry," she mumbled, cheeks glowing, eyes wide. "I just…I needed to know what she wanted. It's been driving me insane watching these letters arrive every week and not knowing. Knowledge is power, Kyle. Fail to prepare, prepare to fail…" She shrugged her shoulders and sighed. "I needed to know." Well...shit.

We'd been doing well with the past few days. No arguments, no goddamn drama. And now, two weeks before Christmas, my woman decides to turn into Sherlock Holmes. Christ…

"And what did she want?" I asked as I sat on the edge of our bed. How the hell did she know about the letters? I'd been so fucking careful about hiding them from her. *Dammit…*I wasn't pissed with her for opening my mail–what's mine was hers–but I was worried. I couldn't understand why she would want to read anything Rachel Grayson had written.

"She wants to see you," Lee whispered as she sat cross-legged on our bed with the letter resting on her legs. "She says it's important. She has some…information." She paused and pulled her bottom lip into her mouth and glanced down at the letter before back at my face. "She says we're in danger."

Here we go…

"For Christ's sake." I blew out a breath and twisted around to face her. I had a nice day planned for the three of us. I had planned to take the girls out to get a tree and some gifts, but from the look on Lee's face I guessed those plans were about to change…She held the letter out for me and I tried to take it as gently as I could from her hand, but my temper was rising. My brain felt like it was about to explode in my head. This was crap. Pure and utter bullshit. Unfolding the letter, I glanced down at words scrawled across the page.

Dear Kyle,

I'm assuming since you haven't barged into the prison, and demanded to see me, you haven't read my letters. For your family's sake, I hope you read this one. I have something to tell you. Something important. He's planning something. I know. I know his plans. You aren't safe. Or the baby. And her …She's even less safe. Danger is watching you. Lurking where you least expect it. I know. I know it all. Every tiny detail. Trouble, Kyle. More than I have ever caused. Your world is about to come crashing down on you. Everything will be gone. You will lose everything. She will be gone. Come see me. Let me explain. You need to know. You don't have to trust me. But if you don't hear my words, you won't have time. No time. Not enough time. You don't know what he's capable of. What they are capable of. I need to see you. See you soon. As soon as you can. Your world will crumble. You'll be better off dead. She'll pray for death when they are finished with her. She'll wish she died that night. She'll wish my bullet killed her. That was the intention. The plan. Not Camryn, just her. Cut off your lifeline. Your little princess. Stab you through the back by shooting her through the heart. It went wrong. So wrong. The plan's... The plan is set. It will happen. You have to stop it from happening. We need to talk. Time is of the essence.

I'll love you forever, Kyle.

Rachel

x.x

"You shouldn't have read this, Lee," I groaned. There was a reason I didn't read these fucking letters. Every drop of ink on those pages was laced with poison. "She's just messing with our heads."

"Are you sure?" she whispered.

No…no I'm not.

"Of course I'm sure," I lied. The only thing I *was* sure of was what I intended to do with this letter. "I need to go out," I blurted as I stood quickly and grabbed my keys off the bedside table and my hoodie off the chair.

"Are you going to see her?" Lee croaked out, causing me to freeze.

"What?" I shook my head. "No baby, of course I'm not." I bent down and kissed her hair. "I'm taking this to Kelsie. Maybe Rachel's done us a huge favor by writing this and they'll lock her up without a trial. No point in pleading not guilty when you write a confession letter."

This was the letter I'd been waiting months for. Only now, I wasn't sure if I felt relief or terror.

"Well?" I asked as I paced Kelsie's office. She was reading the letter and taking her sweet ass time answering me.

"It's good," she said with a grin. "It's very good."

"But is it enough?" I asked anxiously. It better be enough. Time was running out.

"I'm going to make a few calls, Kyle," she said as she pushed her chair back and stood. "I'll contact you as soon as I have more information."

"Wait," I snapped. "That doesn't tell me anything, Kelsie." I ran my hands through my hair and sighed. "Do we have her?"

Kelsie smiled, a cat-like smile, as she stepped towards me. "I think we have, Mr. Carter," she purred as she stroked my arm. *What the fuck?* "And I'm going to make sure that we do."

My phone started to vibrate in my pocket and I pulled it out and glanced at the screen. "I need to take this," I muttered as I backed towards the door. "Call me as soon as you have news," I told her, feeling a little uncomfortable at how close she had inched up to me. "I need to get home to my *fiancée*."

Kelsie nodded professionally and stepped back to her desk. "Will do, Mr. Carter."

"Der, you okay?" I asked as soon as I stepped out of Kelsie's office. His heavy breathing was a sure sign he wasn't anywhere close to being okay.

"He's gonna pay for this," he snarled. His breathing grew deeper–rougher. "I can't take this shit, Kyle," he roared. "They are both going to fucking regret this."

"Who's gonna pay?" I asked.

He didn't reply.

"Derek," I demanded as I rushed down the back stairwell and out to the parking lot through the back entrance of the building. "Who is going to pay?"

The sound of a click in my ear was proof to fact that he'd just hung up on me. "Shit," I hissed as I made a dash for my car. *Yeah, this was turning out to be a really fun day…*

LEE

'She'll wish she had died that night. She'll wish my bullet had killed her.'

My mind repeated those words until I felt like screaming in frustration. I expected myself to feel terrified, and I was, but I was also angry. Really freaking angry.

"That bitch," I mumbled as I sat on the couch, in a state of utter disbelief, with my feet up on the coffee table, and my eyes locked on the photo of Cam.

Who the hell did Rachel Grayson think she was? I would never wish myself dead. Never. Not for her. Not for anyone.

'I'll love you forever Kyle.'

Uh…the woman didn't know the meaning of the word. She had battered Kyle senseless for no reason. Robbed him of his money, his happiness and his freedom. Lied to him for years, faked a miscarriage and had the audacity to say she would love him forever…What a joke.

Hope was still asleep, and I was growing agitated waiting for Kyle to come home.

Dropping my feet to the floor, I sat forward and grabbed the newspaper. The minute I glanced at the cover my eyes bulged in my head and my heart sank in my chest...

KYLE

When I got to the house, Derek was already gone. I ran around the place like a lunatic, checking every room before admitting defeat. I hadn't the slightest clue of where to look for him. Where the fuck would he go, and most importantly, who the hell was going to pay? Sliding my phone out of my pocket, I dialed his number. It went straight to voicemail. Just as I was sliding my phone back into my pocket it started to ring and the name *Princess* lit up the screen.

"Lee." I tried to make my voice sound as calm as possible. "You okay, baby? I can't talk for long. I'm...in a meeting with Kelsie." She didn't need to be worrying. If she even got a hint of how fucked up Derek was it would crush her. She was probably scared over that stupid letter. No. She needed to be protected from this.

"Have you read this morning's paper yet?" she asked in an urgent tone of voice.

Holding my phone to my ear with my shoulder, I fastened my seat belt and started the engine. "No," I muttered as I reversed out of the driveway. "And I hope you haven't either." Jesus, I could barely control the steering wheel. My hands were shaking so badly. If anything happened to Derek I would never forgive myself. Never.

"Your father gave an interview to a journalist," Lee whispered.

Her words were enough to make my entire body stiffen.

I swerved to the roadside, killing the engine. I took a few

calming breaths before speaking. "What did he say?" I managed to ask through clenched teeth. Rage was an understatement for how I was feeling.

"I...um...it's really strange..." She stopped talking and I could tell she was panicking.

"What did he say, Lee?" I said slowly. "Just tell me, baby?"

"I'm just going to read it out..." She paused and I could hear papers shuffling in the background before her soft voice drifted into my ear. "This is a direct quote from your...from David," she told me before continuing. "I love both of my sons with all my heart. I was appalled and devastated for my boys when the news broke about their girlfriends being shot by that grotesque woman. As a father it is your worst nightmare to discover one of your children has been subjected to such a calculating transgression, but to find out both were hoodwinked by that loathsome woman makes my blood boil. One of my son's has buried his beautiful girlfriend, Camryn–the woman he had planned to spend his life with..." Lee's voice broke and I heard her inhale deeply before continuing. "My other son's girlfriend has been left in-inca-incapacitated," she stuttered. "As a result of that vile woman's actions, my grandchild was left motherless for months. My wife and I have tried our best to support both Kyle and Michael during this difficult time, but it hasn't been easy for our family..."

"Stop," I hissed. Rubbing my face roughly with my palm, I tried to get myself under control. "Don't read another word," I whispered. What the hell was he playing at? Who the hell was he trying to fool?

Both of my sons.

As a father...

Our family.

Like he had the slightest clue about being a father...I didn't have a father. I had a fucking sperm donor.

"Where are you, Kyle?" Lee asked quietly. "You're not in a meeting. I can hear traffic."

Groaning, I leaned forward and rested my forehead against the wheel. "Thirteenth Street."

"Why did you lie to me? We promised each other," she whispered and I slumped in my seat. *No more lies* we had promised each other. No more fucking lies and I was still lying. Goddammit to hell.

"I can't find Derek," I confessed guiltily. My tone was gruff. My whole body was on fire. " I didn't wanna worry you." I heard her breathing hitch and I flinched.

"Can you come pick me up?" she asked quickly. I could hear rumbling noises in the background and I suspected she was pulling on her clothes. "I think I know where he is."

LEE

I felt horrible for calling Linda to come over and watch Hope for me when she obviously wasn't at her best, but I didn't have any other option. "Thanks so much, Linda," I mumbled as I shrugged on my coat, ignoring the huge swell of guilt filling my heart from the sight of her washed out face, and rushing to the door. Kyle was waiting outside in his car and I didn't want my daughter coming with us. She didn't need to be exposed to all of this misery and Kyle was too temperamental to go on his own. We needed to talk about this. He needed to stop lying to me. I didn't care if he thought he had my best interests at heart or not. He needed to be straight with me. Lying to each other and hiding the truth had wrecked our relationship before. It was a horrible repetitive habit that we needed to nip in the bud.

"Take care of him, Lee," Linda called after me.

"I will," I replied as I pulled out the door and rushed down the steps to where Kyle was waiting in his car.

"I'm sorry," were the first words Kyle said when I climbed into the passenger seat of his Mercedes. "I panicked…Fuck." His face held the world of remorse. I wasn't angry with him, but he needed to stop hiding things from me. I understood why he did it, but I needed to make him understand why he had to *stop* doing it.

Lowering my hood, I dusted off the flakes of snow that had landed on my shoulders before turning to face him and reaching for his hand. "We've screwed this up before by not communicating. Let's not go down that path again." Stretching across my seat, I planted a soft kiss on his lips before pulling back. "I'm not a porcelain doll, Kyle Carter." I rubbed my thumb over his lip and watched as he closed his eyes and sighed heavily. "We're a team and I will help you when you're in trouble. Do you understand me? Consider me your Tails."

"As in Sonic the hedgehog?" He grinned and shook his head in amusement. "So, I'm Sonic and you're Tails?"

"What?" I said with a shrug as I sat back in my seat and fastened my seatbelt. "Cam had a Gameboy when we were kids. It was the best analogy I could think of."

Kyle smirked at me before revving the engine and speeding off. "So, Tails," he mused as soon as we arrived at the hill. "Where's our golden hoop?"

He wasn't going to like this. I sighed heavily before saying, "I think he's at your father's house."

Kyle slammed his hand on the blinkers and made a highly dangerous–highly illegal–U-turn. "Goddammit. Why the hell would he go..."

"Because he's more than likely after reading the paper and freaking out over what David said about Cam," I said calmly. I had just about fallen off the couch when I opened the newspaper and read what David had said. *Incapacitated.* That stung. That hit me hard... "Take a deep breath and slow down. It will be okay, Kyle."

I didn't believe a word of what I was saying.

I had a really bad feeling about this.

Dread was rising in my heart...

"I don't know if I can do this, Lee," Kyle muttered as he pulled the car to a stop outside the most prodigious house I'd ever seen. It was *huge*–at least four stories tall–snow white in color and completely intimidating. It was snowing heavily now and instead of making the property look endearing, the snow seemed to have the opposite effect. *This was a cold home with no love...*

Kyle unfastened his seatbelt and drummed nervously on the steering wheel with his hands, as his eyes flickered between the house and my face. "I haven't been inside that house in eleven years...and Derek might not even be here."

He was going to do this.

I didn't need to coax him or persuade him to do this.

"I'm with you," was all I said and it seemed to break him out of his panic.

His hand darted from the wheel to my chin. "I know you are," he said in a soft contemplative tone of voice, as he stroked my jaw with his thumb and nodded in what looked like determination. "Come on, princess," he said as he opened his door. "Let's do this shit."

KYLE

"Stay calm," Lee coaxed in a soft tone of voice as she stood by my side, with her small hand wrapped around mine, at the front door of what I liked to call *the manor*. "I'm with you." I knew she was and that knowledge alone made the butterflies that were fluttering around my stomach die down.

I would never admit it to Lee, but this place made me as uncomfortable as Thirteenth Street made her. I felt out of control here. I *had* no control here. This was his turf and I was unwanted. Standing on David Henderson's doorstep made me feel like a vulnerable twelve year old boy again. The last time I stood on these steps was with my grandfather, the day he brought me home. I quickly learned that day that I didn't have a dad and I never would have one. The look of revulsion on David Henderson's face when he looked at me was burnt into my memory. I would never forget the way that bastard had looked down his nose at me like I was a piece of shit on his shoe. I would never forget the words that came out of his mouth.

"Am I supposed to know who he is?" David scorned.

"You're not blind, David," Frank growled as he clamped his huge hand down on my shoulder. "Open your damn eyes. His name is Kyle. Kyle Carter. His mother was Sarah Carter?"

David looked straight in my eyes, his expression impassive, as he raised his brow and said, "Am I supposed to care?"

"Fuck you asshole," I hissed, my temper getting the best of me.

"Calm down, Kyle," Frank coaxed as he stepped towards his son. "This boy is your flesh and blood," he told David, his tone gruff. "Please tell me you didn't know..." Frank's voice broke. He looked down at me with kind blue eyes, blinking back the tears that were pooling in them before facing his son once more. "David, tell me you didn't know about him? Tell me you didn't knowingly allow your own son, to spend nine years of his life as an orphan."

David's brow rose in surprise. There was no flicker of any other emotion on his face besides a glint of amusement. "So, she's dead?" he mused. "Can't say I'm surprised." He shook his head and smirked down at me. "Your mother had a nasty little habit...thought that would've taken care of you."

"You knew she was pregnant..." Frank snapped, but I was already moving.

Shrugging Frank's hand off my shoulder, I stepped forward and got right up in my father's face. "You make me sick," I snarled, shoving his chest with my hands. Even though I was only twelve, he staggered backwards from the force I used. "I'm gonna make you so fucking sorry for this."

David threw his head back and laughed. "Do your worst, runt."

"He's very posh, isn't he?" Lee whispered, breaking me out of my reverie. "You two are like chalk and cheese." I cracked a smile. Only she could make me smile when I was standing here. David's choice of home was just another difference in our personalities and it made me happy to know that she noticed we were nothing alike.

Where I liked the things in my life to be simplistic, David liked extravagance. He valued luxury over practicality. I liked to think that I was sensible when it came to money, but that man was fucking wasteful. He could take fifty homeless people off the streets with the amount of money he spent on lighting this monstrosity of a house each month. I squeezed her hand. "You have no idea, baby."

The front door swung inwards and I was faced with the bane of my fucking existence. "Well, if it isn't Boulder's very own broken lovers," David said with a smirk as he opened the door wider. "I have something that belongs to you, Kyle. Take your shoes off." Turning around, he stalked down the hallway without as much as a backwards glance.

Lee looked up at me with a nervous expression. "Are we supposed to follow him inside?"

"Probably," I muttered, sounding like a petulant teenager but not giving a fuck.

Stepping inside, Lee dragged me back by the hand. "Wait," she mumbled. Pointing at the white carpet in the hallway, she looked up at me with the most innocent expression. "Should we...you know, take our shoes off?"

I snorted and hoped to god that I'd stepped in dog shit on my way here. "Stamp your feet hard, baby," I said with a grin and she nodded eagerly, her smile mirroring mine. *God, I loved that girl...*

Taking a deep breath, I wrapped my arm around her shoulders and stepped inside. With each step we took into the house, Lee moved closer and closer until she was welded to my side. I tightened my arm around her. "It's okay," I whispered. "You're safe. I'm with you."

Lee's hand started to shake and I rubbed my thumb across her knuckles to try and soothe her. "I'm worried for you," she replied quietly.

We rounded a corner to find David standing outside the door of the living room with a scornful expression on his face. Closing the door, he shuddered before glaring at me. "You owe me for the carpet cleaning," he growled.

The loud moans and groans coming from behind the door confirmed to me the fact that Derek was here. I'd know his fucking groaning noises anywhere. I'd heard them often enough. The walls were thin at the house on Thirteenth Street.

"What's going on, Mr. Henderson?" Lee surprised me by asking. She surprised me even further by stepping forward, nudging David out her way and putting her hand on the door knob. The look of anger on her face matched mine when she swung the door open and saw Derek lying limply on my father's couch. The only positive thing about this whole picture was the pile of vomit sprayed all over his white carpet.

LEE

"What the hell did you do to him?" Kyle demanded as he stepped forward and shoved David out of our way. I couldn't hear David's reply. I was too busy trying to wake Derek up–and trying to avoid the vomit.

"Derek," I whispered as I knelt next to the couch and shook his shoulders. He was slumped on top of an immaculate white couch and for the briefest of moments I felt a twinge of sympathy for Mike. It must have been horrible growing up in an igloo. Because that's what this house felt like and looked like to me. Everything was white, cold and clinical. My god, even the Christmas tree in front of the bay window was decorated in white ornaments and tinsel. I dreaded the thought of what happened to children with sticky fingers in this house…

"Cam," Derek mumbled as he threw his arm over his face and groaned. "Make it stop…everything…hurts." My heart cracked open as pain for Derek flowed through me, but fear quickly took its place when his hand shot out and grabbed the back of my neck. "You…broke me," he sobbed, eyes closed, chest heaving. He pulled my face so close to his that I felt drunk from the fumes of alcohol that wafted from his breath. "You…I love you…"

"Derek," I coaxed as I pulled at his wrist with both of my hands. "Please let me go. I'm Lee."

"Whoa," Kyle shouted from behind me and in the next moment I was free and being pulled into Kyle's arms. "You okay?" he demanded as he ran his fingers all over my face and neck.

"Yeah," I whispered even though I was pretty sure we were standing in vomit. "What's wrong with him? He's completely out of it."

"That would be the sedative," David chimed in.

"You drugged him?" Kyle spat as he rushed over to Derek. Kneeling down beside him, Kyle shook Derek gently before swinging his gaze around to his father "Are you insane?"

"Insane, no. Fond of my property, yes," he mused with a shrug. "Stupid fool showed up intoxicated and shouting abuse. What did you expect me to do, take it?" David shook his head and sighed. "I don't take kindly to threats, Kyle. You should know that. He showed up at my house, damaged my property and intimidated my wife. He's lucky all I did was stick him with a needle. I haven't forgotten about him punching me, Kyle. Crying and whining over a woman who didn't want him. He's a pathetic excuse for a man…"

"He is a good man," I snapped as I pressed down hard with my feet. *Let's see how easily he gets that stain out...* "Derek is hurt and he is grieving. Your son ruined his life and *your* thoughtless comments are no doubt the cause of this."

"He is a dangerous man," David countered, glaring at me with a look of pure disgust. "A danger to himself and to anyone he comes into contact with. He needs to be locked up." He turned to look at Kyle and I noted that his expression softened. I narrowed my eyes in distrust. "If he steps foot on my property again, I will have him arrested. I don't want to upset you, Kyle, but I can't allow this kind of behavior. Not on my property. Is that clear?"

"I'll tell you what's clear," Kyle snarled as he hoisted Derek off the couch. "It's clear that you're still a heartless bastard." Carting Derek out to the front door, Kyle turned around and glowered at David. "You even think about causing trouble for him and I'll personally see that you lose everything you value."

"Don't threaten me, Kyle," David warned. "I am not your enemy."

"Don't fucking tempt me, David," Kyle shot back before glancing down at me, his expression softening. "Open the door, baby." I obliged and Kyle shuffled me out first before following with Derek.

"If I was heartless, I would have had him locked up hours ago," David said in a condescending tone of voice as he trailed after us. "Check your phone, Kyle. You'll see that I made several attempts to call you. I am trying to mend fences with you…Look at me when I'm talking to you, will you?"

Kyle didn't turn around. He kept his eyes focused on his car, his jaw rigid. I hurried ahead of him, my feet crunching on the snow and gravel, as I rushed to open the back door of the car. With a gentleness that only Kyle was capable of, he maneuvered Derek into a sitting position in the back seat before fastening his belt. Kyle crouched down and began whispering something to Derek as he cupped his cheeks and inspected his face, but I didn't eavesdrop. It looked too personal.

Instead, I backed away from the car and kept backing up until I hit something hard. Staggering slightly, I steadied myself before turning around. I focused my gaze–more like deer-in-the-headlights stare–on Kyle's father, who was standing less than a foot away from me. His eyes locked on mine and I tried to give him my best evil-eyed stare, but I wasn't feeling half as brave as I had been earlier–when Kyle was standing next to me.

I ran through all the possible things I could say to Kyle's father, but his cold stare was knocking the breath out of me. When he folded his arms over his chest, stepped forward and smirked, I lost all courage and edged away from him. I could have sworn I saw his lips twitch. He was enjoying this…He wanted to scare me. "I don't like you," I blurted out, still stepping away from him.

"I don't like you either," he said softly, so softly I wasn't sure if he'd actually said it or mouthed the words.

"I don't trust you," I countered, feeling a little better when he remained where he was standing. "You're calculating, deceitful and a very bad man."

"You're guileless, unkempt and annoyingly bulletproof," he tossed back at me. "What's your point, Delia?"

I registered the sound of a car door banging and footsteps approaching about two seconds before Kyle stalked past me, not stopping until his fist connected with his father's jaw. David's head snapped back as he fell backwards, landing on his butt on the snow coated ground. "Say that again to her," Kyle snarled as he towered over his father, his chest heaving, his whole body shaking. "I dare you."

"Kyle," I yelled as I rushed over to him. Grabbing his arm, I tried to pull him away, but the man was like a rock. "You crossed a line when you drugged my friend," Kyle roared, eyes fixed on his father in menace. He didn't even seem to feel my hands pulling him. "But you crossed a goddamn continent with her." His hand shot out and he grabbed his father by the collar of his shirt before pulling him to his feet. "You think you can insult my woman? Talk to her like she's a piece of shit? The mother of my child?" Kyle shook his head. "Not fucking happening."

I heard another door slam and watched in horror as Kyle's step-mom, Anna, came rushing towards us. "Kyle," she said in a stern tone of voice. "Let your father go."

Kyle didn't answer her.

I didn't think he could even hear us.

He had flipped.

Pushing David back, he threw another punch and hit David directly in the nose. "There will be no fences mended," Kyle spat before hitting him again and then again. "I am not your son."

Oh god…

My stomach churned at the sight of the blood spurting from David's nose, dribbling down his face. Droplets of blood landed on the ground, darkening the snow, and bringing with it every tormenting memory of that night to the surface of my mind…

I was bleeding, my hands, my stomach… I could see a river of dark blood, spreading over the fabric of my red dress...

The steady flow of blood coming from the back of her head, staining her golden hair, pooling on the kitchen floor...

"Kyle stop," I screamed as I forced the images of that night to the back of my mind and focused on the present. Kyle didn't even twist his head in my direction.

"I hate you," he snarled as he punched his father again and again. "I fucking hate you."

Dammit...

Coming around behind him, I jumped and grabbed onto his shoulders before hoisting myself onto his back. "Let go baby," I whispered into his ear as I wrapped my arms around his neck and my legs around his waist. "Please, stop Kyle," I begged. "You're scaring me."

Kyle's body shuddered, his whole frame sagged, and he dropped his hands to his sides for the briefest of moments before moving them to rest on my thighs. "I'm sorry, princess," he whispered, bowing his head. "Lee, I'm so fucking sorry."

"Shh," I coaxed as I tried to calm him down. "It's okay."

"It is *not* okay," Anna shouted as she helped her husband to his feet. His face was swollen, his nose was bleeding heavily. "You need help, Kyle," she snapped. "You need anger management treatment. You could have killed him. Your own father." She shook her head and pointed a manicured fingernail at us. "I have a good mind to have you arrested for this, Kyle Carter."

Wiggling down Kyle's back, I stepped up to his side and took his blood encrusted hand in mine. "Don't you dare speak to him like that," I growled. My words caused Anna to blanch. "Don't even think about threatening him," I snarled. "You two are disgraceful and if you even think about calling the police on him, I will have your husband arrested for drugging my friend."

Anna's eyes darted towards our car at the same time as Kyle's head snapped up. He gazed at me with a look of pure astonishment. His eyes…oh god, the pain in his eyes just about broke my heart.

This had been about more than just David insulting me and drugging Derek. Kyle's outburst had been stimulated from twenty-three years of neglect and abuse, and coming here was his trigger. Others might not understand–and obviously Anna didn't–but when a human being has been consistently wronged, from infancy through to adulthood, the pain, anger and resentment that builds inside eventually comes to the boil. I understood exactly how he felt.

"Stay out of this, Lee," Anna warned, but her voice wavered slightly. "This isn't your concern. This is a family matter."

"*He* is my concern," I spat. "He is *my* family." Turning to face Kyle, I reached up and cupped his face before whispering, "Walk away from the pain. Leave it all here, okay?" He nodded slowly, his eyes locked on mine.

Tugging on his hand, I led him back to the car, ignoring every red-flag warning my brain was tossing at me.

He's dangerous.

He's just like your father.

He's going to destroy you…

I blocked it all out and concentrated on my heart, and my heart was screaming for him.

My heart trusted him.

That was enough for me.

"I wanna go home," Derek mumbled from the back seat of the car as Kyle tore off, speeding like a lunatic. "Take me home… Thirteenth Street."

"No way, Derek," I said in a stern tone of voice. "You're coming home with us, isn't he, Kyle?" I stared at the side of Kyle's face, willing him to back me up. "Isn't he, Kyle?"

Kyle didn't answer me.

He didn't even glance in my direction.

Dread filled my gut when I realized the direction we were going.

"Kyle, you can't," I begged. "You can't take him back to Thirteenth Street."

LEE

"What am I going to do, Linda?" I whispered.

We were in the kitchen of our house and I was close to climbing up the walls with worry. Kyle was in his office–where he had been for the past six hours. He hadn't come out once and I wasn't sure what to do with him. When we left his father's house this morning, Kyle had driven Derek back to Thirteenth Street–against my wishes–in complete silence. When we got home he went straight into his office, locked the door, and hadn't come out since.

Linda had stayed with me all day and I was grateful. Kyle was in catatonic mode...

Was it me? Had I done something? Was he mad?

Should I have done what Anna said and kept out of their business?

Oh god, not knowing what was going on with him was killing me. I felt like I was about to burst with panic...I paced the floor with Hope in my arms. "He won't answer the door to me..." My voice broke and I brushed away a tear from my cheek as I bobbed around with Hope in my arms. Hope was fussing and I knew it was because she could sense my fear. "He won't talk to me."

Linda stood slowly and made her way to the kitchen door. "Go and settle Hope down, Lee," she mumbled. "That child's exhausted. I'll deal with her father."

KYLE

I couldn't face her.

How the fuck could I look her in the eye again?

I was no better than her father.

I promised that girl a life free from pain and violence and I'd let her down.

My behavior…Jesus, Anna was right. I needed to see someone.

I didn't regret hitting David and I never would. I regretted losing control around Lee. I always knew I had a temper, but in all my life, I'd never felt as out of control as I had this morning. I knew Lee was worried about me, and that made the disgust that was pooling in my stomach grow. I didn't deserve her worry. I didn't deserve her, period. And Derek…I'd let him down, too. I should have brought him home with us. I shouldn't have left him in that state…in that house.

"Please stop, Kyle. You're scaring me…"

My whole body shuddered and I dropped my head in my hands, my elbows resting on my desk.

How the hell could I make this up to her?

If Lee hadn't stopped me, how far would I have gone?

I wasn't sure and that terrified me…

The loud tapping noise on my office door stirred me from my self-wallowing. "Kyle Anthony Carter, you better open this door now, boy," I heard Linda say in a stern tone of voice. "Or so help me, I will knock it down."

I had no doubt that Linda would do exactly what she threatened. Pulling myself up, I walked over and unlocked the door, I took a deep steadying breath before opening the door inwards. "Good boy," Linda said with a smirk, patting me on the arm, as she marched into my office. "I thought I was gonna have to get a chainsaw."

"I screwed up today, Linda," I mumbled. "I messed up so bad…"

"Tell me something new," she chuckled before coughing loudly. "Never would've classed you as a coward, Kyle."

"I'm not a coward," I growled as I closed the door and sagged against it. Letting my head fall back, I exhaled heavily. "I'm a fucking liability and she's been through enough."

"Yes, you are, Kyle," Linda agreed, her voice wheezy.

My head snapped up and I narrowed my eyes at the woman who had spent the past eleven years of her life bailing me out of trouble. "Yes, I'm a liability, or yes, I'm a coward?"

"Yes on the former and the jury's still out on the latter," Linda countered as she leaned against my desk, eyes locked on mine. "Verdict depends on you getting your sorrowful butt out of this room." She shook her head and shuffled towards me. "Lee filled me in on what happened with David…and there's only one thing I'm having a hard time getting my head around..."

"Oh yeah, and what's that?" I asked in a weary tone.

"I'm confused as to why you're hiding from a woman who is so deeply in love with you that she has spent the best part of the day worrying about you, fretting over you, and to be quite frank, crying her damn eyes out because you've pushed her away."

"I'm ashamed of myself," I admitted quietly. I was ashamed of myself. I was fucking disgusted with myself. "I've spent months pushing her about her mother…not listening to her pleas or point of view…" My voice trailed off and I clenched my eyes shut as remorse filled me. "Lee…she stood up for me today, Linda…the girl is afraid of her own shadow and she defended me…even when I was wrong." All the times I'd pushed Lee about her mom, bullied her…Jesus, I'd never put myself in her shoes.

Until now.

I opened my eyes and stared at Linda. "How the hell am I going to make this up to her? Why the hell is she still with me?"

"Kyle," Linda chuckled as she stepped closer to me and

stroked my arm. "She's with you because she loves you, and you're going to make it up to her by holding her in your arms. That's all that poor girl wants. She just wants you. It's that simple, kiddo."

"You make it sound so easy," I muttered.

"It's as easy or as hard as you make it," she replied as she pushed me aside and opened the door. "Now, go and be with your family. I'm tired and I'd like to get some sleep before your next drama. I'm getting too old for this."

"Linda, wait," I said as I grabbed her arm. Another type of fear was building inside of me and looking at Linda's withered face intensified it. "What's wrong with you?" I reached out and touched her cheek. "Are you sick, Linda?"

"I am fine, Kyle," she said with a smile–a fake as fuck smile. "Stop worrying about me, will you?" she chuckled softly. "I told you before, you're gonna give yourself wrinkles."

"Are you lying to me?" I whispered as I stared down at her pale face, her sunken eyes. She was. I knew she was. She could deny it as much as she wanted. Something was very wrong and I felt like an asshole that she was in my house, fixing my goddamn mess, when she looked so exhausted…

"Have I ever lied to you?" she demanded as she rested her hands on her hips.

"No, but…" My voice broke off as Linda grabbed my arms and hugged me tightly.

"Then stop doubting me," she said in a husky tone. "I love you, Kyle Carter, and I'm damn proud of the man you've become."

I held her in my arms and fought down the feeling of dread that was filling me. "I love you, too."

Lee was curled in a ball on our bed. I stood in the doorway, drinking her in. She was still here. I'd lost control and she was still here. For me…

"Princess," I choked out.

Her head snapped up and she sat straight up, eyes unblinking, as she wiped her cheeks with the back of her hands, staring at me. The light coming from the hallway behind me illuminated her tear stained face.

"Lee…" I shrugged my shoulders and dropped my hands to my sides. I stepped closer. "I'm so sorry, baby…" I didn't get a chance to say anything else because Lee scrambled off the bed and hurled herself into my arms.

"Are you okay?" she cried as she kissed my neck. Grabbing my face with her hands, she kissed me hard. "Oh, Kyle. I was so worried…I love you. I love you so much."

"I love you, too," I whispered against her mouth as I hoisted her into my arms and carried her back to bed. "And I'm so fucking sorry for scaring you," I mumbled between kisses as I lowered her down on the bed and stretched out over her. "And for forcing your mom on you…"

"I forgive you," she gasped as she kissed me hungrily. "I understand." Her tears soaked my face, her fingers threaded through my hair, and her hands pulled my neck closer to her. "Just…let it all go, Kyle. All the pain with your dad. Let it all out...I'm on your side," she vowed as she kissed my lips, my neck, my cheeks… "I'm always on your side and don't you ever forget it."

God, I was drowning in her love…

"The things you do to me," I mumbled against her neck. "The things you make me feel…" I pulled back to look at her. "It feels like someone is ramming a red hot poker into my heart and all I feel is the burn." I brushed the tears away from her cheek with my thumb. "The fucked up thing is, I want more. I want the pain, Lee. I want it all. This pull...it's addictive. I wasn't wrong when I said you'd ruin me," I admitted. "Thank you, Lee…for sticking it out with me. For loving me."

"I'll be sticking it out with you for the rest of my life," she vowed, looking up at me with those beautiful gray eyes. "And I want you to know that I'm so proud of you, Kyle. I am so proud of every single part of you. I couldn't love you more if I tried."

"Jesus Lee," I choked out. "There's nothing on this fucking planet that shakes me up like you do, baby."

"Please don't push me away again," she whispered. "Ever. I mean it, Kyle."

"I won't," I vowed as I stroked her nose with mine. "My little Tails."

My phone vibrated on the bedside table next to my head. I gently rolled Lee off my chest and onto her back before reaching for my phone. "Yeah," I mumbled as I rubbed my eyes with my free hand, then glanced at the alarm clock. 04.25.

"Kyle..." Derek slurred. I could barely make out his voice because the line was so fuzzy. "I'm lo...Ky...help..."

"Der?" I whispered, sitting up quickly. "Where the hell are you, man? I can barely hear you."

"Gone...Kyle. She's...aw shit," I caught him say before the line went dead.

Goddammit.

Kissing Lee on the forehead, I slipped out of bed and carried my jeans and shirt into the hallway to dress. Opening Hope's door I peeked inside. The pink glow worm shaped night light Cam had bought illuminated her room. Content that Hope was safe, I rushed down the stairs and grabbed my keys.

LEE

The sound of a car engine roaring to life woke me from my sleep. Reaching for the lamp on my bedside table, I flicked it on and looked around. Oh god…

Kyle was gone.

Dressing quickly, I rushed down the hall to check on Hope. She was sleeping soundly and I breathed a huge sigh of relief. She was my first thought most mornings and even though I could see she was fine, I still had a bad feeling in the pit of my stomach. Something was very wrong. I could feel it.

Creeping down the stairs, I turned on each light switch I passed in the process.

"Kyle?" I called out when I made it downstairs to the kitchen. Uh, I closed my eyes when I switched the light on and kept them closed for a few seconds before slowly opening them. I knew nothing would be there, but sometimes my eyes played tricks on me and I saw things that weren't there.

Especially when it came to kitchens…

KYLE

I found him in Cam's bedroom.

It was trashed and his fist was in an even worse condition. "I'm sorry," Derek slurred from where he was huddled on the floor in a pool of blood and vomit. "I couldn't stop the...blood."

"Come on, dude," I said as I bent down and hoisted him up. Regret filled me. I should have taken care of him this morning... but I'd left him on his own. I was a piss-poor excuse for a friend. "Let's get you cleaned up."

I half-carried and half-dragged him across the hall to the bathroom. Helping him out of his shirt, I sat him on the toilet seat and turned on the shower. "I'm dying, Kyle," he sobbed as he wrapped his arms around himself.

Jesus, his whole body was shaking violently and I thought I would fucking collapse from the sight. I'd only seen Derek cry three times in my life. The night Cam died, the day she was buried, and the day I found him on the side of the road...

"The pain is killing me," he told me as he pulled at his hair. "I can't breathe. It's going to kill me. I'm going under."

"I'm gonna fix this," I told him as I took his shoes and socks off for him. "I'm gonna get you better, I promise."

Hoisting him up, I got his jeans off and held him under the shower until the blood and vomit washed off his body. "I'm sorry you have to do this for me," he mumbled as he bent his head in shame.

"I delivered a baby, dude," I told him. "This is a piece of cake."

"Ah shit," he sobbed. "The girls…"

"The girls are fine," I assured him as I stretched over and grabbed a towel off the rail. "They're missing you though."

"I'm no good for them."

"You are our family," I growled as I helped him out and draped the towel around his shoulders. "It's time you came home to your family."

Derek's shoulders sagged as he sighed. "Yeah."

Lee was sitting at the table when we walked into the kitchen. Her eyes fell on Derek and she was moving before I had a chance to open my mouth to explain.

"You're home," she whispered as she wrapped her arms around him. I watched as he shuddered and held my fiancé tightly. He ducked his face into her neck as she stroked his hair and whispered into his ear. He was nodding and with each nod he squeezed her tighter.

If this was any other guy, I would be pretty fucking pissed. But this was Derek. He loved my girl like a sister and she loved him with the fierceness of a lioness to her cub.

She was comforting her brother. He had come home.

EIGHTEEN

LEE

"CAN I ASK YOU A QUESTION, KYLE?" I asked as I sat on a garden swing, watching as he pushed Hope on the baby swing-set in the backyard. It was the first week of January and the weather was bitter cold, but we were all wrapped up and Hope looked adorable in the pink snowsuit Kyle had bought her when he took us on a day trip to Aspen last weekend.

It had been over a month since the David incident and the change in Kyle's behavior had been quite drastic. He spent all his time at home with us and I wasn't sure if he was doing this because he was upset over the way he had reacted with his dad or because he wasn't busy with work. I guessed it was the former, but I wasn't complaining. I wanted him at home with us, especially when he was being so attentive. He hadn't brought up the topic of my mother– not once–and we were getting along really well. And now, courtesy of my fast-track fiancé, I was the proud holder of a learner's driving permit.

But the best thing about the past month was the fact that Derek was currently snoring his head off in his new room in our basement. Thank god…He wasn't anywhere close to his old self, but he was getting there. *Baby steps…* He was eating three meals a day again–courtesy of Chef Carter–and he hadn't touched a drop of alcohol since the night Kyle brought him home. He spent a lot of his time tucked away in his room, but at least he was with us for now, and that was the most we could ask from him. I never found out what happened between Derek and David, and neither had Kyle. We'd both–on several occasions–tried to coax it out of him, but Derek wasn't talking…

Christmas had been a quiet event, just the three of us and Hope. The same went for New Years. For Hope's benefit, we had put up a tree, but none of us were really feeling festive. Derek had struggled with it being his first Christmas in five years without Cam. I'd silently mourned the one year anniversary of miscarrying our baby, and Kyle…Kyle had spent half the day arguing on the phone with Linda's sister Patty. According to Patty, Linda had flown out to Michigan to spend the holidays with her family, but every time Kyle phoned to speak to Linda, Patty had fed him excuse after flimsy excuse. He'd tried to hide his pain, but I knew he was hurting…All three of us had been in apprehensive moods that day and ended up eating pizza instead of turkey We'd celebrated bringing in the new year with a game of monopoly–Kyle had kicked our butts–and I was beginning to think that we were making our own tradition of boycotting tradition…

"If it has to do with tasting more of your cookies, then no Lee. They suck, baby," Kyle chuckled as he grinned at me. His nose was red, his hair was covered with a gray beanie hat, and I wanted to growl in appreciation. I sent a small prayer up to his momma, thanking her for creating such a beautiful man.

"It doesn't, but the cookies weren't that bad, Kyle," I said, even though I knew they were. I had attempted to make a batch of chocolate chip cookies last night, and I really didn't know what happened, but somewhere during the process I'd made a terrible mistake with ingredients and Kyle, being my taste-tester, had ended up in the bathroom with his head in the toilet bowl for the best part of an hour.

"Tell that to my stomach," he muttered as he gave Hope another push. "So, what's your question?"

"I was just wondering if you ever think about the other baby." I wasn't sure whether I should bring it up or not. It was a raw subject for both of us, but for Kyle the topic of my miscarriage was taboo. I knew he felt responsible, and in the past I'd selfishly put the blame on him. It wasn't his fault though. It wasn't anyone's fault. It was…it just was. I didn't want to say it was just one of those things, because that phrase disgusted me. It wasn't just one of those things. I thought about the baby I'd lost every time I looked at Hope.

Kyle's hand faltered for a moment before he continued to push Hope. "Yeah, princess, I do." He sighed heavily. "Every day."

"Really?" I whispered, feeling deeply comforted with the knowledge that we were both in this together. He felt it, too. We felt the same pain. We were connected through it.

Pushing Hope once more, Kyle stepped away from the swing and came and sat beside me. Wrapping his arm around my shoulders, he kicked his foot on the grass, making our swing move gently. "I think about whether they would have been identical…hair color, eye color, temperament…I think about all of it, Lee," he said quietly. "I think he would have been a boy."

"So do I," I whispered as I placed my hand on his denim-clad thigh. "Do you ever feel like we were robbed, Kyle?"

"Constantly," he replied, his arm tightening around me as he stared straight ahead, his eyes locked on our baby. "I look at Hope now, and all I can think of…is my son should be sitting on the swing beside my daughter."

"I love you, Kyle," I told him as I tucked into his warmth.

He chuckled softly before saying, "Ah, but will you still love me later?"

"Why?" I eyed him suspiciously. "What are you planning?"

"Lesson number ten," he said with a grin. "How to change gears without fucking up the clutch of my car…maybe this time you won't take out half the house."

"It was one flower pot, Kyle," I retorted as excitement bubbled inside of me. Kyle had started teaching me to drive a few weeks ago and he was referring to the one teeny-tiny incident we happened to have–which had been *his* fault in the first place. He pulled the damn wheel when I was trying to shift gears. Yeah, I was a little close to the house, but I had it totally under control until he started to scream like a girl, claiming that I was going to drive into the side of the house. If his car was an automatic it might be easier to learn, but no, of course, Kyle freaking Carter was old school and had to drive a top of the range *manual* Mercedes Benz…

"It was four fucking flower pots and half the goddamn

hedge," he growled as he jerked off the swing and stalked over to where Hope was now fussing. "Actually, forget the lessons," he said in a teasing tone. "I happen to value my body…"

"Ha," I snorted as I stood up and followed him. "I have my permit, remember? You can't stop me now."

KYLE

This was a mistake. This was a huge motherfucking mistake and I was fairly certain I was going to die. My only consolation was that my daughter would live on in my memory, because I had a feeling her mother was about to kill me…

"Slow down," I said as calmly as I could, covering my eyes when Lee took the corner of our driveway with more speed than required on a goddamn race-track. "It's dark, Lee. It's icy. Jesus Christ, you need to slow down."

"I'm trying," she growled as she furrowed her brow in concentration and if I wasn't so worried about staying alive, I would be seriously turned on by how hot Lee looked driving my car… "It won't shift," she hissed as she pulled hard on the gearshift. "It won't freaking shift, Kyle."

"Press your foot on the clutch pedal," I shouted. The car lunged forward. "No, Lee…No…goddammit, take your foot off the gas." Oh sweet Jesus, I covered my face as the car veered dangerously close to a tree. "Keep your eyes on the fucking road, baby."

"Stop shouting at me, Kyle." She gripped the wheel tighter and swerved away before pulling to a stop and killing the engine. "I can't do this with you," she snapped as she unfastened her seatbelt and climbed out of the car. "You make me nervous." She slammed the car door shut before marching off towards the house.

"Good," I shouted as I climbed out and stalked after her and followed her inside. "When you're behind the wheel of a ten thousand pound death machine, you should be nervous."

"You have zero patience, Kyle," Lee growled as she stormed into the kitchen and opened the fridge.

"You two at it again?" Derek chuckled from behind me and I swung around to grin at him.

"You know what they say, Der," I said before winking at Lee. "The bigger the fight, the better the fu…"

"Don't you dare say that word, Kyle Carter," Lee hissed, as she slammed the refrigerator door and poked me in the stomach. "We've talked about this. Some things are *private*."

"Yeah Kyle," Derek said in a sarcastic tone as he leaned against the doorframe. "I think the phrase you're looking for is 'break her bed, not her heart'." We both burst out laughing and Lee threw her hands in the air in obvious frustration.

"Oh my god," she growled as she stormed past the both of us. "You're both as bad as each other."

"Good to have you home, man," I chuckled as I slapped him on the back.

"Yeah," he said with–what I hoped was–a contented sigh. "It's good to be home."

LEE

"How are you so fit?" I asked Kyle when he came out of the bathroom, wrapped in a towel. I was sprawled across our bed ogling him shamelessly. Twisting onto my stomach, I looked up and asked, "How do you keep your body so…tight?"

"I swim," he replied, giving me a look that said this was the stupidest question I'd ever asked him.

"You do?" I asked resting my elbows on our bed and my chin on my hands. "Where?"

Kyle frowned at me for a moment before he dropped his towel. "The hotel pool," he said as he slipped on a pair of white boxer shorts. God, he was so beautiful…the white of his shorts emphasized his golden skin. "How do you not know this?"

"I didn't know," I said defensively. I didn't know a lot of things about Kyle's life and it bothered me. "I guess so much has happened in the past year that we've never really taken the time to learn the little things."

"You're right," Kyle said after a moment. Pulling back the covers, he climbed into bed and shifted me onto my back. He rested on his side and leaned over me. Trailing his fingers up and down my arm, he whispered, "I want to learn the little things, too."

"First kiss?" I asked him as I turned on my side to face him.

"You're my last," was all he said before kissing my nose. He probably didn't remember and to be honest I didn't want to know. I shouldn't have touched that one…

"You're my first and last," I told him. I didn't count Perry Franklin's rough mouth trying to kiss me. It didn't count. Not anymore.

"Favorite band?" Kyle asked as he laced his fingers through mine.

"Kings of Leon," I told him. "Luke Bryan is my favorite singer."

"My little country girl," he teased as he drew me closer to him. "What was your best day," he asked before adding, "And you can't use the day Hope was born."

"It's going to sound bad," I said nervously. It sounded freaking terrible in my head. "You'll think I'm crazy."

"I won't think you're crazy," he said before smirking. "Well, no more than I already do..."

I poked him in the belly. "Fine. I'm not telling you."

"I'm joking," he chuckled. "Come on, baby."

"It was the day I was shot," I told him. Kyle's whole body tensed. "Not the getting shot part," I added quickly. "Everything before that." I rolled onto my back and sighed. "Remember that day, Kyle?"

"I haven't thought much about it, Lee," he said in a gruff tone. Lying on his back, he rubbed his face with his hands. "I try not to."

"We had the best day," I whispered. "We did."

We lay side by side in silence until Kyle finally spoke. "I remember you waking me up with burnt pancakes." He chuckled softly. "You also burned the omelets for lunch, but I ate them anyway because you looked so adorable with flour on your cheeks." He sighed heavily before adding, "I nearly choked on a piece of shell, too."

"I was so excited that day." I turned my face to smile at him. He was already looking at me with such love in his eyes that my heart started to hammer in my chest. "I was going to ask you to repeat the question that day, Kyle. I spent that entire day in a state of euphoria because I knew you loved me and I trusted you. After all the drama and our rough start...we had finally made it." I twisted on my side and stroked his cheek. He shivered under my touch and dragged me on top of him. "It was my best day because of you."

"Until everything went to shit," he mumbled.

"Yeah," I sighed and rested my head on his chest. "Until everything went to shit."

He held me tightly to his chest for a long time before speaking. "You faze out sometimes, baby. Did you realize that you've been doing that?" My face reddened and I was glad it was dark so Kyle couldn't see my embarrassment. I hadn't realized I did that in front of people. "Where do you go, Lee?" he murmured. "Where do you go inside that head of yours?"

"If I'm having a bad day, I sometimes ask Cam for advice," I confessed.

Kyle's arms tightened around me. "Princess…"

"I'm not crazy," I whispered defensively. "I know she's dead, but sometimes I feel incredibly lonely and I miss her so much... She was my best friend, Kyle, and now she's dead. Sometimes I like to pretend she's still with me."

"You're lonely?" Kyle asked and I could hear the hurt in his voice. I didn't want to hurt him, but I wasn't going to lie to him either.

"Yes," I said quietly. "All I have is you, Derek and Hope. And I love the three of you with all my heart, but it's been tough without her. Before you, she was all I ever had. And now you're all I have." I kissed his chest. "You're all I want."

"How can I fix this for you?" he asked in a desperate tone. "How can I make you happy again?"

"You can't fix grief, Kyle," I whispered. "And you do make me happy. I smile through my sadness because of you."

Kyle stroked small circles on my lower back. "I've been thinking…"

"Yeah," I whispered when he stopped mid-sentence.

He paused for a long moment before saying, "I think we should have another baby."

Seven words was all it took to kick me into flight mode.

"You're kidding right?" I whispered, waiting for him to laugh. He didn't.

"No, I'm not."

My mouth fell open as I scrambled off his chest and gaped at him. Oh my god, he looked serious. His blue eyes held no humor. Shit, he was deadly serious. "Tell me you didn't just say we should have another baby," I begged as anxiety tore at my gut. I prayed he was joking.

Kyle shrugged as he pulled himself into a sitting position. Reaching for my hand, he stroked his thumb over my knuckles. "Calm down. I didn't mean right this instant. I was talking about the future, maybe a year or two. After we're married. It would be nice for Hope to have sisters and brothers."

Sisters and brothers? Plural?

I shook my head in disbelief. "No," I whispered. "No way, Kyle."

His brow furrowed as he stared at me challengingly. "Why not?"

"Because I can't," I almost shouted. Aware that Hope was sleeping down the hall from us, I lowered my voice and threw my hands up in frustration. "You know I can't have more children. Why would you even suggest this? You know it's impossible."

"It's less likely, Lee," he said calmly. "But it's not impossible. No one said it was impossible. You heard what Dr. Michaels said. You're getting better. Maybe things will start…happening again."

Climbing off the bed, I paced the floor as I tried to calm myself down. I couldn't have more children. I physically couldn't and the thought of going through all of that…the miscarriage. The pain and the fear… My head was spinning with the fear that he wanted more children. Where was this coming from? Kyle wanted more children? I thought he was joking a few weeks back…He wanted more and I couldn't give him more than I already had. Did I even want more children? Another child with Kyle? My heart fluttered in excitement and I mentally slammed my fist down on the small feeling of joy that was attempting to possess me. Heck, I threw my bible at it. I was not going there. No getting my hopes up. I needed to be logical…rational. What I wanted and what I could have were two very different things…

"There will be no more babies," I said shakily as I swung around and faced him. "If you want another child you'll have to find a better model with all her bodily organs intact. A woman who's not broken."

"Don't you dare pull that crap with me," he snapped as he threw the covers off himself and jumped out of bed. "Is that what you think of me?" he demanded as he stood in front of me. "That I'd fucking leave you after everything we've been through? Dammit, why would you even think like that?"

"Why would you ask me to give you something you know I'm not physically capable of giving you?" I shot back. My whole body was shaking. I had never anticipated having this conversation with Kyle. I couldn't comprehend why he was bringing this up. Fear ripped through me. "I can't give you more children, Kyle," I said with a sigh. Walking over to the bed, I sank down on it and rubbed my head with my hand. "I love you so much...but if having more children is a deal breaker for you, then you need to tell me now before..."

"Jesus Christ, you piss me off worse than any woman I've ever met," he growled as he paced the room. "Deal breaker my ass." He swung around to glare at me. "Do you seriously think I would, that I even could, walk away from you?"

I shook my head and sighed. "You said..."

"No, you freaked the fuck out before I had a chance to speak," he countered. Sighing heavily, he came over to where I was sitting and crouched in front of me. "I meant we could try, Lee. It doesn't have to be right away and it's not a fucking deal breaker for me if it doesn't happen."

"I. Can't. Get. Pregnant," I said slowly enunciating each word. "I haven't had a period since before I fell pregnant with the tw... with Hope. You *know* this. I don't work right anymore. I thought you understood that. I didn't realize you were...broody."

"Bullshit," he said in a softer tone. "You know I love our daughter. You know I want to have a family *with you*. So, what's the real problem here, princess?"

"I'm afraid," I admitted. I was. He had scared the life out of me with that request. This was just the first in a long list of things he'd realize I either couldn't do or wasn't good enough to do. "You've just stated something you want that's not going to happen for us. I know you mentioned having more children when you proposed, but I...Oh god, Kyle, how many other things will there be that we won't be compatible with? What if we hit a wall? One we can't break through."

"I'm not going to leave you, Lee," he told me as he stared into my eyes. "Ever. You need to stop over-thinking things. I'm in and I'm not backing out. I am *in,* Lee. One hundred percent. I'll break down any goddamn walls that stack up against us. Even the ones you put up to block me out."

"I'm sorry," I whispered as a huge wave of guilt flooded me.

"If I could give you more children, I would." I bit down on my thumb as I tried to think of how to phrase my feelings. "I'm worried I'm not enough. What if I'm not enough?"

Shaking his head, Kyle moved to sit beside me. "You're enough for me, Lee Bennett. Believe me, you're more than enough," he whispered as he rested his hand on my thigh. "Do you know what my best day was?"

"I have a fair idea," I muttered nervously. "The day Hope was born."

"Apart from that," he shot back with a crooked smile. "My best day was as screwed up as yours. It was my best and worst. It was the night I walked into that hospital room and saw you curled in a ball pretending to be asleep."

My mind worked at a furious pace as I tried to register which incident he was talking about. We had so many hospital incidents it was hard to pinpoint which one he was thinking of.

"It was the night after the party. Christmas Eve. I came home and couldn't find you. I saw the blood in the…so I called Derek," he continued, but he closed his eyes as he spoke. "He told me that you were pregnant and that you'd miscarried." I shuddered and Kyle wrapped his arm around my shoulder and tucked me into his side. "My world collapsed in the minutes it took me to end that phone call and get to you. And when I got to your hospital door I was faced with the lioness."

"Cam," I sighed.

"Yeah," he chuckled. "Slapped me so hard I saw stars."

"Cam slapped you?" I gasped. I hadn't known that. It sounded like something she would have done. She'd been furious that night.

"I deserved it, Lee," he said with a small smile. "I'm just glad all I got was a slap. For a moment I'd thought she was gonna castrate me."

"Okay," I mumbled as I shook my head. "How in god's name was that your best day?"

"You walked away from me that night, Lee," he admitted with a sigh. "You broke up with me, ripped me apart and woke me up all at once. It was the biggest reality check of my life. I went home after you kicked me out and started going over and over every second I'd spent with you from the night I'd kissed you in my kitchen to the night of that stupid party. I didn't like the person I was. I was a liar and a fucking cheat and I couldn't stand the thought of being those things with you–to you. The way I treated you..." His voice broke off as he ran a hand roughly through his hair before sighing heavily. "All I could see was this young, vulnerable, amazing girl who I'd broken. I've never felt shame like that before. You were so good and I wasn't. I wanted to be good for you, Lee, good enough for you." He turned to face me. Stroking my cheek, he pressed his forehead to mine. "Me loving you has never had anything to do with babies. You saved me from myself a long time ago and Hope saved us from me. I clung to the hope that you might need me, that there may be a possibility that you'd give me another chance. The pregnancy was my way back to you. I wasn't going to let you down again, not intentionally. I knew it, I just needed you to know it. So yeah, that's my best day. The day I woke up."

"You," I breathed as I tried to form a straight sentence. I was drowning in the emotion I felt from hearing his thoughts on that night. "You are a dangerous man with words."

Kyle laughed softly as he stood up and stretched. "And you have no reason to feel insecure. I'm going nowhere. Whether we have fifty more kids, or only have Hope, I'm yours. Have a little faith in yourself. Have some confidence." Leaning forward, he gripped me under my arms and picked me up like I weighed nothing. "Because, baby, if you could see yourself through my eyes you'd never put clothes on again," he purred as he walked around to my side of the bed before setting me back down on my feet.

"Snap," I said with a small smile.

"So, are we cool?" he asked as he stood in front me smirking, with his hands on my hips. "No more tantrums?" He grinned widely, causing the dimple in his cheek to deepen. "No more meltdowns?"

"Ha-ha," I grunted as I crawled into bed. "But seriously, Kyle, *that* isn't going to happen for us again."

Kyle snorted as he climbed over me and settled down beside me. "Relax your brain, woman. Let's just take every day as it comes, okay?"

"Do I have to worry about you piercing holes in the condoms?" I asked with a smirk.

"Smart mouth," he chuckled as he rolled onto his side and

pulled me into his embrace. I rested my head on one of his arms and he snaked the other arm around my waist, resting his palm against my stomach. "Don't over analyze this," he murmured softly, his lips brushing against my neck as he spoke. "Don't worry about condoms. Don't worry about a damn thing. I've got you, baby. I'm gonna take care of you."

"It won't happen," I warned him as I snuggled my back against his front. "I won't get pregnant."

"Yeah princess," he yawned as he kissed my shoulder. "Whatever you say."

DEREK

"Hey, man." Kyle grinned as he sank onto the couch next to me. "Can't sleep either?"

"Something like that," I mumbled as I lowered the volume on the TV. Kyle had a habit of sneaking downstairs to check on me at night when Lee was asleep. He pretended it was because he couldn't sleep, but I knew it was because he was worried. He checked the locks on the doors, and the alarm system at least twice a night, and still hadn't given me the access codes. He was afraid I would break out and go drinking. I couldn't blame him for his lack of trust. My previous antics hadn't exactly inspired his trust in me. I would earn it back–and his respect.

I was seeing things a lot more clearly since I left the hill. I felt like I could breathe again. I felt like I was breathing for the first time in months, but with my awakening also came my shame...

I was so fucking ashamed of myself. Kyle had saved my life repeatedly for months. I'd hit him, pushed him away and insulted the hell out of him and he never walked away. He kept coming back and he had pulled me away from the edge. I could never repay the guy. He was one in a million. If I died trying, I would earn back the right to call myself his friend.

"You hungry?" Kyle asked as he folded his arms behind his head and stretched his legs out in front of himself. "I couldn't eat a damn thing at dinner." Kyle laughed quietly. "Dude, I love that girl to death, but I have a real fear she's gonna poison me someday."

"Yeah," I chucked. Lee couldn't cook to save her life. She was a liability in the kitchen, but she had these big, glassy gray eyes that were a fucking deadly weapon. One damn puppy dog gaze and she could make you do whatever the hell she wanted you to do–even if that involved eating incinerated chicken.

"By the way," Kyle said before yawning loudly. "Thanks for keeping an eye on Hope for me tonight."

"Dude," I growled. "I am living in your house, rent free. The least I can do is watch the kid for an hour." Hope had gone to bed willingly for me tonight, which made a change from when she lived on Thirteenth Street. The nights Kyle had gone to check on Lee in the hospital, I'd sang every nursery song I could think of until I'd discovered Hope was a reggae baby. *No woman no cry* was more her style than *humpty dumpty*.

And Hope made me feel better. I knew that sounded stupid since she was a baby and couldn't talk, but she did. I loved that kid and she seemed to provide exactly what her name suggested. When I was at my lowest, and felt like I couldn't lift a finger from the pain, that little girl's innocent face made me drag my ass up and keep going. In my eyes, Hope was a miracle baby. She had survived almost impossible odds. The day she was born was a pretty damn good day–blood and goo aside.

It was the last time we were all together and smiling. Even though Cam and I were broken up when Hope was born, I'd felt so fucking close to her. We stood side by side and watched a family being born. The volume of pure love that had spilled from the backseat of that car was indescribable and had cloaked over the both of us. She'd held my hand for the briefest of moments as we watched our two best friends transform into parents right in front of our eyes. It was instantaneous. It was humbling... "I did something, Kyle," I whispered. I needed to tell him. I didn't think I'd ever sleep again if I didn't get it off my chest. "And I think you're gonna hate me for it."

"Okay..." Straightening in his seat, he turned to face me. "Is this a conversation where you need to be at least ten feet away from me before you tell me?" He smiled but it was an anxious one. "'Cause I gotta tell you dude, I'm trying real hard to rein it in lately, and I really don't wanna mess up my clean sheet. For Lee's sake."

"I fucked Anna," I blurted out. Jesus, the weight that fell from my shoulders was huge. Kyle's face remained impassive, his eyes unblinking, and I wasn't sure if he was in shock or if he was planning all the ways to make me bleed. "I'm sorry," I added as I edged away from him.

"Anna?" Kyle whispered.

I nodded.

"As in Anna, my stepmother?"

I nodded again.

Kyle groaned. "You fucked my step mother." He shook his head and shuddered. "What the fuck…Uh, I think I'm gonna puke."

"How mad are you?" I asked as I watched him lean over and clutch his stomach. "Should I start running?"

"I'm not mad," he growled. "I'm fucking repulsed."

"She is kinda hot, dude," I said with a smirk, feeling a little better now that it was out there. "She's a beautiful woman."

"She's a geriatric woman," Kyle countered as he glared at me. "How did this happen…No, no, don't tell me." He leapt off the couch and started pacing. "I really don't think my stomach can handle it…Wait, does he know?" Kyle glared at me. "Is that why he fucking drugged you?"

"No," I said calmly. Bringing Kyle's asshole father into this conversation could make him flip. "I don't think he knows…at least, I didn't tell him. He drugged me because I slashed the tires on his Lexus and barfed on his cat." I wasn't proud of myself–especially for throwing up on the white Persian cat–but from the way Kyle's eyes lit up when I told him, I guessed he was.

"Nice," he said in an appreciative tone and for a moment I thought he was going to high-five me. "Mr. Tinkles is a sly son of a bitch."

"Mr. Tinkles?" I asked as I burst out laughing.

Kyle nodded, his eyes gleaming with mischief. "Yeah," he chuckled. "He belongs to Mike. Idiot used to take that fleabag with him everywhere when we were younger…" he stopped talking immediately and I tried to pretend that it didn't hurt when he spoke about Mike. It did hurt. It annoyed the hell out of me that Kyle had promoted him, but I didn't own him. I could hardly say 'you're my friend, you can't be his friend too.'–even if I wanted to. I hated his guts and I always would, but Kyle… dammit, he was too fucking forgiving. The one small perk was that Lee was still boycotting all things Mike Henderson. It shouldn't make me feel smug, but it did…

"Okay, tell me," he blurted out as he resumed his pacing. "Not in any detail." He shuddered. "Just the bare necessities."

"She came onto me a couple of times in the past," I told him. He paled and if he wasn't such a temperamental fucker I would have laughed at his expression. The memory of one of his punches sobered me. There would be no smiling. "I was drunk and missing…" I forced myself to say her name. I needed to talk about her–according to Lee. "I was missing Camryn and I wanted revenge."

"And now?" Kyle asked quietly.

"I haven't slept with her in months," I promised him.

"No." He shook his head. "I meant Cam."

I sighed heavily. I hated what I was about to say, but I needed to say it. It was the only way forward. "I'm always gonna miss Cam," I admitted. "I'm always gonna be in love with her..." I stopped and stared straight in the eyes. "But I am also going to live. I am going to live my life, Kyle. I am going to survive this and…" I closed my eyes and inhaled deeply. "I am going to move on."

Kyle's face broke out in the biggest smile. "You asked me a question before," he said, his smile indulgent. "You asked me if I believed in god."

"Yeah," I muttered in embarrassment. *The shit I'd spurted…*

"And I told you I didn't know," Kyle continued. "Well, I've changed my mind. I believe now, Der."

"Do you think she's looking down on us?" I asked quietly. "Do you…do you think she'd be happy for me?"

Kyle sighed heavily and sank down on the couch beside me. "She's probably bossing the hell out of every other poor soul as we speak," he said with a chuckle. "And if there's anyone Camryn Frey is looking down on, then it's Derek Porter."

"But she left …"

"Doesn't matter," Kyle said as he nudged my shoulder with his. "One love, Der," he said simply. "You were hers."

"Yeah," I whispered.

And she was mine…

NINETEEN

KYLE

"I'VE BEEN THINKING about what you said," Lee murmured as we sat in the car having just come from the courthouse. I'd passed Rachel's mom in the corridor and I felt so bad for the woman. She'd looked at me first, and when she looked at Lee her whole face had caved. I'd rushed Lee out the door before Mrs. Grayson had a chance to say anything. She didn't need to be apologizing to anyone. The woman had done the best she could. She'd brought a child into the world and had loved her with all her heart. It wasn't her fault, nor was it in her power to prevent Rachel's actions. The trial was drawing closer, and Kelsie still hadn't made progress with getting Rachel to change her plea, and to be honest, I was starting to doubt we would. I was beginning to accept the fact that there would be a trial, where my girl would be interrogated and terrified...

Forcing all thoughts of the trial out of my mind, I turned my face to look at Lee. There was a determined glint in her eyes. "Which part?" I asked as I stashed my strawberry milkshake in the cup holder in my car.

"About speaking to Tracy." She inhaled deeply. "One meeting to thank her. Nothing else, Kyle. I don't want to hear her reasons, excuses or whatever else she's had twenty years to think up. I want to thank her for coming forward and saving my life, then walk away with a clear conscience."

I sat in my seat absolutely dumbfounded. Was she serious? I'd been pushing her for months and then when I finally grew a few brain cells and backed off, Lee decided she wanted to meet her…

Jesus, I would never understand the female mind.

"I'll set it up," I told her as I pulled out my phone. "When do you want to do this?"

"As soon as she is able to meet me," she replied. "If I don't do it soon, I'll chicken out and I don't want this looming over us. I want us to have a good life. One with no regrets or sadness."

"I'm proud of you, baby." I leaned over and kissed her lips. "Very proud of you."

"I have one tiny prerequisite," she said in a teasing tone as she brushed her lips to mine.

"Whatever you want, princess," I mumbled as I pulled her mouth back to mine.

"I want to drive," she smirked. "Both ways."

I was nervous as hell on the drive to the hotel, partially because we were meeting Tracy, but mostly because Lee was driving. I conceded control of the car in exchange for dinner with her mom – including dessert. That was the deal. "Which turn off do I take?" Lee asked. Her brow creased in concentration as she maneuvered my CL550 through Saturday night traffic. She was doing pretty well. She hadn't stalled or fucked the handbrake like last time.

I needed to get her a car of her own though, something small and girl friendly, because the thought of her denting my car fucking pained me. "Keep going," I told her. "Then take the next left. There should be some parking available on the street."

She nodded in response and took the turn sharply, tossing me sideways. Her cheeks reddened as her eyes met mine in apology.

I craned my neck to check Hope had survived the turbulence. She grinned at me from her car seat. "Are you nervous?" I asked, stretching a hand out to rub her knee. Lee jerked and the car veered sharply. I snatched my hand back, and counted back from ten.

"I'd have to feel something for her to be nervous," she growled. "So, no. I'm not nervous."

"Okay." I made a mental note to keep my mouth shut for the rest of the car ride.

Probably safer...

LEE

I was such a terrible liar and Kyle knew it. Every inch of my body shook with anxiety as Kyle held the door of the hotel for me. "Come on, Princess," he coaxed. "We made a deal. Dinner with your mom in exchange for driving my car."

"Yeah, well I think you got the sweeter end of that deal." Not really, since I was fairly certain I'd left a modest sized dent on the trunk of his car. He'd been grabbing a parking disc and I'd gotten a little too excited clutching and accelerating in reverse. I thought I'd been doing a pretty good job…until I reversed too quickly. I only hoped I could get the car home before Kyle noticed I'd left half the body paint on a street lamp.

"Walk your hot ass in there," Kyle grumbled impatiently. "Or I'll fucking carry you."

I rolled my eyes at his threat. "And they say romance is dead."

"It will be fine," he said in a kinder voice. "I'll call you in an hour. If you need me just send me a text and I'll come get you."

"Okay," I whispered when all I wanted to say was 'don't leave me.' But I had to be a grown-up about this. I needed to do this alone. I had decided that if Derek could move forward then so could I. I just wished that it was easier done than said…

DEREK

Derek was putting the trash out when I pulled into the driveway. Climbing out of the driver's seat, I ran around to the trunk and groaned.

I knew it.

I fucking knew she hit that street lamp.

"Hey man," Derek said as he picked Hope out of her car seat and gave her a kiss. "Is everything alright?"

"Yeah," I growled. "If you consider a dent the size of the titanic on my baby."

Derek moved to stand beside me. "Damn." He let out a whistle. "You drive like a bitch. What'd you reverse into? Bambi?"

"It was Lee," I said through clenched teeth. "She's gone to the hotel to meet her mom," I told him as we walked inside to the lounge.

"Are you sure this is what she wants?" Derek asked as he handed me Hope. "Did Lee agree to this or did you push her until she cracked?"

I gave him a cold stare as I sat down on the couch and propped my baby girl next to me. "What the hell kind of question is that?" I hissed in disgust. "I might want her to clear the air with her mother, but I'd never force her, Derek." He flinched and I felt like a dick. I needed to work on being more tactful. He was only getting back on his feet…

"Da...Da…Da."

"Holy shit," I shrieked as I turned Hope around to look at her face. She was grinning at me with her little gummy mouth. "What did you say, angel?" I crooned. "Did you say da-da?"

"Say it again," I coaxed as I held her out in front me to get the right view. "Say da-da. Come on, sweetheart, talk for daddy…"

"Dada," she babbled.

My heart melted.

I was ruined.

This girl would have me wrapped around her little finger for the rest of her life.

Her first word.

I was her first word.

Me...

"Dude, you look like that monkey from the lion king," Derek chuckled from where he was perched on the coffee table. "You wanna coconut? Maybe you can crack it open and spread some of that gunk on her forehead."

"You better start running," I said through clenched teeth as I grinned at my daughter. I couldn't take my eyes off my daughter.

Damn, she was going to be a genius.

LEE

This was a mistake. I should have stuck with my gut feeling. It had been screaming 'don't do this' all day.

'She'll let you down' it screamed. But I'd pushed it aside and had gone with the part of me that wanted to make Kyle happy. There was also a small part of me that wanted to meet her.

It was now six-thirty and she wasn't here. I wasn't sure if I was annoyed with myself for agreeing to this when I knew it was a bad idea, or with the part of me that had wished she cared. Her absence only proved her intentions. Her interest in getting to know me was to get closer to Kyle. I sent a text to let Kyle know.

Two minutes later my phone started ringing and I answered it immediately. "She's not here," I told him. "I guess you were wrong about her wanting to talk."

"Who's not there, Delia?" The familiar angry voice bellowed through the line and my blood ran cold. A tremor ran through my body as I leaned forward and rested my elbows on the table.

"Daddy," I whispered, breaking out in a cold sweat. "I'm sorry…I thought you were Kyle. I'm waiting for his call." I inhaled a shaky breath and tried to stay calm. I hadn't spoken to him in months–nor did I want to. *Oh god…* "I should probably hang up and wait for his call. He'll be worried if I don't pick up..."

"Don't you dare hang up on me, girl," daddy warned and even though there were hundreds of miles between us I nearly peed my pants. "I ain't done talking with you. Not by a long shot."

My eyes searched around the bar as I tried to keep my breathing calm. "What did you want to talk about?" I asked quietly.

"I wanna know what the hell you ain't been telling me," he snarled. "Goddammit, Delia. What did I tell you about that boy?"

"Are you drunk?" I whispered appalled.

"WHAT DID YOU TELL HIM?" he roared down the phone. "You better answer me now, girl."

"I have no idea what you're talking about," I cried as I pressed my hand to my forehead. "What boy? What are you talking about?"

"Perry," daddy spat. "People in town are talking about some incident last year. Damn boy's on the television as we speak. What the hell did you tell that piece of shit you've shacked up with? What lies have you been spreading?"

"What has Perry been saying?" I asked, almost too terrified to know.

Last year when my father had his heart attack, Kyle and Derek had followed Cam and I to Montgomery. I wasn't sure of what had happened at the bar that night, but there had been some type of altercation. Kyle and Derek had been black and blue the following morning...

"Only that your pretty boy went and smashed his face in, avenging your worthless ass," daddy growled. "He's gone and sold his story to some gossip channel on TV. You've gone and shamed me with your whoring antics, girl. The whole town knows what kind of a tramp I raised. You're just like your momma. A dirty little slut. Like mother, like daughter."

"I told you the truth about that night," I hissed. My knee was bouncing so hard the table started to shake. This couldn't be happening. Oh please god stop this from happening…"I wasn't lying about what he tried to do to me. Perry Franklin nearly raped me, daddy. He tried to rape me. He nearly did."

"Nearly never milked a cow," daddy said in a sarcastic tone of voice. "You tell that son of a bitch lies 'bout me, too, girl?" he demanded. I could hear banging noises in the background. I guessed he was rearranging the furniture. If I was at home it would be my face he would be rearranging.

"I haven't told lies to anyone." My voice was shaking. I could barely hold my phone in my hands. "And I am not a whore. You d-don't get to c-call me things like that anymore. I'm not afraid of you."

Daddy laughed. "You think that boy's gonna protect you when I get my hands on you?" he snarled. "I'm gonna snap that mouthy little shit in two, and then I'm gonna teach you a lesson in behavior. You're gonna be sorry, you ungrateful little whore. You forget who raised you, girl?" He laughed and it was cruel. "I made you. I sure as hell can break you."

My phone was torn from my hand and I looked up in shock as Mike stood over me, red faced and fuming. "Listen to me, you piece of shit," he snarled. "Call this number again and you'll be ordering your own fucking execution." He hung up and handed me my phone. "Sorry," he mumbled. "I couldn't listen to that."

"You heard?" I asked mortified.

His eyes were full of sympathy as he nodded his head. "Yeah, me and half the bar." He gestured for me to look around. I swung my face and locked eyes with several curious looking customers. "You need to phone Kyle and tell him to take you home," he said in a worried tone. "There's a story running on channel scoop. You should go upstairs and wait there until he comes to get you. Trust me."

KYLE

My phone vibrated, alerting me to an incoming text message.

Princess: She didn't come.

Three words.

Three fucking words and I was ready to tear this goddamn house apart. "She didn't fucking show. I gotta go, dude," I told Derek. I could barely keep my temper under control. Derek didn't say a word as he opened the door for me and followed me down to the car. He was good like that. Knew when to keep his mouth shut. One word and I was about the flip the fuck out.

Opening the car door, I slotted Hope into her car seat and strapped her in. My head snapped up when I heard another car door shut. "What are you doing?"

Derek, who was sitting in the driver's seat, turned his head to look at me. "I'm coming with you," he said simply.

I was too fucking agitated to argue.

In truth I was grateful. My hands were shaking.

We drove in silence until we reached the hotel and the anger vibrating inside of me needed an outlet. "Will you take her inside for me?" I asked as I climbed out and got Hope. "Tell Lee I'll be back in one hour."

"Yeah," Derek said as he plucked Hope out of my arms. "But you're running to the wrong woman, Kyle. Just saying..."

"I need to fix this," I snapped. Pressing a kiss to Hope's forehead I walked around to the driver's side. "I've been pressuring her for months to meet her mom. She finally agrees and gets screwed over. Fuck that. I want answers."

DEREK

There was no point trying to talk Kyle down. He wouldn't hear me and it was too cold to stand outside and argue with him. Snuggling Hope against my chest, I walked into the foyer.

"Are you looking for Lee?" some dude in a suit asked me as I stood at the door of the restaurant. "She's upstairs," he said before I had a chance to speak. "Top floor. Their old room." With that he strolled off and left me standing there confused as hell.

What the hell was she doing upstairs?

Christ, I hoped she wasn't crying.

I was not in the mood to deal with tears.

Taking the elevator up to the eighth floor, I walked over to the double doors and knocked. "Who is it?" I heard Lee call out.

Aw damn, she sounded all choked up.

"Mommy, it's me," I said in a squeaky voice, hoping I could cheer her up before she soaked my shirt. "I puked on Uncle Derek." That part was also true. Babies and moving floors did not mix.

The door opened and Lee stood before me with a red nose and puffy eyes. Shit…"What's wrong, Ice?"

Taking Hope out of my arms, she sniffled loudly and pointed towards the television behind her. I wasn't sure I wanted to see this, but I forced my feet into the suite. When I saw the man on the TV my head started spinning. What the hell?

"Ladies and gentlemen, tonight on channel scoop, we're talking to Perry Franklin from Montgomery, Louisiana," the presenter said as

she flashed the screen with a fake smile. The camera zoomed in on the shithead Kyle had beaten the hell out of last year. *"Perry is a local of Montgomery, and last year he was the victim of a vicious attack. Our sources have discovered that the survivor of the thirteenth street shooting, Delia Bennett, isn't quite as sweet and innocent as has been previously reported. Perry, please tell us what happened to you."*

"Well," he said in an injured tone of voice. *"I'm sorry, ma'am, this is a little hard for me."*

"Go on, Perry," the presenter crooned. *"You're completely safe."*

"I was the victim of slanderous accusations, ma'am. I'm here tonight to set the story straight," he said with fake hurt in his voice. *"I took Delia to our high school prom. We had sex in my truck after prom. It was completely consensual. I'd tried to hold her off, but the girl was all over me. Afterwards she accused me of raping her."* I looked at Lee. She was crying so hard and I didn't have a clue what to say. She ran out of the room with Hope in her arms but I couldn't move. My eyes were glued to the piece of shit on the TV screen

"Were the police involved?" she asked.

"Yes ma'am." he nodded his head solemnly. *"Her lies were dismissed. Everyone here in Montgomery knows how flirtatious Delia is. She sets her eyes on a man and she doesn't stop until she gets him. Even her daddy knew she was lying about me."*

The reporter nodded in sympathy. Fucking bitch. *"So let's fast forward eight months to the night you and your friends were attacked at the bar."*

"Yes ma'am," Perry said as he shifted in his seat. *"I was having a few beers with a couple of buddies, minding our own business, when her boyfriend burst into the bar and attacked us without provocation."*

"When you say boyfriend, you mean Delia's lover?" the reporter asked. *"Hotel tycoon, Kyle Carter?"*

Lover?

Who said that word nowadays?

Yuck. I wanted to puke.

"Yeah," the asswipe confirmed as he wiped his brow with his hand. *"He went nuts. Broke up the bar. Picked a fight with all three of us. We were only defending ourselves when we fought back. But he had back up. Some bald guy and a friend of hers who used to live 'round here. Cammy Frey."*

My heart stopped.

The camera zoomed back on the female presenter. *"Camryn*

Frey is the twenty-two year old student from the University of Colorado, who was shot dead on June twenty-eighth last year. Her body, along with the unconscious body of Delia Bennett, was discovered in a house owned by hotel tycoon, Kyle Carter, in University Hill, Colorado. The women were found on the floor of Mr. Carter's kitchen. The paramedics who were called to the scene described what they saw as heartbreaking. The young women were found holding each other. Miss Frey was pronounced dead at the scene. Both women were taken to the St. Luke's hospital in Boulder…"

I grabbed the remote and switched off the TV. Rubbing my hands over my face, I grabbed my phone.

This shit was too much.

TWENTY

KYLE

"OPEN THE DOOR, TRACY." I knocked harder. "I know you're in there. I can see your shadow."

The door creaked open and Lee's mother peeked her head out from behind the frame. "I'm sorry," she whispered as she gestured for me to come inside. I stalked inside and watched as she closed and bolted the door.

"You better have a damn good reason for letting her down again." I paced the kitchen, unable to keep my feet in one place, before I bumped into something hard. "And why the hell are we in the dark?"

"He knows," she whispered. The light came on and the anger I had inside multiplied. Rapidly. There were boxes all over the floor, nothing on the walls or the countertops. "Jimmy knows," she said in a louder tone. "He phoned me…my house phone. I have to leave."

"So that's it?" I demanded as anxiety filled my gut and my brain tried to make sense of this shit-bomb. "You're just going to run away again?" What the hell was it with this man…He was just a man. A drunken fucking bully.

Goddammit.

"I have to," she sobbed. "You know what he did to me."

"I know if you run he wins," I sighed heavily. "Don't do this, Tracy. Take control of your life. Of your future."

"What am I supposed to do, Kyle?" she snapped. "I'm just a woman."

"What the fuck?" I demanded in disgust. "Just a woman? That's the worst excuse for being weak I've ever heard."

"That's easy for you to say," she hissed. "You've never had to worry about someone being stronger than you. Being more powerful than you. Having control over you."

"Yeah I have," I shot back. "I do. Your daughter is my fucking kryptonite and that scares the daylights out of me every single day. She *is* and *does* all those things to me. Do you think I like feeling overpowered like that?" I shook my head. "You're not the only person in the world who's afraid of something, Tracy. There are some things in life worth fighting for, and some things in life are worth fighting. Period. For me it's the former. For you it's the latter."

"I'm sorry," she whispered.

"She'll never forgive you," I warned her. "You walk away now and that's it. There's no coming back, Tracy."

My stupid damn phone started ringing and I growled in frustration. Derek's name flashed across the screen and I answered immediately. "Is she okay?" I asked him.

"Turn on channel 837 right now," he roared. "Get the best damn lawyer your grandfather's money can buy and take him out. Annihilate each and every one of them."

The line went dead and I stood, staring at my phone for a moment before my brain kicked into gear. "Where's your TV set?" I asked a confused looking Tracy. "Is it packed up?"

"N...no," she stuttered. "It's in the living room."

I barged through her small cottage until I reached the room and turned on the channel.

"So there you have it, folks, right from the horse's mouth," some blonde, with a set of teeth that resembled Gnasher's from the Dandy comics said. *"It makes one wonder just how far Delia Bennett pushed Rachel Grayson in the months before the shooting. Tonight we heard from Perry Franklin about her compulsive lying and promiscuity.*

Just what happened in the run up to the shooting to make Rachel Grayson snap? Is Delia Bennett more responsible than has previously been reported? Does she feel guilt for causing the death of her friend? From where we're sitting, it certainly seems that she should. She embarked on a love-affair with a man who she knew was involved with another woman. She snared him with a child and is now sitting pretty on her throne at the top of a multinational hotel chain, haven gotten exactly what she wanted. My question for all of you watching tonight is how far would you go to snare a multimillionaire?"

"Oh my Lord," Tracy cried from behind me. "Turn it off."

I didn't move.

I couldn't.

I was frozen to the spot.

What the hell had just happened…What the fuck had I just heard? I turned my head to look at Tracy. "Are they blaming Lee?" I shook my head and stared at the television again. "Did I hear that right?"

"They're liars," Tracy snarled through her tears. "How can they do this? Isn't there a law against this kind of thing?" she demanded.

"Why do you care?" I roared. I knew I was taking my anger out on the wrong person, but this was too fucking much. This had to stop. I had to make this go away. "I have to go," I muttered as I moved towards the door. "If you want to be the next person in a long fucking list of people who've let her down then be my guest. But if you run away this time, don't ever ask me to help you again."

LEE

I curled into the tightest ball and covered my ears with my hands. Derek was still in the lounge area of the hotel room. He came and took Hope away earlier. I was grateful. I couldn't function. I was a mess and she didn't need to see me like this. I was numb and I was ruined. This was never going to be over.

Never.

"Cam," I whispered into the darkness. "Cam, please help me…" I shoved my fist in my mouth to stop myself from crying. I bit down hard. The physical pain was easier to deal with than the emotional pain. It was a distraction. I couldn't live like this anymore. "Cam, please come back…I'm so afraid." I squeezed my eyes so tight they started to ache. "I need you."

The door creaked open and a shadow loomed in the doorway for a brief moment before the door closed out. I heard the light pad of feet moving closer just before the mattress dipped and I was being pulled into a pair of strong arms. "Shh baby. I got you."

"Make this end," I begged as I curled my body into his. "Please…take me away from this." I let the tears fall as his hand gripped the back of my head and pulled me closer. "I can't live my life like this anymore."

"I'm gonna fix this," he whispered, as he kissed my face. "I'm gonna end all of this, baby."

"It's too much, Kyle," I whispered as I held onto the frail tether of my sanity. "I want it over."

"I know, princess," he choked out. "I'm so fucking sorry that you're going through this."

"He called me." I dug my nails into Kyle's shirt. I was probably tearing his skin, but he didn't complain and I needed the anchoring. I needed him.

"Who called, baby?" he whispered, as he folded me into his arms. The heat of his body calmed me. The weight of his arms around me gave me comfort.

"Daddy," I managed to say, though my voice was shaky. "He threatened me..."

"When," Kyle demanded and his arms fell away from me. Jumping off the bed, he flicked on the light. "When Lee?" he asked again as he grabbed my purse and tipped it inside out.

"When I was in the restaurant," I sobbed. "Kyle, don't..."

Grabbing my phone, he tapped at the screen then held it to his ear. "No Lee," he shouted. "This is not happening to you again. You are mine. Mine. He is not fucking with you anymore."

KYLE

My whole body was on fire. I was burning the hell up and every sob, sniffle and tear that was coming from Lee's body was adding fuel to that fire.

"You see the news, girl?" Jimmy snarled as I held Lee's phone to my ear. "Ain't so white now, are you? The whole world knows what kind of slut you are. I should have kicked your momma down the stairs. Saved myself years of trouble…"

Jesus Christ. Is this what she was listening to all her life?

"I'm not your daughter, you worthless piece of shit, and you've pushed me too far," I snarled as I locked eyes with Lee. She was kneeling on the bed with her hands in her lap. Her eyes were wide and fearful. I had to look away or I would snap. "I'm only going to say this once, so listen very clearly." I paced the floor in a bid to calm myself. "The next time you see my face it will be when I'm standing over your fucking body."

"Well, if it isn't the city boy with the fat wallet." Jimmy's cruel laugh filled my ears. "Brave words, boy. Did your daddy teach you how to talk like that?" He laughed harder. "No, that's right, you ain't got no daddy, do ya, boy?" he snarled. "I know all about you, Carter. All about your whore of momma." He whistled down the line. "Sixteen, wasn't that what I read? Must've fucked her up real bad to make her kill herself…"

"I'm going to end you," I vowed. "Before you take your last breath on this earth, I will have found a way to make you suffer for what you did to her."

"Not if I kill you first," Jimmy roared. "You, your whore and your little bastard..."

I hung up.

I'd heard enough.

I'd said enough.

I meant every word.

He'd been warned.

My gaze landed on Lee, crying on the bed, and my whole body shuddered. "Come here," I mumbled as I held my arms out for her.

"I'm sorry," Lee whispered as she scrambled off the bed and rushed towards me. I caught her just as she flung herself into my arms. I hoisted her up as she wrapped her legs around my waist and clung to my neck. "I'm sorry he said that to you…"

She was apologizing for him…

I turned around and pressed her back to the wall. "Look at my face, Lee," I told her. Sniffling, she lifted her face to mine. Her eyes. Jesus, the fear I saw in her eyes crippled me. "I love you." I wiped her tears with my thumb. "You are everything to me. No one is going to hurt you again. Not while I'm breathing. I'll take the whole fucking world down before I let that happen. Got it?"

She sighed heavily and closed her eyes. "I love you too. So much." Tucking her face into my neck she whispered, "I think we're cursed, Kyle. Every time we get back up from one blow, someone comes along and knocks us back down. I'm so afraid that the next blow will end us."

"We'll get through this," I promised her. "We've survived worse than an asshole gossip station and that drunk piece of shit."

"Look at the odds though," she whispered. "Kyle, they're all stacked against us."

"So fucking what?" I growled, pulling back so I could see her face. "Let me tell you something, princess. The odds were never in our favor, but we're doing it. We beat those fucking odds every second of the day. I'm damn proud of us for it. I'm so fucking proud of you, and I love you. I *more* than love you, if that makes any sense." I pressed my forehead to hers and tried to slow my breathing. "I'm not good with words or expressing my feelings and shit, but that's the best definition I can give you. I more than love you, Lee. I am more than in love with you. Every day. Every night. I can guarantee you that won't change."

"You're right," she whispered as she brushed her lips against mine. "I'm proud of you, too. I more than love you, too. This won't break us."

"There's my girl," I said, as I smiled at her. "Now say it for me..."

"Fuck the odds," she said with a small smile. "I'm keeping you."

"Hell yeah." I grinned at the sound of a swear word coming out of her mouth. "Fuck the odds and the whole damn world. You, baby, are permanent. You are cemented, glued and fucking nailed to everything inside my body that pumps life into me. The odds and every other asshole that tries to interfere with that will lose, because I'm betting my money on us. And I always win."

"I love you, Kyle," she whispered as she buried her face in my shirt.

"I love you, too, princess," I murmured as I kissed her hair. "I'm always gonna protect you, I promise."

Even as I said the words, the fear of tomorrow flooded my veins.

Trouble was brewing.

I could taste it.

But I would keep my promise to her.

If I had to die trying.

THANK YOU SO MUCH FOR READING!

Kyle and Lee's story continues in
Forever we Fall
Available now.

Please consider leaving a review on the website you purchased this title.

Broken series in order:
Break my Fall
Fall to Pieces
Fall on Me
Forever we Fall

OTHER BOOKS BY CHLOE WALSH:

STANDALONE NOVELS:

Endgame – An Ocean Bay Standalone Novel

Seven Sleepless Nights (TBR)

THE FAKING IT TRILOGY:

Off Limits – Faking it #1

Off the Cards – Faking it #2

Off the Hook – Faking it #3

THE BROKEN SERIES:

Break my Fall – Broken #1

Fall to Pieces – Broken #2

Fall on Me – Broken #3

Forever we Fall – Broken #4

THE CARTER KIDS SERIES:

Treacherous – Carter Kids #1

Always – Carter Kids #1.5

Thorn – Carter Kids #2

Tame – Carter Kids #3

Torment – Carter Kids #4

Inevitable – Carter Kids #5

Altered – Carter Kids #6

Nothing Else Matters – Carter Kids #6.5

THE DIMARCO DYNASTY:

DiMarco's Secret Love Child: Part One

DiMarco's Secret Love Child: Part Two

BLURRED LINES:

Blurring Lines – Book #1

Never Let me Go – Book #2

THE BROKEN SERIES AND CARTER KIDS SERIES READING ORDER:

1. Break my Fall
2. Fall to Pieces
3. Fall on Me
4. Forever we Fall
5. Treacherous
6. Always
7. Thorn
8. Tame
9. Torment
10. Inevitable
11. Altered
12. Nothing Else Matters

THE BLURRED LINES DUO READING ORDER:

1. Blurring Lines
2. Never Let me Go

THE DIMARCO DYNASTY READING ORDER:

1. DiMarco's Secret Love Child: Part One
2. DiMarco's Secret Love Child: Part Two

THE FAKING IT TRILOGY READING ORDER:

1. Off Limits
2. Off the Cards
3. Off the Hook

BROKEN SERIES/CARTER SERIES COUPLES:

KYLE & LEE

Break my Fall

Fall to Pieces

Fall on Me

Forever we Fall

NOAH & TEAGAN

Treacherous

Thorn

Tame

Torment

JORDAN & HOPE

Always

Torment

Inevitable

Altered

LUCKY & HOPE

Torment

Inevitable

Altered

Nothing Else Matters

ABOUT THE AUTHOR

Chloe Walsh is the bestselling author of The Boys of Tommen series, which exploded in popularity. She has been writing and publishing New Adult and Adult contemporary romance for a decade. Her books have been translated into multiple languages. Animal lover, music addict, TV junkie, Chloe loves spending time with her family and is a passionate advocate for mental health awareness. Chloe lives in Cork, Ireland with her family.

Join Chloe's mailing list for exclusive content and release updates.
http://eepurl.com/dPzXM1

Made in United States
North Haven, CT
30 April 2024